A HUNDRED LITTLE FLAMES

Celebrating
30 Years of Publishing
in India

PREETI SHENOY

A HUNDRED LITTLE FLAMES

HarperCollins *Publishers* India

First published in 2017

This edition published in India by HarperCollins *Publishers* in 2022
4th Floor, Tower A, Building No 10, DLF Cyber City,
DLF Phase II, Gurugram, Haryana – 122002
www.harpercollins.co.in

2 4 6 8 10 9 7 5 3 1

P-ISBN: 978-93-5629-354-0
E-ISBN: 978-93-5629-363-2

This is a work of fiction and all characters and incidents described in
this book are the product of the author's imagination. Any resemblance to actual persons, living or dead, is entirely coincidental.

Preeti Shenoy asserts the moral right
to be identified as the author of this work.

Printed and bound at
Thomson Press (India) Ltd

For my grandfathers
S. Gopala Pai
and
Vasudeva Kamath

BOOK ONE

Thekke Madom

Your house shall be not an anchor but a mast.
It shall not be a glistening film that covers a wound,
but an eyelid that guards the eye.

—Kahlil Gibran, 'The Prophet'

1

There were two completely unrelated incidents that happened on Sunday, which would change Ayan's life forever.

1. He attended an office party thrown by his boss in a swanky uptown pub in Pune.
2. More than a thousand miles away, in a small village in Kerala, not identifiable by Google Maps, his grandfather had a fall.

On Monday morning, unaware of anything but the clock on his computer ticking, Ayan took a sip of the horrendous office tea with over-boiled tea leaves, too much milk and sugar. He had only forty-five minutes left before the meeting was to begin. Beads of perspiration trickled down his forehead into his eye, and he blinked. His brow furrowed, he sat hunched, with an ache in his neck, his fingers flying across the keyboard. He felt as though somebody was raining blows inside his head. His throat was parched despite the tea, and now his stomach began to feel queasy as well.

He regretted having that fourth tequila last night. But Randhir had insisted. You can hardly refuse your boss, that too when you are out for a celebration dinner for exceeding the quarterly targets. The venue was a popular one, very much in demand, and they had managed to get a booking only for Sunday. The women at the party were downing alcohol like athletes drinking water after a race. Ayan had never met such stunning women, so gorgeous, stylish and sexy. He could have sworn they had stepped straight out of an upmarket lingerie catalogue.

All of that was irrelevant now. What mattered was this lengthy presentation, which had to be ready for the meeting.

Dhiraj peeped over the padded grey wall divider.

'Not now,' said Ayan even before Dhiraj could say a word.

'Ha. I was about to ask you if you wanted me to do a few slides,' said Dhiraj.

'Buzz off! You don't even know anything about this,' Ayan gritted his teeth as he placed his teacup back on his desk. He missed placing it properly and it went crashing to the floor, shattering into pieces, the half-finished tea splashing across Ayan's grey trousers, staining them.

'Fuck,' he said, 'I am screwed! How do I present this now, in these trousers?'

He reached out for the bottle of water on his desk, grabbed a tissue, wet it, and dabbed furiously at his trousers. That made it worse and the stain grew larger.

'Look, I can go back home and get you a new pair of trousers,' said Dhiraj.

For the first time that day, a look of relief crossed Ayan's face.

'Really? Would you do that?' he asked.

Dhiraj was a good flatmate. Ayan was glad they lived just five minutes away from work.

'Only if you give me the phone number of at least one of the babes at the party yesterday,' said Dhiraj.

'What? How did you know about the women?'

'When you don't get to attend the parties that Randy throws, you check out the pictures on social media. Chabra posted pictures,' Dhiraj shrugged.

Ayan was temporarily distracted.

Then he said, 'I am in no mood to discuss this. I left the party early, as I wanted to work on this. Also, even if I did give you the numbers of any of those women, which I don't have by the way—what would you tell them? That you are the flatmate of the guy at the party from last night?'

'Chill bro, I was only kidding. Leaving now,' said Dhiraj.

By the time Dhiraj got back, Ayan had only a few more slides left.

'Here,' said Dhiraj, as he handed Ayan a freshly laundered grey pair of trousers. He had also got him a pair of fresh socks.

'Thanks, bro,' said Ayan, as he continued working furiously. His head was still pounding, but the thought of finishing the presentation spurred him on. He kept looking at the clock on the computer, and finally, when there were five minutes left, he was done. He raced to the restroom, changed and ran to the conference room with his pen-drive.

Randhir was already there, looking fresh and dapper, with no traces of last night's party at all on his face. Ayan had no idea how he managed that.

'Ayan, my boy, all done?' he asked.

'Yes, Randhir. It's all done,' he answered.

'Let's run through it quickly, shall we?' he asked.

Ayan ran him through it and Randhir admitted he had done a good job.

'You can present this today,' said Randhir.

'Eh—oh ... okay,' said Ayan, taken aback. It was an unexpected development.

It was always a senior member of the team who made these presentations. Today, Randhir wanting him to do it, indicated that he trusted him completely, thought him capable and that he was moving up in the team. Ayan considered it an honour and he was glad he got an opportunity. He was nervous now and the hangover was making it worse.

'Here, have this, it helps,' said Randhir as he slid a bottle of water across to him.

Ayan gulped it down and Randhir smiled.

The presentation went off smoother than Ayan expected it to. His nervousness did not show at all. He knew his data well and was able to answer all the questions that the clients raised, in great depth. If they clinched this deal, it meant that they would be setting up a major production facility in Sabriya, Kuwait. Their company would also be dealing with every single process, from project inception and system design to installation and after-sales support. The revenues this deal would bring would be a milestone achievement, catapulting the company into the top league in its class. It would be a feather in the cap for the Projects Team which Randhir headed.

Later, after the client lunch, and after the clients had left, Randhir walked over to Ayan's cubicle and patted him on the back.

'Well done, my boy. I think I should get you to attend some more parties. Looks like your performance increases after a party, eh?' he winked and walked away, even as Ayan muttered a 'thank you'.

When Randhir was out of earshot, Dhiraj popped up and made a gesture with his fist moving it up and down, and said, 'Performance increases, eh? And you say you didn't get phone numbers?'

'The truth is, I did not. If you hadn't slept over at your girlfriend's place last night, you would have known when I got home.'

'How do I know? And how do I know who came home with you last night?'

'I am telling you the truth. My mind was only on this presentation and boy, am I glad it's over!'

'Good. Now you can tell your father that you did him proud,' said Dhiraj.

'Not sure if he would be proud of me or anything. But at least, it will justify the favour he pulled with his classmate, for getting me in here. Now they will know I am not entirely useless,' said Ayan wryly.

* * *

'Hey bro, Nishi wanted to meet today. She wanted me to ask you if you wanted to join us. She has a friend with her and we could go grab dinner at this new place which has been getting great reviews,' said Dhiraj.

'I am exhausted. I want to just go home and sleep. I am really in no mood to meet a woman and entertain her.'

'Oh, I will tell Nishi to bring her home, then. We can order in pizzas and watch a movie. That's settled.'

Ayan groaned. This was the third friend that Nishi was bringing over. What was with Dhiraj and Nishi, trying to set him up? He had made it clear that he wasn't interested. He had been burnt once and he did not intend going there again.

But he knew that Dhiraj and Nishi would not take no for an answer. They would wear him down with their sheer persistence. It would be futile for him to protest.

'Whatever,' he muttered as they both packed up for the day and headed towards's Dhiraj's car.

'We have to hurry, bro. My dad said he would call at 8.30 p.m. today,' said Ayan. Dhiraj had insisted that they take a detour to buy cans of beer. He had stopped off at a liquor store while Ayan fidgetted restlessly, hurrying him along. Dhiraj bought a crate of beer cans.

'Just tell him you are busy. Nishi will probably already be at the flat with Shivani,' said Dhiraj, as he placed the crates in the rear seat, and they both got into the car fastening their seat belts.

'Eh? Who Shivani?' asked Ayan.

'Her friend—duh! She said she is bringing her friend, remember?'

'Oh. You know I can't avoid my dad's call, right? Also, I promised my mother as well as Askhu that I would video call them.'

'Oh yes, your weekly call with your family. How could I forget! You can't disappoint Akshu for sure. That kid is something else,' said Dhiraj.

Dhiraj had chatted with Akshay many times on video, whenever Ayan had spoken to his family. He thought that Akshay was smart and articulate and he had been very impressed with him. Dhiraj had also found it odd that there was such a huge age difference between Ayan and Akshay. Akshay was just eight, a good eighteen years younger than Ayan. 'This is our Bahrain addition,' Ayan's mother had joked, when she had first introduced Akshay to Dhiraj on a video call with Ayan.

One drunken evening, at their apartment, Ayan had confessed to Dhiraj how bad he felt about his father's constant taunts about Ayan being useless at everything.

His father never failed to remind Ayan, how much he had to help him with every step he had taken. His father also constantly commented that Ayan had no focus, no goals. Ayan had not wanted to do mechanical engineering in the first place, but it was his father who had pushed him towards it. Ayan had failed two subjects in his class twelve and had then given the supplementary exams and cleared them. When he said he wanted to go to a fine arts college, his father had scoffed.

'A degree in fine arts? Are you going to be the next Hussain or the next Arakkal? Why don't you walk about in bare feet too?' he had ridiculed. He had then enrolled him in coaching classes for engineering entrance exams. Ayan detested them. But he was given no choice in the matter.

He managed to get into a lesser known engineering college in Navi Mumbai. He spent four years hating every minute of it. After he scraped through engineering, his father decreed that he was to do an MBA. This time, Ayan, determined to get into a reputed college, put his heart and soul into his preparations, worked hard and managed to secure a place at Symbiosis in Pune.

But his father was far from happy. 'If you had put in more effort, you could have cleared the CAT and got into the IIMs,' he had said. Ayan knew then—no matter what he did, it would never be enough for his father.

On the day of the placements, Ayan was offered a job at his present company, which was into design, manufacturing, and distribution of emission solutions and electrical power generation systems. He would be based out of Pune. The pay package was good. The perks they offered were great. He had accepted the offer. It was when he called up his father to tell him the news, when he discovered that his father already knew. The CEO was his father's classmate.

'You know, it was Balki who had got me on this company in Bahrain. That was thirty years ago. And look at us now. He is the CEO of his company there, and I am the CEO of my company here. I had put in a word for you. There was no way you were not getting the job,' his father said.

All the joy that Ayan had felt evaporated that instant. He wanted to scream at his father. Couldn't his father have stayed away from this one at least, and let him get an offer on his own merit? But he had said nothing. Three weeks later, he had started working as a management trainee, which was where he met Dhiraj. They had hit it off and had rented an apartment together. It was a little over a year now, and both were doing well at their jobs.

* * *

Nishi was already in the flat when Ayan and Dhiraj let themselves in.

'Hey babes, where's your friend?' asked Dhiraj, as he greeted her with a kiss on the cheek.

Ayan turned away, rushed to his room, took out his laptop from his backpack and turned it on. He found these little displays of affection and the little terms of endearment between couples in love, annoying.

'She is in the restroom, she will be out in a minute,' he heard Nishi say.

Ayan logged in. He saw that his father was already online. An incoming video call came in and Ayan accepted it. He smiled when he saw Akshu sitting in front of the computer, his chin resting in his arms, waiting to talk to his elder brother.

'Hi *chetta*[1],' he said. He had lost his molar. He opened his mouth wide and came right towards the camera, showing it proudly to Ayan. Ayan laughed and asked him if it hurt. 'Of course not, I am a big boy now,' said Akshu.

After Akshu had finished filling him in on his latest escapades at the Bahrain International School, the antics of his PT instructor whom he hated, and those of his English teacher whom he loved, Ayan's mother came online.

'You look so tired, Ayu. Are you taking your food on time?' she asked.

'Ma, you always ask that. I am fine! The food in the canteen is great. Why do we always have to start these conversations this way?' replied Ayan.

His father piped in. 'You know how she is. Always worrying about you.'

'Yes *accha*[2], I know,' said Ayan.

His mother told him that his father's sister and her husband were planning to visit them in Bahrain and that she was excited

---

1. Form of address for 'older brother' in Malayalam

2. Accha/Acchan—forms of address for 'father' in Malayalam

about it. Ayan was very fond of his Aunt Shaila and his Uncle Ghanshyam, who was in the IFS. He was currently the Indian High Commissioner in Pretoria, South Africa. Growing up, Ayan had spent many summer vacations at their home in whichever part of the world they happened to be. They had a daughter Nithya, who was a few months older than Ayan, and together, they had planned and plotted many pranks. Any news about them always made Ayan happy.

Nithya was now doing her Masters at UCLA. She and Ayan messaged each other only occasionally, as both were busy with their lives.

His mother filled him in on all the activities of the Indian Malayalee Association in Bahrain. Ayan was happy that she was involved in all of it. Soon Ayan's father came on the line again.

'So how is your job going? All well?' asked his father.

Ayan told him about the presentation and the deal that was clinched because of it.

'Let it come through. Then we will see. There is no need to count your chickens before they hatch.' His father's reply was quick and curt.

Ayan did not react to that. Couldn't his father be happy for him, at least one time? He said that his friends were waiting and he had to go.

'Don't go binge drinking,' his father said. All Ayan could do to hide his annoyance was pick up the stress ball sitting on the bedside cabinet and squeeze it hard. He then said a 'bye to Akshu and his mother and hung up.

'Done with the call, bro?' called Dhiraj.

Ayan had almost forgotten about the girl they had invited.

'A minute,' he said, as he washed his face, changed his clothes and walked out.

Shivani was on the couch, leaning back with her legs stretched out. Nishi was next to her. Dhiraj was on a cushion on the floor. They had already opened the beer cans. The pizzas too had arrived. Contemporary pop music streamed through the speakers.

'Ayan—meet Shivani. Shivani—this is Ayan,' said Dhiraj.

'Hi, I know a lot about you,' said Shivani and smiled.

That was when Ayan looked at Shivani. Her eyes sparkled. Her dusky clear skin glistened and she had a nice smile. Ayan thought that she looked like an actress in a movie he had seen recently and he racked his brain to remember the name of the actress. The red shirt she wore was a striking contrast against her black linen pants. He noticed the many thin metallic bangles on her wrists and her nose ring. She was attractive. Ayan found himself liking her almost instantly. She seemed very different from the other two girls that Dhiraj and Nishi had introduced him to, earlier.

'So what do you do, Shivani?' asked Ayan.

'Oh—I thought you might know! Didn't Dhiraj tell you?' Shivani sounded surprised.

'Er ... He might have. Sorry, I was preoccupied. Had this monster presentation today at work,' said Ayan.

'She works in features with me,' said Nishi.

'Oh, media people,' remarked Ayan.

'Yes, the dreaded journalists whom everyone hates,' smiled Shivani.

Shivani then asked Ayan about his work and they chatted, munching on pizzas. Ayan learnt that Shivani had lived in Bangalore her entire life. After her schooling, she had gone to the National School of Journalism, and then had moved to Symbiosis at Pune, for her post graduation. She had got this job in the *Pune Gazette*, which was where Nishi worked. She lived in the same hostel as Nishi and they had become friends quickly.

It was a pleasant evening, and by the time the girls left,

Ayan was exhausted and ready to sleep.

'See? It wasn't as bad as you thought it would be, isn't it?' asked Dhiraj.

'Yeah, she was better than the last two,' confessed Ayan.

'Did I detect a spark between you two?'

'Come on, it's too early for that. I have just met her.'

'All great love stories start with that single meeting. Of all the gin-joints in the world, she walks into mine,' said Dhiraj clutching his heart dramatically.

Ayan laughed. '*Casablanca* is passé. What you should be saying is: You know how they say we only use 10 per cent of our brains? I think we only use 10 per cent of our hearts.'

'*Wedding Crashers*,' Dhiraj said and laughed.

It was a favourite game of theirs to quote random dialogues from movies, and the other person had to guess the name of the movie. The one who failed to guess bought beer for the other person.

* * *

On Tuesday morning, when Ayan reached the office along with Dhiraj, he saw a bright pink post-it note stuck on his computer, right on the monitor, where he could not miss it.

'URGENT: Leena from HR wants to see you as soon as you are in. Go to the conference room,' it read. The note was from Juliet, the woman who did all the administrative jobs in HR.

Ayan was surprised. This was an unusual request. Perhaps Randhir had told them about the presentation and the deal he had clinched for the company. Leena headed HR and Ayan couldn't imagine why she would want to see him, and what the urgency was about.

He walked over to the conference room and gently opened the door.

'Come in,' Leena called out.

When he walked in, he saw that there were two senior HR

managers sitting around the oval-shaped table with her. He was puzzled. This seemed like an interview set-up. Why were they all here?

'Have a seat, Ayan,' Leena said.

Ayan glanced around uneasily and fiddled with the button on his shirt.

'Ayan, do you have any idea what this meeting is about?' asked Leena.

'Er … No. I have no idea,' said Ayan.

'We are speaking to everyone who attended the celebration party on Sunday night. You had attended it, right?' said one of the senior managers.

'Yes, I had. Why?' Ayan asked, puzzled.

'We will come to that,' said Leena. 'What time did you leave?'

'I left at around midnight as I had a presentation to work on, the next day.'

'Do you know until what time the party went on?' asked one of the senior managers.

'No, I have no idea,' said Ayan.

'Are you aware of what happened at the party? Did anyone who was there tell you about it? ' asked Leena.

'No, I really have no idea. Could you tell me what this is about?' Ayan's palms were cold and he curled his fists into a ball under the table.

'Were you introduced to any women at the party?' Leena's tone was grave.

Ayan felt his heartbeats racing. He knew there was something very wrong, but he couldn't grasp what it was.

'Yes,' he replied.

'Did any of them come with you when you left?' asked one of the men.

'No, nobody did. I left alone,' said Ayan.

'Ayan, this is a very serious issue and it is a breach of company policy. If you have any information about any of the activities of that day, you are required to disclose it, right now, in the best interests of the company,' said Leena.

'I already told you, Leena, I left early. I did not speak to anybody about the party. In fact, I attended it only because Randhir insisted.'

'Ayan, this company has the highest standards of ethics. The women who attended the party that day were all escorts. Randhir put it under entertainment expenses and claimed it from the company. Not only that, someone has posted a picture on Facebook, of cannabis joints being handed around. It was posted on a private page, but is going viral now, as someone has leaked it. This has put us in a very embarrassing position. We have no option but to sack all the people who attended the party that evening. We have already spoken to Randhir and he has agreed to put in his resignation. We strongly recommend you do the same. That way, it will be off the records,' said Leena.

Ayan's eyes widened and he shook his head. He was at a loss for words. He absently curled and uncurled his fists. This was a bolt from the blue.

Finally, he spoke.

'I am innocent, Leena! I didn't even know about the escorts. I ... I presumed they were socialites who were invited. That's what they told me. And ... and I haven't touched cannabis in my life. This is just not fair,' Ayan was speaking fast.

Leena leaned back and clicked her pen shut.

'Sorry, Ayan. These are non-negotiable policies. The company's reputation is at stake. We are sure you will get a new job elsewhere. You can pack your things and leave. You can serve out the rest of your notice period, which is what it will be on paper, from home. All your dues will be cleared by the end of the month,' Leena said.

And with that, the meeting was concluded.

Ayan walked back to his cubicle, his shoulders slumped, looking down at the floor. He sat for a minute staring blankly at the computer screen.

Dhiraj peeped from the next cubicle and asked, 'What happened, bro? Why did they want to see you? All good, I hope?'

Ayan did not look up from the computer screen. 'I am fucked. That's what happened,' he said.

Then he quietly cleared out his desk, packed his bag, and walked out of the office.

He walked on in a daze. He did not know when he reached home, and how he let himself in. He also did not recognise the cry that emanated from his mouth, as he flung himself on his bed.

2

With rains, the greenery took on a new hue hitherto unseen, and transformed the scene in front of Gopal Shanker into a watercolour painting. The fragrance of cardamom wafted across the air. Myriad crickets chirped. The trees in the rubber forest nearby swayed to the wind, making 'whoosh' sounds, as though they were dancers moving their limbs to a musical rhythm that only they could hear.

The miles and miles of green paddy field stretched out like carpets, contrasting against the endless light blue sky dotted with fluffy white clouds, till the horizon. It was a picture perfect setting, ideal for advertising Kerala as God's Own Country. Anyone who arrived here as a tourist would gasp in delight when they first set eyes on this picturesque scene. But the beauty of all of this was lost on Gopal Shanker.

He was an angry man most of the time, his temperament brought on by age, creaky bones and most of all, a slow realization that navigating his eighties would not be as easy as his seventies. For one, his joints hurt and it was a constant ache that accompanied him every waking hour. No amount of oil massages with *dhanvantara tailam*[3] by his trusted aide Velayuthan helped. The relief was only temporary and the moment the massage stopped, the ache came back.

---

3. A type of Ayurvedic massage oil commonly used in Kerala.

It was Velayuthan or Velu as he was called, who bore the brunt of his anger all the time. But Velu was a patient man. He was also fiercely loyal, his father having served Gopal Shanker's father, and later Gopal Shanker himself.

Now Gopal Shanker's right foot was in a cast, and it rested horizontally on the long arm of the easy chair where he sat and surveyed the paddy fields which the verandah of his house faced. He had a cup of hot *naadan chaya* [4] in his hands, which he sipped as he stared gloomily at the paddy fields.

He did not like being dependent on anybody. This fall that he had two days ago, had rendered him almost immobile. He had to call Velu even to go to the bathroom.

'Velu!' he roared. A wary-looking Velu appeared almost instantaneously. He did not want to risk angering Gopal Shanker. He was bare-chested, dressed in a *mundu* [5] folded up at the knees. He unfolded it immediately and stood with his head slightly bowed, a mark of respect for Gopal Shanker.

'Where is today's newspaper? Why is it delayed?' asked Gopal.

'I think it is because it rained,' said Velu.

'Pah! Haven't they heard of tarpaulin sheets and plastic covers? Did it rain inside the printing press at Kottayam?'

'It will be here soon,' said Velu, used to Gopal Shanker's sharp words. 'And today is the day of your check-up,' he reminded him.

'What check-up? I am perfectly fine! This is just a cast and it will heal,' said Gopal.

'Jairaj Sir has instructed me to take you,' said Velu.

'Hah! Jairaj Sir! The great Jairaj *Sir*. He sits in Bahrain and gives orders. Who does he think he is? If he was so concerned,

---

4. Tea made in rural parts of Kerala, typically strong, sweet and thick.

5. Traditional Kerala lower garment worn by men, tied at the waist.

don't you think he would have come and seen me, as soon as he heard that I had a fall? In fourteen years, he has not found some time to see his father. *Soooo* busy he is,' he sneered.

'I will call for the taxi at 8.30 a.m. The appointment is for 9.30 a.m. That will give us ample time to get there,' said Velu, ignoring Gopal's outburst. He knew how to deal with him. Gopal had to be cajoled, like a difficult child.

'And how do you suppose I will rest my foot there? If I keep it down it hurts. You know it has to be rested only horizontally,' grumbled Gopal.

Velu knew that he had won the first battle—of getting Gopal to agree to go to the hospital. They would have to travel to Kottayam, which was where the nearest hospital was. Poongavanam village had only a small government health centre. Jairaj had insisted on *Marthoma Hospital* in Kottayam, as one of the doctors there was personally known to him. A part of Velu's duty after each of Gopal Shanker's health check-ups, was to read out the medical reports to Jairaj on the phone.

Neither Gopal Shanker nor Velu knew how to use the Internet. They had no computers, no laptops; and cable television had not yet invaded their village. Very few houses had a television, and the ones that did, had DVD players attached to them. The only development that the village could boast of, was the construction of a temple in the Kerala traditional style. The village was the place where Gopal Shanker had spent his early years.

A long, paved cement driveway, flanked on both sides by overgrown hibiscus bushes which were in full bloom, led to *Thekke Madom,* the ancestral home, where Gopal Shanker and his siblings had grown up in a large joint family along with their many cousins. Little by little, the joint family had disintegrated, with members moving away to different cities to make a living.

He had outlived his two brothers and his sister, and was the sole occupant of the massive home. It was an old, ornate, beautiful double-storied mansion, with sloping red tiled roofs, built in the traditional Kerala fashion, with a central courtyard open to the sun. It was a behemoth—about 10,300 square feet. It consisted of two double storeyed blocks, with rich, intricately-carved wooden pillars, wooden ceilings, attics and cellars. A verandah ran around all the four sides. Even during the peak Kerala summer, it was cool inside the house.

Most of the rooms were now locked up, as nobody used them. Once a week, a hired help opened all the rooms, swept and mopped them. Even though the structure was more than a hundred and fifty years old, it was maintained impeccably. Velu took care of the routine repairs, like broken tiles, crumbling plaster and rotting wood. During monsoons, the cement tiles were scrubbed and sprinkled with bleaching powder so that they would not be slippery.

This large house was the bone of contention between Jairaj and Gopal Shanker. Jairaj felt it was too large for his father to be living in alone, and Gopal Shanker did not see himself living in a flat in the city. They never ceased to argue about it.

'People like to live in matchboxes, where there is not even a piece of land. You should always live in a structure where you can step out and feel Mother Earth, not be half-suspended like *Trishanku*[6] in the sky,' Gopal Shanker always said.

The steps of the staircase that led to the first floor of the *tharavadu*[7] were steep and made of wood. The structure was like a little ladder and had no railings. Gopal Shanker could not climb them anymore. There were steps made of stone to

6. A king from Indian mythology who was suspended halfway to heaven

7. Ancestral home

get into the inner courtyard as well as to get out of the house. Those he managed to navigate by himself.

'What is the use of a house, where you can't even go into every room?' Jairaj had asked.

'What will you know about memories and sentiments? You have made Bahrain your home. What do you know about the smell of earth when it rains; the fragrance of cardamom; the cool breeze of the branches of rubber trees; the paddy from the fields and coconuts from the trees? You are used to your supermarket conveniences and you will never understand,' Gopal had retorted.

* * *

The taxi that Velu had called for, arrived.

'Gopal Sir, shall we leave?' asked Velu.

'How will I rest my foot there? And how will I get down the steps?' asked Gopal. After his leg had been put in a cast, the orthopaedic department had given him a foldable walker which he used to get around.

'We will help, sir,' said the taxi driver.

'I have taken the wooden stool. It is already inside the trunk of the car. We can use that to rest your leg, when you are waiting to see the doctor,' said Velu.

As much as Gopal Shanker hated it, he had to be half-carried by both Velu and the taxi driver, as he made it to the car.

The doctor said that the cast would come off in about three weeks. He was advised to rest, after which he could slowly resume walking.

Jairaj called as soon as they were in the car. Gopal answered the phone.

'Yes, yes. I am still alive, not dead yet and so nothing to worry,' he said, instead of the customary hello.

'I have told you so many times, that those steps are difficult to navigate. At your age, the healing takes longer. See, in a flat, all these problems will not be there,' said Jairaj.

'I have told you so many times that you can live in your city matchboxes. I will not move from here. I will decide what to do with the house after my death, seeing that you are simply not interested in this building or this legacy. How many years has it been since you visited Kerala? You did not even come for Subadhra's granddaughter's wedding. You don't have to utter a word about this place. You don't have any right to!' Gopal Shanker's voice was shaking. There was pain and anguish, which Velu recognised. Velu felt the same way about *Thekke Madom*.

Too bad Gopal Shanker's son or daughter didn't see it that way.

'No *accha*, nobody told you to sell it. It is just that I feel bad about you being all alone there,' said Jairaj.

'I have Velu. And I have the birds that come every day, the ducks and fishes in the pond, the chickens and the dogs too. I am not alone. And I must tell you, Lakshmi and Saraswathi keep me company too,' said Gopal Shanker, changing the topic. He did not want to discuss the house any further.

Jairaj was puzzled. He didn't remember any relatives called Lakshmi and Saraswathi.

'Eh? Who are Lakshmi and Saraswathi? I am sorry I don't remember them?'

'How will you, the busy city-dweller, even remember? They are our cows. Your grandmother looked after them like her own children. And by the way, how are Akshay and Ayan? And how is Kamakshi?' asked Gopal Shanker.

'All are fine. Kamakshi is busy with her Indian Bahrain Association activities. Akshay is doing well in school and Ayan was telling me the other day about a deal that he had clinched in his job,' said Jairaj, a little puzzled that his father mentioned the cows. He didn't remember any cows at all. Did they get new cows? He made a mental note to check with Velu.

'Good. Tell him to call me some time. I would like to speak

to him,' said Gopal Shanker.

'Yes *accha*, I will do that,' said Jairaj as he hung up.

Velu had overheard the entire conversation and he gently decided to broach the topic to Gopal Shanker.

'Ehhh—sir, you mentioned Lakshmi and Saraswathi to Jairaj Sir,' he said.

'No, I didn't,' said Gopal Shanker.

'Sir, I heard you telling Jairaj Sir about them.'

'So what? They are the only ones who care about me.'

'Sir, they existed a long time ago. They aren't there now. They were around when you were a little boy,' said Velu.

'Of course, I know that,' said Gopal Shanker.

Velu did not know what to say to that. So they completed the rest of the journey in silence. When the car pulled into *Thekke Madom*, the taxi driver and Velu once again assisted Gopal to his bedroom. His bed was a four-poster one with intricately-carved rich brown rosewood pillars. By the side of the bed stood an ancient desk. On it were a few books and a fountain pen. Gopal loved to read and write. Velu would see him scribbling in diaries, late at night and early mornings, when Gopal couldn't sleep. Once or twice while Gopal was sleeping, Velu had opened a diary and looked inside. They were all tiny spidery scrawls in English and Velu couldn't read a word. He had shut them then and let them be.

After he was certain that Gopal Shanker had fallen asleep, Velu dialled Jairaj's number and cut it after a couple of rings. The standing instructions to Velu were that whenever he had anything to report, he had to give a 'missed call' and Jairaj would call him back at his convenience.

Today, after giving the 'missed call', Velu simply couldn't wait. He dialled again, and then again.

Jairaj called him back almost immediately after the third time...

'Yes Velu, what happened?' asked Jairaj.

'Sir, Gopal Sir mentioned Saraswathi and Lakshmi. That is something from his childhood. He was a little boy, of maybe fourteen or fifteen, when *Thekke Madom* had two cows by those names. I remember my father looking after them. I don't know why he brought them up in the conversation with you. And when I mentioned that it was a long time back, he said he knew. I thought I should inform you about it.'

'Has this been happening often? Does he talk about the past like this?' asked Jairaj.

'No sir, he is sharp and alert. This is the first time he has said something like this,' said Velu.

'Oh, I see. Let's see what to do about it. Meanwhile, keep a close watch on what he says,' said Jairaj.

Velu nodded but he was not happy at all.

3

Ayan was in a daze. He had no idea what had hit him or how he was going to break the news to his father. But it turned out he did not have to. His father already knew. The entire unit working under Randhir, and Randhir himself, had been asked to put in their papers. The scandal had managed to make its way to the pages of all newspapers.

"Engineering Giant rewards staff by hiring prostitutes"
"The red walk of shame"
"Smoke up, have sex, we clinched a deal!"

...read some of the headlines in the newspapers and the online portals. They went into the details, with many of them running the pictures that Chabra had posted on social media. He had taken them down as soon as HR had connected with him, but the archives and screenshots had gone viral. Ayan wasn't in any of the pictures. They must have been taken after he had left. He was thankful for that. But all the others in the unit were in the pictures.

The CEO of the company, Balki, called up Jairaj and told him that he was helpless, that he couldn't do anything about this one. It was company policy which they had followed and to save face, they had no option but to ask all those who were at the party to resign.

Jairaj called up Ayan as soon as he heard this.

'Wonderful. Is this how you celebrate your clinching the deal?' he roared.

Ayan hung his head in shame.

'But ... but *accha* ... this ... this was before the deal. And I was ... I was not involved,' his voice was barely audible.

'Oh ho ho, listen to yourself. How can you *not* be involved? Are they crazy to fire you without reason? Weren't you present at the party? '

'Yes. But I left early.'

'That is like saying you attended a wedding, but did not stay to see the groom tie the *thaali*[8] around the bride's neck. There are no two sides to this, Ayan. You were there and you are guilty. You should not even have gone to such a party. You should have had the courage to say no. You should not simply follow the herd.'

'I ... I am ... I am sorry, *accha*,' said Ayan, his cheeks flaming. He grimaced.

'So what are the future plans of the great man who clinched the office deal?' asked Jairaj.

Ayan winced. He had barely recovered from the shock of losing his job. And here was his father asking him about his future plans.

'I haven't thought of it yet ... I will ... I will apply for jobs,' said Ayan.

'And who would hire you? Do you think people don't read the papers? The moment they know which company you had worked for, they will know you were involved.'

'I am innocent, *accha* ... I did not do anything.'

'Try telling that to those who will interview you to hire you, if you manage to get any interview calls, that is.'

'I ... I don't have any plans. And I ... I will be looking for a job. I really don't have any other option now,' said Ayan.

---

8. An ornament on a chain which the groom puts around the bride's neck during the wedding ceremony

He wished his father would leave him alone. He just wanted to lie down and think. He did not know what to do. He was in so much pain that he could barely breathe.

'I will think of something soon. Once I have finalized something, I will call you back,' said Jairaj as he hung up.

Ayan gritted his teeth and kicked the plastic bottle that contained drinking water resting on the floor at the foot of his bed. The bottle went flying across the room, hit the wall and cracked open. Water poured out and spread across the tiled floor.

'Aaaaargh!' screamed Ayan. The scream echoed through the room, bouncing off the walls. When it subsided, the silence was sepulchral. He sat for a while with his head in his hands. At last, he looked up. Having nothing to do, he decided to make himself a cup of tea. As he got off the bed, he stepped into the puddle of water, slipped and unable to maintain his balance, he fell down. He wasn't hurt as he landed on the floor on his bottom. The water seeped through his shorts forming a wet patch. He didn't bother to change out of the wet shorts. He walked to the living room, switched on the TV and plonked himself on the sofa. A national news channel came on and he saw that one of the headlines on the ticker was his company scandal. It was being shown over and over again. Footage of the office building was being shown, with a crowd of reporters, with their hysterics and drama. Randhir's photograph was also being flashed, with all his career details. Thankfully, the rest were spared and were only referred to as 'Randhir's team'. Ayan switched the TV off and waited for Dhiraj to get home.

'So sorry, bro,' said Dhiraj as soon as he entered. 'Everyone at work had only this to talk about. The hot topic of conversation.'

'The thing is, Randhir has thrown these parties before. How is it that only this time it became an issue?' asked Ayan.

'Apparently, he had been warned twice by HR to tone it

down. They had agreed to turn a blind eye as long as it was kept private. But that damn Chabra posting it—that caused the problem. The company could no longer pretend not to know and they had to take a stand,' said Dhiraj.

'Yeah, I guess from the company's perspective, it makes sense. But I am in a fix. I don't know what to do. It's not like this will not be brought up when I apply for other jobs,' said Ayan.

'Right now, this is everyone's favourite topic. Give it a few weeks, and it will die down. Start applying for jobs. You can always tell them the truth about what happened. They will respect you for it,' said Dhiraj. This gave Ayan hope and in a strange way, he felt comforted.

'Beer?' asked Dhiraj as he walked to the fridge and popped open a can.

'Sure, thanks,' said Ayan.

* * *

A week passed and for Ayan, each day was same as the previous day. He lost track of time. Each morning, Dhiraj would leave for work and Ayan would be still asleep. When he woke up, he would wander around the house not knowing what to do. One morning, out of sheer boredom, he decided to paint. He used to paint well in school and had won prizes for his art. But once he left school and got into engineering, he had given it up completely.

Ayan went shopping and got canvas, oil paints and turpentine. He then began to paint, without even knowing what he would be creating. He was so engrossed in the painting that he forgot to eat, and this was how Dhiraj found him when he came back from work.

'Whoa—you've got talent!' he exclaimed.

Ayan had painted a night scene, with dark skies full of a thousand stars. There was a silhouette of a forest, and a lone wolf howling at the full moon. It was an arresting picture.

'Thanks,' said Ayan. He didn't tell Dhiraj that he had painted what he felt. He felt he was enveloped by darkness and he was the lone wolf howling. His savings were fast running out, and with no income coming in, Ayan calculated that it would last him another two months, at the most. After that, he wouldn't be able to afford to live on his own. He would probably have to be funded by his parents for his daily needs. Ayan detested the thought and hoped it wouldn't come true.

It was the day of his weekly call with his family, and Ayan dialled in. After the usual conversation with Akash, his father came on the line.

'I have arrived at the perfect solution for your situation, Ayan. You will agree that there is no point in staying on in Pune,' he said.

'And what is it?' Ayan asked with dread. He was certain that his parents were going to ask him to return to Bahrain.

'You can go to Kerala for a while and stay with your grandfather. He has had a fall, and his foot is in a cast. I don't think he can manage alone there. If you are there, I can have buyers coming in, to look at the property and all the things inside it. At some point, it will have to be sold. It's best to do it at this point, rather than...' Jairaj trailed off.

'Oh! But ... but *accha*, what will I do in Poongavanam?'

'What are you going to do in Pune? And who do you think will pay the rent for the apartment that you are living in? Your being in Poongavanam will help me manage your *muttachan*[9]. He needs to be convinced about selling the house. Pack your bags, and you can fly out this weekend. That will give you ample time to close all the things there,' said Jairaj, with an air of finality.

There was no arguing with him. His mother came on the line and tried to convince him that this was for the best.

---

9. Muttacha/muttachan—a term of address used for 'grandfather' in Malayalam

Dhiraj felt terrible for Ayan, about the entire episode.

'Look, if you live here and watch me go off to work every day, you will only feel worse. Maybe this Kerala break will be a much-needed change?' he suggested.

Ayan simply shrugged. It was not like there was anything much he could do. He accelerated his job hunt and sent out his resume to a few companies. He also uploaded his CV on many job portals. So far he had heard nothing from any of the companies. Perhaps his father was right. Maybe he had become a corporate pariah. And perhaps Dhiraj had a point.

Shivani messaged him the day that he was leaving.

'Got your number from Nishi. So sorry to hear about all of this. Don't take it to heart. And be in touch,' her message read.

'Yes, it's a bummer. But thanks!' he replied.

He had packed all his belongings into two large suitcases and one backpack. He couldn't help reflecting that it was his life, neatly packed, waiting to be transported to a different world.

* * *

By the time, the flight landed at Nedumbassery International Airport, Ayan felt his spirits lifting. He was surprised that he was actually feeling excited. The view from the plane just before landing was spectacular. There were miles and miles of greenery that stretched out below. Velu was waiting at the airport with a placard and a car. He had seen Velu only once, when he was a little boy. When he saw the placard, he walked towards him and Velu greeted him enthusiastically.

'Ayan Sir! So much you have grown. I saw you when you were about this high,' he said extending his hand out at his waist level.

As the car sped towards *Thekke Madom*, Ayan found himself relaxing more and more. Kerala was beautiful. Ayan remembered the vacation that he had taken here once, when he was a child. His father had sent him to stay at *Thekke*

Madom. His cousin Nithya too had been sent. They had created unforgettable memories, catching fish in the pond and putting them in glass jars; climbing mango trees and eating the raw mangoes with chilli powder and salt; borrowing Velu's cycle which was too big for them, and yet riding it expertly, standing up on the pedals, for if they sat on the seat, their legs wouldn't reach the pedals. Ayan remembered the fragrance of pepper and cardamom, and the sweet taste of the mulberries that they had plucked from the mulberry tree. He remembered the deep red *jambu*[10] fruits that they used to pluck and eat, and his mouth watered.

'Velu *chetta*, are the *jambu* fruit trees and the mulberry trees still there?' he asked.

'Ooooh, yes. Nowadays we sell it all at the weekly bazaar as there is no one to eat them. We have a surplus. You can eat all you want!' Velu answered.

'Oh lovely,' said Ayan, and he felt like a little boy again.

Gopal Shanker was waiting for them on the verandah, as the car pulled up. Ayan got out of the car and walked towards him. He was shocked to see how old he looked. It seemed like his grandfather had aged a lot, since the last time Ayan had seen him. He still had his mop of white hair though. He was frail and he seemed to have lost a lot of weight. Gopal Shanker frowned.

'*Muttacha,* it's me, Ayan,' said Ayan, as he greeted him.

Gopal Shanker stared at him, as though trying to ascertain that he was not dreaming. Then his face broke into a smile.

'Why did you have to come all the way here? I can manage fine with Velu,' he said.

'I wanted to spend a few days with you,' said Ayan.

'Wanted to or were you forced to, by the great Bahrain Lord?' asked Gopal Shanker. The old man was sharp.

---

10. A kind of fruit, 'rose apple' in English, found commonly in Kerala

'I am here now, *muttacha,* and I am happy to be here. Kerala is just beautiful,' said Ayan, refusing to be drawn into an argument. The beauty of the place had that effect on him.

'Give him the guest bedroom upstairs. The young man can have some privacy too, then,' said Gopal.

'Yes ... Ayan Sir. We have made everything ready for you,' said Velu, as he carried Ayan's suitcase and proceeded up to the bedroom, climbing the steep wooden stairs with no railings, expertly.

The four-poster bed in the guest bedroom was so high, that you needed a little stool to climb on to it. A picture-window looked out at the paddy fields. An antique wooden desk stood in the corner, next to an ancient, large wardrobe. The roof had dark wooden panels that crisscrossed each other, and just looking at them brought back so many childhood memories for Ayan. Nithya and he would lie on these beds, after having had their fill of green mangoes, stare at the ceiling and talk about their futures. The room was dark, cool, soothing and welcoming.

'Do you want me to bring you tea?' asked Velu.

'No, just give me a few moments, and I will join you downstairs,' said Ayan.

He unpacked his paints and canvas first and left them on the desk. Then he sat on the bed and stared at the paddy crops swaying in the breeze. After the events of the past few days, this felt like a protective shell to retreat into. Ayan felt it was just what he needed.

He felt a faint stirring in his heart—and he recognised that feeling. It was peace and calmness that he was experiencing—something he hadn't felt for a very long time.

4

To Ayan, *Thekke Madom* felt like a resort. When he finally made his way downstairs, he saw that Velu had kept tea ready for him.

'Would you like to have rice or *parotta* for dinner?' Velu asked.

'*Parotta* please,' answered Ayan mimicking the way Velu pronounced 'paratha'. 'Where's *muttachan*?' he asked.

'He always takes a nap at this time. He has dozed off. He wakes up exactly at 4.30 p.m. And if hot tea isn't beside his bed at that time, he creates a ruckus,' said Velu.

'Is that so? You better be ready with the tea then,' said Ayan.

'Yes, I will. What would you like to do in the meantime? Do you need anything?' asked Velu.

'Oh, I will be fine on my own. I remember this place from my childhood. I think I will take a walk around and explore,' said Ayan.

'If you get lost in the village, you can just ask anyone where *Thekke Madom* is and they will point you in the right direction,' said Velu.

'Ha ha, I am sure there will be no need for that,' said Ayan and he walked down the long driveway, to the road that led to the village.

He crossed a small shop, and the shop owner, an old man, called out to him in Malayalam, 'Jairaj Sir's son, aren't you? When did you arrive?'

Ayan was surprised.

'Yes! How did you recognize me? I arrived a little while ago,' said Ayan.

'Oh, Velu has been going on and on about it. You were in Pune, right?'

'Yes, I was.'

'So, what about your job? Are you on leave?' asked the shopkeeper.

'Um ... no, I quit,' said Ayan.

Then he bid a polite farewell and walked on.

He was astonished that he was stopped by at least three more people, who asked him the same questions that the shopkeeper had. The villagers were such a friendly bunch, and inquisitive too. Their genuine smiles on seeing him warmed his heart. In Bahrain or in Pune, nobody cared about who he was or what he did. In Poongavanam, it was a different world.

By the time he got back, Gopal Shanker was awake and had finished his tea, and *etha pazham*[11], which Velu had served.

'Where did you go exploring?' he asked Ayan.

Ayan made himself comfortable on the large flat wooden swing that hung from the ceiling. The swing was as big as a bed, and Ayan loved it.

'I took a walk around the village, *muttacha*,' he said.

'And did you meet any pretty girls?' asked his grandfather and chuckled.

'Eh ... ha ha, no, I did not,' said Ayan.

'That is because all the pretty girls have gone to the city to study and work. Nobody wants to live in Poongavanam anymore. It is only old relics like me who stay on here. See your father? He abandoned all this,' said Gopal Shanker, as he made a large sweeping gesture with his hand.

---

11. A long variety of banana commonly available in Kerala

'Well, people have to make a living, *muttacha*,' he said.

'Living? You call it living? When there is fresh air to breathe, and pure water to drink, and produce from the fields, what more do you need? Why do you have to go and slave in the desert? Fools, you people are. That's all I can say,' said Gopal Shanker. His mood suddenly changed and his face darkened in anger.

Velu was standing behind him, and he made a silent gesture to Ayan, asking him to leave.

'Errr ... I need to have a shower after my walk,' said Ayan, as he made his way upstairs.

Velu joined him a few minutes later.

'He is like that. He suddenly flares up and gets angry for no reason. Please don't take it to heart or feel bad. If you had continued sitting there, he would have gone on and on about the evils of city life. That's why I asked you to leave. I am sorry if I overstepped my limits,' said Velu.

'Of course, not. I understand. And I am glad you rescued me,' said Ayan.

Velu then handed him a towel and soap. The bathroom, to which no modern additions had been made, was outside the main house the way it was in traditional homesteads. There was a massive copper vessel which held about 200 litres of water, and it was embedded inside a cement tank. On the other side of the wall was a narrow opening, which was a mini-tunnel that led to the bottom of this copper vessel. The 'tunnel' was full of wooden branches and sticks, and it was lit. It was like a concealed fireplace. The water in the copper vessel was boiling hot. Next to this, was another cement tank that stored cold water. There was a bucket, and a 'mug' made of aluminium that had a long wooden handle. In order to take a bath, one had to mix hot and cold water in the bucket, using the mug. Ayan had found it cumbersome when he had visited *Thekke*

Madom as a child. As an adult, however, he found it quaint. He was also surprised that this old-fashioned way of having a bath had not been replaced by a modern convenient shower, with running water, and he commented about it to Velu.

'Your grandfather still prefers this. He says all the firewood around the house will go waste if he doesn't use it this way. Thankfully, he agreed to get an LPG connection, and we have cooking gas. Else we would have been using firewood in the kitchen too and I would be blowing my lungs out trying to light a fire using coconut shells as before,' laughed Velu.

Ayan had to admit that having a bath this way felt refreshing.

His grandfather was waiting to talk to him, while Velu was in the kitchen, cooking. Ayan hoped that he would be able to stick to the 'safe topics' as he didn't want to set the old man off on another rant.

Ayan needn't have worried. Gopal Shanker had his own ideas on what to converse about.

'Do you know, I left Poongavanam when I was eighteen years old? I was sent to work in Mumbai under my uncle, in a cotton mill.'

'Oh, did you like it in Mumbai?' asked Ayan.

'I did not know a single soul there. I lived with my uncle for a week, and then my aunt made it clear that she did not want me there. I rented a place along with three other employees. By the twenty-fifth of the month, our salaries would run out. We would then subsist on eating only bananas for dinner, as we didn't have money for a meal,' said Gopal Shanker.

Ayan nodded. He couldn't imagine a life like that. He had heard his own father's accounts—about how he had struggled in his early days in Bahrain, but he had never thought of what his grandfather's life would have been like.

'And let me tell you a secret,' said Gopal Shanker suddenly, in hushed tones. He looked around as though to make sure no one was listening. He lowered his voice and said, 'You know, both my children—Jairaj and Shaila, they are waiting for me to die.'

Ayan was taken aback at the sudden change in topic. One moment he was reminiscing, and the other moment he was talking about his children waiting for him to die.

'*Muttacha*, that's not true. Nobody is waiting for you to die.'

'Oh, what do you know? You are an innocent little kid. Do you know how much this property is worth? Crores. Not lakhs. It is worth crores. That is all they are interested in.'

'*Muttacha*, they all are really successful and they have their own homes. I am sure they are not eyeing the property,' said Ayan. He felt compelled to defend his aunt and his father.

'Ooooh, just because Shaila's husband is an IFS officer, don't you dare think that they don't care about money. They all do. That's all they want. Both my children. Pah! Selfish to the core. I am telling you, it's true. They are waiting for me to die, and you know what? I don't intend to die so soon. Hahaha!' Gopal Shanker started laughing.

Ayan did not know what to do. He looked around helplessly, looking for Velu.

Velu had overheard the conversation from the kitchen and came into the drawing room.

'It's time for the evening news. Don't you want to watch it?' he asked.

That was enough to distract Gopal Shanker.

'Yes, yes, switch it on,' he said.

Velu switched on the television and retreated to the kitchen.

As the news started, Gopal Shanker turned to Ayan and said, 'Go and feed Lakshmi and Saraswathi.'

'Eh?' Ayan asked.

'Don't tell me you have forgotten them? Your father already

has. But you will most certainly remember them,' said Gopal
Shanker.

'Mmmm … sorry *muttacha*. I don't recall Lakshmi and
Saraswathi,' said Ayan, trying hard to comprehend what his
grandfather was saying.

'Go to the cowshed, and feed them. Then come back here.
They are waiting,' said Gopal Shanker.

Ayan went into the kitchen and asked Velu if there were
cows on the property.

'Cows? What cows? Has he been talking about Lakshmi
and Saraswathi again?' asked Velu.

'Yes, he wants me to feed them.'

Velu shook his head. 'It's a new thing he has started. He
mentioned them to your father too, the other day. They did
exist—but we sold the cows a long time back, when your
grandfather was a little boy.'

'Oh—is that so? Isn't that a bit worrying? He talks about
them like they exist.'

'I know, I think he just gets confused. After all, he has
hit his eighties. I don't think we need to worry about it too
much,' said Velu.

Dhiraj called Ayan that evening.

'How is it going?' he asked.

'Life here is so slow and sleepy, so different from what I
have been doing my entire life. You have to see this place to
believe it,' said Ayan.

'I have never visited Kerala.'

'You must. It truly is God's own country. What the tourist
brochures say is right. And hey, has the buzz in the office died
down?'

'Not entirely. They are still talking about it. And that Gupta
from admin—he was joking that he wanted invoices, as they
will have the number of the agency that supplied the escorts,'

said Dhiraj.

'Not even funny,' said Ayan.

'I know. And there's news to cheer you up,' said Dhiraj.

'What?' asked Ayan. He hoped it was a job offer. If so, it would be great. He would take anything that came his way. It was better than being dependent on his father financially.

'Shivani told Nishi that she really likes you.'

'Aaaah! I thought it would be a job offer. You got my hopes up there for a second.' The disappointment was evident in Ayan's voice.

'A 25 per cent slice of something big is better than a 100 per cent slice of nothing.'

Ayan recognised the movie quote instantly.

'*The Hustler*, Paul Newman. But hey—Shivani isn't anything big.'

'You dog, you. You actually checked her out?' laughed Dhiraj.

'Please. That's not what I meant, and you know that! Talk about projection. You must have checked her out and you are projecting your inner fantasies onto me.'

'I shall take refuge in the clause of plausible deniability here. But don't tell me you didn't like her?' Dhiraj's tone was cheeky, probing. Ayan knew that he was dangling a bait, hoping to get him to say something about Shivani, so he could report back to Nishi.

'Listen, I haven't even thought about it. Really. There's been so much happening in my life, as you know.'

'Then I would suggest, a distraction would be great. I am sure she will get in touch with you.'

'Let's wait and see. And I will handle that if that happens,' said Ayan.

* * *

Gopal Shanker called out to Ayan and asked him to join them

for dinner. Velu had made Kerala *parotta* and chicken curry for Ayan. He had made oat porridge and a bowl of mixed fruits chopped into small pieces for Gopal Shanker.

'Gopal Sir always has oats and fruits for dinner,' said Velu, when Ayan looked questioningly at him.

Ayan was relieved that his grandfather seemed to have forgotten all about feeding the cows. He loved the food that Velu cooked and complimented him on it.

Gopal Shanker said, 'Eat up, young man. I am glad you like Velu's food. He has been cooking for me, ever since I moved here.'

'When did you move here, *muttacha*?' asked Ayan.

'I moved here in 1990. It was 1st April. April Fools Day. I will never forget that date,' said Gopal. He had a faraway look in his eyes now. Ayan's question seemed to have transported Gopal to a different era, a different time.

'She never lived here, not even a single day. I wanted her to see the place very badly, she never got a chance to,' said Gopal.

'Oh. But didn't you get married here?' asked Ayan.

Gopal Shanker looked at him uncomprehendingly. He blinked a few times.

'No, Padmaja and I were not married here. We were married at her place. And it was in Hyderabad that she passed away. The year was 1988. You were not born then, am I correct?' asked Gopal Shanker.

'Yes, *muttacha*. I was born in 1989. I feel sad that I never even got to see *muttashi*[12],' said Ayan. He had seen pictures of his grandmother. She was beautiful.

'Ha. You know only what is on the outside. I have one piece of advice for you, young man. Do not ever get married. Marriage kills things. Marriage, it kills everything,' said Gopal

---

12. Grandmother

Shanker.

They finished the rest of their meal in silence.

When Ayan went upstairs after dinner that night, his grandfather's words played around in his head. Why had his grandfather said that?

His phone buzzed. He reached for it and checked the message. It was from Shivani.

'Hi! What are you doing? How is Kerala?' she had typed. There was a smiley at the end of it.

He noted that there were complete words typed, no vowels eaten up, and the grammar was perfect, just the way he liked it. He disliked the way most people typed these days, substituting 'Thnx' for Thanks, and 'Vot' for 'What'.

Perhaps Dhiraj was right after all. She seemed to be interested in a conversation with him. He decided to play hard to get. He knew that she would get a 'message read notification'.

He turned off his phone and lay on the bed looking out of the window. The moonlight streamed in. It looked like a scene straight out of a fantasy movie—the paddy fields luminous, swaying gently, reflecting the moonlight. Ayan could imagine a werewolf howling. Finally, after tossing and turning for a very long time, he fell asleep.

5

'Ayan Sir … Ayan Sir.'

Velu was standing at the foot of the four-poster bed with a steaming tumbler of coffee placed in a small steel bowl with a flat base, the typical manner in which coffee is served in many traditional South Indian homes.

Ayan stirred in his sleep. It took him a few minutes to even comprehend where he was. Velu's voice seemed to be coming from somewhere far away. For a moment he was not sure whether he was dreaming or whether it was real.

He opened his eyes and then sat bolt upright, seeing Velu.

'So sorry to startle you like this, Ayan Sir. I didn't mean to wake you. But Gopal Sir is asking for you. He told me to wake you up, and he said he wanted to speak to you urgently. I tried stalling him, distracting him, but nothing worked. He is insisting on you coming downstairs right now.'

'Uh, okay. No problem. Give me ten minutes and I will be there,' said Ayan, taking the tumbler of coffee that Velu handed him.

He took a sip and the hot coffee scalded his tongue mildly, but it tasted like heaven. Ayan looked at the sunrise across the paddy fields, which he could see from his picture-window. He realized that even to brush his teeth, he would have to go downstairs where the bathroom was located, that too outside the house. He finished his coffee, and headed downstairs with his toothbrush, the toothpaste squeezed on it. He was dressed in a sleeveless vest and shorts.

As soon as he went downstairs, Gopal Shanker pounced on him.

'Aaah, there you are! I have been waiting for you. Did you sleep well?' he asked.

'Yes, *muttacha*, let me just brush my teeth, I will join you soon,' said Ayan, as he headed towards the doorway at the back of the house, which led to the bathroom.

'Okay, be careful. She isn't always nice to new people,' said Gopal Shanker.

'Eh? Who?' asked Ayan.

'You will see,' said Gopal Shanker and chuckled.

Ayan was a bit puzzled, but he said nothing. When he finished his morning ablutions, he went to his grandfather, who was perched in the easy chair on the verandah, in his usual place, his leg resting on the arm of the chair.

'Did she try any tricks on you?' asked Gopal Shanker.

'Who, *muttacha*?' asked Ayan.

'Shyamala. She killed herself by sticking her head in the tunnel in the bathroom fireplace.' Gopal Shanker paused and lowered his voice. 'When the fire was burning,' he whispered.

A chill passed through Ayan. He shuddered.

'What? Who Shyamala?' he asked.

'It was a long time back. But if any new person uses the bathroom, she makes her displeasure known. But if she didn't do anything to you, perhaps she likes you,' said Gopal Shanker and smiled.

'Yes, perhaps she does,' said Ayan as he cracked his knuckles and stood up. His heart was beating fast. He had no idea what his grandfather was talking about. He also did not know whether he was joking or not.

'Where are you going? I am not done yet. Sit down, young

man or don't you have time for your grandpa too?' said Gopal Shanker.

Reluctantly, Ayan sat down.

'There are many things you do not know about this house. I grew up here. In those days, the house was full of people. My father's three brothers and their families—all of us lived here, and they all raised their children here. We were four—my two older brothers and a sister. All are dead now. Only I am waiting for the royal passport and once that arrives, I too take off,' he said as he made a gesture with his hand, mimicking a plane taking off and laughed.

'Did you enjoy growing up here?' asked Ayan.

'Oh, we never thought about enjoying it. It was the only life we knew. It was a home full of noise and laughter. But there was acute poverty too. We had no electricity back then. We used kerosene lamps. I am sure you wouldn't even have seen those, would you?'

'No *muttacha*, I have never seen those. Do you still have any?'

'They must be in the attic. There are a lot of things lying around in the attic. You can go and have a look if you like,' said Gopal Shanker.

'Oh yes, I will. And when you finally got electricity, it must have been great?' asked Ayan.

'When electricity first came to the village, we were all excited. But the voltage was very low. Still, we did not mind. Nobody had ceiling fans then. We only had electric bulbs, and we were fascinated by them. It was a company called Kannan Devan which was owned by the British East India Company, which first brought electricity to the state.'

'Wow, I can't imagine living without power,' said Ayan.

'When that is all you have known your entire life, it does not become a big deal. We managed fine those days. All of us had to be inside by 6 p.m., as it would be too dark outside. We ate our meals here, by the light of the kerosene lamp,' he said, pointing to the verandah.

Ayan tried to imagine how the many rooms of this house must have been—filled with children, their laughter, the voices of women at their various chores, the aromas from the kitchen, and the members of the family gathering in the central courtyard to talk. He noticed that each of the bedrooms opened up into the courtyard. The house itself was designed to bring people together. He wondered how Gopal Shanker felt now, about all the rooms being locked up. Ayan was suddenly filled with a curiosity to see the other rooms in the house.

'*Muttacha*, do you think I can go around the house, and also up the attic and explore?' asked Ayan.

'Oooooh, feel free to do so. Only be careful of Shyamala,' said Gopal Shanker and laughed.

'Sure, if I see her, I will convey your regards,' laughed Ayan, nervously.

'I have more to tell you, young man. But I will not keep you from your breakfast. Please eat and come back here. I have already had my breakfast.'

'Sure, *muttacha*,' said Ayan, as he sped towards the kitchen where he found Velu busy making *puttu-kadala*, a dish which Ayan, like any true-blue Malayalee, loved.

'Velu *chetta*, was there anyone called Shyamala living in this house, who died here?' asked Ayan.

Velu frowned as he concentrated. 'Shyamala, eh? There was no one here by that name. Not that I recall.'

'*Muttachan* says she stuck her head into the firewood tunnel of the bathroom and killed herself,' said Ayan.

'Eh? No! Nobody has killed themselves like that here, in this house! I would have definitely remembered if something that shocking had happened,' said Velu with certainty.

'Do you think it could have been before your time?' asked Ayan.

'If it was such a shocking incident, my parents would have told me about it. I am sure of that,' said Velu.

'I think *muttachan* is messing with me then,' said Ayan.

'Yes, most likely he is doing that. He must have been just joking,' said Velu.

But it nagged Ayan. Why would his grandfather say something that outrageous? Perhaps Velu was mistaken or perhaps he did not know.

* * *

Now that Ayan did not have an office to go to, the days stretched before him endlessly. He asked Velu if there was any way he could get an Internet connection set up. Velu said that he would have to visit Kottayam for that, and as far as he knew, nobody in the neighbourhood had a computer, let alone an Internet connection.

'Really? How do people manage then?' asked Ayan. What Velu said confirmed his suspicion that getting a connection through optic fibre cable, like the one he had in Pune, would be impossible. It didn't seem like Poongavanam had that option.

'What do we need Internet in the house for? We have our *Akshaya Kendras* set up by the government. You can go there and they do everything for you through computers. We can pay our electricity bill, do train bookings—anything that you people do with your Internet, they do it for us there,' said Velu.

'I guess I will have to make a trip to Kottayam then. I need to get a dongle for Internet.'

'Dongle? What is that?' asked Velu.

'It's this little thing Velu *chetta*, which you can plug into the laptop, and get Internet in your laptop.'

'Oh, you brought your computer with you?' asked Velu.

'Yes, I did,' smiled Ayan.

'Oh, *kollaam*[13], Ayan Sir,' said Velu.

'So, how do I get to Kottayam from here?' asked Ayan.

'We will have to book a taxi. Or you can walk to the junction and take a bus. The bus will take you an hour to get there,' said Velu.

'I think I will take the bus. I would like to explore the place,' said Ayan.

Just as he was getting ready to leave for Kottayam, Gopal Shanker called out to him again. 'Ayan—where are you off to?' he asked.

Ayan explained his need for Internet and that he was going to see if he could buy a dongle. He then had to explain to Gopal Shanker what a dongle meant.

'Do buy fruits on your way back. Murali and his family are visiting this evening. He called me up yesterday,' said Gopal Shanker.

'Oh, sure. Er ... who is Murali, *muttacha*? I am sorry I don't remember them,' said Ayan.

'Murali—our Murali. He is a big man now. He hasn't forgotten me. You will meet all of them when he comes this evening. He has two daughters, very smart girls. Very pretty too,' said Gopal Shanker.

* * *

It was 4 p.m. by the time Ayan returned from Kottayam. The search for a dongle had taken him longer than expected, as he had to furnish a few details and fill up forms. He had also decided to explore Kottayam a bit and had discovered a nice cafe with free wifi, where he spent some time. Kottayam was a modern town compared to Poongavanam.

'Oh, you have brought so many fruits! If you had told me, I would have got it from the weekly market, and it was today.

---

13. A term used in Malayalam, indicating approval

I have just got enough for a week. Plus of course, our own fruit trees give us a lot. All what you have bought is in excess of all that, Ayan Sir,' said Velu, taking the bags from Ayan.

'Oh! *Muttachan* told me to buy these as he said Murali and his family were visiting this evening.'

'Murali? Who Murali? I don't know anyone by that name. And no one called Murali has visited in all the years that I have worked here. Let me go and check with Gopal Sir. If we are having visitors, I can prepare *bondas*[14]. That will be better than these fruits,' said Velu, as he walked to Gopal Shanker's bedroom. Ayan followed him.

Gopal Shanker was sitting at his desk, his back facing the door. He seemed to be writing something.

Velu cleared his throat and waited.

Gopal Shanker stopped writing and turned towards them.

'Ah, there you are, Ayan. Come, come and sit,' he said gesturing to the wooden bench that was to the side of the room. Gopal Shanker told Velu to assist him and with Ayan and Velu helping him, he sat on the wooden chair, next to the bench, resting his foot on the centre table. Ayan sat on the bench next to his grandfather.

'Er ... Gopal Sir, are we having visitors today? Shall I make *bonda*?' asked Velu.

'Eh? What visitors? My own children don't come to see me. Where will I have visitors from? No, there are no visitors for me,' said Gopal Shanker, shaking his head.

Ayan gasped involuntarily. It took him a couple of seconds to find his voice.

'What?! *Muttacha*! You told me Murali and his family were coming to visit. You said he had two daughters, and that he has become a big man now. You were pretty excited about his visit,' exclaimed Ayan.

---

14. A deep-fried delicacy with potato filling

'What? I never said any such thing! Murali? Who is Murali?' asked Gopal Shanker.

Ayan darted a worried glance at Velu. Velu looked back helplessly.

'Anyway, you make the *bondas*. Ayan here will love them,' said Gopal Shanker.

'All right, I will have some,' said Ayan to Velu.

Gopal Shanker did not speak about Murali at all again that day. It seemed as if he had completely forgotten about making that statement. He wanted to see the dongle that Ayan had bought. He insisted on seeing Ayan's laptop, and Ayan was glad to finally get connectivity. His browser opened to Facebook and Gopal Shanker asked him what that was. Ayan patiently explained to him how Facebook worked. Gopal Shanker listened intently and had a lot of questions, which Ayan answered. When Ayan showed him the photographs that various relatives had posted, Gopal Shanker was delighted. He clapped his hands and said, 'Oh, so anyone you want will be on this? Do you mean to say you can find anybody?'

'Only those who have opened a Facebook account, *muttacha*,' he said.

'Oh. I thought it just could find anyone,' said Gopal Shanker, the disappointment evident on his face.

After his interaction with his grandfather, Ayan opened Google Maps to explore the areas around the neighbourhood. He saw that Poongavanam was not even listed. He selected 'satellite view', zoomed in and clicked on 'add a missing place'. Then he submitted his location co-ordinates. He received an automated notification thanking him, stating that it would be reviewed and added.

* * *

Jairaj called Ayan later that evening.

'How are things there?' he asked.

'*Accha*, *muttachan* mentioned someone called Shyamala, and then someone called Murali. He said Shyamala had killed herself in this house, and that Murali would be visiting soon with his family.'

It took a moment for Jairaj to even understand what Ayan was telling him.

Ayan had to repeat himself.

'Shyamala? I have never heard that name before. Nobody killed themselves in that house. Nor do I know any Murali,' said Jairaj.

'Velu said the same thing. I think *muttachan* is imagining things,' said Ayan.

There was a pause at the other end.

'If that is the case, then we need to get medical help. I will speak to Shaila too regarding this, and we will see what to do,' said his father.

6

Shaila called Ayan the next evening.

'Shailammayi! How are you? What is news?' said Ayan, answering her call.

'Truth be told, I am getting tired of life in Pretoria. Can't wait for Ghanshyam to get his next posting so we can move out of this blessed country,' said his aunt.

She then enquired about his job. Ayan narrated the whole incident, including how he had been fired and how the job search was not yielding any results. He confided that he was beginning to get disheartened.

'It's early days yet, Ayan. Don't worry, it will all get sorted out,' Shaila consoled him.

Then she asked about her father, the real reason for her phone call. She mentioned that Jairaj had told her what had happened and she asked Ayan how serious he thought the issue was.

'I am not sure, Shailammayi. He seems perfectly normal but for these two incidents.'

'It could be old age. Maybe he is just confused. I do remember someone called Murali who visited us a long time ago, when we were living in Jaipur, before we moved to Hyderabad. He had two daughters too. They were twins and were very cute. I was a child and I was convinced that these two little girls were porcelain dolls that walked and talked,' said Shaila.

'Oh! So this Murali person is not entirely fabricated then. That's a relief,' said Ayan.

'Yes, your father might not probably remember them, as he was too little at the time.'

'That probably explains it. But what about Shyamala, who is she?' asked Ayan.

Shaila was silent for a minute.

Then she said, 'No, I do not know anyone like that.'

Ayan asked if there was any way they could find out if there was someone called Shyamala.

'Leave it Ayan, it doesn't matter. I think because of age, he is just getting confused. How is he otherwise? Jairaj said all his medical reports were normal. How is his leg healing?'

'He is recovering. The cast should come off soon. I think he is lonely. He seems to be wanting to talk to me a lot these days,' said Ayan.

'I am glad you are around for him. Take care of him Ayan,' said Shaila.

It was only after she hung up that Ayan realised that she hadn't spoken of when she would be coming to Kerala to look her father up. Ayan found it odd that both of Gopal Shanker's children did not want to come and see him. But in any case, he was here now, and he decided he would talk to his grandfather every chance he got, and he would try and alleviate his loneliness. He remembered reading that one of the main things that the elderly suffer from was the feeling of being useless and uncared for. He didn't want his grandfather to feel that way. The best way to get him talking was to ask him about his past, and Ayan started mentally preparing all that he could ask him.

As if on cue, Gopal Shanker called out, 'Ayan, what are you doing? Come here!'

Ayan went to his grandfather and sat down opposite him, in his usual place on the verandah, leaning against the pillar.

'Velu, come and light the lamp. It is dusk already and the lamp is not lit,' said Gopal Shanker, pointing to the small kerosene lamp kept on the verandah.

'Yes, Gopal Sir,' said Velu as he hurried out to light the lamp.

Ayan remembered this ritual from his childhood. As soon as the sun set, the lamp kept on the verandah was lit. The children then had to stop playing, go inside, wash their faces, hands and legs. Then they would have to say their prayers. Ayan was strangely comforted to see that the tradition of lighting the lamp still continued.

'*Muttacha*, it is so nice to see this lamp still being lit,' he said.

'In the olden times, when there was no electricity, this was important. Now it is more out of habit, than anything else. I like to watch the flame dance,' said Gopal Shanker.

'Me too,' said Ayan and then after a pause, asked, '*Muttacha*, I wanted to ask you about your life. When did you go to Mumbai?'

Gopal Shanker leaned back in his easy chair and thought for a moment.

'Aaaah, those days it was called Bombay. Let me see—I was just eighteen when I left home,' he said.

He then talked about how overwhelming Bombay was in those days, and what a major change it was for a village boy from Poongavanam to arrive in that city and find his way around. Once Gopal Shanker started talking, he just wouldn't stop.

Ayan listened to him, asking questions at appropriate places, which would spark another memory in Gopal Shanker, and he would start narrating another story from his past.

When Gopal Shanker got tired, he said he wanted to go to his room for a while and read. Ayan helped him to walk to his bedroom and settled him down on his bed.

He then remembered that he had left his phone charging

upstairs. He went upstairs to his room to get it. He saw three calls from Dhiraj that he had missed. Ayan couldn't remember a time when he had put away his phone for even five minutes, and now he had not even remembered his phone for the past three hours. He could see that life in Poongavanam was changing him. He was surprised to discover that he was actually liking the unhurried pace of things here.

When he called Dhiraj back, his call went unanswered.

*   *   *

The next morning, after breakfast and after chatting with Gopal Shanker for a while, Ayan decided to explore the rest of the house. He went to the kitchen and asked Velu for the keys to the rooms that were locked. Velu took a large bunch of keys from a drawer in the wooden almirah placed outside the kitchen. They were large, heavy and made of copper. Ayan had never seen keys like these.

'How do you know which key opens which room?' asked Ayan.

'Aaah, I know them by sight. There is a slight difference in each of these keys,' said Velu.

Ayan inspected them closely and saw that they were indeed different in design. Velu offered to come with Ayan to each of the rooms and open them for him.

'Don't worry. I will try each one and open them myself,' said Ayan.

'Okay, leave the doors open after you are done. Today is the weekly cleaning day,' said Velu, as he went back to the kitchen.

*   *   *

Ayan set about exploring the house. The locks themselves were beautiful, made of copper, embedded in the door frames, ornate, intricately carved with motifs. He loved them. Most of the rooms he opened were similar to his own. There was a picture-window at one end facing the door, a four-poster bed, and an antique writing desk. It was only the position of the bed that differed. Some of the rooms also had old wooden trunks. Ayan opened each one, and all of them were empty. One of them had an old black cardboard folder that was falling apart. Ayan opened it to see what was inside. It was empty.

There was a long narrow corridor at one end of the house which led to a smaller room. As Ayan was walking towards it, his phone rang, startling him. Ayan saw that it was Dhiraj. He answered the call.

'Hey! I have news for you. Nishi and Shivani are coming to Kerala. They asked me to join them!' said Dhiraj.

'Uh? What? Why are they coming here? And which place are they coming to?' asked Ayan.

'Not sure. I think we land in Kochi. How far is your village from there?'

Ayan instantly felt the muscles in his neck stiffening up. He couldn't understand this sudden negative reaction that he felt. 'Uh—I have to go. My grandfather is calling me. I will call you back,' said Ayan, as he hung up.

He didn't want Dhiraj or Nishi or Shivani to visit Poongavanam. It was almost as if Poongavanam was his protective shell, and he felt safe here, sheltered from the real world.

Dhiraj's phone call telling him that they would arrive soon was a little too close for comfort.

Ayan sat down on the verandah which faced the inner courtyard, thinking about what he could possibly tell his friends, so that he wouldn't have to meet them.

Velu came to him with a glass of freshly squeezed lemon juice.

Ayan thanked him and sipped it gratefully.

'So how is our home? Did you like it?' asked Velu.

'It is beautiful, Velu *chetta*. The antique furniture, the

intricately-carved locks, the low doors, the flooring—all of it is so charming. The energy in this place is so calming. I feel good here,' said Ayan.

'You will find that in all the old homes. All of these were designed keeping in mind that a home has to shelter you from the harshness of the outside world. Did you notice that all the doors are made in such a way that you have to bend to enter each room?' asked Velu.

'Yes. I was curious about that. Why did they make the doors so low?'

'You see, humility is the first virtue that we must all imbibe. Our elders ensured that when we bend our heads to enter a room, we are forced to remember to be humble.'

'By bowing our heads?'

'Yes, it is a sign of respect. It makes us pause for a second,' said Velu.

When Velu left with the tumbler in which he had given Ayan the lemon juice, Ayan decided to continue his exploration. He walked to the end of the corridor, tried the various keys, and finally opened the door. He had to step over the large wooden step and bend his head to enter the room.

This room was very different from the others. Ayan drew in a sharp breath when he opened it. It was a long, cavernous room about fifteen feet by twenty feet, lined with bookshelves on both sides. It also had various assorted pieces of furniture. An antique dresser, with a circular mirror in the centre, with wooden shelves on either side, stood by the entrance of the room. At the far end was a low bed. An intricately-carved wooden cradle lay at another end.

Next to the cradle were several rocking horses. Ayan was delighted when he saw them and couldn't help exclaiming, even though he was alone. 'Oh my God!' he said. He remembered rocking on one of them as a child, when he had spent a summer at *Thekke Madom,* along with Nithya. He and Nithya had named the horses Harvard and Stanford, which were the 'grandest names' they could think of as children. He was Sir Ignatius the Brave and she was Lady Constance. They had rocked back and forth till the horse he was rocking on had toppled. He had to get two stitches on his forehead and Nithya had got a scolding, even though it was not her fault. Ayan was amazed at how vividly he recalled the incident as soon as he saw the rocking horses. He smiled at the memory.

There were also many old lamps that lay scattered at one end of the room. They were made of copper but had blackened with age. Next to the lamps stood a Malabar treasure box shaped like a small house, with copper embossing, and a lock. In one corner, a gramophone and many records lay, all covered with a thin coat of dust. There were dusty picture frames stacked up against a wall.

Ayan felt like he had entered a magic land of forgotten items. The bookcases did not have glass doors like the modern ones in his home in Bahrain. Instead, these had wooden doors, with carved motifs. He could not see what was inside them till he opened them. Two of them were empty. But there were five bookcases filled with books from top to bottom. The leather-bound volumes yellowing with age were well preserved, and Ayan found himself looking through a couple of them with awe, turning the pages carefully. Right from classics to history books to text books—there were so many.

'What a treasure!' thought Ayan as he walked to the picture frames. They had a fine layer of dust and he sneezed as he picked them up one by one. The black and white portrait photographs were visible beneath all the dust. He recognized his father and Shailammayi in one of the photos. They stood proudly staring into the camera. In another photo was Gopal Shanker and his wife Padmaja. Ayan had never met his grandmother, as she had passed away before he was born. He stared at the photograph now. She looked beautiful. Her hair was braided into two plaits. She wore a saree and a blouse with short sleeves. Her back was towards the camera but she was looking over her shoulder and smiling at the photographer. He wondered what she was like, as a person. His father rarely spoke of her.

Next to the picture frames, on the floor, rested a large rolled-up bundle of burlap. When Ayan looked inside it, he discovered two thick photo albums. He was delighted to find them, and he eagerly looked at all the old photographs. There were many of his grandmother, as well as pictures of other relatives. He had no idea who the people in the photos were.

Just as he was placing the albums back in the burlap, he spotted a broken mirror lying with its face up, next to the albums. The light that it reflected made pretty patterns on the roof, like disco lights. When Ayan glanced up, he saw a little trap-door in the roof. It was the attic.

There had to be a ladder somewhere here, to climb up. Then he spotted it. It was behind the book shelves. Ayan carried the ladder to the trapdoor and pushed the trapdoor upwards with the ladder. It opened easily. Ayan saw two hooks on the wooden panel. He saw that the ladder he was carrying had grooves at one end, which fitted into the hooks.

What a neat idea to make the ladder fit firmly, he thought. He attached the ladder to the hooks and began to climb up.

7

Ayan poked his head up the trap-door and sneezed. A single circular window at the far end was the only source of light. The motes of dust danced in the shaft of light streaming in. He held his breath for a brief while—the musty smell was an assault on his nostrils. Ayan was sensitive to smells and he had a strong dislike for unpleasant odours. When he couldn't hold it in anymore, he exhaled. He wanted to explore the attic. He decided that he might as well get on with it, smell or no smell.

He heaved himself up into the loft and dusted his hands. The roof was so low that he couldn't stand to his full height of 5'11". He had to bend slightly to walk around. He noticed the cobwebs on the wooden beams and tried to avoid them by bending even more as he passed them. The attic seemed mostly empty, a direct contrast to the room downstairs. There was barely anything here.

The attic went around the whole house. As the house was built around the courtyard, the attic ran its length too. Ayan decided to explore a bit further. He switched on the flashlight on his phone and walked on. One of the floorboards creaked as he walked. He pointed his flashlight to the corners and spotted a few dried coconut husks and shells. He also saw a couple of old jars which were about three feet in height. He recalled seeing miniature jars like these in his home in Bahrain. His mother called them *bharanis* and used them to store pickles.

Sometimes she also churned buttermilk in them. There were also two large, heavy, shallow, bowl-shaped vessels. They were almost black, but he knew they were made of copper. *Uruli*—that's what these vessels were called! He was surprised how these names were coming to him easily. There was nothing interesting in the attic.

Just as he turned to leave, he spotted an aluminium trunk at the far end. Ayan walked towards it. It was fairly large. He recalled this trunk being in his grandfather's room when he was a child. He and Nithya used to drag it from under his grandfather's bed. They would climb on it to reach the top shelf of the cupboard in Gopal Shanker's room, where he kept a jar of 'cream biscuits'. Whenever Gopal Shanker was pleased with Ayan and Nithya, he would tell them that they could take two biscuits each from the jar. These were a coveted treat. Ayan and Nithya loved to take apart the two biscuits stuck together and lick the cream that was in the centre. The trunk was about a foot high. When they climbed on it, they could reach the biscuit jar easily. Once they helped themselves, they would sit on the trunk and savour their treat. The trunk was large enough to seat two children comfortably as it was about 4' by 3'.

Ayan remembered that it used to be a deep blue colour. The colour was now faded. It was rusty in patches where the paint had peeled off. It was coated with a thick layer of dust.

He remembered opening this trunk as a child. Back then, it had held his grandfather's hat, his umbrella and his galoshes, which he wore whenever he went out in the rain. It wasn't locked in those days. But now there was a large lock on it. He inspected the lock. It was rusted too. He tried lifting the trunk, but it was heavy. So he dragged it to the trapdoor of the loft. He would need Velu's help in getting it downstairs. He would also have to ask him for the key to the trunk. He was curious now and wanted to see what the trunk held. Why was it locked?

When Ayan climbed down, he detached the ladder from the trapdoor and shut it.

'Ha! Look at you. You need a bath for sure. Found anything interesting up there? Was your exploring adventure worth it?' asked Velu, when he saw Ayan walking towards his room, his head covered with cobwebs, his T-shirt dirty with dust.

'Yes, I do need a bath, Velu *chetta*. And yes! I found *muttachan's* old trunk up there. Nithya and I have had many adventures on that trunk. Sometimes it used to be our bus, sometimes our sofa, and sometimes a ship on which we sailed. It holds such fond memories,' said Ayan.

'A trunk? Up there?' frowned Velu. 'As far as I remember, the loft only has *bharanis* and *urulis*.'

'Yes, Velu *chetta*. This trunk was at the far corner. If I hadn't switched on the flashlight on my phone, I would have missed it. Do you remember, it was a deep blue aluminium trunk which used to be under grandfather's bed?'

'Ooooh yes, I remember it now. I recall asking your grandfather where it was, when I discovered that it was gone. He had laughed and asked if I noticed only then. He mentioned that he had got rid of it long back. So this is what he had meant! That he got rid of it by shoving it upstairs!' exclaimed Velu.

Ayan laughed at his expression of indignation.

'I think Gopal Sir must have asked the hired help who come to clean the place, to keep it in the attic. He must have done it when I was at the market. Else there is no way he could have got a trunk up in the attic without my knowledge,' said Velu.

'Do you know where the key to that trunk is?' asked Ayan.

'Oh. I didn't even know it was locked,' said Velu.

* * *

After Ayan showered, he noticed another message from Dhiraj.

Ayan read it with dread.

'*Hey, call when free. Want to tell you about the Kerala trip,*' it said.

Ayan did not want to know about their Kerala trip But if he ignored this message, there was a chance of him being caught by surprise as they could turn up suddenly. As much as he hated it, he had no choice but to call Dhiraj.

'Hey! How is the Kerala native doing?' asked Dhiraj.

'Good. Why are you coming and when?'

'That doesn't sound very friendly or welcoming.' Dhiraj did not miss the curt, abrupt tone which Ayan thought he had managed to conceal.

'No, I was asking as I could hire a local band to welcome you with music and garlands,' Ayan improvised quickly, forcing a laugh, knowing that Dhiraj had caught him out.

'Oh, I see. Throw in a few elephants too and have them garland us at the welcoming party,' said Dhiraj.

'Ha! Great idea. But seriously, how did this sudden Kerala trip come up? Don't tell me you miss me so much.'

'Nishi has been asked to do a story on the Kerala monsoon, by her editor. It's a tie-up with the Kerala Tourism Corporation and the hospitality partner is a resort called *River Creek*, which is in a place called... um... let me think... Oh yes—it's in Aluva. They are paying for air tickets and two days' complimentary stay. Now she isn't going to turn down that offer, is she?' said Dhiraj.

'Of course! That's great,' said Ayan, desperately trying to squeeze enthusiasm into his tone.

'Shivani managed to coordinate this one with the Tourism Board and make it happen. So when this came through, the editor said Shivani could go too. Since you are there now, when Nishi asked me, I jumped at the chance. I have always wanted to visit Kerala. Have heard so much about it,' said Dhiraj.

'Oh, I see. Aluva is a bit far from Poongavanam—that's the

name of my village by the way.'

'Spell that for me, please. The name itself is a tongue twister,' said Dhiraj.

That annoyed Ayan—he had no idea why.

'You won't be able to pronounce it easily. It's a village near Kottayam,' said Ayan.

There was a pause at the other end. Then Dhiraj said, 'Kottayam isn't that far from Aluva. Google Maps shows me that it's about two and a half hours' journey. We must meet up while we are there,' said Dhiraj.

'Sure, I will come over and see you guys,' said Ayan, before Dhiraj could say anything. It was better to preempt their visit to *Thekke Madom* by offering to meet them where they were staying. He did not want to have them over at Poongavanam.

* * *

After his usual post-lunch siesta, Gopal Shanker called out to Ayan to join him at the verandah. Velu brought tea.

'*Muttacha*, do you remember the blue trunk that used to be under your bed?' said Ayan.

Gopal Shanker took about two minutes to think about that.

Then he said, 'Rohini. She was the most beautiful girl I ever saw. I was in the second form when I noticed her. She was in class four, or maybe five. Such a little girl she was. I can still see her clearly, wearing her little frock and two plaits, carrying that cloth satchel which she wore across her shoulders.'

'Eh ... so Rohini was in your school?' asked Ayan puzzled.

He wondered why Gopal Shanker was telling him about a girl in his class when he had asked about the trunk.

'Yes, we went to the same school. She was my junior. It was when Mannathu Padmanabhan visited Poongavanam that I got my chance to speak to her alone. I think it was in 1946. He was giving a speech for equality. Have you heard of him?' asked Gopal Shanker.

'No, *muttacha*, I haven't. And what is second form? I haven't heard of that too.'

'In those days, after standard five, we went to first form, second form and so on. The final year of school was the sixth form. It is the equivalent of class 11 these days. Those days, after the sixth form, we could go to college,' said Gopal Shanker.

'Oh, okay. I never knew about that,' said Ayan.

'Anyway, this Mannathu Padmanabhan—he was a social reformer. Rohini and I, as well as many children from our school, had gone to hear him speak. It went on for very long, much longer than we had anticipated. And then it got dark. I offered to walk her home. When she reached home, I let her go inside by herself. Her parents were furious with her. I hid in the bushes and listened. She got a thrashing from her father. He hit her with a cane, and I counted the thwacks. He hit her four times. Each time he hit her, I winced. I heard her wailing. Her wail still rings in my ears. But I stood frozen. I couldn't do anything. I sneaked away. It was a cowardly act,' said Gopal Shanker. Ayan could see the sadness clouding his eyes.

'You were a child yourself, *muttacha*, what could you do?' said Ayan.

'Child? I was no child. I was twelve, running thirteen. I should have stood up for her and told her father that I had walked her home. I think it was on that day that I knew how I truly felt about her,' said Gopal Shanker.

Velu appeared then with *pazham pori*[15], that Ayan loved.

'Velu *chetta*, you are going to make me fat,' said Ayan.

'Eat up, young man. At your age, you can digest even iron. You should not be worrying about your weight. There's plenty of time for dietary restrictions,' said Gopal Shanker.

Ayan took a bite of it. 'Mmm, delicious! This is divine!'

---

15. A deep fried banana delicacy

he exclaimed.

'Anyway, you were telling me about Rohini,' said Ayan.

Gopal Shanker looked at him and blinked.

'Eh? Rohini? Who is Rohini? I don't know anyone by that name,' said Gopal Shanker.

'*Muttacha*—your classmate. The one you went to see Mannathu Padmanabhan with,' prompted Ayan.

'Oh! You know Mannathu Padmanabhan? I am impressed, young man. Most people your age haven't even heard of him. How do you know of him?' asked Gopal Shanker.

'Oh *muttacha*, you mentioned him just now,' said Ayan.

'Oh, did I? How forgetful of me,' said Gopal Shanker.

He did not mention anything more about Rohini.

Ayan thought he would gently probe him about the key to the trunk.

'*Muttaccha*, I found that blue aluminium trunk in the loft,' said Ayan.

'Blue aluminium trunk?' asked Gopal Shanker speaking each word slowly, as he scrunched his eyes and tried to remember. Then he said, 'Aaah yes. It used to be under my bed for a long time. Then I decided to get rid of it from there.'

'Do you recall where you kept the key?' asked Ayan, as he held his breath. He was hoping his grandfather would remember and tell him.

'The key ... the key to that trunk. I think I hid it. I will look for it. But there's nothing of value in the trunk. It's all old files and things which I have no use for,' said Gopal Shanker.

'Would you mind if I opened the trunk to look?' asked Ayan.

'Be my guest young man! It will give you something to do I suppose. Are you getting bored in Poongavanam?'

'No *muttacha*! On the contrary. I am really liking it here,' said Ayan.

* * *

Later that night, Shaila called Ayan once again to enquire how

Gopal Shanker was doing.

'He is fine, Shailammayi. He told me all about Mannathu Padmanabhan and how he went to listen to his speech. I couldn't have imagined grandpa having a crush on a girl!'

'Really? His crushes in school? That's just incredible. You have got him really talking to you, haven't you?'

'Yes. He was talking about a girl in his school called Rohini, who he walked home with and then he claimed he didn't say any such thing!' said Ayan.

There was a death-like silence at the other end. Ayan thought the call had dropped.

'Hello-hello! Shailammayi?' he said.

He heard the sound of water being poured into a glass at the other end. He heard his aunt drinking it.

Then she spoke. 'Ayan, if he raises that topic again, please steer him away from it.'

'Oh. But why?'

'I think it's time to tell you the truth. Your grandfather—he is schizophrenic. There's nobody called Rohini. If he mentions the name again, please let me or your father know immediately. He ... he ... well ... All these years, he never brought it up and so we thought he was fine. But now that he is talking of her, it looks like his schizophrenia has come back.'

8

Ayan couldn't sleep that night. The conversation with Shailammayi had disturbed him no end. Why hadn't he been told that his grandfather was schizophrenic? When had the condition started? Had he been treated for it? He had pressed Shailammayi for details, but she hadn't given any. She said it was best to speak to his father and she had hung up.

Ayan texted his father saying he wanted to speak to him, but he got no response. He looked at the world clock on his phone. It was past 10 p.m. in Bahrain and most likely his father was asleep. Ayan was restless. Shailammayi's words kept playing around in his head.

When he couldn't bear it any longer, he decided to message Nithya. It was noon in California and she must surely be awake.

'Hey, how is it going?' he typed.

He got a response in minutes.

'Hi!!! What is up with you? Heard you are in Kerala. How is *muttacha*?' she typed.

'Talk?' typed Ayan.

'Sure,' came the reply and Nithya called.

'Ayan!' she said, the joy evident in her voice.

'Nithya! It has been so long. How are things with you?' he asked.

She told him about her workload and how she was finally taking a day off after many weeks. She told him all about her cooking attempts, and how she was tired of eating out and partying. When he asked her about her love life, she said she was casually dating, but hadn't found anyone yet. Then she asked about his love life.

Nithya was the one who had consoled Ayan endlessly after his last girlfriend had dumped him, during his engineering days. She asked him if he had a girlfriend now.

'Nobody, Nithya. I learnt my lesson after you-know-who,' he said.

'Come on! That was three years ago. Don't tell me you haven't got over that.'

'I don't think about it. You tell me, what is up with you?' he said, shifting the focus to her. He didn't want to discuss his love life with her.

'I am growing old, Ayan. Nowadays I look forward to sleeping at 10 p.m., can you imagine!' she said.

'Welcome to the club. I am liking the quiet life in Poongavanam too. And guess what I found today?' he said.

'What?' she asked.

'Do you remember Stanford and Harvard? And do you remember the blue aluminium trunk?'

'Hahaha, of course, I do! How can I forget them? I got such a scolding because you fell off the horse,' she chuckled with unsurpassed mirth.

'You know, I found that blue trunk in the attic.'

'Oh! Did you?! Does it still have his hat and umbrella?'

'I don't know. It was locked! He can't remember where he kept the key.'

'It must be in his bookcase. That's where he used to hide it. Put your hand inside and feel around the inner edges of the top shelf. You will feel a little concealed depression. Just slide it and it moves. It's a secret compartment. He used to keep the key there.'

'What? Really? How do you know this?'

'Remember, when I was in class ten, I spent my entire summer there? I didn't want to stay with my parents as I was tired of Nairobi. You didn't come that year. He used to lock his trunk and keep the key there.'

'All the bookcases have been moved to the room at the far corner of the house. There's no bookcase in his room anymore. But I will look for the key tomorrow. Thanks for the tip,' said Ayan.

'No worries! And how *is* the old man?'

'Nithya, I had actually pinged you to speak about him. I had a conversation with your mother a little while back. Tell me, did they ever mention to you that he is schizophrenic?'

'What? No way!'

'That's what your mother said. She said he had it many years back, and they thought he was fine now. But they suspect it has come back.'

'Oh no! That's terrible.'

'I know. That's why I called you. How is it that they never mentioned this before?'

'Er … I don't know. Maybe we were too young? Maybe there was no need to? There could be so many reasons, Ayan.'

'Hmmm, yes, you are right. Anyway, I am waiting for my father to wake up. I want to talk to him. Your mother told me to keep a watch on whatever *muttachan* says and report back.'

'Do keep me posted too,' said Nithya.

Ayan lay on his bed and stared out of the window. He stared at the thousands of stars twinkling in the night sky. He listened to the sounds of the crickets chirping. He saw the fireflies hovering around the window. He watched them fascinated. But no matter how hard he tried, sleep eluded him. He was inundated with thoughts that raced around inside his head.

How did his grandfather give so many details about Rohini? Did people with schizophrenia have an innate ability to do that? He opened his laptop and read up all about it. There were many symptoms of schizophrenia. He discovered that his grandfather did not exhibit most of them. They listed aggression, compulsive behaviour, or nonsense word repetition as some of the symptoms, none of which were applicable to his grandfather's behaviour. He also didn't seem to have paranoia or incoherent speech. Of the many symptoms listed, only one which was 'making things up', was applicable. But would people with schizophrenia make up such vivid stories? He could actually see the sadness in his grandfather's eyes when he spoke of Rohini. Why did Shailammayi say that such a person didn't exist? What were they keeping from him?

Ayan fell asleep after very long time, with all these thoughts still running inside his head.

He overslept and was woken up the next morning with the phone ringing in his ear. He fumbled around and took a few seconds to find it. It was his father. There was no cursory small talk. He came straight to the point.

'So Shaila called me this morning. Is he talking about Rohini again?' asked his father.

'Only once, *accha*. He talked about walking her home when they were in school.'

Ayan now felt a little foolish repeating the details to his father. In a strange way, he also felt he was betraying his grandfather. Neither his father nor his aunt had seen the emotions on his grandfather's face when he had spoken about Rohini. There was rawness and vulnerability there, which Ayan had seen. He couldn't explain this to his father. He now regretted even mentioning this to his aunt.

'He used to have these episodes in the past, but he hasn't mentioned anything after your *muttashi* died. Anyway, keep a close watch, Ayan, and let me know if he talks about Rohini again,' said his father.

Ayan had already decided that he would do no such thing. Neither of the siblings had bothered to visit Gopal Shanker in the past many years. If they were so concerned, why hadn't they at least looked him up?

But Ayan didn't want to say all of this to his father. So he simply said, 'Yes *accha*, I will.' That satisfied his father and he hung up.

* * *

Ayan decided that he would try and look for the key to the trunk. He would also take Velu's help in getting the trunk down from the loft.

He couldn't wait to get through breakfast, so that he could get the trunk down and search for the key. Velu would be free only after breakfast.

Gopal Shanker joined Ayan for breakfast. Ayan wanted to see if he could get more information about Rohini out of Gopal Shanker. He knew better than to ask him directly. So he tried another approach.

'*Muttacha*, this Mannathu Padmanabhan, did he speak well?' asked Ayan.

'Oh yes. He was a great orator. The day he came to speak, I remember going to Joseph's shop, as my father had asked me to buy shaving blades for him. He wanted 7 *O'Clock* slotted blades, double-edged. They were 12 annas for a packet of ten. When I got back home after listening to Mannathu Padmanabhan, the first thing my father asked me was, 'Did you get the shaving blades?' Fortunately, I had. Joseph and I still laugh about it,' said Gopal Shanker.

'Is that the shop just around the corner when you exit *Thekke Madom*? You know, he called out to me that day when I went for a walk. He knew me and I was surprised.'

'Yes, yes, that is our Joseph's shop. We go back a long way. I used to buy candies for Rohini from there. He would always smile and say, 'Using sugar to get a sugar-girl.' I have no idea what that phrase meant,' Gopal Shanker was now smiling at the memory.

Ayan was instantly alert. He had mentioned Rohini again.

'Did Rohini like the candies?' Ayan asked.

Gopal Shanker's expression instantly changed. He squinted his eyes and called out to Velu.

'How many times do I tell you to clean the cobwebs, Velu? Haven't I made it clear that the cleaning has to be spotless? What are those cobwebs doing there?' he demanded, pointing to the corner of the room.

Velu rushed out of the kitchen and looked at where Gopal Shanker was pointing. There was indeed a tiny cobweb there.

'Oh sorry, Gopal Sir. I missed that spot when I cleaned yesterday,' said Velu.

'Are you the eighty-year-old here? I can see it so clearly and you can't. See that it is cleaned up immediately. And has the newspaper arrived? Help me up, I want to go and read it,' said Gopal Shanker.

Ayan told Velu that he would help his grandfather. He placed the walker next to him and helped him up. Once he was seated in his favourite chair in the verandah with his legs outstretched, Gopal Shanker immersed himself in reading the newspaper. He always read the Malayalam papers back to back. After he was done, he would read the English newspaper too. It was one activity which he enjoyed tremendously. Ayan did not want to interrupt him.

Ayan's phone buzzed. He looked at the message. It was from Dhiraj. 'We arrive on Friday. Shall we meet on Saturday?'

Ayan read the message and decided to ignore it for now. He put the phone away without replying.

Then he went into the kitchen and asked Velu for help to bring the trunk downstairs.

Ayan climbed the loft once more using the ladder. Velu got a flat table and climbed on top of it, standing next to Ayan. Ayan carried the trunk down, supporting the weight on his head. It was heavy. A thin film of sweat coated his forehead. Velu took it from him and Ayan climbed down. Then he helped Velu, and between both of them, they managed to gently lower the heavy aluminium trunk on to the floor.

'Velu *chetta*, have you ever met this Rohini that *muttachan* mentioned?' asked Ayan.

'No. Never. I was not even born when your grandfather was in high school,' said Velu.

He asked Ayan if he wanted anything else from him. Ayan said he did not.

'How are you going to open it?' asked Velu.

'I have a good idea where the key might be. I am going to look for it,' said Ayan.

Once Velu left, Ayan decided to go over each bookcase thoroughly to see if he could find the secret compartment that Nithya had told him about. Ayan was tempted to take out the books, and start reading them. They looked so good in their leather-bound covers. There were many titles that he had not read. But he pushed that thought aside. Finding the key to the trunk was more important. He had no idea why he was so eager to find that key. His grandfather had clearly said that there was nothing of value in the trunk. Still, he wanted to open it and see.

He felt along the inner edges of the top shelf. There was nothing. He was meticulous. He ran his hands under the plank of each of the lower shelves too. The first three bookcases yielded no results. Inside the third bookcase, he felt the depression, just like Nithya had described. Excited, he moved it. It slid easily open. He switched on his phone torch light and looked into the compartment. There was a little circular tin. He examined it and discovered that it was a tin that had held cigarettes at some point in the past. He had never seen anything like it before. He prised open the lid.

Inside it was the key.

9

Ayan's heart beat faster as he held the key in his hand. There was a flutter in his belly as he walked to the trunk. He had no idea why he was this excited at finding the key. Maybe it was a sense of adventure; or maybe it was because he felt like a child again, discovering something new. All he knew was that he wanted to look inside the trunk.

Ayan tried the key, but the lock was so rusted that it just wouldn't turn. He tried it a couple of more times, wiggling the key back and forth. Then he tried to gently twist the key, but it was futile.

'Damn!' swore Ayan. He went to find Velu to ask him what to do.

'Oh, we can put coconut oil into the lock. After that, we have to wait for about a day. It should soak in and lubricate the insides. The lock will definitely open then,' said Velu.

'Okay, let's do that,' said Ayan.

Velu told him that he had a machine-oil container with a long nozzle, which he kept in the bicycle shed to oil his bicycle parts. That would do the trick.

Ayan got the machine-oil container and Velu carefully dribbled a few drops into the slot of the lock where the key would go, as well as on the shanks. He concentrated and pressed the nozzle carefully, so that the oil would slide down the movable parts.

'All right. Now we have no choice but to wait,' said Velu. He then excused himself as he had to cook lunch.

Ayan looked at the bookcases and decided to choose a few books to read. He chose a classic, 'The Scarlet Pimpernel'. He opened it and saw his grandfather's name in his neat handwriting. Below it was written '1949' and on the next line *'Thekke Madom'*.

The pages were yellow with age, but Ayan did not mind that at all. It was such a long time since he had lost himself in a book. He loved the feel of the leather cover and the gold embossed lettering. He ran his hands up and down over the cover. He carried the book to the verandah, and rolled out a straw mat kept on the side of the verandah. He spent the whole morning lost in the book and looked up only when Velu called him for lunch.

* * *

In the evening, after tea, Ayan decided to watch a football match on television. The television set itself was an ancient one. It was nothing like the flat-screen TVs that he was used to. This one was a like a box with a curved screen. His grandfather sat by his side, solving a word puzzle on a newspaper.

'Does the television disturb you, *muttacha*?' asked Ayan.

'Television is for dumb people. Smart people read books and newspapers,' said Gopal Shanker.

'Haha—I only watch sports on it,' said Ayan.

'What do you gain out of watching sports? If you ask me, you should join the local football club here and play with the others. Not sit like a couch potato and watch others playing. Those who can, do. Those who can't, watch,' said Gopal Shanker.

'Oh—is there a football club here? Can I join?' asked Ayan.

He had last played football in his school, in Bahrain. He had been on the school team. After he had joined college in

Mumbai, there simply had not been time for sports. Though the college had a football team, Ayan did not qualify for it. Most of the players in college were the ones who did not bother about academics and were hoping to pass the exams because of the extra marks given under the sports quota. Ayan had been forced to make a choice between sports and academics, and sadly, he had given up football. The prospect of playing football once again made him happy.

'There's no 'Can I'. There is only 'I will'. Do you understand? Ask Velu to show you where they play. Go and speak to the secretary. They are sure to take you in. I know all those boys. They come here for an *Onam*[16] *Sadhya*[17] each year.'

Velu said that he would accompany Ayan to the local club. It was just a five-minute walk from *Thekke Madom,* when you crossed through the paddy fields.

'If you walk around from the main road, it will take you fifteen minutes. This is a shortcut,' said Velu.

'And such a beautiful walk too!'

'I grew up here. So I suppose the beauty is lost on me. Incidentally, this used to be your grandfather's favourite walking route too, till he had the fall. He was telling me that he can't wait for the cast to come off, so he can start his walks again.'

'What do the doctors say?'

'Two or three more weeks and it will come off. They will do an X-ray first, of course.'

When they reached the football field, the game had not yet started. There were many young guys in football jerseys, warming up. The 'football club' was a small room with a tiled roof at the side of the football field. On one side of the

---

16. One of the major festivals of Kerala

17. Feast

room was an iron rack with hooks, on which T-shirts, jeans, shorts and trousers were hanging. Many pairs of footwear lay scattered next to it. It was evident that this room doubled up as a changing room as well.

Velu introduced Ayan to the secretary of the club, Biju, who spoke in Malayalam.

'Welcome, welcome,' he said. He asked Ayan at what level he had played. Ayan said he was a part of the school team and had not played since.

'That's okay. You will quickly pick up. There are a few district-level players here,' said Biju. He said Ayan could start straight away if he liked.

Ayan replied that did not have football boots just yet, but he planned to get one, and that for today, he would play in his usual sports shoes.

Velu didn't stop to watch as he had to make dinner. Ayan told him he would find his way back home.

The game was exhausting. These players were very good. Ayan discovered that his level of fitness was way below what it used to be. Still, it was a great game. After the game, he thanked them and promised to join them every day. They all introduced themselves, and Ayan tried hard to remember all the names. There was Biju the secretary, Roshan, Vinod, Peter, Joshua, and then a short guy with spectacles whose name he forgot, and some more.

'Don't worry, gradually you will get all our names,' Roshan smiled.

It was with a happy heart and a tired body that Ayan left the club. He was drenched in sweat. He felt charged up, elated. He didn't remember feeling this satisfied in a long time. It was as though the vigorous game of football had reminded him of the good things in life. After he had lost his job, this was the first time he was feeling happy.

Velu had already heated the water for his bath. He had also kept a scrumptious dinner ready. Gopal Shanker asked Ayan how the game had been. Ayan said that he had loved it.

The next morning, Ayan went rushing to the trunk and tried to open it. But the lock still would not budge. Velu said that they would lubricate it a bit more, and that perhaps it just needed some more time.

'If it doesn't work tomorrow too, we will call a locksmith and cut open the lock.'

'But Velu *chetta*, it's such a beautiful antique lock. Why destroy it?' asked Ayan.

'Let's wait and see. Many a time, things have a way of sorting themselves out. We just need to be patient,' said Velu.

* * *

Ayan discovered that he had now settled down into a routine. His days were divided into neat slots that involved chatting with his grandfather four times a day, after breakfast, lunch, tea and dinner. In between, there were fixed pockets of time for his job search—where he was hitting a dead end everywhere; his football, which he thoroughly enjoyed; and his reading. During one such talk-session with his grandfather, Gopal Shanker spoke about his days in Baroda, which was one of the places where he had been posted during the course of his tenure with the bank. Ayan was a good listener and he knew to ask the right questions. Ayan noticed that when his grandfather spoke of his professional life, there was no mention of Rohini at all. But when he spoke of his school days, he mentioned her. He told Ayan about a school programme which he had taken part in, along with her.

'It was 1949. The princely states of Travancore and Cochin had just merged. My headmaster wanted me to give a speech about it. My teacher wrote it for me, and I just memorized it without even understanding what I was talking about. But

I got a thunderous applause. Then there was a group song, which she and I were both a part of. She stood right in the front, as she had a lovely voice. I was right at the back. I did not know the words of the song and so I was just mouthing them. Nobody found out,' said Gopal Shanker, as he guffawed at the memory.

Ayan joined in the laughter. 'You know, *muttacha*, I had done the same thing in my school when the teacher forcibly put me in a group song!' said Ayan,

'After all, whose grandson are you?' said Gopal Shanker and smiled.

*   *   *

In the evening, Ayan couldn't wait to get to the football club. He discovered that his skills were slowly coming back. He loved playing with these guys. After the football session, all of them were going to Kottayam, to a restaurant which was newly-opened. They asked Ayan if he wanted to join them. Ayan said that his grandfather would be alone, and he hurried back home.

His father called that night, after dinner. He wanted to know how Gopal Shanker was doing and whether there were any more mentions of Rohini.

'No *accha*, absolutely no mentions,' lied Ayan.

He did not know why he was lying to his father. He was simply going by his gut-instinct. Whenever his grandfather mentioned Rohini, he could see him transform before his eyes. There was that sparkle in his eyes, and he seemed to take great pleasure in narrating all the Rohini episodes. His father asking about his conversations with his grandfather, felt like an intrusion to Ayan.

'I think he is getting too old to live in the *tharavadu* alone. Shaila agrees with me. It is time we sell that property. I already have buyers who are very interested. I called to tell you that I have given your number to a few of them. If they contact you, I want you to show them around,' said Jairaj.

That felt like a stab to Ayan. He had no idea that his father was thinking of selling *Thekke Madom* this soon. How could he? It was so beautiful and this was where his grandfather's roots were. Agreed, most of the rooms were locked. But it *was* his grandfather's home, and Gopal Shanker was happy here.

'But … but *accha*, where will grandpa live if this is sold? And is he okay with it?' asked Ayan.

'What is there to be okay or not okay? Who is going to live in that huge house, after him? The property prices are up right now. It is a good time to sell. I will speak to him and convince him,' said Jairaj.

Ayan knew his father had a point. He was being practical. But the sadness Ayan felt was profound. He felt waves of grief engulfing him. It took him a few minutes to compose himself after the phone call with his father.

His phone rang and it was Dhiraj. Ayan did not feel like answering the call, but he picked up anyway.

'Bro! We just checked in. This place is awesome! You are meeting us here right?' asked Dhiraj.

'Yes,' said Ayan.

'Great! Be here by 11.30 a.m.?'

'Okay, will see you tomorrow,' said Ayan and hung up.

He didn't want to go. He wanted to stay here with his grandfather, read books, and play football with the boys in the club. The conversation with his father had put him in such a dark mood.

His phone buzzed again and it was a message from Shivani. 'See you tomorrow! So excited to finally be in Kerala,' she had typed.

He typed a smiley back but he did not mean it at all. That was the thing about messaging. You could easily convey what you didn't feel by typing a few emoticons.

He sat quietly for a while, staring out of the window. It was pitch black outside, being a new moon. He thought about *Thekke Madom* and all the rooms with the beautiful antique furniture. He couldn't imagine it being sold. And what about all that furniture that lay in the room? He guessed they would fetch a great price as they were genuine antiques. With a heavy heart, he found himself walking to the room at the far end of the house, where the trunk lay. He once again tried to open it. This time after a few wiggles, the key turned and the lock opened.

'At last!' thought Ayan, as he slipped the lock out. At least there was one nice thing to look forward to, after that miserable phone call with his father.

But he was disappointed when he opened the trunk. His grandfather had been right. There were only a few old folders with nothing in them.

The trunk was empty.

It matched how he felt inside.

10

It was with a heavy heart that Ayan woke up the next morning. His grandfather was on the easy chair in the verandah, sipping his morning tea. The paddy fields swayed in the morning breeze. The bulbuls and mynahs chirped.

'Good morning, *muttacha*,' greeted Ayan.

'Good morning, young man! Just look at that,' said his grandfather, pointing to the tamarind tree which rose high above *Thekke Madom*, its branches with tiny leaves, casting a web of greenery over the red tiled roof.

Ayan squinted and turned to look in the direction his grandfather was pointing. He saw a small bright blue bird with a flaming orange chest. The bird had a long pointy beak. Ayan's eyes lit up. It was a beautiful sight. He instantly took out his phone, zoomed in, and clicked a couple of pictures.

He then showed them to his grandfather.

'That is a lovely capture. Do you know what bird it is?' asked his grandfather.

'No, *muttacha*, I don't,' admitted Ayan.

'He is the kingfisher. He hunts fish. He waits, sitting very still for his prey. Once he spots it, he swoops down and takes off with it. So fast, so sharp. No distractions. He knows what he wants and goes after it. Then he gets it. You should be like that in life,' said Gopal Shanker, as he took a sip of his tea.

His grandfather looked so happy and content, sitting there, watching the birds and sipping his tea. Ayan's heart sank further. It would be very unfair to uproot him from this place. He debated for a second whether he should discuss his father's plans about selling the property. Then he decided against it. He simply did not have the heart to break the news to his grandfather. Let his father do the talking. He didn't want to get involved in this.

Ayan announced to his grandfather that his friends from Pune were visiting Kerala, and he had to go and meet them.

'Friends? Who are they? Boys or girls? What are their names?' asked Gopal Shanker.

'One boy and two girls, *muttacha*. Their names are Dhiraj, Nishi and Shivani,' said Ayan.

'What do they do?'

'Dhiraj and I used to work in the same company in Pune. Nishi—well, she is seeing Dhiraj. And Shivani works with Nishi. Both work for a newspaper.'

'Oh, newspaper? That is impressive. And what is this 'seeing'? What does seeing mean? Are they engaged? Or boyfriend and girlfriend? Or testing the waters?'

'I think they plan to get married. They are not engaged. Waters have already been tested,' said Ayan, smiling at his grandfather's choice of words. He found it amusing that he was discussing his friend's love life with his grandfather.

'Do their parents know?' asked Gopal Shanker.

'I have no idea, *muttacha*! I don't ask them such things.'

'But I thought you were friends? Friendship in my times meant, you knew everything about each other. And you would support each other, no matter what.'

'It's the same for me too, *muttacha*. It's just that I don't know the details—about whether he has spoken to his parents or not.'

'I see. And what is that other girl doing? Is she your

girlfriend?'

'No, *muttacha*! Of course not! I have met her only once.'

'Prospective then?' Gopal Shanker's eyes twinkled.

Ayan laughed. He decided to humour his grandfather. 'Well, we never know, do we?'

'She is welcome here. They are all welcome here. Bring them over and we can offer them a grand tour of Poongavanam. In fact, all of them can stay here if they want to. We have plenty of rooms. It is not like we have any visitors, ever,' said his grandfather.

'Mmmm … I think their itinerary is already planned, but I will keep it in mind,' said Ayan.

He didn't have any intention of bringing his friends over. He didn't know how to explain to his grandfather that he wanted to protect his time at *Thekke Madom*. It was *his*. He didn't want his friends to be a part of it. Yet, clearly, his grandfather would probably enjoy the company, which was evident from the manner in which he suggested he could bring over his friends.

'Where are you meeting your friends?' asked Gopal Shanker.

'Aluva, at the resort where they are staying, *muttacha*.'

'If you stay out too late, you will not be able to get a taxi back to Poongavanam. So keep that in mind.'

'I will,' said Ayan, as he walked to the bus stop to take a bus to Kottayam. Velu had told him that he could get a taxi from the taxi stand there, or he could take any bus which was going to Aluva, from the KSRTC bus station. There were also plenty of trains available. Ayan checked online and discovered that there was one at 9 a.m., which would get him to Aluva in time to see his friends.

Ayan took the train and then a cab from the station. He reached *River Creek* a little past quarter to twelve. Dhiraj had called him thrice by then.

'Get here fast! This place is incredible,' he said.

When Ayan reached the place, his first reaction was that of disbelief. An unpaved road led to the resort, which was constructed in the style of an old Kerala house. In fact, it looked a lot like *Thekke Madom*! Nestled in a serene pocket of greenery, with a stream running right through the resort, it was breathtakingly beautiful. He was welcomed with a drink—cool, tender coconut water, which refreshed Ayan. The reception lobby was decorated in the traditional Kerala way. There were *urulis* full of water, in which lit lamps floated amidst red hibiscus flowers. Intricately painted Kerala murals adorned the walls. Brass lamps with miniature peacocks, which were about four feet tall from the ground, stood on either sides of doorways. The carved, polished, deep brown rosewood beams on the ceiling, made square patterns, crossing each other at right angles. Just as Ayan was finishing his tender coconut water, Dhiraj arrived.

'Toto, I have a feeling we are not in Kansas anymore,' he greeted Ayan with a half hug.

Ayan couldn't help smiling at that greeting.

'No, we're in a better place,' he said.

'Which movie?' asked Dhiraj.

'It's so easy that it's an insult to my intelligence—*Wizard of Oz*,' said Ayan.

'Correct,' smiled Dhiraj.

A short walk led Ayan and Dhiraj to the two-bedroom cottage which had been allotted to them. Right next to it was a stream. Ayan saw both Nishi and Shivani, sitting on tiny wooden chairs, dipping their feet into the stream. Nishi raised her hand in greeting and smiled at Ayan, as he and Dhiraj joined them.

'Hello!' greeted Shivani.

'Hey there,' said Ayan.

'Isn't this place something else?' said Nishi.

'It has an amazing vibe. Actually, the whole of Kerala does,' said Ayan.

* * *

River Creek was so splendid that it was impossible to be in a bad mood here. The place had a kind of magic, soothing and calming to your nerves.

Dhiraj opened a bottle of beer. He poured out a mug for himself, for Ayan and Nishi. There was also a bottle of wine. Shivani said that she preferred that to beer. The menu also listed the local alcoholic drink—toddy. It was described as a palm wine. They ordered it, and all of them savoured the slightly sour, tangy taste. The menu had all kinds of Kerala delicacies like *appam-stew, puttu-kadala* and fried stuff like *pazham pori, parippu vadas* and onion *bhajjis*.

All of them found the food delicious. Ayan couldn't help thinking that while his friends could savour this food only when they were on vacation, this was what Velu *chetta* had been making for him on a daily basis. He felt lucky.

After a while, Nishi said she was drowsy and wanted to catch up on her sleep. She disappeared into a bedroom. Much to Ayan's annoyance, Dhiraj too said that he was sleepy. He stood up and followed Nishi, leaving him alone with Shivani.

Ayan wanted to leave right away. But he thought it would be impolite. Besides, he could see that Shivani was feeling as awkward about it as he was.

'Want to go see the duck pond?' asked Shivani.

He jumped at the offer. Anything, to not just sit there with her and do nothing.

'So how are you liking the life in Kerala?' she asked, as they walked through the verdant green property. Everywhere they looked, there were carpets of greenery. They walked by the stream, on the grass. Shivani had taken off her sandals and was walking barefoot.

'It's great actually,' he answered.

When they reached the duck pond, they saw a little bridge across, which led to a wooden platform on which you could stand and view the ducks.

There were at least fifty ducks swimming peacefully in the pond.

'Wow. Just look at that!' exclaimed Ayan.

'You know, this whole thing is so romantic. Too bad we are not in a relationship,' smiled Shivani.

Ayan avoided meeting her eyes. He looked away, not knowing what to say. Shivani instantly realised how that might have come across.

'Hey. I wasn't flirting with you. Nor am I looking for a relationship. Have had enough of relationships to last me a lifetime!' she said.

Ayan was taken aback by her forthright statement.

'Oh!' he said.

Then he said, 'Me too. Although Dhiraj and Nishi won't give up trying to set me up.'

'Yes. They are hoping we will hit it off. What a relief to talk about it,' she laughed. He joined in.

With that, the ice between them was broken.

The attendant at the resort came to them and asked if they would like to feed the ducks.

'Sure,' said Ayan.

He brought them a paper bag each, which contained corn, seeds and a certain kind of small cylinderical black pellets. There were benches by the pond, shaded by large leafy trees. Ayan and Shivani walked towards one and sat down.

As soon as they sat down, the ducks clamoured towards them.

Shivani laughed in delight as they pecked hungrily and gobbled up the pellets that Ayan and she were throwing at them.

'So what made you tired of relationships?' asked Shivani.

'Oh, I had just one relationship. It ended badly. She not only left me for another guy who was my close friend, but they joined together and bad-mouthed me to our common friends.'

'They couldn't have been much of friends, if they chose to believe her.'

'To my face, they wouldn't say anything. But I know they were talking about me,' Ayan found himself saying. He was surprised as to why he was telling Shivani these details which he had not shared with anyone. Perhaps it was the combination of beer and toddy that was hitting him and loosening his tongue. He found that he was relaxing completely in her company. She was easy to talk to.

'I know what that feels. I had a similar experience,' said Shivani. 'I was in a relationship with one such toxic idiot. I think I have an invisible antenna inside me, that attracts all the wrong guys.'

'I think we all accept the love we deserve,' said Ayan.

'*The Perks of Being a Wallflower*,' Shivani's reply was instantaneous.

'Wow! I am impressed. I didn't know you were a movie buff too.'

'Big time. I loved that movie.'

'Oh me, too!'

'So you think you deserve more love than what Mr. Toxic offered you?'

'I don't know about 'deserving love', but I think it is important to be with people who make us feel good, make us feel loved. Don't you think so?'

'Of course. Else, what's the point of a relationship?'

'Ummm ... sex?' said Shivani.

Ayan laughed. 'You don't need a relationship for that,' he said.

'You are right. But it helps to cut to the chase and avoid the small talk,' she said.

They chatted easily about all the movies that they had seen. They discovered that they shared a common taste when it came to movies. Shivani had seen some movies which Ayan hadn't, and she excitedly told him what they were about, urging him to watch them. Ayan shared her excitement as he came up with a list of movies which he had enjoyed but she hadn't seen. They discussed the dialogues and the scenes in the ones that they both had watched.

It was only when the setting sun cast its orange light on the shimmering waters of the duck pond, and the lights came on at the resort, that Ayan realised how late it was.

'Fuck! I didn't intend to stay here for this long! I won't get a taxi back to Poongavanam now. That's my grandfather's place by the way,' he said, as he stood up with a start.

Shivani held his arm and pulled him down.

'Sit,' she commanded. 'It's no big deal. We have two bedrooms at the resort. You can stay here, and leave tomorrow morning. And don't worry, I won't get into a relationship with you, even if we have sex,' she said, as she met his eyes and smiled.

Ayan couldn't tell if she was joking or not.

11

They walked back to the cottage with the golden light from
setting sun illuminating their hair, casting long shadows
sideways. The shadows that danced along with the swaying
branches of the trees crisscrossed the shadows that walked
with them.

Ayan felt like he was in a trance. It was as though an entity
had taken possession of his body, and he was merely a shell
carrying out actions controlled by someone else. Shivani was
merrily chatting about her work now. She was talking about
how the architecture of the resort had got her interested in
ancient Kerala houses. She said she wanted to do a project
on it. Ayan was only half-listening to her, his mind elsewhere.
Should he really stay here? Would it be difficult to get a cab
back? What did Shivani expect him to do? All these questions
raced through his head.

When they reached the cottage, they found a spread of more
toddy and more food. Dhiraj was sprawled out on the sofa.
Nishi was sitting on the floor, her face close to his, munching
on roasted peanuts and feeding him some.

'Mmmm. There you are, you two love birds. We were waiting
for you to join us. We ordered more food. Gastronomical
excess, I know—but we were ravenous when we woke up. And
this... this is heaven,' she said, sipping toddy and extending a
glass to Shivani, motioning her to sit down.

Shivani sat, accepted the glass and took a sip.

'Can't agree more,' she said.

'Listen guys, I ... I think I should leave. Let me check if they have cabs,' said Ayan, as he walked to the telephone and dialled reception. He asked about getting a cab back to Poongavanam. The receptionist told him that all the cabs had to be booked at least six hours in advance. They had only two hotel cars and both were on airport duty that evening. His grandfather was right. No cabs would be willing to travel that distance at such a short notice. Ayan was stuck. So he just made a booking for the next morning.

Ayan made a quick call to *Thekke Madom's* landline but nobody answered the phone. He then called Velu on his mobile. He told him to inform his grandfather that he would be coming only the next day, and that he would be staying with his friends.

'Don't we have to inform the resort that I will be staying here?' asked Ayan.

'No, it's cool. We can have as many people over as we want. They have given us the whole cottage. The numbers are up to us. Besides, I had already made a booking for you as well,' said Nishi.

'What? How could you do that?!'

'We knew you two would hit it off,' winked Dhiraj.

Ayan made a face.

His friends were conversing, joking and having a great time. But Ayan was not really participating. He didn't want to be staying here. Dhiraj was now narrating a funny story from his childhood about a practical joke he had played on his cousins. Shivani and Nishi were laughing uproariously. Ayan pretended to laugh.

Shivani poured him a glass of toddy. He drank it, finishing it in a gulp almost. He extended the glass for a second helping.

He needed to be inebriated to get through this unexpected situation. Ayan just wanted the morning to arrive fast, so he could go back to *Thekke Madom*. The earlier relaxed mood he was in, was now replaced by impatience. It made him uncomfortable.

After a couple of hours, Dhiraj and Nishi decided to call it a night, retiring to their bedroom. Ayan was irked that they were acting as though he and Shivani were a couple, but he suppressed his irritation. It wasn't something that he could even create a scene about. He had wanted to say that he would share a bedroom with Dhiraj and the girls could share a room. But the way Nishi and Dhiraj had taken for granted that he would be sharing a bedroom with Shivani, Ayan knew there was no point in suggesting that.

Ayan and Shivani were alone once more.

'Let's go for a walk,' said Shivani.

He followed her like a little lamb.

She was chatty. As they walked around the resort and talked, he felt his irritation slipping away. He found himself gradually relaxing. All the toddy that he had consumed was having an effect on him. She asked about his grandfather and he told her about *Thekke Madom*, how he had settled so quickly and how he was actually liking it there. She asked him about his job hunt, and he said he was hitting a dead end there.

'But you know what—strangely when I am in Kerala, it doesn't even bother me,' he confessed.

'I know what you mean. This place—it's like a suspension of reality, isn't it?' she asked.

They walked on and saw that all the copper lamps in the reception area were now lit. A hundred little flames danced. It was a mesmerizing sight.

'You know, this reminds me of the summer I had spent at my grandpa's place when I was a child. We had gone to the

Shiva temple. Outside the temple, all across the four walls, were thousands of little lamps. It was called *Aayiram Villaku,* which translates to 'thousand lamps'. All the devotees participated in this little ceremony of filling the lamps with oil and lighting them. It was a breathtaking sight to see the walls illuminated with tiny flames,' said Ayan

'Wow, I want to see it!' cried Shivani.

'This practice still exists in temples in Kerala. I will check with my grandfather and tell you the dates and the names of the temples where it happens,' said Ayan.

'That would be great, although I don't know if I can make it on those dates. But hey, who knows what tomorrow brings, right?' she said.

They walked back, watching the moonlight shimmering on the water in the river. The ducks were nowhere to be seen now. It was quiet, the stillness of the night accentuated by chirping insects and a layer of darkness.

*　*　*

They reached their cottage and went inside.

The sofa in the living room was a narrow two-seater. Ayan quickly saw that he wouldn't be able to sleep on that one.

'Shall I ask the resort for an extra mattress? I can sleep here in the hall,' said Ayan.

'Why?' asked Shivani, her voice barely audible. She ran her fingers through her hair. She was wearing a white peasant top and one of the sleeves had slipped off a shoulder, exposing her bra-strap.

Ayan couldn't help staring at her. Her eyes didn't leave his. It was as though he was under a spell. There was no doubt about what she had in mind. His heart thumped in his mouth. He swallowed.

'Are you sure?' he asked.

'Positive,' she whispered.

Shivani led him to the bedroom and shut the door.

Slipping off her top and shorts seemed like the most natural thing in the world. Her body was firm, voluptuous. They kissed each other hungrily, and he was taken aback by how passionate she was. He pushed her on the bed, stripping off his shirt, cupping her breasts, and nuzzling her neck. Her hands went around his hips and she drew in a sharp breath, as she pulled him towards herself.

When they finished, they lay side by side panting. Ayan had forgotten how good this felt.

She reached out for his hand and held it tight.

He turned towards her and stared at her. Her dark skin glistened with perspiration. There was a glow on her face. Her eyes sparkled.

'You are beautiful,' he said, as he tucked a strand of hair behind her ear.

She smiled. Her teeth were so white.

'You are supposed to say that to try and get me into bed. Not after the deed is done,' she giggled.

'Shall I just roll over and go to sleep then?' he joined in her laughter, adding, 'You know, I have never done anything like this.'

'What? Complimenting a girl after sex?' her eyes twinkled.

'No, sleeping with a girl I just met.'

'We hadn't just met. We have met before.'

'Yes. But we barely know each other.'

'Let's make amends then. You first. Why did you sleep with me?' she propped her head on her elbow, pulling the quilt up to cover her breasts and looked at him.

'You left me with no choice. You did a "Take me to bed or lose me forever" and I responded with a "Show me the way home honey". Which movie?'

'*Top Gun*. Meg Ryan. Who can forget that scene where she sits on his lap?'

'Full points! You are a girl after my own heart!'

'What? Do you quiz all the women you sleep with on their knowledge of movie lines?'

'All—but nobody passed the test. You are the first,' said Ayan with a poker face.

'What? Seriously?' Shivani's eyes widened in surprise.

Ayan began to chuckle. She laughed and said, 'Dumbo! I believed you for a moment.'

'Your turn now, why did you sleep with me?' asked Ayan.

'You are kinda' cute.'

'Kinda'? What's that supposed to mean?'

'Okay. You are cute. Admitted. Happy?'

'Thank you. That's what they all say.'

'All?' she raised an eyebrow.

'Okay, most. The others turn around and go to sleep,' Ayan said, and she laughed again.

'You know, this has been so good. I feel so light and happy with you,' said Shivani.

'Yes, me too. Although, I must admit I was apprehensive about staying over.'

'I know. I sensed it. I think we all try too hard to do the right thing and stay in control. Once in a way, we should just let go and see where it takes us. Don't you agree?'

'Mmm … never really thought about it. But when you put it that way, yes. It does make sense.'

'I don't know about you. I so needed this. I am going through hell at the moment. This is like an escape from reality.'

'What's going on so bad that you need to escape from?'

'My life, Ayan. The last few months have been hell. My divorce proceedings are going on. Am escaping the most terrible relationship I have ever got into. The Mr. Toxic who we talked about earlier—well, he is my husband. Soon to be ex-husband.'

Ayan's jaw dropped.

'What?! Fuck! Oh, my God—you are married?'

'Yeah.'

'I had no idea ... Holy Cow ... you ... you never mentioned it.'

'You never asked,' she replied calmly. 'And how does it matter? Do you need to know somebody's marital status to have a good time with them?'

Ayan was silent for a few seconds. Then he said, 'Yes, you are right. You don't.'

Shivani nodded.

'Was it an arranged marriage? How did things deteriorate? You don't have to tell me if it's too personal.'

'No, I don't mind sharing at all. But it's a long saga. Are you sure you want to hear?'

'Yes, of course. I want to know.'

Shivani inhaled and then began.

'It was a perfect match—at least in my parents' eyes. We met a couple of times and he seemed like a nice guy. I had been working for two years at a media house in India. He was in the US on an H1-B visa. I joined him in Dallas, where he had a job, within ten days of my marriage.'

'Uh huh,' Ayan nodded.

'You know Ayan, I didn't even think twice about quitting my job and following him to the US. My parents, relatives—all were over the moon. I was happy too. But the thing is, I was on an H4 visa. I had no idea what that meant. All I knew is, I was going to the US. I did not realize that I would lose my independence completely as soon as I landed. Since I wasn't allowed to work, I was dependent on him for every single thing. I felt so useless. I had no credit card, was not allowed to have a bank account and had to ask him for money on a daily basis. And I was a successful working professional when I was in India.'

'Couldn't you get a job there? And get a company to sponsor your visa?'

'Oh, believe me, Ayan, I tried. For weeks and weeks, I would meticulously set up interviews, send out applications. I got many interview calls too, but the moment they heard my visa status, they would back out. I hit a dead end everywhere. This went on for two years, can you imagine? I felt like a piece of furniture. Those were really terrible days. I had nothing to do other than cleaning the house and waiting for him to come back. His niceness was vanishing and the way he was talking to me was changing too. It ... It was terrible. It was slowly eroding my confidence...'

Shivani was speaking slowly now, and there were tears in her eyes. 'Then ... then I got pregnant. I was happy for a brief while. But he ... he didn't want the baby. That was when the abuse started. Initially, it was just verbal. He would use foul language and say nasty things when I called him at work, to ask him something. I guess things turn out the way they have to. I had a miscarriage. Lost the baby. And then the physical abuse started. He would get annoyed if the house wasn't cleaned. He would find fault. Bang doors. One night he hit me. I could have reported him. But by then, I was so emotionally battered that I just couldn't. That was when I left the US. It's a long story, Ayan. Finally, with the help of my father's friend, I came back to India. And we have now filed for an ex-parte divorce.'

'Good Lord! I ... I had had no idea ... You have been through such a lot,' said Ayan.

'Sorry if all this is too much for you.'

'No ... No. I am glad you shared it. But why was he treating you like that?'

'I have no idea. We heard later through common friends that he had psychiatric issues and he was being treated for them.

His parents had insisted that he get married, as they felt that marriage would help him get over the issues.'

'Awful...'

'Anyway, it only made me stronger. I am determined now to live, to enjoy life. To be present fully in the moment. It is so important,' she said.

They slept after that, cradled in each other's arms.

The next morning, when Ayan opened his eyes, she was still sleeping. She was lying on one side, curled up like a child. He tip-toed out. Dhiraj and Nishi's bedroom door was shut. He was definitely not waking them either. He looked around and found the hotel stationary on the table in the bedroom.

'Thank you for an amazing time. It felt like a movie!' he wrote. He then propped it against the radio alarm clock on the side table, so that Shivani would see it as soon as she woke up. He went to the bathroom, quickly washed his face, wore his clothes and went out.

He inhaled the fresh morning air, as he walked to the reception and took the hotel cab to *Thekke Madom*.

Ayan kept thinking about Shivani on the way back. Her personality was so bubbly, so effervescent. He would have never guessed that she had been through such trauma, had she not told him. There was no trace of her past in the way she carried herself. She was such fun to hang out with.

* * *

When he reached *Thekke Madom*, he found his grandfather on the verandah in his usual spot.

'You find your friends and you forget your grandfather, is it?' he asked.

'No no, *muttacha*, I meant to come back last evening itself. I am so sorry, I lost track of time and then I didn't get a taxi.'

'It's okay, young man. I was only teasing you. Go have a shower. Velu has kept breakfast ready. I have already had mine,' said Gopal Shanker.

Ayan bounded up the stairs with his backpack. His phone buzzed just as he placed his backpack on the bed.

It was a message from Shivani.

'Thank YOU. And thank you for listening,' it read.

'You are amazing. When are you leaving?' he typed back.

'Tomorrow,' she replied.

As soon as Ayan read the message, he realized that he very badly wanted to see her again.

12

'Want to come over to my grandfather's place? This place is amazing,' Ayan typed out in the Instant Messenger of his phone and pressed send.

He got a reply from Shivani after fifteen minutes: 'That would have been lovely, but will take a rain check. Got work to catch up on,' it said.

Ayan was a little disappointed. But then he thought that had she agreed to visit him, he would have had to invite Nishi and Dhiraj too. He didn't really want that. After Shivani opened up with her story, he felt he could let her into his world. But as far as the other two were concerned, he was not ready yet, to have them over.

He got a message from his father that his mother wanted to speak to him on a Skype call—that they would call soon. The message asked him to login and be ready for the call. Ayan decided to Skype from the verandah. He told his grandfather that he would be able to see his family when they called.

'Pah! Video call. I have read about it. People have time to video call but do not have time to visit. That is the reason I don't even use a mobile phone. The best meetings are always face-to-face,' Gopal Shanker waved his hand dismissively, shaking his head.

'*Muttacha*, they are just substitutes for face-to-face meetings. I haven't spoken to Akshu for so long. But now when I see him and speak to him, it feels like I have met him,' said Ayan.

'Do you know, I have not even seen him?'

'Oh! Is it, *muttacha*?' Ayan was angry on his grandfather's behalf. He hadn't until now considered the fact that his grandfather had not even seen Akshu.

'Yes. Jairaj hasn't come here for thirteen years or maybe more. I have stopped counting. He hasn't come here even after Akshu was born. The family tradition is to give a *thulabharam*[18] at the *devi kshetram*.[19] He hasn't done even that.'

The call came in and Ayan answered it with video.

Akshu was grinning into the camera. 'Ayu *chetta*, see-see,' he said, showing him a tiny card shaped like a phone, which he had made.

'What is it, Akshu?' asked Ayan, leaning forward to take a closer look.

'It's my paper phone which opens up. Inside is a message. We are making this as a part of the class project in communications. We write out thoughts inside this phone and we stick it on a big chart that the teacher is making. The messages we write on our 'phone' goes to a satellite. Then the satellite sends it to the phone of the person who we want to send the message to. Isn't it cool?' he asked.

'It indeed is. That's how we are able to see each other now too. Our computers communicate via satellite,' said Ayan.

Akshay then spotted his grandfather.

'*Muttacha*!' he called out.

Ayan moved the laptop so that Gopal Shanker could see Akshu.

'*Muttacha*! How are you?' asked Akshu.

---

18. A ritual in Kerala temples where an offering is made as bananas, or jaggery or pulses. The offering has to be equal to the weight of the person in whose name it is made

19. Temple of the goddess

Gopal Shanker adjusted his glasses and as soon as he saw Akshu, his face broke into a grin.

'Never been better, young man! Now, when are you coming to see me?' asked Gopal Shanker.

'When my parents bring me. I am too small to come alone, says my mother,' said Akshu.

'Tell your father and mother to bring you soon. Don't you want to see Kerala?' asked Gopal Shanker.

'Yes, *muttacha*! I want to come there. I have seen photos on the Internet. It is so beautiful.'

'What Internet? You should see all this in person,' said Gopal Shanker.

Ayan's mother came on the screen and greeted Gopal Shanker. She asked him how he was doing and how his leg was healing. Gopal Shanker said that the cast would come off soon. She asked if Velu was taking care of him and Gopal Shanker snorted.

'Velu's loyalty can never be questioned. He has been with me for years. He is trustworthy and he will never betray me,' he said.

She realised she had touched a raw nerve and hurriedly asked for Ayan.

'Ayan *mone*[20], see who is here,' she said.

Ayan peered into the screen and spotted his aunt and uncle. Shaila and Ghanshyam were waving to him, saying, 'Ayan! Hello.'

'Shailammayi! When did you guys arrive there?' he asked.

'The day before yesterday. We will be staying here for a few days,' said Shaila.

Shaila then spotted Gopal Shanker behind Ayan.

'*Accha*,' she called out.

---

20. Malayalam for 'son'

Gopal Shanker stared straight ahead, refusing to look at the laptop, refusing to look at Shaila.

'*Accha*, it's been so many years. Isn't it time to let go?' she said.

Gopal Shanker clenched his fists and gritted his teeth. His face was slowly turning red with rage. He seemed to be breathing faster.

Then he spoke. It seemed like he was finding it difficult to not yell. His tone was controlled, measured. 'Tell her I do not talk to those who don't put the family first,' he said.

'*Accha*—have you forgotten—it was you ... you who ...' said Shaila,

'SHUT UP... NO MORE...' thundered Gopal Shanker.

Ayan was startled. He had never seen Gopal Shanker like this before.

'NOT FIT TO BE MY DAUGHTER ... PAH! Just GO ... GO ...' Gopal Shanker shouted. He hurled his empty tumbler of tea in anger. It landed with a thud on the mud in the garden.

Velu came running out to see what the commotion was.

Ayan didn't know what to do. He could see Shailammayi crying and then she disappeared from the screen. Ayan walked with the laptop to the drawing room inside the house, so that his grandfather wouldn't get angrier.

His mother said, 'Why did you include *muttachan* in the call?'

'How was I to know I was not supposed to? You knew where I was. You should have told *accha* to mention it explicitly. In any case, didn't you see how happy he was to see Akshu? What's going on between him and Shailammayi?' asked Ayan.

'You don't have to put your head in matters that don't concern you,' said Jairaj, making an appearance on the laptop screen.

'*Accha*, you were the one who called me. I wasn't interfering in anything.'

'Look at him. Doesn't even have a job and he is trying to explain things to me. Just mind your own business. You better step up your job hunt. Sitting idle there and trying to teach me. You are a disgrace. I found you a job and you lost that too. Fool,' said Jairaj and walked away in anger.

'Can't you just shut up?' asked his mother.

'But ... but ma ...' said Ayan, trailing off. He had no idea what to make of all this drama that had just unfolded. He told her he had to go and hung up.

* * *

He went to find his grandfather. Gopal Shanker was still sitting in the easy chair on the verandah, staring out at the paddy fields, breathing hard. Velu was sweeping the garden.

'*Muttacha*, what happened? Are you okay?' Ayan asked.

'Everyone thinks they know what is best for everyone else. That is the problem. Bloody interfering pests,' said Gopal Shanker.

'*Muttacha*, you keep saying that they don't come to see you. But if this is the way you talk to them, how will they?' Ayan's tone was gentle. It was like the tone you use while talking to a child that was being unreasonable.

'Let them come here. Let them all come here. Shyamala will get them,' said Gopal Shanker. He began to laugh.

Ayan was worried. There was clearly something that was not right here. He didn't know what to do. He darted a worried glance at Velu. Velu looked back at him, clueless.

Gopal Shanker stopped laughing and looked at Velu. Then he said, 'Better get that coconut climber soon. We don't want coconuts dropping on anyone's heads. Look at them. All ready to be plucked,' he said, looking up at the coconut tree in the garden.

'Yes Gopal Sir, I will call him,' said Velu.

There was no mention of the morning's incident after that. By the time Ayan got ready for his football, it seemed as though Gopal Shanker had forgotten all about it.

When Ayan returned after a very satisfying game of football, Gopal Shanker wanted to know all the details about the players.

'Who all were there today? I know all of them,' he said.

'There are so many of them, *muttacha*. I don't know all their names yet, but the ones I hang out with and talk to the most, are Biju and Roshan,' said Ayan.

'Aaaah—Jacob's grandson and Vijayan Nair's son. Vijayan is a lawyer and a very successful one. Let me tell you Ayan— Roshan's and Biju's grandfathers were my classmates,' said Gopal Shanker.

'Is it?'

'Yes, and that Jacob, do you know he actually liked Rohini too?'

'Oh, is that so?'

'Yes, but he did not have the guts to ask her if he could ever walk with her, to her house. I did. Those who can, do. Those who can't, watch.'

The morning's incident which had enraged his grandfather, was playing on Ayan's mind. After dinner, when Gopal Shanker had gone to bed, Ayan went to talk to Velu.

Velu was putting away the leftovers in smaller containers.

'Why doesn't *muttachan* talk to Shailammayi? Why did he get so angry seeing her today?' asked Ayan.

'She hasn't set foot in this house ever since Gopal Sir moved here, after your grandmother's death. He hasn't once spoken about her. Whenever she has called, he has refused to speak to her. I don't know what it is that she has done that is so terrible, that he wants no contact with her.'

'Isn't that strange?'

'I don't know, Ayan Sir. But Gopal Sir must have his reasons. His children aren't exactly the paragons of virtue. Whatever it is that they did, can't they fall at his feet and ask for his forgiveness? I can only tell you the incidents that happened after he moved here, into *Thekke Madom*. I do not know what happened before that.'

'When did *muttachan* move here? '

'Ummm … let me see… It was in 1990. I remember the year, as my father died the following year. And soon after, I lost my mother too. Gopal Sir was a huge support.'

'He was talking again about Shyamala.'

'I think he does that when he is upset. Today he was very upset.'

'Yes, he indeed was.'

'Let's not remind him of that phone call. Do not mention Shailammayi's name in front of him.'

'No, I certainly won't,' said Ayan.

* * *

Gopal Shanker seemed perfectly fine after that incident. One evening, when they were sitting on the verandah having their tea, Ayan remembered the conversation that he had with Shivani, about the flames in the temple.

'*Muttacha*, do you remember, once when I had come to stay here for my summer vacation, you took Nithya and me to the temple? All the lamps outside were lit?'

Gopal Shanker leaned back in his chair and closed his eyes as he thought about it.

'Aaah, yes … I remember well. You had said there were a hundred little flames and Nithya corrected you saying that there were a thousand. You got annoyed at being corrected and you asked me who was right.'

Ayan had forgotten *that* memory. He smiled as he remembered it.

'Oh, yes! I remember that now. You answered that it did

not matter if it was a hundred or a thousand. You told us how wonderful it is that all of the thousand flames originate from a single spark. A single spark and a flame is lit, you told us.'

'Yes', nodded Gopal Shanker. 'Once a flame is lit, it can burn brightly and divide into a hundred little flames—or it can die down. Just like the connections we form.'

Ayan took a minute to think about what his grandfather had said. It was so profound.

'Yes, *muttacha*, so right,' he said.

* * *

Shivani and Ayan now had a nice little chat going back and forth. It was more than two weeks that they had been doing this. She would reply to his queries within minutes of receiving his messages. He would do the same. He learnt that she was applying for a job as a senior features editor at an architectural magazine, as one of her areas of interest was interior design. She shared pictures of a friend's house that she had designed. It was chic and contemporary, and Ayan liked how she had done the house up. She sent more photos of a store that she had designed. He wanted to see the place where she lived. She sent him pictures of her flat which she had styled with beautiful colours and modern furniture. Her flat overlooked an empty field where donkeys grazed.

'Donkeys, in Pune?' he had typed.

'Haha. They keep increasing,' she typed back.

He sent her pictures of *Thekke Madom* and she admired the natural beauty of the place. She wanted more pictures. Ayan began looking for photos to click, so he could share them with her.

One day his grandfather noticed him clicking photos and typing away on his phone.

'Ummm ummm ... sending messages to your girlfriend, are you?' he asked.

'No, *muttacha*! She is just a friend,' said Ayan.

'Isn't she the same friend who you stayed over for, when you went to meet her?'

'I didn't meet her alone, *muttacha*! There were other people too.' But he didn't meet his grandfather's eyes when he said that.

The fact was that he looked forward to his phone buzzing these days. Shivani and he were gradually developing a very good friendship over text messages. They sent each other interesting things that they came across during their day.

One evening, when Ayan returned from football, grubby and drenched in sweat, he was surprised to see a car coming up the driveway to *Thekke Madom*. He wondered who it could be. Velu had certainly not announced any visitors, nor had his grandfather mentioned anything.

The car stopped and the door opened. Ayan stood there, wide-eyed, gaping.

Getting out of the car was his father.

13

Ayan took a moment to recover. How in the world had his father decided to visit suddenly? Why hadn't he let them know he was arriving?

He rushed towards the car and greeted his father, who was paying the cab driver. The driver put his luggage out.

'*Accha*! How come suddenly?' asked Ayan, as he picked up the suitcase.

Velu rushed out of the house.

'Jairaj Sir! So suddenly! You didn't even call?' he exclaimed, as he took the suitcase from Ayan.

'It came up all of a sudden. One of my friends in Mumbai lost his wife. I flew in to attend the funeral, which was this morning. I wasn't sure of whether I would be able to make it to Kerala, as I was supposed to rush back to Bahrain for a meeting. But the meeting got cancelled, and so I could make this trip,' said Jairaj.

'Welcome Jairaj Sir, welcome. I will get a room ready for you,' said Velu.

Jairaj turned to Ayan and said, 'Look at you. Have you stopped taking a bath, now that you are out of work? You haven't shaved also? What is with the beard?'

'*Accha*—I went to play football. I was going to take a bath when you arrived.'

'Football? With whom?'

'The local football club. I play regularly now.'

'Ah ha ha. Great life isn't it? Don't have to work! You get all three meals served and now football on top of that. Have you any idea what you are going to do with your life?'

'I ... I am trying to get a job ... I haven't had any luck so far.' Ayan looked down at the ground as he spoke.

Jairaj shook his head disapprovingly and climbed up the stairs that led to the verandah. Velu had already taken his luggage inside. He was making the beds and getting his room ready.

'Where is *acchan*?' asked Jairaj.

'*Muttachan* must be in his room, resting. Shall I go and call him?' asked Ayan.

'You go and clean yourself up. I will find him myself,' said Jairaj, as he proceeded to walk towards Gopal Shanker's room.

By the time Ayan had a bath, changed and returned to the living room, his grandfather and his father had already settled in. Velu had laid out a plate of *achappam* and *murukku*[21]. He had also made tea.

'Ayan Sir, I have made chicken sandwich for you. You must be hungry after your football,' said Velu.

'Thank you, Velu,' said Ayan, as he uncovered the plate that was kept for him, and began eating the sandwich.

Ayan could see that his grandfather was ecstatic that Jairaj had come to see him. He could make out from the way he was excitedly asking him about his job in Bahrain, about Akshu and his mother. Ayan noticed that he did not mention Shailammayi or the incident the other day.

'Strange are the ways of fate. You can never predict how long someone is going to live. Poor man—it is hard to lose a wife. But his misfortune made you come and visit me after so long,' said Gopal Shanker to Jairaj.

---

21. Fried savouries commonly served in Kerala

'I have been meaning to come, *accha*. I have been meaning to bring Akshu too. But ... but circumstances were such that I could not leave Bahrain for a longer duration. There was so much pressure at work and many other things. I can stay only for a day. I have to leave tomorrow evening. Have to get back to Bahrain,' Jairaj was apologetic.

'It's okay. What matters is that you finally came. You must go around tomorrow and see our vegetable gardens, the orchards, the farms. And now that you are here, go feed Lakshmi and Saraswathi too.'

Jairaj looked at Ayan and then at Velu.

'Why don't you show me Lakshmi and Saraswathi? They will want to see you.'

'No, no. Velu can show you. With this walker it will be difficult in the cowshed,' said Gopal Shanker. There was confusion in his eyes. It was as though he knew something was amiss.

Velu said gently, 'Gopal Sir, Lakshmi and Saraswathi were there long back. Times have changed now.'

'Don't interfere, Velu. Go—go to the kitchen and see what work remains. I am talking to my son,' said Gopal.

Ayan and Jairaj looked at each other.

Then Jairaj said, 'We will go for a check-up tomorrow. Don't you want this cast off?'

'Uh ... okay. Tell Velu to call the taxi.'

'No, no need for that. I have made arrangements for a taxi. I have booked one for the whole day tomorrow,' said Jairaj.

Gopal Shanker didn't even protest at the hospital visit which Jairaj proposed. There was no cajoling needed, like when Velu had to take him. He readily agreed.

Jairaj told his father that he wanted to go around and have a look outside the house. Ayan told him that he would accompany him. Jairaj looked at all the trees outside the house. There was pride in Ayan's voice as he gave him a guided tour.

'All this is novel for you. You forget that I have spent more time in this place than you have,' said Jairaj.

'Has it changed much since your last visit?' Ayan asked as they walked through the paddy fields.

'It has become lusher. The trees have grown so much. Which is a good thing. It increases the value of the property.'

'Where will *muttachan* live? It is his home you know.'

'Oh is it? I never knew it was his home,' Jairaj snorted.

Ayan didn't speak after that. They completed the rest of the walk in silence.

Jairaj said that he had a few phone calls to make and went to his room. Ayan sat with his grandfather.

'Everything happens in good time. I knew he would come,' said Gopal Shanker.

Jairaj emerged from his room after a while and said to Ayan, 'I have spoken to some of my classmates and my network of people. One of them has a huge company which is into many things. They are doing very well, and have clients across UK and Europe. He has said he will interview you tomorrow. Get ready to go to Ernakulam, early tomorrow morning.'

'Oh! What does the company do?'

'They initially started out in the hospitality industry. The Balan Group of Hotels is theirs. They have diversified into many other things. It's headed by Puthran, who is known to me. He said they will find a position for you, after I explained your situation. Go and meet him tomorrow, and your job will be sorted.'

Gopal Shanker said, 'Tell them to give him a job at Kottayam, son. Then he can stay here with me.'

'We will see about that. Let them interview him first,' said Jairaj.

* * *

Ayan set out at 7.30 a.m. the next morning, as it would take him about three hours to get to Ernakulam. He didn't want to be late for his interview. Jairaj was still asleep when he left.

'All the best, Ayan. Don't keep all the past things in mind. Just answer them confidently and boldly. Speak the truth. You are sure to get the job,' said Gopal Shanker.

Ayan located the office easily. It was a modern structure, with glass exteriors, in a multi-storied building on Marine Drive. The receptionist led him to the waiting area. He noticed that the office was spread over three floors. As Ayan walked in, his eyes took in the stunning views of the ocean from the large floor-to-ceiling windows, which went around the whole office. It was a visual delight. The space was luxuriously done up with pleasant colour schemes, open work spaces, and well-planned seating. It was of international standards. Ayan loved what he saw.

After waiting for nearly an hour, the receptionist told him that he could meet Mr. Puthran.

Puthran was speaking on the phone when Ayan entered.

'Absolutely … Yes … Better get rolling and set up a meeting,' he barked into a phone and then hung up, abrupt in manner.

He glanced at Ayan cursorily, and frowned as though he had forgotten why Ayan was there. Then he made another phone call, and gave specific, short instructions.

Ayan kept standing as Puthran had not asked him to sit. When he finished his phone call, Puthran looked at Ayan and said, 'Why are you standing? Sit.'

Ayan sat down.

'Job, eh?' he asked.

'Yes sir,' replied Ayan.

'Your father said you would be okay with any job. Any experience in the hospitality industry?'

'No sir. I was working for a multinational engineering

company.'

Puthran smirked. 'Yes, we read all about it in the papers.'

Ayan was silent.

'Go and meet Krishnan. He heads our export plant. Get the address from the receptionist. She will guide you with the rest,' said Puthran. And with that, Ayan was dismissed.

Ayan thanked Puthran, but he didn't even acknowledge him, as he went back to making his phone calls. Ayan met the receptionist and asked for the address of the export plant. It was located at Mattancherry. The receptionist said that the fastest way to get there was to take a ferry from the boat jetty which was located at Park Avenue. She said he could walk to the boat jetty, as it was close to Marine Drive.

Ayan had never taken a ferry before. He made his way to the jetty. It was just like a bus station, except that it was by the backwaters. He bought a return ticket to Mattancherry. The sheer beauty of the backwaters took his breath away. He couldn't help taking out his phone and clicking pictures, to send to Shivani, as the boat left the jetty. The other passengers were oblivious to their surroundings. For them, it was a daily commute, but for Ayan, it was an astounding ride. There were many fisherwomen in the boat with their daily catch. Ayan scrunched his nose and moved away from them. He hated the smell of fish. He made his way to the front of the boat and took a deep breath as the boat sped away from the Ernakulam jetty. He wondered if this was how Leonardo Di Caprio and Kate Winslet felt, as they stood on the *Titanic* in that well-known scene. The salty sea-breeze hit Ayan and he inhaled deeply. He savoured every moment of it. The bright blue stretch of sea, the tiny white cranes landing on wooden posts that dotted the sea-scape, the water rushing and splashing against the boat—Ayan loved it all.

When they reached Mattancherry, Ayan was fascinated

with how the boatman moored the boat by expertly lassoing the rope around the rod at the wooden pier. He made his way out carefully, as the boat bobbed up and down. There were young men who assisted the ladies who were old, by helping them get out of the boat. Ayan jumped out and hailed an auto-rickshaw. He gave the auto-rickshaw driver the address which the receptionist had given him.

When the auto dropped him off, Ayan stood staring in shock. GRS Exports turned out to be a large seafood processing factory. It was an old building with peeling paint, which looked more like a barn. There were many trucks in the compound. As he watched, bare-chested men in *lungis* and turbans on their heads, unloaded plastic crates from the trucks. Water dripped from the crates. The crates were full, up to the brim. Ayan could see the ice catching the sunlight, melting in the Kerala heat. He could smell the fish from where he stood. His stomach churned at the smell. The men paid no heed to him as he made his way inside the building, half holding his breath to escape the smell of fish.

There was a tiny cabin to his left and he knocked on it. A person sitting inside looked up. When he explained that Puthran had sent him to meet Krishnan, the man nodded and led Ayan to the factory floor. Ayan saw hundreds of women dressed in blue overalls, peeling shrimps. Ayan almost gagged at the odour that hit him. Krishnan was in the sorting section. When he saw Ayan, he greeted him with a large smile. He was probably in his mid-fifties, surmised Ayan. He also seemed to be a lot friendlier than Puthran.

'Welcome to our factory. Did anyone give you the introduction?' he asked.

'No, I just got here, and they led me to you, straight away,' said Ayan.

'Oh, I see. Then let me give you a quick introduction to

what we do,' said Krishnan.

Ayan nodded.

'We specialise in processing cuttlefish, octopus, shrimps and squids. We are one of the finest in the field and we meet the strictest international standards approved by the European Union,' said Krishnan, as he walked around.

Ayan followed him.

Krishnan led him to the storage facility. They looked like massive steel lockers lining both sides of the wall. He opened one of them, and a drawer slid out. It was full of packets of frozen shrimp.

'We handle about six metric tonnes of individually frozen products per day. We have the facilities for 450 metric tonnes of cold storage at minus 21 degrees. So you can imagine the scale of our operations,' Krishnan said. The pride in his voice was evident.

Ayan realised he was holding his breath, and he exhaled.

'Anyway, I guess that is enough for a day,' he smiled. 'You can start tomorrow.'

'What? Tomorrow? And what would I be doing?' asked Ayan.

'Oh. Didn't Puthran tell you? You can join as the shop-floor supervisor trainee. You just have to keep a count of the crates coming in. And do random checks to see that the shrimps are peeled properly. Ashokan will demonstrate how to check the shrimps. He will also give you your overalls, and take care of all other formalities,' he said.

Ayan's opened his mouth to speak. 'I ... I...' he stammered. Then he said, 'Thank you. I will ...' He couldn't complete the sentence.

'No problem. Anything else, we will sort out slowly,' said Krishnan and he escorted Ayan out of the factory.

When Ayan came out, he kicked a stone that was lying

in his path. His fists were clenched and he walked fast. He couldn't decide what was worse—losing his job in Pune or getting this new one.

He checked his phone. There were several messages from Shivani. She had wished him luck and wanted to know how his interview went. He didn't feel like replying.

* * *

By the time Ayan got back to *Thekke Madom*, it was past 9 p.m. As he walked up the driveway, he spotted Velu pacing the verandah like a caged tiger, in circles.

As soon as he saw Ayan, he said, 'Ayan Sir. I have been calling your number so many times for the last one hour. Why didn't you answer the phone?' His voice was shaking. He was trembling.

'Oh. I had put it on silent as I didn't want it to ring during the interview. I forgot to unmute it. What happened, Velu? Is everything okay?' asked Ayan.

That was when Velu broke down.

'He ... he isn't here anymore ... I ... Jairaj Sir left... I...' Velu was incoherent.

'Who, Velu? Calm down. What happened?' asked Ayan.

Ayan's heart froze when he heard Velu's answer.

'Gopal Sir. They have admitted him to the mental hospital.'

BOOK TWO

Gopal Shanker

It was a long time ago.
I have almost forgotten my dream.

—Langston Hughes, 'As I Grew Older'

14

Ayan stood there staring incredulously at Velu, his heart racing. Velu sat down on the verandah and put his head in his hands. He couldn't speak.

Ayan's mind was in a turmoil. He struggled to rein in the chaotic thoughts swirling inside his head. What mental hospital? When? Where? Why? What was happening?

He dialled his father's number immediately. But his phone was switched off. Ayan guessed he must be in the flight.

'What happened, Velu? You have to calm down and tell me,' said Ayan, taking off his backpack and sitting down next to Velu.

Velu let out a long sigh. Ayan could hear him taking shallow breaths.

'Sorry, Ayan Sir ... I am ... I am too upset. How could Jairaj Sir do this?' he finally managed to force the words out of his mouth.

'Come inside, Velu. Let me make you a cup of tea,' said Ayan.

The suggestion managed to shake Velu out of his current state.

'Tea, at this time? No, no Ayan Sir. I will make you something to drink. You must be tired after the long journey,' said Velu, as he got up.

Ayan followed Velu inside and sat on the stool by the door in the kitchen.

'Shall I give you hot chocolate?' asked Velu.

'Yes Velu *chetta*, that will be good,' said Ayan.

He needed to think with a cool head. He also needed to get more information from Velu.

Velu made the hot chocolate in silence. Ayan sat quietly, trying to make sense of it all. He cupped his hands around the mug and took a sip. It was delicious. And oddly comforting. The branches of the tamarind tree swaying gently in the breeze made a whooshing sound. Insects buzzed and chirped. The needle of the clock on the wall made a ticking noise as it went around. Every single click was magnified in the silence of the night.

Velu stood, leaning against the doorway of the kitchen, his shoulders slumped, his face downcast.

When Ayan drained the last drop of hot chocolate from the mug, he said, 'That was delicious, Velu *chetta*. I didn't realize how much I needed it. Now tell me, what happened after I left?' asked Ayan.

'Jairaj Sir said he was taking Gopal Sir for a check-up. I asked if I should call a taxi and Jairaj Sir said he had already arranged one. Gopal Sir got ready without any fuss. They had breakfast together. I wanted to go along with them. But Jairaj Sir said that he would take him and that he wanted to speak to the doctor personally.'

Ayan nodded encouragingly.

'Then they left together. Gopal Sir was happy that his cast would come off today. I expected them to be back for lunch. So I kept lunch ready. But they were not back. I tried a few times to give a missed call to Jairaj Sir's number, but it was unreachable. So I waited, thinking that maybe the doctor was late or there was a crowd at the hospital or something. Finally, at around 4 p.m., Jairaj Sir returned alone. He was in a hurry to leave.'

'So did you ask him about *muttachan*?'

'Of course, I did, Ayan Sir. That was the first thing I asked. Jairaj Sir said that the doctor there had made a detailed assessment and that Gopal Sir is suffering from ... from ... some condition—*demonta*—*demonsha*—something like that.'

'Dementia?'

'Yes, Ayan Sir. Yes! That was what he said. He said if we don't admit him, it will worsen into a bigger disease. Again, I forget the name.'

'But why didn't he call you to join them there? How can he admit *muttachan* there and push off to Bahrain?'

'He said that place takes care of old people with similar conditions. He said there is nothing to worry. He had made all arrangements.'

'But you said he was at a mental hospital?'

'It is a mental hospital, Ayan Sir. Jairaj Sir mentioned that it was a special home which has mentally ill people. He said Gopal Sir needed treatment. The hospital we go to regularly is just a small hospital and it does not have a psychiatry ward.'

'Which hospital is this?'

'The one at Kottayam. I am the one who takes him there always. I know all the doctors there.'

'Oh, I see. And did you ask any more details from my father? Like the name of the place where he is admitted?'

'Yes, Ayan Sir, I did.'

'And? What did he say?'

'He told me not to interfere in things that do not concern me,' Velu's voice was hoarse as he said it. 'Can you imagine Ayan Sir—I have looked after Gopal Sir since 1990. Nobody can take better care of him than me. I told Jairaj Sir that I can go there and take care of Gopal Sir.'

'Yes. We can't leave *muttachan* alone in a place like that. Why didn't you insist, Velu?'

'I tried. He said he needed me here to take care of *Thekke Madom*. Also, I had to be here, as you were not yet back. He also said they don't permit visitors, Ayan Sir. Relatives can see patients only once a week as otherwise it will interfere with the treatment. What kind of hospital is that, Ayan Sir? '

'I don't know, Velu. Let me talk to my father. I will get all details as soon as he lands. His phone is switched off.'

'I can't bear it, Ayan Sir. Gopal Sir is all alone there. What kind of a son shoves his father into a mental hospital and pushes off? Heartless he is, Ayan Sir. I am sorry, I am cursing your father. But honestly, I have no words. This … this is not okay, Ayan Sir.' Velu shook his head in disapproval, an angry frown on his face.

'Velu *chetta*, we will go and see him tomorrow. There is nothing we can do tonight. We don't even know where he is. And in any case, no hospital will allow us to visit at this time,' said Ayan, reasonably.

After that, there was nothing left for Velu or Ayan to do but retire to bed.

Sleep was elusive. Ayan was still smarting from the job offer. Did they really expect him to join work tomorrow as a supervisor in a shrimp factory? Thoughts of his grandfather were haunting him as well. Where was *muttachan*? Was he okay? He didn't even have a mobile. Ayan wished he had got him one, and taught him how to use it. Then he could have easily called him now. He decided he would speak to his father, as soon as his father landed.

Ayan kept dialling his father's number every fifteen minutes. He lost track of how many times he tried. Finally, after what seemed to him like the hundredth attempt, his father picked up the call.

'*Accha*! How many times have I tried you!'

'I just landed. What is it?' His father's voice was gruff.

'Where is *muttachan*?'

'In a safe place, where he is well looked after. Didn't Velu tell you?'

'He doesn't know the name of the place.'

'How does it matter what the name is? He needs care and he is getting it there.'

'Of course, it matters, *accha*! I will visit him tomorrow, first thing.'

'They don't allow visitors till the weekend. I will let you know when you can visit. I am in touch with the doctors.'

'What kind of a place is that? He is so old. How can they not allow visitors?'

'Do you know better than the doctors? '

'Which home is this, *accha*?'

'It's a private home for the aged who suffer from dementia and other mental conditions. It's attached to *Marthoma Hospital*. Anyway, what happened to your interview? And hold on, I am getting my luggage.'

There was a pause at the other end. Ayan could hear his father take off the suitcase from the conveyor belt. After a few seconds, Jairaj said, 'Yes, so what happened to the job? Did you get it? What did Puthran say?'

'He sent me to another person called Krishnan.'

'And?'

'Well ... I got the job ... They are telling me to start tomorrow.'

'That is wonderful news, son! I didn't expect something positive so soon.'

'No, *accha* ... It is the position of a trainee supervisor in a shrimp factory. I ... I can't do it.'

'Shrimp factory? Oh ... You mean *GRS Exports*. Do you have any idea what their annual turnover is? It is more than 400 million US dollars. They are market leaders and have the best practices in their field.'

'They want me to work on the factory floor, *accha* … I just … I just can't do it.'

'What? What can't you do? What do you expect then when you start out? An AC cabin?'

'It's the smell of the fish that I can't stand. And the job—it's really counting the crates that come in. I can't … I really can't work there, *accha*.'

'Are you refusing this job?' bellowed his father. 'First of all, you go and get fired from your job—that too in a scandal. Then you are happy sitting idle and playing football. Now I get you a job and you say that it is below your dignity? What the hell?' His father was yelling now.

Ayan kept quiet.

'I am getting into the taxi now … I am hanging up. USELESS you are, that's what. I took a favour from my friend, Puthran. And what do I tell him now? I have no face to show him because of you. You are an ASS! Not even grateful.'

The line went dead.

Ayan immediately called his father back. But his father cut the call. Ayan tried two more times and his father did not answer. It was clear that Jairaj had nothing to say to Ayan.

Ayan barely slept. He kept waking up every hour or so and glancing at the time. The night seemed to be never-ending. As soon as he saw the light from the sunrise flooding in through his window, he went rushing downstairs. Velu was already up.

'Ayan Sir, did you speak to Jairaj Sir?' was the first thing Velu asked. It looked as though he had a restless night too.

'Yes, I got the name of the home. It's a private home attached to the *Marthoma Hospital*. Get ready Velu, we are going there.'

'Now? Now it won't be open, Ayan Sir. Let's wait till 9 a.m.'

'Okay, we will wait.'

'But Jairaj Sir said that they allow visitors only on weekends?'

'We will find a way, Velu. How can we just let *muttachan* be there? I want to talk to the doctors.'

Ayan and Velu took a taxi and reached *Marthoma Hospital* at around 9.30 a.m. Velu already knew the way around. He asked for Dr. Varghese who was Gopal Shanker's doctor.

'Do you have an appointment?' asked the receptionist.

'No, we just have to speak to him for two minutes,' said Velu.

'Who is the patient among the two of you?'

'Neither of us. I want to talk to him about my grandfather who is admitted here,' said Ayan

'Name of your grandfather?'

'Gopal Shanker. But he isn't admitted to this hospital. He is admitted to the private home attached to this one.'

That was when the receptionist looked up.

'Oh. Psychiatric case. You better speak to his doctor. But you will have to wait till he finishes seeing all the patients.'

'Okay, we will wait,' said Ayan.

It took about three hours for the doctor to finish seeing all his morning patients. Finally, when the last patient left, Ayan rushed in with Velu.

Dr. Varghese, an elderly gentleman, was clearing his desk and packing up for the day.

'Good morning, doctor. I mean, good afternoon. I just wanted to have a quick word with you about my grandfather, Gopal Shanker,' sputtered Ayan.

'Ah! Velu, how are you? And you are Gopal Shanker's grandson? Nice to meet you,' said the doctor. He had kind eyes and a gentle voice. 'Do sit down.'

Ayan and Velu, both sat down.

'So, how is he doing? He didn't want to come and see me, is it?' asked Dr. Varghese.

Ayan and Velu looked at each other puzzled.

'I thought you saw him yesterday?' said Ayan.

'Yesterday? No, you are mistaken. I didn't see him yesterday,' the doctor frowned. 'The last I saw him was when Velu brought him. It must be time for his cast to come off, isn't it?'

'But ... but ... my father said he was admitted to the home attached to this hospital.'

'Oh,' said Dr. Varghese. There was a pause. Then he spoke up. It was as though he was carefully considering his words. 'The home? It's not really attached to this hospital. It is a private arrangement which Dr. Babu has. You will have to speak to him.'

Ayan thought he detected a faint note of disapproval in Dr. Varghese's voice. But he wasn't entirely sure.

Ayan thanked him.

He went back to the receptionist and said he wanted to talk to Dr. Babu.

'There he is,' said the receptionist and pointed outside.

Ayan spotted Dr. Babu getting into a jeep which was parked outside.

He broke into a run. 'Dr. Babu ... Dr. Babu ... wait ... wait,' he yelled.

Velu rushed behind him.

Dr. Babu, a youngish-looking bald, overweight man, paused and waited till Ayan reached him.

'Yes?' he said.

Ayan was panting. 'I am ... I am Gopal Shanker's grandson. I wanted to speak to you about him. He was admitted to the home you run, yesterday,' said Ayan.

Dr. Babu looked at Ayan as though he was insane.

'I have never heard of that name and I have not admitted anybody in the last one month, in the care centre that I run for the mentally challenged. Incidentally, even if I did, I would not be at liberty to talk to you about my patients. It is highly confidential.'

With that, Dr. Babu got into the jeep and drove away, leaving Ayan and Velu gaping after him.

15

Ayan's shoulders slumped. Velu gently touched his elbow and said, 'Come Ayan Sir, let's go home.'

'How can we, Velu? We have to find *muttachan*.'

'Yes, but we need to think what to do. We have hit a dead end here,' Velu was pragmatic.

Ayan knew he was right. But he was not ready to give up that easily. He walked to the receptionist and asked her if she had seen an old man yesterday, who had come in with the support of a walker, along with another person.

'So many patients come every day. I don't remember,' she said and she continued working.

* * *

Once they reached *Thekke Madom*, Ayan decided to call his father once again. It was his mother who answered.

'Ma, I went to the hospital where *acchan* said that he had admitted *muttachan*. Look, they are not giving me any information. I have to meet him. Please ... please tell *accha*,' The desperation and helplessness in Ayan's voice, was not lost on his mother. He was pleading. But there wasn't anything she could do.

'Your father does not even want to talk to you. Why don't you just take up the new job, Ayan? Work for three to four months and then we will see. Your father is FURIOUS,' said his mother.

'Ma, don't you understand? *Muttachan* is all alone there. I *have* to see him. Don't you get it? And that job—it is supervising a factory floor, full of stinking fish. What kind of a job is that?'

'Ayan, that is only temporary. They might move you out. And *acchan* said that *muttachan* is being taken care of. What is your problem? Why can't you just listen to your father once in a way?'

Ayan could feel a vein throbbing on his forehead. He took a deep breath, exhaled, and closed his eyes. There was no point talking to his mother. She just didn't get it.

'Look Ma, I will talk to you later,' he said and hung up.

He sat for a while, thinking what he could do. He looked at the time. It would be a little past 12 a.m. in the US. Would Nithya be awake? He took the chance and decided to call her.

She answered almost immediately.

'Hey! What's up?' She sounded bright and cheerful.

'I wasn't sure if you would be awake. I took a chance.'

'Was taking a break from my research notes. Your call is a welcome distraction,' she said.

'Nithya—please tell me if I am overreacting to this. *Muttachan*—they have put him in a home. Nobody has any clue where, except my father, of course. And he ... he is refusing to talk to me,' the sentences just tumbled out.

'Wait ... wait ... slow down, and tell me everything,' said Nithya.

Ayan then narrated the entire sequence of events of the last few days. Nithya listened intently.

Then she said, 'Wow ... This is just crazy. Shall I call my mother and ask her what's going on?'

'You could do that, but I don't think that will help much. She would have got the news from my father. And he would have told her the same thing that he told me and my mother.

The problem here is that I don't want *muttachan* to be alone. I want to speak to the doctor who treated him. Dammit ... I just want to see him,' Ayan was growing more and more agitated as he spoke.

'Hmmm ... I get what you are saying,' said Nithya. She was silent for a few minutes, as she pondered over the problem.

Then she said, 'I have an idea ... I read this article the other day. It was in the *New York Times*. There was this adopted guy, raised in Australia who found his biological mother in India, from whom he was separated when he was a baby. This guy zoned in on the possible locations, and then google-searched, combing through entire areas. Why can't we do that?'

'What do you mean?' Ayan frowned, rubbing his chin.

'See Ayan, from what I understand, Jairaj *ammavan* (Uncle), went and came back the same day, and then left for the airport—am I right?'

'Yes, so?'

'So, he couldn't have gone far, could he? We can ask Velu what time he went. And what time he came back. He would have spent approximately an hour at the home or hospital or wherever *muttachan* is at the moment. So we deduct that. And divide it by two. We get his approximate travel time, one way. We draw a radius, and then zone in on ALL the hospitals, and homes in the vicinity. *Muttachan has* got to be in one of them,' Nithya sounded triumphant.

'Good Lord... Nithya—that is a great idea. You ... you are a genius. Let me talk to Velu straight away. Thank you!' Ayan was excited, now that he had something to go on with.

'Keep me posted. Leave me messages,' said Nithya.

'I will,' said Ayan as he hung up.

Ayan rushed to find Velu. He found out that his father had left around 11 a.m. and he had returned by 4 p.m. It was safe to presume that his father had taken an hour at the home/

hospital where *muttachan* was. This meant that his father had travelled for approximately two hours to reach the place. If he took longer at the home, maybe he had travelled even an hour or less. But it was better to err on the higher side. Ayan took a paper and did quick calculations.

Muttachan was likely to be in a radius of 120-150 kilometres from Poongavanam. Ayan logged onto maps, and did a quick search for old age homes and mental health care hospitals. He was surprised to discover that there were about forty-three of them. His heart sank. This wasn't going to be an easy task at all. Who would have imagined that there would be so many? He took out his notebook and meticulously wrote the name of each one, the address and the phone number. There was *Mission Valley*, *Puthupally Care Home*, *Mercy Home*, *Alphonsa Home*, *Sacred Heart*, *St. Camillius*, *Karuna*, *Vaanaprastha*, *Veliyanad Home*—the list seemed to be endless. He kept writing, one after the other. Finally, when he finished listing all of them, he leaned back in the chair, exhausted.

He had no idea how to even begin. He thought he would start by calling each one and asking if they had any patient by the name of Gopal Shanker. He called the first six on the list and soon realised it was futile. They wanted to know who he was, why he was enquiring, and then said that they were not at liberty to give out the names of their patients. To his own ears, his explanation of why he did not know which home his grandfather was in, sounded unbelievable. Over and over he had to explain the same thing, and he was met with variations of the same response.

'Sir, you will have to ask your father, as he is the person who admitted him.'

'We cannot give all this information on the phone, without verifying your identity.'

'Patient information is confidential, sir. It is the hospital policy.'

Ayan was exasperated. He sat for a while with his hands behind his head, resting his feet on the desk. After a while, he took his laptop, went downstairs and called out to Velu.

'Velu … Velu,' he said.

'Yes, Ayan Sir,' Velu emerged from the kitchen, wiping his hands on the kitchen towel.

'Look at this, Velu,' said Ayan, as he pushed the list that he had made towards Velu.

'What is this, Ayan Sir?'

'It is a list of all the possible places where *muttachan* could be.'

'How did you get this list?'

Ayan opened out his laptop, explained Google Earth to Velu, and how he had zeroed in on these places. Velu was awe-struck.

'Oh my God, Ayan Sir, what all we can do with a computer!' he marvelled.

'Yes Velu, but a computer can't tell us which among these places that *muttachan* has been admitted into. I called about six of them and have met with no luck,' said Ayan, sadly.

'What if we start visiting these homes, Ayan Sir?'

'There are so many, Velu. It will take us weeks to investigate them all. Also, will they even let us inside?'

'We can just say that we are there to visit Gopal Shanker. If he is there, they will tell us that we can see him during the visiting hours. If he isn't, we know that is the wrong home.'

'But even if we do that, I think we would be able to cover just two homes at the most, in a day. If we are extremely lucky, then three. It is a mammoth task, Velu.'

'You are right. But let us keep the faith, Ayan Sir. We should do something about this. We can't just let it be,' said Velu.

Ayan was frustrated. He told Velu how he felt and said that he was going out for a walk. He needed something to do. This feeling of sheer helplessness was engulfing him to such a great extent that he felt lost. He passed the outer verandah where Gopal Shanker always sat and looked at the easy chair. Ayan missed his *muttachan* very badly.

He walked through the paddy fields, not really thinking about where he was going. The greenery soothed him. He saw a kingfisher perched on a tree, and he remembered the picture that he had clicked.

Without knowing where he was headed, Ayan walked on, thinking of *muttachan*. Would he have eaten? Was someone there to serve him his tea? Would *muttachan* be thinking about *Thekke Madom*? Was he happy? Was he getting his oats and fruits for dinner? How was his leg? Were they taking care of him?

* * *

'Ayan!' said a voice. He was startled to see Biju, Roshan and the gang waving out to him. He had reached the embankment that bordered the football club.

Ayan waved to them. They gestured that he join them. He walked towards them. As soon as he walked closer, the gang knew that there was something terribly wrong.

'What happened, Ayan? Is everything okay?' asked Biju.

'No … it isn't,' said Ayan.

He explained to them his predicament, of finding his grandfather and how he couldn't possibly check out each and every home and hospital that he had found listed.

Biju, Roshan and the others, listened to Ayan in rapt attentiveness. They were shocked that *muttachan* had been taken away like this. Ayan discovered that all of them had a great liking for Gopal Shanker. They recalled how he would invite them for an *Onam Sadhya*, after the annual football tournament, and how Velu would cook for all of them.

'Listen, Ayan, there are twenty-two of us. Include yourself, and we are twenty-three. Don't you think that each of us can cover two homes which are located close by, in one day?' asked Roshan.

Ayan stared at him for a few seconds. Then he thumped him on his back.

'Bro! That is a FANTASTIC idea,' he said. 'But is everyone in?'

'Yes, yes, we are all in!' they said in a chorus.

Each one on the team was very earnest and more than willing to join in. Ayan was touched by their sincerity. This would have never happened in Pune or any other city. There was something very close knit, a certain bond among people who lived in villages.

Roshan took charge and divided them into pairs.

'Where is the list of homes we have to cover, Ayan?' asked Biju.

'It is at *Thekke Madom*,' said Ayan.

'Let's all go there, then. We have no time to lose,' said Roshan.

* * *

It was a very surprised Velu who looked through the window and saw the entire football club, all twenty-two of them, and Ayan, marching down the cemented driveway of *Thekke Madom*. They were talking excitedly amongst themselves. He rushed out to greet them.

'Velu *chetta*, we have a plan. All of them are going to help us find *muttachan*,' said Ayan.

Velu's face broke into a wide smile.

'Sit, sit all of you. Let me make tea and *bhajjis*[22] for all,' he said.

'Thank you, Velu *chetta*,' said Biju.

'This feels like Onam, with all of you here. And I too want

---

22. Deep fried fritters

to join in the search,' said Velu.

'You can be my partner then. We have divided ourselves into pairs and we were one person short, to complete a pair,' said Ayan.

Ayan got the list he had made and showed it to Roshan. He also got his laptop and they peered into the map. Roshan and Biju divided the location of the various homes into zones, and he allotted each pair a zone.

'So, the plan is to turn up there and then tell them that one of you is Gopal Shanker's grandson and you are there to visit him,' said Roshan.

'Can't we just ask if he is there?' asked one of the boys.

'No. They won't tell you that. Ayan already tried calling them. I don't think it would be any different face-to-face. But if you say you are his grandson and you are there to visit him, then it sounds a bit more authentic.'

'What if they find out that we are lying?' asked another boy.

'How will they? They aren't going to ask for any id or anything. Remember, they have no reason to suspect that you are *not* his grandson,' said Roshan.

'This is not a bar where they ask for id proof and age proof,' said Biju and everyone laughed.

Biju made a WhatsApp group and added everyone so that they could send updates about what was happening.

Mission 'Finding Muttachan' had officially begun.

* * *

Ayan set out with Velu at 8.30 a.m. the next morning. He had been allotted a place called Erumeli, which would take them about an hour and a half to reach. They were to visit two homes. They set out in a state transport bus.

'We should have taken a cab, Ayan Sir,' said Velu.

'I think the cab would take the same time. This is a direct bus. I checked on the Internet,' said Ayan.

'Mmmm. Do you hope to find him in one of these two places we are checking out?'

'I don't know, Velu *chetta*, but someone is bound to find him today. He can't vanish just like that.'

They started getting messages on the newly-formed group even before they reached their destination. Those who had been allotted places closer to Poongavanam, had already reached. About six messages had come in and all of them had no luck.

When Ayan and Velu alighted from the bus, they took an auto to both places on their list. The first was a home which cared for the elderly who were mentally ill. The second was a luxurious retirement home. At both places, they hit a dead end. At the first place, they were made to wait for about ten minutes, while the receptionist flipped through the names of the people who were admitted there.

'You cannot visit now, as it is not visiting hours,' the guy at the counter stated flatly.

'We will come during visiting hours. We just wanted to know the room number. Name of the patient is Gopal Shanker,' said Ayan.

They waited while he checked the records,

'Gopal ... Gopal ...There is a Gopalan Nair. But no Gopal Shanker,' he said.

Ayan and Velu thanked him politely and left.

At the second place, they did not even have to consult the register.

'We know each and every resident of ours as well as their family background. There is no resident by the name of Gopal Shanker,' the lady smiled.

It was on the way back, just as they were almost reaching *Thekke Madom*, that they got the message from Shibhu, one of the boys of the football club whom Ayan had not interacted with much. Ayan sat bolt upright when he read it, his heart pounding.

'Found *muttachan*. He is in the *Ashrayam Mental Hospital* at Erunjipally. But they are not permitting us to see him. They said only weekends, and only approved visitors. The approved person is Mr. Jairaj.'

16

Ayan showed the message to Velu.

Velu shook his head. 'If anyone is an 'approved person' it should be me, Ayan Sir,' he said.

'Sadly, my father doesn't seem to think so,' said Ayan.

Once they reached *Thekke Madom*, Ayan logged into his laptop and searched for *Ashrayam Mental Hospital* at Erunjipally. The centre did not have a website of its own. But from the few write-ups which had a mention of it, he learnt that it was heavily funded by the government. He came across a blog post by a citizen's initiative which said that they had taken steps to identify sponsors and redesign the centre. They had appealed to the district administration for budget allocations. Campaigns to create awareness about mental health were also being run. It had a division for mental health care for senior citizens. There were a few more mentions on Wikimapia, and a few pages he saw, had listed the phone numbers. He found the names of a couple of doctors who were on the management board of the hospital. One was Dr. Hariharan, and another was Dr. Jomon. There wasn't much else that Ayan could dig up from the Internet.

Ayan wanted to know something more about the mental health centre. So he called up Shibhu.

'That place—they were such grouches, Ayan. They wouldn't even let us inside the compound, to go up to the reception,' said Shibhu.

'Then how did you find out that *muttachan* was there?'

'The security guards have a cabin at the entrance gate. One of them called the receptionist and said that a patient's grandson was there to see him. They wanted to know the name of the patient and I gave your grandfather's name, just as we had decided.'

'And then?'

'The receptionist must have checked the patient roster. They told the security guard to inform us that only authorized family members are allowed to visit and that too on weekends. So I told them to check and tell us the names of the authorized family members. Turns out your father has not given your name or Velu's.'

'Hmmmm ... I see ... Anyway, I have to thank you, Shibhu. You took the trouble of going up there, and finding him.'

'It's no problem, really. I hope you speak to your father soon, and you get to bring your *muttachan* home'.

'I hope so too,' said Ayan.

Talking to Shibhu hadn't really given him any more information. But at least now he knew where *muttachan* was.

Just as he was hanging up, a message popped up from Shivani.

'Hey, all well? I haven't heard from you in two days now. No pictures for me either?' she had typed.

Ayan immediately called her up.

'Hey, there. Didn't expect you to call! So not all that busy, eh?' she sounded pleased to hear from him.

'Hey, Shivani. Sorry, *yaar*. Got caught up in many things.'

'Oh, don't apologize. It's the same here.'

'Is it? What's happening at your end?'

'I am going through a lot of work-related stress... Plus my court case... I just wish I had someone Ayan—someone to go with me to the courts. My hearing comes up on Monday,' she said in a small voice.

'Isn't your father there with you? Can't he come? Or your mother?'

'Dad isn't keeping well. Else he would have flown in. In fact, his tickets were booked from Delhi. But he is in hospital now and mom is with him.'

'Oh, what a bummer. Sorry to hear that. How is he? What happened?'

'Chest infection. It is severe and he had to be given oxygen. He will be fine. They will discharge him once it clears up. There are no complications fortunately.'

'I wish I was there. I would have come with you to the courts, you know.'

'Really?'

'Yes, I would have. And hey—don't worry. It will all go well.'

'You are a true friend, you know. By the way, how are things with you?' she asked softly.

'Don't even ask, Shivani. Not too good at all. I am at my wits' end,' Ayan sighed.

'What happened?' she asked.

Ayan filled her in, telling her everything about how he had spoken to Nithya, how they had executed the idea she had given, and how he had finally succeeded in locating *muttachan*, but couldn't go inside.

'God, Ayan! I had no idea that you were going through such turmoil. You never mentioned in our chats. All we were doing was sending each other pretty photos. I had no clue.'

'Those photos—I liked clicking them for you! It was one thing that gave me joy,' he declared.

'Me too,' she confessed.

'Funny, how small things matter, right?'

'It is the smallest things that take up the largest space in our hearts. Who said it?' she asked.

'Oooh, I know this one ... wait ... Winnie-the-Pooh!'

'Spot-on! Ten points for you,' said Shivani.

'Put it on my points card. I will redeem them someday,' smiled Ayan.

They chatted some more and reminisced about the time they had spent at the resort.

'Know what? I miss you, Ayan,' said Shivani.

Ayan paused.

And then he said, 'I miss you too.'

But he wasn't sure if he meant it.

* * *

A few hours later, Shivani called up Ayan again. Ayan was pleasantly surprised to see her call.

'Hey, I have been mulling over what we spoke. And I have sent you something that will probably help you. Open your email,' she said.

'Sure, I will check after dinner,' said Ayan.

'No, Ayan. Now, now, now. I spent so much time on this.' Her excitement was palpable. And infectious.

'Okay, okay ... hold on, let me login,' said Ayan as he opened his laptop.

When he checked his mail, he saw a message in his inbox from Shivani, with an attachment. All it said was: 'Open it, rest when we speak.'

'See it yet?' asked Shivani.

'Wait a second. Opening it,' said Ayan.

When he opened the attachment, it took him a few seconds to even understand what it was. He peered closer at the screen to study it.

'Like it? Like it?' she asked.

Ayan stared at the screen and blinked for a few seconds. He couldn't believe what he was seeing. Right before him, was an identity card issued by the Newspaper Association of India. It had his photograph and his name. His profession was listed as "freelance journalist" for print and electronic media.

'Ohhh! ... Oh my God ... wow ... what is this? How did you manage this?' he asked, stunned, still trying to make sense of it.

It seemed a little surreal to him.

Shivani laughed at his reaction. 'Photoshop! I learnt it at my previous job,' she chuckled.

'But why make this? ' asked Ayan rubbing his jaw.

'Ayan, as a journalist you have to find innovative ways to get your story. This press card which you have—it's such a powerful thing. It gives you access everywhere. Doors magically open for you.'

'I ... I still don't get it. Why should I pretend to be a journalist?'

'To get inside that hospital silly. Don't you want to see your *muttachan*?'

Then the penny dropped.

'Ooooh ... Shivani. That's just crazy. How can I do that? Also, how will I get him out?'

'We will think of something. The first hurdle for you is to get inside that blessed building, isn't it? Everyone is afraid of the press. They all want nice things to be written about them. This will at least give you access inside. Once you are there, maybe you can talk to the doctors? Who knows? At least you get to see him,' said Shivani.

Ayan thought for a minute.

Then he said, 'You know what Shivani—that's just what I will do. I just ... just HAVE to see *muttachan*. At any cost.'

'That's my boy. And don't worry. They won't find out that you are not a journo. Just take someone with you, with a DSLR, to click pictures. Carry a little pad and a pen with you. You will seem authentic.'

'God ... Shivani, I am nervous about this ... What if I get

busted? I have ... I have never done anything like this before.'

'Have you ever played a role in a school play? Or at college?'

'Yes, I have ... But I was the tree. I had no dialogues. I just had to stand in the background and sway my arms,' said Ayan.

Shivani laughed. 'Okay, here you will have to do a little more than that. You just take a writing pad and a pen along and ask a lot of questions. Remember, you can ask anything. I think you will be fine. Now go and print out your new ID card, and get it laminated. Pick up one of those lanyard straps that you wear around your neck, along with a card holder. Slip your new ID inside and voila—you are done. '

'Tell me, won't my 'photographer' need an ID card as well?'

'No, Ayan. Press photographers generally go with the reporters, and nobody really checks their ID. They only deal with the reporter.'

'All right. I will go get it laminated and pick up the strap first thing tomorrow morning. Now I have the whole night to be nervous about this.'

'Don't worry. It will be fine,' Shivani assured him. 'And this was the least I could do. I would have come with you, if I could.'

'Really?'

'Really, Ayan.'

'You are a true friend, Shivani,' said Ayan and Shivani chuckled.

'Yes, we are both true friends. Happy?' she asked.

'Will be happy if this plan works,' said Ayan.

He wished her luck for her court hearing. She, in turn, asked him to keep her posted about the happenings at his end. Then they hung up.

Ayan wondered who he could ask to accompany him, as the photographer. He didn't want to ask Shibhu, as the security guard would probably recognise him. He decided he would ask Roshan, and called him. He explained the plan to Roshan.

'What an idea, Ayan! This I think, will definitely work,' said Roshan.

'You think so?'

'Of course! And you know what—I can do better than being a photographer. I can be your video film person,'

'What?'

'Don't you know? Moonshine Studios, which is the best photo studio in Poongavanam—it belongs to my brother-in-law. I always accompany him for all the wedding shooting. We do both video and photos. I can get the equipment, which sits there idle, when we have no assignments. I don't even have to ask my brother-in-law. It will all look very professional then. '

'But video film? What would we tell them?'

'Tell them you are making a documentary.'

'Hmm ... okay. From a reporter to a documentary film-maker.'

'All for a good cause,' said Roshan.

He definitely had a point there, thought Ayan.

Ayan asked Roshan to be ready at 8.30 a.m., and said that he would pick him up. Roshan told him that he would wait for him at the bus stop.

He then explained the whole plan to Velu. Velu booked a taxi for the next day.

'Do you think this plan will work, Velu *chetta*?' asked Ayan.

'We will at the very least, get to see him, Ayan Sir. I wish I could come along too. But I don't think I will be as convincing as Roshan would be. You call me as soon as you can and keep me informed, okay?'

'I will,' promised Ayan.

* * *

Roshan was punctual and waiting for Ayan the next morning. Ayan was impressed when he saw that Roshan was smartly dressed in a pair of freshly-ironed jeans and tucked-in shirt. He was wearing a light grey hat, the typical attire of a videographer. The equipment that he was carrying looked very professional indeed.

The cab driver got out and opened the boot. Roshan put his paraphernalia inside and got into the car.

'Let me see your press card,' said Roshan.

'It's in my laptop. We need to take a printout and then laminate it. Do you know any place where we can do that?'

'We will have to go to Kottayam for that. You will find one on the way to Erunjipally,' said Roshan.

'Sure, let's go there first then.'

They located a shop easily. It was just opening when they reached. Ayan took out his laptop and explained what he wanted.

By the time they were done, nobody could tell that the card was fake. It looked authentic.

Ayan took deep breaths to calm himself. Roshan told him to not worry, and that it would all be fine.

Ayan wasn't so sure, as the car sped towards Erunjipally.

When they reached the destination, the cab driver parked the car at the entrance of the *Ashrayam Mental Hospital*. The walls of the centre were very high, just like prison walls. Ayan shuddered involuntarily when he saw them. A massive arch led inside. Just inside the arch, to the left, was the security cabin.

Roshan took out his equipment from the boot of the car. Ayan wore his ID card around his neck. They walked towards the security guards. Ayan's heart was in his mouth. His throat was dry and he forced himself to concentrate on the task at hand.

The security guard looked at them as they got close.

'We are from *The Gazette*. We are here to film a documentary on senior citizens in mental health care centres,' said Ayan, as he flashed his card.

'Have you got permission, sir?' asked the guard.

'Yes,' said Roshan, before Ayan could answer.

'Who did you speak to?'

Ayan racked his head to remember the name of the doctor. Fortunately, his memory served him well. 'We spoke to Dr. Jomon and he said it was fine. He said we could film today,' said Ayan. He was surprised at how easily the lies flowed.

'One moment, please. Dr. Jomon isn't coming today. But let me check with the office,' said the security guard.

Ayan and Roshan looked at each other. The security guard went inside and called the reception. Ayan prayed. His head was beginning to hurt with all the stress.

Finally, the guard emerged. 'Sign this register. Then you can go inside,' he said, as he pushed a register towards Ayan.

Ayan put down the purpose of visit as official.

'You can go inside, sir,' said the guard.

'Thank you,' said Ayan and Roshan, simultaneously.

The guard opened the gate.

And just like that, Ayan and Roshan walked into the precincts of *Ashrayam Mental Hospital*.

17

Ayan and Roshan looked at each other as they walked in. Ayan did not realise he had been holding his breath. He exhaled.

'I had no idea it would be this easy,' he muttered.

'Me too,' admitted Roshan.

Once they crossed the arch, right in front of them stood a large banyan tree with dense foliage—its branches extending out and making a shady canopy that cast dark shadows on the ground. Around this was a circular platform made of cement. Beyond the tree stood a pale yellow building, with red sloping tiled roofs, shadows criss-crossing all over them, making them look an even deeper red. It had a porch with a few straggly-looking plants in old terracotta pots, that were chipped and covered with grime. It looked like an old British bungalow. Around this old bungalow, conjoining it on three sides, were slightly modern single-storied structures that had seen better days.

Not a single person was seen outside. A chill ran down Ayan's spine as he walked towards the dark entrance of the old building. He hated the very sight of it. This place was clearly in need of urgent maintenance. What the hell was his father thinking, putting *muttachan* in a place like this?

They walked inside and to the left, an arched entrance led to a large room, which Ayan guessed was the administrative office. The ceiling fans with long rods whirred noisily. A few people sat at their massive, ancient wooden desks, working. Ayan and Roshan approached the first person, an elderly gentleman who was making entries into the computer on his desk.

He continued typing, ignoring Ayan and Roshan. He looked up after a full five minutes.

'Yes?' he said, raising his eyebrows, as he peered over his glasses, his curly salt-and-pepper hair falling over his forehead.

'From *The Gazette*. We are here to film the documentary. Dr. Jomon said we could shoot today,' said Ayan, repeating exactly what he had told the security guards. He found that it was easier to say it this time around.

'From where?' he blinked.

'*Gazette*. It's the Indian division of BBC which focuses on small towns, and we are from the youth wing,' said Roshan.

Ayan groaned inwardly. BBC! Youth wing! Where was Roshan spouting all this nonsense from? Couldn't he have come up with something better? He was certain Mr. Curly Hair would call their bluff now.

But no such thing happened. Mr. Curly Hair nodded understandingly.

'It's no use,' he said shaking his head.

'Excuse me?' said Ayan.

'Dr. Jomon—he is a good man. I know what he is trying to do. Just a few months back, there was the French documentary-maker who shot extensive footage. Dr. Jomon said, once the documentary was released, we would get funding, as the government would sit up and take notice. What happened? Nothing,' he shook his head.

'But this one will get extensive coverage in India and most likely, internationally too,' said Roshan. He had slipped into the role so easily. If Ayan didn't know any better, he would have believed him, himself.

'Okay ... a minute,' he said. Then he turned to the

back of the room and shouted, 'Prakash ... Prakash!' while simultaneously pressing the little bell on his desk a few times.

A young, bearded lad, dressed in a white shirt and white pants appeared. Ayan guessed that he was the office-assistant.

'Show these people around. They want to shoot a documentary. Be sure to show them the general ward. Everyone should know the reality.'

'Yes sir,' said Prakash.

'We have the capacity for just 450 beds. And we have 672 inmates. Can you believe that? Mention that and highlight it in your documentary,' he said.

Ayan remembered that he was supposed to be the reporter. He fished out the writing pad, and wrote that down, just as Shivani had instructed him to.

'Sir, can we have you make that statement on film for the documentary?' asked Roshan. Roshan was improvising on the spot.

'Why not? I am not afraid of anyone. I will say things as they are,' Mr. Curly Hair said.

Roshan turned on the camera. He took a microphone from the pocket of his camera bag. He asked Mr. Curly Hair if he could clip it on his shirt. The man clipped it on his collar. He then preened and adjusted his hair.

'Should I look into the camera?' he asked.

'Yes, sir. Please tell us your name first and then something about this hospital,' said Roshan.

Mr. Curly Hair nodded.

. '1... 2 ... 3 ... rolling...' he called out as he began filming.

Ayan looked at him impressed. He certainly appeared very professional.

'My name is Sebastian, and I am the Administrative Superintendent of *Ashrayam Mental Hospital*. I have been working here for the past thirty years. We have both male and female patients here. We treat all kinds of mental conditions, from mild illnesses to very serious conditions.'

'How do patients come here?' asked Ayan.

'They are admitted by their relatives. Most mentally ill patients have no idea about their condition. This is not a place where people come voluntarily,' he said, and flashed a smile, revealing slightly yellowing, uneven teeth.

A wave of horror passed through Ayan and settled in the pit of his stomach.

'What are their ages?' asked Ayan.

'We have patients right from eighteen years of age to ninety. In fact, recently, one patient, a man in his eighties was brought in.'

Ayan's heart began to beat faster.

'Eighties? That old? So what about their care? And what about their family members? Patients that old must be needing special care, right?'

'Oh yes. We have a Senior Citizens' Wing. They are mostly patients abandoned by their families. The families admit them here, and never come back. Some of the patients can be cared for at home. But who has the time for all that these days? This is an easy solution,' scoffed Sebastian.

Ayan felt a lump in his throat when he heard this. He swallowed. But this was no time to get emotional. His goal was to somehow get to *muttachan*.

'What do you do with such patients?' asked Ayan, with no trace of emotion in his voice.

'We get in touch with their families as soon as they get better. But mostly, there is no response. Then there are so many cases where people get better. Especially women. But their families are not willing to take them back. Often, the husband has abandoned the wife, and remarried. They are banished from their own homes and have nowhere to go,' said

Sebastian. His face reflected the sorrow he felt. 'We have to remember that these so-called mental conditions—they are just a state of mind. At that moment, for that period of time, the mind perceives certain things in a certain way. It can change anytime. And to isolate people like this because of that, it … it's just not right,' he continued.

Ayan nodded understandingly.

Roshan said he had enough footage from Sebastian and asked if they could film inside. 'We would like to see the Senior Citizens' Wing, and talk to a few patients if possible,' said Roshan.

'You can talk to the ones who have recovered. Whenever a TV crew comes, they are eager to talk, in the hope that someone they know will recognise them, and hopefully take them home. You will see for yourself. Prakash will take you around,' he said.

Prakash led the way. Ayan and Roshan followed him.

'We can start with the general ward,' said Prakash.

Ayan and Roshan looked at each other in shock when Prakash fished out the key to an iron grill door and opened the lock. The door was at the entrance to a corridor lined with rooms on one side. As soon as they entered, Prakash locked the door again.

'You … you lock them up?' Vocalizing it was hard.

Prakash looked at him. 'First time in a mental hospital?'

Ayan nodded.

'We have to lock them up. They are not of sound mind. Else we will be chasing the escapees all over town,' said Prakash.

The stench of unwashed human bodies in a small crowded space hit them as they entered. Ayan tried hard to not let the disgust and horror show on his face. The 'rooms' that lined one side of the corridor were tiny, about 10'x10', almost like prison cells. In each tiny cell, there were two basic beds made of iron. There was barely space for anything else.

Women wore long, loose dressing gowns made of printed polyester fabric. They sat around various spots. Some were bald. Some had shoulder length hair let loose. Some were staring vacantly into space. Three were playing a game of carrom with a hospital attendant who was dressed in white.

'This is the Women's Wing. Opposite this is the Men's Wing. But right now, it is common time for recreation,' said Prakash.

As they walked on, they saw the men. They all wore the traditional *mundus*. Some were bare-chested. Some wore shirts over the *mundus*. One person sang as they arrived. Then he began to dance.

'Quiet, Vignesh. These people are here to film you all,' said Prakash.

He turned to Roshan and said, 'He is the resident dancer.'

Vignesh did not listen to Prakash. He broke into a crazy dance, to a rhythm which only he could hear inside his head. The song that he was singing was tuneless, and the words were incoherent.

'Don't dance so well. They might cast you in the next movie and make you the hero,' smiled Prakash.

Vignesh came close to Ayan. His breath smelled like a sewer. He had two missing front teeth and the rest of his teeth were yellow.

'Will you cast me?' he asked, peering into Ayan's eyes.

Ayan was frightened. It was the first time in his life that he was seeing insanity up close.

'Hahahaha … Look at him … I scared him,' said Vignesh, and began to laugh.

'Just ignore him. He isn't really insane. He is just pretending to be. He owes a whole lot of money to his debtors. He used to run a successful business and he went bankrupt. This is his way of rebelling,' said Prakash.

'Rebelling?' asked Roshan.

'Things are easy in here. You get three meals. You can be whatever you want to be. This is a kind of liberation, don't you think?'

Ayan looked at the dingy rooms, the unwashed bodies, the general miserable atmosphere. He couldn't imagine in what way this was liberation.

'Where is the Senior Citizen's Wing?' asked Ayan.

'You see those trees there? It's located there—a little ahead,' said Prakash, pointing to an isolated building about 800 metres away.

'Is that locked as well?'

'No—the entrance to that wing is only through this one. Even if the oldies wander around, they cannot get out.'

Ayan felt sick to the pit of his stomach.

Roshan looked at Ayan. Then he told Prakash, 'Prakash, I want to interview and film some of the patients. I also want to talk to the staff. Do you think you can help me?'

'Yes, of course. I know all of them and the ones who are not severely ill—they will respond to me. Come this way,' he said.

'Do you mind if I go ahead and have a quick look at the Senior Citizens' place?' asked Ayan.

'Not at all. Do you want me to come with you?' asked Prakash.

'But I thought you were helping me,' said Roshan immediately.

'I can find my way around,' said Ayan, just as quickly.

'You can go on, then. Talk to them. They are all grateful for company. They will tell you their stories themselves. Most of them there are not completely insane. They are just forgetful. They all love to talk,' explained Prakash.

Roshan told him that he wanted a few aerial shots of the complex and Prakash said he would lead him to the terrace.

It gave Ayan the perfect opportunity to walk towards the

Senior Citizens' Wing. Ayan had to control his pace, and not break into a run. He forced himself to walk casually.

The dried leaves made a crunching noise under his feet as he walked. He made his way up the steps and discovered that he was in a massive hall, furnished with iron-framed beds. They were set in four rows, one next to the other, with narrow gaps between them, forming pathways for walking. The room must have easily had about a hundred people, both men and women. As he inhaled the staleness in the air, he involuntarily held his breath. His heart plummeted. Is this where his *muttachan* was?

He looked around the room, his eyes quickly scanning the area for a hospital attendant. He found a nurse at the far end, giving an injection to an old woman. He approached her and said that he was from *The Gazette*, and that he was doing a film on this centre. He said that he had a few questions for her.

She regarded him for a moment. Then she said, 'Sure, ask away. I will answer to the best of my ability.' It seemed as though this centre was very used to reporters asking questions.

Ayan nodded.

'Do mention in your film that we are very short-staffed here. You can see for yourself how crowded this place is. We have been running petitions to get the attention of the government to employ more staff. So, the more media talks about it, the better it is for us.' She was echoing what Sebastian had mentioned earlier. Ayan could sense the desperation of the staff.

'How many people are here, in this division for senior citizens? Is this where they all live?' he asked.

'There are about 120 residents here. This is the general ward. We house both men and women here, as we don't have facilities for separate sections.'

Ayan nodded. As she spoke, he was scanning each bed in the room carefully, to see if *muttachan* was there. He was nowhere to be seen.

'Then there are about twenty patients in the private wards,' said the nurse.

Ayan's ears perked up.

'Private wards—where are they?' he asked.

'Down this corridor, you will find the rooms. But the patients have R&R now,' she said.

'What is that?' he asked.

'See—our routine is like this. We wake them up in the morning. We make them brush their teeth, and send them for their morning ablutions. Then we give them all baths. The bed-ridden ones, we give sponge baths. We have to look after them like children. After that, we feed them breakfast. Some of them eat on their own, and some have to be fed. Look there,' she pointed at a bed.

An old man was sitting up, and a male attendant was feeding him a kind of a gruel from a bowl. It dribbled down his chin. The attendant seemed to be patient and was coaxing him to eat.

'It's a task to get him to eat—ah, where was I? Yes, I was explaining R&R. It is 'rest and recreation'. Now after breakfast, they can do whatever they like, until lunch time. The ones who are able can wander around, go for walks. That's called R&R.'

'After that what happens?' asked Ayan.

He hadn't yet found *muttachan*, and he was growing desperate by the minute.

'Then the bell goes. It's for lunch. After lunch, they are not allowed to leave their beds. The doctors come on rounds then,' she said.

'Mind if I see the private rooms?' asked Ayan,

'Please carry on,' she said.

Ayan walked to the private rooms. They were stark, spartan and bare. Each of the rooms had a single iron bed and a tiny steel stool. The windows were shut. The rooms looked exactly like the rooms that he had seen earlier—except that these had just one bed. Prison cells, Ayan thought.

He walked into each of the rooms. They were empty. Where was *muttachan*?

Then, as he turned, his eyes fell on a lone figure sitting on a rock at a distance. Could it be his grandfather? Ayan's heart began to beat fast as he moved towards the figure. He went closer.

There was no doubt in his mind now.

Ayan had found Gopal Shanker.

18

Ayan broke into a run when he saw Gopal Shanker sitting on the rock, staring at the trees. He looked bewildered, lost, confused.

'*Muttacha*!' called out Ayan, as he approached him.

Gopal Shanker looked at him uncomprehendingly.

'*Muttacha*, it's me!' said Ayan.

Gopal Shanker stared as though he was seeing an apparition. He looked so much older than when Ayan had seen him, just a few days ago. He seemed to have aged overnight. His eyes were vacant. He kept looking at Ayan, befuddled.

'Aaaa ... Ayan? Is ... it ... really ... you? Where ... where is Jairaj?' Gopal Shanker enunciated each word slowly. It seemed like he was grappling with his words, trying hard to form them into coherent sentences.

Gone was the earlier confidence, the certainty. *Muttachan* now seemed a broken man. He looked frightened. Like a beaten animal.

Ayan felt like his heart was being plucked out and squeezed.

'*Muttacha*—it's me. Don't worry, *muttacha*. I will get you out of here,' said Ayan with a confidence that he was not feeling.

'Where is Jairaj?' repeated *muttachan*.

'He ... he has gone back to Bahrain.'

'But he told me that ... that he would come back in a few hours.'

Ayan didn't know what to say. Was there an explanation

to this? Why did his father do this? Ayan couldn't believe that his father had turned out to be one of those who abandoned their aged parents. Hatred, rage and sorrow rose like waves within him. He wanted to kill his father. Yet, one part of him still wanted all of this, not to be true. Perhaps his father meant to come back and there was something else that had happened which he didn't know about?

In any case, the top priority here was to get *muttachan* out. He took in a deep breath and said, 'I think something urgent came up, *muttacha*. Anyway, I am here now. I will get you out.'

Gopal Shanker was silent for a while. Then shook his head sadly and gestured for Ayan to sit next to him, on the rock.

'No, I think he wanted me locked up. You think I don't know what is happening? I heard him talk to the doctor … I suspected it then. But I didn't think it would come to … come to this. I did not believe he would actually do this. He … he fed the doctors some nonsense.'

Ayan couldn't bear to hear the pain in his grandfather's voice. Each word stung him like a needle.

'What did he tell the doctors, *muttacha*?' asked Ayan, as he sat down on the rock next to Gopal Shanker.

Gopal Shanker was silent again.

Then he said, 'I heard it clear as day. I heard Jairaj tell them that I was talking about an imaginary person called Rohini. He said I talked about things that didn't exist. Imaginary, eh? Bloody bastard! As though I have lost my senses. I am perfectly sane.'

'And then what happened?

'I told him to shut up. I told him to hold his tongue and that he very well knew who Rohini was. It was at that moment when I sensed this was a trap. I knew it then … I knew it when he exchanged that knowing look with the doctor. But I didn't think he would actually—actually would abandon me. Shove

me into this asylum with these crazy people. The bastard!'
Gopal Shanker's voice shook as he spoke.

'Did he ... did he send you to come and get me?' he asked
with a glimmer of hope. It was as though he was looking for
the smallest chance to believe that his son wasn't as terrible
as he thought he was.

Ayan debated for a minute whether to protect his father.
Then he decided to speak the truth.

'No *muttacha*. It's a long story how I found you. He didn't
even tell me where you were admitted.'

'He ... he ... is not my son ... The bastard! He very well
knew that talking about Rohini would get me angry. And he
used that to rile me up ... How could he?'

'But why would that rile you up, *muttacha*? Wasn't Rohini
someone you went to school with? I ... I just don't understand
any of this.'

'It's a long story, Ayan. I think it's time to tell you something.
Something I don't talk about. Do you remember the box you
took out of the attic?' asked Gopal Shanker.

'Yes. Of course, I do. But it was empty,' said Ayan.

'Aaaah—that's where you are wrong. The box—it has a
false bottom. Feel around the sides, and open it. It contains
a few of my diaries from 1987 onwards. You can read what
Rohini meant to me and who she was. Read it Ayan, and then
you will know ... I ... I cannot speak about it. But I can tell
you, Rohini is not a figment of my imagination.'

Ayan could sense the urgency in his grandfather's tone.

'I will, *muttacha* ... Now, please listen to me carefully ... I
pretended to be a journalist to get inside this centre. No one
here knows I am your grandson. I just told them I am speaking
to the patients. So we will have to maintain that.'

'Eh? You pretended to be a journalist to get in here?' Gopal
Shanker blinked.

'Yes, *muttacha* ... I will explain everything, once I get you safely to *Thekke Madom*. I promise I will be back soon. Just trust me, okay?' said Ayan.

Gopal Shanker nodded.

'And I almost forgot. How is your leg, *muttacha*? Are you able to walk now? When did they remove the cast?' asked Ayan.

'The day Jairaj brought me here. He sent me in for the cast removal after that altercation we had. After that, they said they had to take x-rays. And then he vanished. I should have suspected something was amiss, the moment he brought me here. He said there was an excellent doctor here, and that he had made all arrangements. This ... this was the 'arrangement' he made. Pah!' His face darkened.

Ayan could see a glimpse of the old Gopal Shanker now. He no longer seemed as frightened as when Ayan had first seen him. Ayan took that as a good sign.

'So how are you going to get me out? They think I am senile. The doctors here think I have lost my mind. They think I am talking about some imaginary person. Your father ... He set me up for this...'

'I don't know how, *muttacha*. I will figure something out. Who is your doctor here?'

'Dr. Balakrishnan. He is the geriatric psychologist. He comes on rounds every day. But I think your father is hand-in-glove with him. We need a doctor who knows me well. Who can vouch for my sanity? Nobody here even knows me...' Gopal Shanker was thinking out aloud.

'What about your regular doctor, *muttacha*? Dr. Varghese?'

'Yes! That's what you have to do. Go and speak to Dr. Varghese and see what he can do.'

'I will, *muttacha* ... I will. I will also check at the office, what the procedure for discharge is. '

'God bless you, Ayan,' said Gopal Shanker, as he stood up. It was the first time he had said that. All these days when

Ayan was at *Thekke Madom*, *muttachan* had not said such a thing.

Ayan and Gopal Shanker walked back to the private rooms. Gopal Shanker walked slowly, but steadily. It seemed like his leg had healed completely.

'I will be back soon, *muttacha*. Do not worry,' said Ayan.

He didn't want to leave his grandfather. He wanted to somehow take his grandfather and make a run for it. But the logical part of his brain told him that if he did that, it would ruin everything. They would probably alert his father. This would have to be done in the proper manner.

He walked back, past the general ward of the Senior Citizens' Wing. When he entered the common recreational area, he saw Roshan and Prakash on the terrace of the building.

'Ayan!' called out Roshan and waved.

Ayan waved back.

'Wait. We are done with shooting here. We are coming downstairs,' said Roshan.

Near the common area, Ayan noticed Vignesh from the corner of his eyes, shaking his head and looking at him. He looked away. He didn't want to be confronted by him again.

A minute later, Prakash and Roshan emerged. 'Got everything you wanted?' asked Prakash.

'Yes, thank you very much. Can you show me the restrooms?' asked Ayan.

'Outside,' said Prakash and he motioned them to follow him.

Prakash unlocked the iron grill door and let them out. Then he locked it behind him. Ayan gestured to Roshan with his eyes.

'I want to use the restroom too,' said Roshan.

Prakash showed them where it was.

'Can I leave this equipment in the office?' asked Roshan.

Prakash said they could. They left the equipment there and

went to the restroom. Once they were sure they were alone, Roshan asked Ayan in hushed tones, 'What happened? Did you find him?'

'Yes, I did. We need to get him out. How much money do you have on you?'

Roshan took out his wallet and counted the notes. There were two five hundred rupee notes and a couple of hundreds. Ayan had about a thousand on him.

'Give it to me,' said Ayan.

'What do you have in mind?' asked Roshan.

'Look, we can't do this without inside information. I think Prakash will be a good ally to have on our side.'

'What about Sebastian? He seems friendly too.'

'I don't know … Prakash is the one who does the ground work here. He has the keys. Let's talk to him. You go get him, Roshan. I will wait here.'

Ayan waited in the restroom while Roshan went to get Prakash. A few minutes later, he appeared with Prakash in tow. Prakash was darting swift glances at the door.

'What …? What do you guys want?' he asked.

'We just want co-operation. Don't worry. Nothing illegal,' said Ayan as he slipped the notes into his hand.

Prakash glanced at the notes and his eyes widened in surprise. Then he quickly pocketed it.

'Yes?' he said.

'Look—one of the patients admitted here—he is my grandfather. I have actually come for him,' confessed Ayan.

'What? So all this documentary and all that was pretence?'

'No, no—I am actually filming for the BBC,' said Roshan.

Ayan looked at him and decided to go along with whatever Roshan was saying. There was no point in contradicting him anyway. Roshan was so convincing and had slipped so much into the role, that Ayan didn't want to blow it all up by admitting the truth.

'See, the reason we chose this centre to make this documentary is because my grandfather is here. Kind of a vested interested, you see,' laughed Ayan nervously, quickly improvising on the spot.

Prakash didn't seem to detect anything amiss. He nodded.

'So, here's the thing. My father is the authorized signatory for getting my *muttachan* out. But he is in Bahrain. I want to take him home. We need your help. What is the procedure?' asked Ayan.

'Oh! Is that all? It's very simple. You just need a discharge certificate from the concerned doctor. And you need proof of your identity, and where you are taking him. You don't need my help for that.'

'See Prakash, my father, he has kind of abandoned my grandfather here. I think he is hand-in-glove with Dr. Balakrishnan. That's why I need your help.'

Prakash considered all this for a minute. Then he scratched his head. 'There is one way we can do this,' he said.

'How? Anything ... I want *muttachan* out of here, as fast as possible.'

'Dr. Balakrishnan takes his weekly off on Tuesdays and Saturdays. I can ... you know ... give you the key and you can take him out. There's a gate at the back. Come there with a van or something, and I will let him out from there.'

'But that will raise suspicion, won't it?'

'No, it will be treated as an escapee case. This won't be the first time that something like that has happened. We are very short-staffed, and it will be put down as a slip-up from one of the staff.'

'No, we want to do it in a proper manner. We don't want any hassles later.'

'Then you will have to speak to Dr. Jomon. He will be here

on both those days. He is a very reasonable man,' said Prakash.

Ayan and Roshan thanked Prakash, and they left. Ayan felt that he was leaving a piece of his heart behind.

'Roshan, you were very, very convincing, I must say,' said Ayan.

'I got a lot of footage. I do intend to make a documentary on this. We can see where we can screen it later. If nothing, we can release it on YouTube. Some of the stories I got on film were incredible,' said Roshan.

'Good ... good,' said Ayan.

'What do we do now, to get *muttachan* out? Do we speak to Dr. Jomon?'

'Let's rush to Kottayam and meet Dr. Varghese,' said Ayan.

* * *

By the time they reached Kottayam and went to the hospital, Dr. Varghese had left for the day.

'Can you please give me his mobile number? It's extremely urgent. My *muttachan*, he needs help and we need to reach Dr. Varghese urgently,' Ayan pleaded with the receptionist.

She stifled a yawn and thrust a laminated sheet at Ayan. It contained the emergency contact numbers of all the doctors. Ayan scanned the document quickly and saw Dr. Varghese's number. He handed his phone to Roshan and read out the number. Roshan keyed it in. Ayan thanked the receptionist.

As soon as they were in the car, Ayan called up Dr. Varghese. He answered immediately.

'Dr. Varghese? This is Ayan, Gopal Shanker's grandson. I had met you the other day, remember?'

'Yes, yes, I remember. Did you see Dr. Babu? How is your grandfather?' he asked.

'This is where we need your help, Dr. Varghese,' said Ayan.

'Yes. Tell me what I can do,' said Dr. Varghese.

Ayan told him about how his grandfather was admitted to

the mental hospital, and how his father was the only authorized signatory.

'Say no more. I know the hospital very well. Dr. Jomon is a dear friend as well as a colleague. These things are so common in Kerala nowadays. Old people are dumped like waste. I am not sure if you are aware—so many old people are abandoned at the Guruvayoor temple, as they serve two free meals a day. And this trend is rising even in well-educated families. But honestly, I never thought Gopal Shanker would fall a victim to this … He is … he is so feisty.'

'It broke my heart to see him there, Dr. Varghese. Can you help in any way? I would be so grateful.'

'I tell you what—I will make a phone call to Dr. Jomon. I will be more than happy to appraise him of Gopal Shanker's mental health and write you a recommendation letter for immediate discharge. You can come and collect it tomorrow.'

'Thank you, Dr. Varghese. Thank you very much!' Ayan was so overcome with emotion, that he could barely speak.

He hung up and sank back into the seat of the car, heaving a huge sigh of relief.

Then he dropped Roshan off.

When he reached *Thekke Madom*, Velu was waiting eagerly to hear the news.

When Ayan told him, Velu couldn't hold back his tears.

'I can't even curse that wretched Jairaj Sir … You know Ayan Sir, the curses affect the children. I don't want anything to affect you. You … you are a good lad,' he said, as he dabbed his eyes with the thin cotton towel that was hanging on a shoulder.

'We have a lot of work tomorrow, Velu. Make me some tea please,' said Ayan.

Ayan sat on the verandah sipping his tea and thinking about *muttachan*. At least he was safe. His anger at what his father had done was bubbling inside him like a dormant volcano. But he had to stay calm for now. Confronting his father would serve no purpose. His father might even call up the hospital authorities if he discovered that Ayan had found *muttachan*.

It was only after he had eaten his dinner, that Ayan remembered what Gopal Shanker had said about the trunk. He made his way to the storage room. He opened the trunk, and felt around the edges of the bottom, just like his grandfather had told him to.

Muttachan was right. There was a tiny little flap, towards the edge, at the centre on both sides. Ayan touched it gently and it sprung up. The bottom of the box was indeed a false one. He removed it carefully. He couldn't believe what he saw.

Arranged neatly in a single row, were his grandfather's old diaries, each of them identical, leather-bound in black, with the year neatly handwritten and stuck on the cover.

With his heart pounding, Ayan carefully took out the diaries. There were three of them, from 1987 to 1989, one for each year.

Ayan carried them like a treasure to his bedroom and arranged them neatly on his desk.

He took out the one that said 1987. Then he began to read...

19

It was with a sense of trepidation that he turned to the first page. Even though his grandfather had given him permission to read his diaries, Ayan felt like he was trespassing on somebody else's property. He recalled a time when he was fifteen when he had poured his heart out in his diary with typical adolescent angst and naivety. His father had discovered them, and to his chagrin and horror, he had read them. Then he had got a lecture about how he should focus more on his studies, and not worry about what Susan, whom he had a crush on, did or thought.

Ayan hesitated for a moment. Should he really read this? Did he have a right to? Then he heard his *muttachan's* voice in his head, urging him to read it. His *muttachan* knew very well where the diaries were hidden, and he had shared it with Ayan. *Muttachan wanted* him to read what he had written.

Ayan's hesitation lasted only for a few seconds. He was mesmerised by the diaries and what they held. He could feel the flutter of excitement in his belly as he turned the pages.

The first thing he read was a quote neatly written in grandfather's tiny precise handwriting:

What lies behind us and what lies before are tiny matters compared to what lies within us.

—Henry Haskins

The diaries were in excellent condition. It was evident that Gopal Shanker was a careful man. As Ayan turned the pages, he realized that these were not the usual diaries which were bought off the market. It was actually a custom-bound leather notebook with unruled pages. Gopal Shanker had not posted an entry every day, but had written when he felt like. The first entry in the diary was on 8th January.

* * *

8th January 1987
Thursday

Starting a new diary like this, in a leather journal, with no dates allocated for each page, makes a lot of sense at this point in time because I am not obliged or compelled to write a page daily. Most of the past years, the page-a-day diaries I wrote in had so many blank leaves at the end of the year, since I couldn't make the time to sit down and write proper entries.

I think Padmaja definitely needs to see another doctor. But if I broach the topic with her, she gets angry. Hence it is best to be quiet.

Today, when I came back from the bank (after a terribly busy day) all I asked her was what she had cooked for dinner. She started crying. I didn't know what to do. I thought back quickly about whether we had had a fight in the morning, before I left for work. But we hadn't! She seemed fine in the morning, although quieter than usual.

I asked her what was wrong and she said she had not cooked anything for dinner. I told her that was fine and we could go over to Malabar House, and have parottas and chicken curry. Jairaj also likes the food there. She said that was not the point. She said I did not care about her anymore. I told her that simply wasn't true.

'What is the meaning of this marriage for you?' she asked.

'What is it for you?' I retorted.

But I should know better than to retort when she is in one of these moods. I should just keep quiet.

This mood of hers—I have dealt with it so many times. I should show a little more maturity.

She seems to be happy to see Jairaj. She fusses over him, asks him how his work was, and what went on at his office. I can see that he gets irritated with her questions. His replies are mostly monosyllabic but she doesn't seem to notice that.

On the work front, visitors from the head-office are due tomorrow. I have to leave early to welcome them. I hope she doesn't throw any tantrums in the morning.

* * *

It felt odd for Ayan to read about his father, and about his grandmother. He had never thought of his father as a young man living with his parents. Learning that his father's first job was in Hyderabad was news to Ayan. He had always thought that his first job was in Bahrain.

Ayan read the next few entries in the book.

* * *

13th January 1987
Tuesday

Sometimes, when you run a race and you are nearing the finish, you feel you have used up the very last reserve of strength within you, and you cannot go on anymore. Then suddenly the finish line looms large. You decide to complete the race. You give it all you have got. You dig deep into yourself, and an extra burst of energy which you never knew was within you, opens up from depths which you didn't know you had. You run with all your might, complete the race successfully and collapse—to rest and recover.

Right now, that is how I feel in my marriage. For the past eight months now, we have had more downs than ups. I am tired of constantly being a support to Padmaja, uncomplaining, smiling and cheerful. Jairaj barely takes responsibility. Can't he see how much it matters to his mother, that he spends just a few minutes talking to her?

I tried broaching it with him. 'This is all I can do,' he says.

Shaila calls only once in a way. She says the residential phone is given by Ghanshyam's office and is also paid for by them. She says it is not right to 'waste' government money on personal phone calls.

'Waste'—when did talking to your mother on the phone become a 'waste'?

* * *

12th February 1987
Thursday

Padmaja has finally agreed to see another doctor. Oh, the relief. The new doctor, Dr. Arasu, seems to be good. He has prescribed an anti-depressant to be taken twice a day. He says it's a very low dose that he has given.

Padmaja was more concerned about the side-effects. All she asked the doctor was whether there would be nausea.

'I can't stand that vomiting sensation. I had enough during my pregnancies,' she said.

I told her that whatever the side-effects, if it helped to make her better, it had to be taken. We almost got into a row, right there at the doctor's clinic. I really should learn to be silent about these things.

I had to tell the doctor about the time in Mumbai, when she had downed a bottle of pills when we were newly-married, when we had a pregnancy scare. She had missed her period, and she thought she might have been pregnant. She had rushed out and bought a tonne of over-the-counter painkiller medications. She had taken about thirty tablets at one go. When I had confronted her about it, she said that at best, it would result in a miscarriage, and at worst, it would result in her death. She had then laughed. I was frightened. I took her to the hospital and her stomach was pumped. She had held my hand throughout in the train as we travelled back home. She had insisted on travelling with me in the general compartment, even though the ladies compartment was empty.

How could I have possibly not mentioned this incident to Dr. Arasu? Yes, agreed, it happened more than thirty years ago, but it is still significant.

Padmaja thinks I was deliberately trying to malign her in front of the doctor.

I think it is important to tell the doctor your entire medical history—especially when you are consulting a psychiatrist, because you cry for no reason.

I hope the treatment given by this doctor works. I just want her to stop feeling so unhappy all the time.

* * *

Ayan leaned back on the pillow and exhaled deeply after he read that. It felt surreal, reading these diaries and imagining what his grandfather must have gone through. He felt transported to an era where his grandfather and grandmother were playing out these roles. Reading these pages felt like the numerous time-travel movies he had watched—*Kate and Leopold*, *Hot Tub Time Machine* and a couple others whose names he couldn't recall. In those movies, there was usually a device which was built which could transcend the fourth dimension—Time. Ayan felt that he was doing just that, but without any complicated machinery. He was doing it with a simple old diary.

The next two entries were short ones.

* * *

14th March 1987
Saturday

Jairaj wants to go to Bahrain. He is excited about it. It is a new company. The salary will not be enough for him to make any substantial savings. But he seems hell-bent on it, as his friend is confident they will raise the capital for it.

Padmaja is very unhappy about it. She mentioned this to Dr. Arasu. He said we have to learn to let the children go.

He also increased the dosage of the medication.

I am uncomfortable with this. It makes her drowsy.

But she seems to be fine with it.

* * *

16th March 1987
Monday

A matrimonial alliance came for Jairaj by post today. It was from Shaila's mother-in-law's sister, for her close friend's daughter. The girl, Kamakshi, is doing M.Sc. in Microbiology in Kochi. They have seen Jairaj, and are keen on proceeding with this. They have sent photographs of the girl—full-length and close-ups. Also listed her hobbies and all that—the usual nonsense.

What can you make out from photos? The couple have to meet first. The personalities have to match. Else marriage just becomes a burden you endure for the sake of the children. You will feel bound, shackled. There will be huge adjustments to make.

The last three alliances, Jairaj rejected. Padmaja is keen on this girl.

But it all depends on Jairaj.

* * *

Ayan's phone buzzed. He almost jumped out of his skin as it vibrated next to him. He had been so lost in reading the entries that he had forgotten where he was. He saw that it was a message from Shivani. That was when he realized he had not updated her at all, even though he had promised her he would.

He read her message immediately.

'Hey, what's the latest with your grandpa? My thing didn't go too well. These courts—they are awful places to be in.'

Ayan picked up the phone and called her immediately.

As soon as she heard his voice, she couldn't hold back the tears. She began to sob softly.

'Hey … hey … it's okay. Don't cry … Is everything fine? What happened? ' asked Ayan.

He could hear the muffled sobs.

She spoke after a couple of minutes. Her voice was barely audible. 'Sorry … sorry for crying like this. Nothing happened. That's all. After the entire hearing, the plea, and asking me a whole lot of questions, it got adjourned for another day. This legal process in India—it's so long drawn. And queues at the family court—it was insane. Like a huge *mela*. You would think half of Pune's population has turned up there. And I don't know. I felt very alone. Sorry Ayan, to dump all this on you. And sorry I burst into tears even before asking about your grandfather. You must be thinking I am an inconsiderate boor.'

'Don't be silly. What are friends for? It's been so crazy at my end, I didn't even message you. I managed to locate *muttachan*. Your identity card—it got me into the hospital.'

'Oh, really? That's good!'

He told her how they had managed to get inside and about Roshan filming for the 'youth wing of the BBC'. They both laughed about it.

'You know what—I might actually be able to put him in touch with a few media houses if he does make that documentary. I have a few contacts,' she said.

'That would be awesome. He was mentioning that he did get some really good footage.'

'Keep me posted about your grandpa. And hey, thank you for making me laugh and making me feel better,' said Shivani, as she hung up.

As soon as she hung up, Ayan went back to reading the diary entries again. He was reading a story which he was a part of.

The next entry surprised Ayan.

* * *

20th March 1987
Friday

Took an off from work today to go watch India versus Pakistan at Lal Bahadur Shastri Stadium. Jairaj came with me. Padmaja didn't want to come with us even though I had got three passes.

It was a THRILLER of a match. I don't think in cricketing history, it has ever happened that both teams score the same runs in a One-Day-International. Pakistan won the toss and chose to field. We scored 212 in 44 overs. Srikkanth retired hurt after scoring 2 runs! Gavaskar scored a pathetic 1 run. It was only Shastri who held fort with his 69.

What a nail-biting match! Qadir was run out, when he tried an impossible second run.

Padmaja should have been there! She missed an exciting time!

* * *

Ayan never knew that his grandfather and his father had actually gone to see a cricket match! He didn't even know they were cricket fans. In all his years in Bahrain, he had not heard his father talk about cricket even once.

When Ayan turned the page of the diary, he saw a letter neatly tucked into an envelope stuck on the page. He opened the envelope and took out the letter carefully. It was on heavy ivory paper and the stationary looked exotic. Ayan had never seen such a letterhead before. His eyes skimmed over the content and he turned it around.

He drew a sharp breath when he saw who the sender was.

It was a letter from Rohini.

BOOK THREE

Rohini

The past beats inside me like a second heart.

—John Banville, 'The Sea'

20

Ayan took the letter out and ran his hands over it. The handwriting was artistic and beautiful. The letterhead was embossed with the initials R.R.

Ayan began to read.

* * *

Madras
18th March '87

Dear Gopal,

Hello.

How are you? How is life treating you? I do not know if I even have the right to write to you anymore, but I am writing anyway.

It has been more than three decades since we last wrote to each other. Three decades—can you believe it? So much has happened since then, that I don't even know where to begin. The last letter I have from you is dated 19th October 1954. I am certain you remember the date. But just in case you have forgotten, let me refresh your memory—it was my last birthday as a single woman. (Your words—that is what you said. I am sure you have forgotten this).

I am so sorry I never replied to that letter, Gopal. I know it is unconscionable on my part. But trust me when I say I had no choice. That letter from you created a huge furore in my home. My father read it, as did my mother and her sisters. I wished I could sink into the earth. My father hit me in front of all the guests and relatives. I still wince at the memories. They berated me—said it was no way for a bride to behave. I was put under a 'watch' till my wedding day. I was not allowed to leave my home. There was no way I could have replied to you back then, even if I wanted to.

After my marriage, I moved to Madras with my husband. We have been living inside the IIT campus ever since. We have moved many houses, but all of them, within the campus. Each time my husband got a promotion, our house got upgraded. My husband Raman, has now become the Dean of Applied Mechanics.

But please don't think I never wrote to you, Gopal. I did. Your Bombay address is imprinted in my memory. (How can it not be? We must have exchanged at least a hundred letters in the two years that you lived there. I want to tell you, I have ALL of them to this day.)

I did send you about twenty-three letters between 1954 and 1961. I wrote to you on your birthday, I wrote on New Year and Onam. But all the letters came back to me, saying 'addressee left'. It was the only address I had for you, Gopal. I kept hoping that by a miracle, you would get the letters. I stopped writing after 1961, as I lost my mother that year. In 1966, I lost my father too. That was the last time I went to Poongavanam. For his funeral.

You must have noticed that I haven't mentioned anything about my children so far. I had a daughter, and I lost her last year. I think the cruellest tragedy God inflicts on someone is making them watch their child die. She was admitted to the hospital with high fever (later we got to know it was meningococcal disease) and she was gone by the end of the third day. She would have been 25 this year in April.

It has been about eight months now since she left us. To this day, I find it hard to believe she is gone. The grief is overwhelming on some days. On some days, it is manageable. But all the time it is constant. Like a stone in my heart.

A friend of mine suggested I join Reiki. She said it would help me. One of the things that we have to do as a part of the course, is write to people whom we think we have wronged, and ask them for their forgiveness. I asked my Reiki Guru, what if we did not know the address of the person. She laughed and said that all I had to do was write. The intention was what was important, not the actual sending of the letter. So I wrote a brief letter to you. It was just a single line, asking you to forgive me.

I have wondered about you for many years now. You disappeared completely. I tried asking around furtively about you. But I never got any concrete information.

Last week, my mother's distant cousin from Poongavanam visited me as she had to attend a wedding. She is a marriage-broker now. She has information and contact details of many eligible boys and girls which she collects from her huge network. I don't think there's anyone in the Poongavanam network that she doesn't know. She keeps all these details in a diary. We left together for the wedding, and she had told me to keep her diary in my bag. She forgot to take it back the day we returned. I couldn't help glance through it, just out of pure curiosity—to see if I knew any of the people listed there.

Imagine my shock and surprise, when I saw your name listed there, as the father of Jairaj Shanker. All details about your family were there as well. I learnt that your daughter is married and is in Delhi. Your address wasn't there, but it said you were in Bharathiya Bank, Somajiguda branch, Hyderabad. So do you know what I did?

I visited their branch here and asked them for the address of the Somajiguda branch. And that is how I am writing to you, at your office address.

My regards to your daughter and to your wife and to your son too.

I guess I shall take refuge under the cliché, 'Better late than never.'

I hope you have it in your heart to forgive me. I hope to hear from you. But if you decide to ignore this letter, I will understand.

Rohini

* * *

Ayan's curiosity was piqued after reading the letter. He could not imagine his grandfather as a young romantic, writing over a hundred letters to Rohini. *Muttachan* must have been about twenty at that time. Clearly, they were in love. And how hard it was those days, to find out an address! Rohini actually had to go to the bank in Chennai to get it. He noticed how back then, the city was still Madras. Today, all it would have taken was a simple Google search. Ayan thought about how easy it was for him to talk to Shivani, even though she lived in another city. How hard it must have been without computers or the Internet! He hadn't even given a thought to all this before.

He couldn't get over the hundred letters! Ayan hadn't drafted a single letter in his life, except the ones he had written for his language exams. And then there were the twenty-three letters which she had written, without even getting a reply. Their love for each other certainly ran deep.

He was eager to know what happened next.

He turned the page and read the next few pages of *muttachan's* diaries in quick succession.

* * *

23rd March 1987
Monday

At around 11 this morning, just when I finished the weekly staff meeting. I got a letter from my Rohini. Thirty-three years! And she decides to write to me now. I am dumbfounded. Excited. Happy. Sad. Elated. Angry.

She said she wrote me twenty-three letters!

How could I explain that it was because I couldn't bear the grief of her wedding that I moved out of Bombay? Every single thing there reminded me of her.

I am sticking her letter here in this diary. This is the first time I am making a personal diary entry while sitting in my office. But I think this is momentous.

It is not every day that someone you have not seen for over three decades, comes back into your life.

She has lost her daughter and her parents. I can't imagine the agonies that she must have gone through. Life has been cruel to her.

Her letter transported me right back to my Bombay days. How many times had we made promises that I would show her Bombay, show her my world?

Perhaps I should have approached her father, and asked for her hand in marriage, as soon as I got that job. But it was she who asked me to hold on. She was terrified.

I am unable to focus on my work right now. I have asked not to be disturbed; my cabin door is closed. And nobody has a clue that I am sitting here and writing this in my diary.

I am giddy with excitement. I feel like a teenager now. I have read her letter at least fifteen times. If she had given a phone number I could have called her.

I think that is what I will do. I will write to her and ask her for her phone number.

I wonder how she looks now.

Rohini—I never knew she would have the ability to turn my world upside down.

A second time.

*   *   *

24th March 1987
Wednesday

I replied to Rohini's letter yesterday. I told her how overjoyed I was to hear from her and how very sorry I was for her loss. I told her about how her wedding drove me insane. I told her how I felt lost and angry. And how I had got married to the first girl my parents suggested.

I didn't tell her that Padmaja's emotional problems started right after marriage. I didn't tell her about how unhappy I am at the moment.

Instead, I told her about how after I returned from Bombay, my uncle had helped me get this job at the bank and how far I had progressed in my career.

(It was a little petty of me perhaps—but she had said that her husband was the Dean. I haven't done too badly for myself either. I don't know why it was important to me, to make that clear to her, but it was.)

I have asked for her phone number.

Jairaj has asked us to go ahead with the marriage proposal. He wants to meet the girl. That is a good sign, I suppose.

* * *

29th March 1987
Sunday

Wonder of wonders, Jairaj has liked the girl. Kamakshi and her parents flew down to Hyderabad yesterday. They seem to be very nice people—honest, humble and educated. Kamakshi seems nice too—smart and convent-educated. The most important thing is, Jairaj thinks she is a perfect fit. The engagement ceremony is some time in May. They will decide an auspicious day.

My parents (God bless their souls) would have been happy to see this day.

Padmaja is excited about the wedding plans. Shaila called yesterday and I heard them both go on and on about the wedding. I am happy leaving all these decisions to them.

I wonder if Rohini received my letter. The earliest I can expect her reply is the 30th, presuming letters take three days to be delivered from Hyderabad to Madras.

* * *

30th March 1987
Monday.

No news from Rohini. I am getting impatient.

* * *

31st March 1987
Tuesday

No letter from Rohini at all. I asked the office peon thrice, just in case he had made a mistake.

'Nahin sahib. I will bring them straight to you if something comes,' he says.

I have to stop writing in this diary during office hours.

* * *

1st April 1987
Wednesday

At last a letter!! I am happy again.

I am pasting it here.

* * *

Madras
29th March '87

Dear Gopal,

How WONDERFUL to hear back from you! I thank you from the bottom of my heart for writing back and being so gracious about it.

Yes, I agree with you that the obstacles life throws in our paths, makes us grow. I only wish it wasn't so painful.

It is terrific to know that you have risen to the position of General Manager and it is great that you have done remarkably well in your career.

You asked about what Raman is like. And how I spend my days here and what I have been upto all these years.

Raman is a very smart man. He is currently doing research work on ion scattering on metal-semiconductor interfaces. Don't ask me what that means—I have no idea! But it's something he gets engrossed in. It helps him cope with the grief.

As regards me—before Lalitha was born (it took about eight years after my marriage to conceive her) I used to teach at a school inside the IIT campus. I taught art. I had to undergo a lot of treatments to conceive her. So you can imagine how protected and loved she would have been.

Once she was born, I resigned my job. I was a stay-at-home mother, and looked after her full-time. I wonder now where the years went.

Once she was off to college, I had some time once more, but I couldn't go back to full-time teaching. They have restrictions on upper age limits for employment.

I worked with a few local artists and helped them showcase their arts. I also worked with Unnati International Rural Cultural Centre (UIRCC) for a while—mainly organizing cultural festivals among rural youth, to provide them opportunities to learn and practise the fine arts. I helped in many national integration camps.

Then my health took a beating. I had to have a hysterectomy surgery two years ago. After that I lost Lalitha. I haven't gone back to work since then.

In the past, I have travelled to Hyderabad and I have helped organize camps there. Now that you are there, I have motivation to join back work.

If I come to Hyderabad, will you meet me, Gopal?

Rohini

PS: I have enclosed my old business card which has my phone numbers. I am reachable on the residence number mentioned there.

* * *

2nd April 1987
Thursday

I replied to Rohini today. How wonderful to be connected again. I love her letters. I want to call her, but I have no idea what she will tell her husband. Meet Gopal—my ex-lover, who has got back in touch with me?

She wants to come to Hyderabad to meet me! She has asked in her letter whether I will meet her. How can I not?

I think it is time I tell Padmaja about her.

* * *

4th April 1987
Saturday

On the way back from the Hanuman temple, I told Padmaja that an old friend of mine had got in touch with me.

'Don't think I don't know it is a woman,' she said.

I was stunned. This is the first time I am witnessing Padmaja's mind-reading abilities. I asked her how she knew.

'Your face is glowing these days and you can't get wait to get to work. She contacts you at office, I presume?' she asked.

Astute.

The way she spat out the words makes it sound like it is a clandestine affair. Cheap. Hidden. In secret.

It most certainly is not like that.

* * *

8th April 1987
Wednesday

I finally mustered the courage and called Rohini today, from office. She answered on the third ring. She recognised my voice as soon as I said, 'Hello? Rohini?'

'Hello, Gopal. I have been waiting for your call,' she said.

I felt I couldn't breathe.

We spoke for about ten minutes, even though I wanted to speak longer. I do not want the bank logging my calls.

Her husband Raman, seems to be a self-absorbed intellectual from what I can make out. He does not seem to understand her grief, her pain. She said she spoke to UIRCC about resuming work. They are more than happy to have her join back. She also said she broached the topic of organizing a cultural camp for rural youth in Hyderabad and they seemed receptive to her ideas.

She asked me if I believed in the power of the Universe conspiring to make things happen. I told her I did not know about that, but we certainly did not control life events.

It will be so good to see her again.

I have promised to call her again next week.

21

Ayan yawned and glanced at the clock. It was already past 1 a.m.

He would have to wake up early and go to meet Dr. Varghese. If he continued to read the diary, he would not get adequate sleep. But he was enthralled by the entries and *muttachan's* life. Each entry that he read revealed a bit more about *muttachan*. What a man! Who would have guessed how deep his love for Rohini was?

Ayan just couldn't put away the diary. He was mesmerized. He promised himself that he would go to bed after reading just a few more entries. He propped a few pillows on the headboard of the bed, wrapped a blanket around himself, curled up cosily and continued to read.

* * *

14th April 1987
Tuesday

I replied to Rohini's letter yesterday. I told her that I would definitely meet her if she came to Hyderabad. I also called her up today. She has not yet received my letter. It takes four or five days for the letter to reach from Hyderabad to Madras.

We spoke for about seven or eight minutes today. When I mentioned that I don't want the bank to log the calls, she said she could call me up from an STD booth just outside the IIT campus as she did not want her calls to me to appear in her telephone bills either.

We talked about whether it was right or wrong to be secretive about our phone calls. Rohini said that Raman would not understand why she wanted to talk to me. I did not mention Padmaja's caustic comments. Instead, I told her that if she came to Hyderabad, she could come over for a meal.

Padmaja told the doctor that she did not think the medications were working. He has now changed the dosage. He asked her if she was taking them regularly and she said she was. I highly doubt it. But I did not utter a word, as I did not want another fight in front of him. From now on, I will make sure that she takes her medication, before I leave for work.

* * *

23rd April 1987
Thursday

Rohini called me up from the STD booth outside the campus. This time, we spoke for about twenty whole minutes. How lovely that was! From now on, I should perhaps call her from outside too, instead of my usual calls from the bank.

She asked me if she was disturbing me, at my workplace. I didn't tell her that there was a client waiting to meet me. I took her call, making them wait outside, till we finished talking. It was a choice between making the client wait, or making Rohini wait. I chose the former.

Rohini said she could come to Hyderabad in the last week of May. UIRCC had organised an exposition for rural artisans to showcase their work and she was helping to co-ordinate it.

'You know, I am coming mainly to see you, right?' she asked.

She sounded sixteen then. Just like how it was when we were a couple.

I asked her if she remembered how I used to get her candies from Joseph's shop. She laughed and said she remembered every detail. She told me how she would hide the candies so that she did not have to share them with her brother and sister. She would later climb high up the mango tree in her courtyard, far away from prying eyes, and sit there to eat the candies.

She asked me if I remembered the ink tablets which we had

to dissolve to make our ink and the dip-pens. We never had fountain pens those days. We had only dip-pens and blotting paper. How can I forget that? She had forgotten her ink tablets on the day of her exam. I had cycled all the way home from school and fetched some for her. She remembered that as well. We spoke about how there was no electricity in Poongavanam, back then. We had to huddle over our kerosene lamps, to study for the exams. She laughed and recalled how she, her brother and her sister had to share a single lamp, and how each one would yell their lessons at the top of their voices, each louder than the other, till their mother asked them all to shut up. It was a vocal-chord competition rather than any actual studies happening. We laughed as we spoke about it.

I asked her if she remembered how we had both gone to the Poongavanam river and sat by the banks just before I told her that my father was sending me to Bombay for a job. I had finished my Intermediate, and those days, you were eligible for employment if you completed sixth form. Having done Intermediate, my employability potential, therefore, was very high. Most boys started working as soon as they finished sixth form. My father felt it was a great idea to work outside Kerala. So he wrote to a relative who got me a job at a cotton mill in Bombay. I felt sad that I had to leave Kerala, but I was also excited about going to Bombay.

We had both taken a bus and gone to the post office just before I left for Bombay. She had gone inside and bought stamps, so that she could write letters to me. I had waited a little distance away, outside the post office, as we did not want the postmaster to ask us questions. I remind her how excited she had been to see the postal stamp with 'Republic of India' on it, with a picture of a quill, an ink-pot and Sanskrit verses. It cost two annas. She had studied the postage stamp closely and then told me that her father had said that India getting independence and becoming a republic, was the biggest thing ever and that she agreed with him. It felt nice to remember these things once again. We had much more to say to each other, but Rohini had to go and so ended the call. But, I continued to think about those days even after I put the receiver down.

I remembered how I arrived in Bombay with just two extra sets of clothes in my suitcase. I stayed in Matunga initially, with my uncle, and then shared accommodation with three others who worked with me in the same factory. We used to dine at Mani's Lunch Home and for 6 annas, we could get a full meal. Each month I sent home fifteen rupees by money order, as soon as I got my salary. By the 27th or 28th of the month, our salaries would finish and we would subsist on eating bananas and drinking water.

Those days, there were tramlines in Bombay. We took the tram from Matunga to Parel every day. And even though I had to send money each month, I always set aside some for buying inland letters, to post to Rohini. I would starve happily if it meant I could write to her, and hear from her.

When I came back from the factory, I would look forward to reading her letters over and over, till I got the next one. I would write to her in detail, and her replies to me were just as detailed. We would tell each other every single thing that had happened since we last wrote.

When I went back to Poongavanam from Bombay, she would be waiting to meet me. I remember how she would tell her parents that she was going to the temple, and how we would sit by the temple pond, our feet in the water, with the fish nibbling at our feet. She would laugh delightedly then.

The Ambal[23] flowers and the lotus flowers intermingled, spread out before us like an interwoven rug of pale pink and white. She said they were talking to each other. I had laughed then.

She was fascinated with the tall lamp outside the temple, which was lit only on special occasions. It was lit that evening. The lamp was about sixteen feet high with several circular layers. Each layer had many tiny flames. 'How do you think they light all these, Gopal?' she had asked. I had replied that they would probably use tall platforms which you could climb on, as oil had to be poured, and wicks had to be put in.

---

23. Water lilies

We had together, watched the flames dance in unison, as if to a cosmic rhythm. Rohini said they were friends, celebrating a happy occasion.

She has a unique way of looking at things, my Rohini.

Once I returned to Bombay, she would send me beautiful paintings of the lotus pond. Her paintings were remarkably accurate, with great detailing.

I used to wait as eagerly back then for her letters as I do now.

How is this even possible? Do some people have a deep soul connection?

I don't know.

All I know is that I feel incredibly happy when I hear from her and talk to her.

I sometimes cannot believe, we have got back in touch again.

* * *

21st May 1987
Thursday

Jairaj got engaged to Kamakshi today. It was a small ceremony, and we hosted it at our residence itself. Shaila has come for a few days. Ghanshyam is travelling abroad.

The wedding will be in January or February next year.

Padmaja is delighted. I can see happiness on her face, after a very long time. She didn't want to take the medicines yesterday. She said she was perfectly fine. But I insisted that she had to. She sulked, but she obliged.

Jairaj seems to be very happy too, about this whole thing. Kamakshi has no qualms about moving to Bahrain and she said she would love to. So all is well that ends well.

Rohini and I call each other regularly now. I have started calling her from an STD booth, a little away from the bank, on the way home. She calls me on Tuesdays and I call on Fridays.

I would have loved to speak to her every day. But the costs are prohibitive.

We haven't been in touch for 33 years, and now I find speaking eight times a month is not enough!

She is coming here on 28th May. I haven't yet told my family. I think I will tell them only on the previous day.

* * *

28th May 1987
Thursday

Good Lord. What a grand day today has been. It will be etched in my memory forever. I met Rohini today, after thirty-three years. I had not even thought in my wildest dreams that our paths would cross again. This joy, this feeling of elation, is a hundredfold more than what it was when we spoke on the phone. This meeting her—it is almost surreal. I still cannot believe it.

Time stood still, as I watched her getting down from the train at Nampally Railway Station. I recognized her straight away as I already knew her compartment number, and was waiting at that spot where it would arrive. She got down slowly, carrying her suitcase, a cloth bag slung over one shoulder. I almost ran to greet her.

She was wearing a starched cotton saree. She still looks the same except for a bit of grey in her hair. We compared our glasses, the grey in our hair and we chuckled. I am smiling now as I write this. I was so happy, I thought my heart would burst.

I then rode with her in an auto to Banjara Hills, which is where she is staying. Her cultural centre has a guest house there. That is such a classy part of the town. But then—everything about her exudes class. Her clothes, her speech, her walk. She told me she was carrying a gift for me. The moment she said that, I realized I had nothing for her. I should have bought something!

Once we reached the guest house, she checked in. We had a cup of tea in the living room, which the staff there served. The guest house looks like a five-star hotel. She gave me my gift then. It was a copy of E.M. Forester's *Passage to India*. I was so overwhelmed I couldn't speak. She remembered after all these years! I had borrowed the book from our village library and I was upset that they would not re-issue the book again to me, when I requested them to, as the librarian knew I would be leaving for Bombay soon. I had argued with him and told him I would return it before I left, but he had not relented. And so, I had not read it completely.

What a thoughtful, rich gift Rohini has chosen to give me. I will treasure this book for the rest of my life.

After tea with her, I went directly to office and worked for half a day. Or rather, I pretended to work. I did what I could. It was so hard to focus, knowing that she was just a few miles away from me. I was also thinking about what gift I could get her.

She came home for lunch and met Padmaja, Jairaj, as well as Shaila. They were polite to her.

But the moment she left, Padmaja threw a fit.

'What kind of friendship is this? All these years we have been married, you never had a woman friend. And she travelled from Madras?' she asked.

'She travelled on work,' I said.

Shaila and Jairaj both said that it was not right.

'What is not right?' I asked. 'I met her and she came home. She is an old and dear friend.'

I told them to mind their own business, and that I would do just as I pleased under my roof. Jairaj banged the door and left the house to show his disapproval. Shaila and Padmaja wouldn't speak to me for the rest of the day.

How absurd they are being! Rohini had even carried gifts for all of them. That was so kind of her. She didn't have to do that. They didn't even appreciate that.

But even their reaction hasn't put a dampener on my ecstasy of seeing her.

I am meeting her again for lunch tomorrow. But I do not think I should tell my family that.

They will not understand.

* * *

31st May 1987
Saturday

Rohini left last evening. I saw her off at the railway station.

I think the last three days were the happiest days of my life. I took an off from the bank yesterday afternoon and went to meet her at the campsite. It was a huge eye-opener. She is working closely with the government to establish an arts and crafts council of some sort. I learnt about Banjara needle work. She told me that the Banjara groups of Andhra Pradesh were previously a nomadic community with roots in Rajasthan. Their style of embroidery is unique and distinct. Rohini told me that the art of embroidery dates back to 2300-1500 BC. I asked her how they could be so sure of the dates. She said archaeologists could date these things. Bronze needles and rich embroidered pieces of cloth had been discovered in excavations.

What Rohini is trying to do, is to establish a body which acts as a kind of formal society to help to develop the skills of these Banjara women, so that they can be empowered to earn from it. Right now, many of them work as labourers in agricultural fields. The needlework they do is beautiful.

Rohini showed me the work that they have done. Stunning. The techniques are handed down through the generations, from mother to daughter, and needlework forms an integral part of the community heritage. Traditionally, these women wear very colourful clothes. Clothes are an important part of the bride's trousseau as well. They showed off her skill and are visual symbols of wealth, with mirrors, coins and cowries worked into the fabric. The motifs that Rohini showed me were geometrical, mostly a combination of squares, triangles and diamonds with contrasting rich colours. Rohini explained all the different types of stitches to me—simple chain stitch, herringbone stitch, long and short stitch, etc. She pointed out how all of it gave the richness to the embroidery.

The body that they intend to establish will understand the urban market and they will develop a new range of products made for use in urban homes, keeping their indigenous style intact. She is so passionate about this. Her face glows when she talks about it. She forgets everything else. I am very proud of the work she is doing because it will benefit thousands of people.

And I had no idea at all about all of this.

After she finished her camp, she had about two hours before catching her train. I took her to see the Charminar. I wanted to buy her a gift and asked her if I could get her Hyderabadi pearls. She said she hated pearls as they came from torturing oysters. I asked her, what if the pearls were natural. 'Oh, they will all say that they are natural, but there is no way of truly knowing, is there?'

Her unique world view is intact even after all these years.

We roamed around the market area. She did not mind the crowd. She said she rarely got to go to places like this, and that she was enjoying this very much. I got her a wooden bangle stand and a set of lacquer bangles that Hyderabad is so famous for. She was delighted with the bangle stand and she loved the bangles. She smiled as she slipped a red one on.

'I will think of this day, whenever I wear these,' she said quietly.

'Wear it every day then,' I replied.

I want to gift her a gold bangle.

But for now, I will have to be content with this.

I felt sad to part from her. She looked sad too.

'Thank you for this, Gopal,' she said. I will never forget the look in her eyes when she said that.

I should be content that I got at least this much time with her.

Yet, the heart longs for more.

Be still my beating heart—be still.

* * *

Ayan read all of it spellbound.

What amazing memories his grandfather had made with Rohini.

He looked at the diary. There were many more entries. He wanted to stay up for more time and read them all. But then, he would probably not be able to wake up at all.

With great reluctance, Ayan switched off the light and closed his eyes, his head full of images of Gopal Shanker and Rohini. What a story theirs was! And how privileged he was to be privy to it.

With these thoughts, Ayan slept.

22

Around 6 a.m., Ayan woke up with a start. The diary rested right next to his pillow. He had barely slept for a couple of hours, and yet he was wide awake. He couldn't believe how enthused and eager he was to read the rest of it. If he began to read now, he would still have a couple of hours to complete reading it. He desperately wanted to know what had happened next in his *muttachan's* life. He rushed to the kitchen downstairs. There was no sign of Velu. Freshly-boiled hot milk stood on the stove. He made himself a cup of coffee, and hurried back upstairs, his footsteps echoing on the wooden staircase.

The first rays of the golden light of dawn were beginning to stream in from the window. The cries of several birds filled the air. He sat up on his bed, propped a few pillows against the headboard, and once again began to read.

* * *

14th June 1987
Sunday

There's been a sudden turn of events. Jairaj wants to go to Bahrain next month end. All his travel arrangements have been made by his friend and his visa too has been arranged. His friend needs him there urgently. Kamakshi's parents are not comfortable with him going off to Bahrain, unless the marriage ceremony has been conducted.

So, after much discussion, we have now fixed the marriage date for 17th July, at Arunodayam, under the aegis of the Kerala Samajam in Hyderabad. It is easier to conduct the wedding there, and her parents are more or less comfortable with it. We have booked three houses near the Samajam, and that should suffice to accommodate all the guests from their side, who will be travelling from Kerala for the wedding.

Padmaja is tense and anxious about it. She wanted a wedding at Kodungaloor, which is the bride's place, and her own native place too. She has told me many times now, that she would prefer that, and how it will not be our primary responsibility to take care of arrangements if we do so. But there is paucity of time, and Jairaj agrees with me that it is practical to have the wedding in Hyderabad. This is the best we can do.

Jairaj and Kamakshi will travel to Kerala after the wedding and take the blessings of all the elderly relatives, who are not able to make it. Padmaja says she will travel with them, although I think she should leave the newly-weds alone.

* * *

27th June 1987
Saturday

It is only the phone calls with Rohini that are keeping me sane. Padmaja snaps or gets angry for the smallest reasons.

The flower seller said that the dark yellow Jamanthi[24] flower would be difficult to procure in the quantities requested. He asked if light yellow was okay. I said it was fine. Padmaja started shouting at me saying I did not care.

Frankly, how does the colour of the flowers matter?

Rohini says that Padmaja is stressed. I still did not tell her about her medication or her problems.

I am happy that it is only rarely that we have missed our weekly phone calls to each other. She is doing a rural artisans camp in Maharashtra soon.

* * *

---

24. Chrysanthemum

20th July 1987
Monday

The wedding went off beautifully. Padmaja was teary-eyed. There were about 125 people, which I think is a good number. Padmaja wasn't too happy though. She said had it been in Kerala, it would have been at least a 500 guests.

Jairaj and Kamakshi couldn't care less.

Ghanshyam and Shaila went back to Delhi the very next day.

Yesterday, Jairaj, Kamakshi and a few others left for Kerala.

I want to buy a colour television set. I have narrowed down my selection to EC-TV which is manufactured by Electronics Corporation, Government of India. I think it is an excellent choice. The colours are rich and vivid. The price is fabulous too.

But Padmaja wants to wait for some more time. I told her that she will not have to go to the neighbour's house and watch the movies on their black and white television anymore. Padmaja says that if we buy a colour TV, we will be the only ones in this area to have it, and so everybody will end up coming here to watch it. I guess she has a point. We will wait for a few months more.

I do want to buy it before the cricket World Cup though.

It is wonderful to have the house to myself. I can't wait for tomorrow—as it's the day to talk to Rohini.

* * *

30th August 1987
Monday

Jairaj left for Bahrain today. Kamakshi says she will stay with her parents till he sends the tickets and visa for her. I think Padmaja liked having both Jairaj and Kamakshi around. She tried convincing Kamakshi to stay with us until such time Jairaj sends the tickets.

'What will I do here without Jairaj, amma? I want to spend a little time with my parents. It has been a while since I saw them,' she said.

Padmaja complained to me about how Jairaj and Kamakshi don't care about her. I tried pointing out that it wasn't true, and that the girl was only being reasonable.

But Padmaja wouldn't have any of it. She says I don't

understand, and all I am interested in, is immersing myself in my work. She asked me if my 'lady friend' calls. I said we spoke on the phone now and then. Padmaja got angry when I said that and she hasn't been speaking to me since then.

Kamakshi leaves tomorrow.

* * *

12th September 1987
Saturday

We bought a colour TV today. EC-TV. It is wonderful!

Sure enough, as Padmaja predicted, the neighbours have come to watch the movie.

All these months, Padmaja has been going to their place. So it's time to return the favour. I can't understand why she grumbles so much. They leave right after the movie—and she watches the movie anyway, whether they are there or not.

I let her deal with it. I go inside and read a book, or I write to Rohini.

* * *

30th September 1987
Wednesday

Padmaja is very lonely. The neighbours have stopped coming over now, as they have bought a colour TV as well.

Jairaj has sent just one letter from Bahrain, so far. He says calling up is very expensive. He said they are working hard, and he is happy there.

'Why can't Kamakshi write?' Padmaja asked.

'Why don't you take the initiative and write first?' I asked her. So she did.

I will go to the post office tomorrow and send it.

* * *

26th October 1987
Monday

I think it is time to probably take a second opinion about Padmaja's condition. No medication seems to be helping. The doctors keep experimenting with the dosage.

This is not how it should be. If it's depression, there has to be an improvement with medication.

They have told her that she should force herself to go for a walk every morning. But she sleeps a lot. She is distraught that Kamakshi has not replied to her letter.

I called up Shaila a week ago and told her to call her mother once in a way.

She said she would, but there have been no calls from her, so far.

I don't know what to do.

* * *

5th November 1987
Thursday

India lost to England by 35 runs. What a shame! Gavaskar made a pathetic 4 runs. We managed to score 219, thanks to Azhar. Our tail-enders should have performed.

When we won the toss and sent them in to bat, I was hopeful of a victory. But I was wrong.

Gooch is solid. He made a 115 and firmly anchored their win.

They deserve this victory. They played so well.

Today, when we spoke I had asked Rohini if she watched cricket. She said she did not. Raman was a fan of cricket, but she couldn't stand the sport.

'Oh, then I think I will get along well with your husband,' I commented.

She laughed and said I ought to meet him, then I would know.

I asked her if she would invite me to her home if I came to Madras.

She said she would invite me at a time when her husband was not home.

'Why?' I asked.

'Because I haven't yet told him about you. And I cannot suddenly spring a surprise on him,' she said.

I have no intention of meeting her husband. I don't wish him ill, but I don't want to see him either. Perhaps it is foolish of me to view my relationship with Rohini 'in isolation'—as a stand-alone thing. After all, we are both married, and have other responsibilities. But for the few moments that I talk to her, it is like nothing else exists. I don't like to think of her 'other life'.

I think about Rohini and me all those years back, and it is laced with regret. We all have regrets in life. Certain things we could have done differently in the past. My biggest regret remains my not approaching her father and asking for her hand in marriage. We could have been together then.

Now we have to settle for weekly phone calls.

That's life, I guess.

* * *

Velu knocked on Ayan's door with a cup of coffee.

'Ayan Sir, slept well? Today you have to meet Dr. Varghese, right?' asked Velu.

Ayan sat up bolt upright and took the coffee from Velu. He glanced at the time on his mobile phone, 'Oh! It's already 7.45 a.m. I better hurry. Dr. Varghese should be there by 9 a.m., isn't it?'

'Yes, Ayan Sir. I want to go with you. Please eat. Breakfast is ready,' said Velu.

Then he noticed the diaries on Ayan's bed.

'What are you reading, Ayan Sir?'

'*Muttachan's* diaries. He told me to read them.'

'He likes writing diaries. I have seen him writing every now and then. He says unless we document the events in our lives, we will have only our memories to go by. He says memory is unreliable and that is why the written word is important.'

'Have you ever read his diaries, Velu?'

'I once glanced through one of them. It was all in English. Had it been in Malayalam, I might have read it,' Velu admitted sheepishly.

'Let's leave by 8.30 a.m. I want to be there when Dr. Varghese arrives, so we can get that letter quickly,' said Ayan.

'You know Ayan Sir, Gopal Sir had left the house with only

the clothes he had on. I will pack fresh clothes for him. I have laundered and ironed all of them,' said Velu.

Ayan couldn't help thinking how thoughtful Velu was. He seemed to care more about his *muttachan* than his own father did.

* * *

When Velu and Ayan got to the hospital, Dr. Varghese had not yet arrived. There were already a few patients waiting. They joined them in the waiting area, taking their seats on the metal chairs placed in rows. Ayan restlessly tapped his fingers on the metal arm rest, till a woman with a baby sitting next to him asked him to please stop.

'Oh sorry,' he said.

He saw Dr. Varghese walking in. He jumped up from his seat and greeted him. Dr. Varghese motioned for them to follow him inside. Ayan was glad that they didn't have to wait till he finished seeing all his patients.

Once they were seated inside, Dr. Varghese said, 'It is a pity what has happened. I shall write a letter of recommendation for immediate discharge. I spoke to Dr. Jomon yesterday. You can take all of Gopal Shanker's medical reports too. It will not be necessary, but carry them with you.'

'Thank you so much, Dr. Varghese. I really appreciate this,' said Ayan.

'It is my duty and pleasure. Gopal Shanker does not have to be in a home. I think during one visit that he was here, almost four years back, he was slightly delusional. I had suspected an electrolyte imbalance. I immediately ordered a complete blood count—blood urea, serum creatinine and serum electrolytes. It turned out he had low sodium. If I remember right, it had fallen below 135, and that's what caused the delusions. I had prescribed medication. Velu—you were with him then. Do you remember?'

'Oh sir—yes, I remember now. I had forgotten about it. At that time too, he was talking about things that didn't exist, and once he took the medicines he was fine,' said Velu.

'Yes. An electrolyte imbalance causes delusions. Once the levels are restored, it vanishes. I have had patients who reported seeing giant dinosaurs when their levels dipped,' Dr. Varghese explained.

'Ah—perhaps that explains why he was talking about the cows which were at *Thekke Madom* when he was a little boy. And then he was talking about a person whom we have never heard of, saying she killed herself in the house,' said Ayan.

'Yes—it is likely. Gopal Shanker is definitely is not senile and has no mental issues. It was only last evening, after your phone call, I remembered that visit from four years ago. You can collect copies of those old reports. I will tell the reception to pull them out.'

Dr. Varghese then took out his letter pad and wrote a letter to Dr. Jomon, recommending immediate discharge, given the case-history. Ayan noticed that Dr. Varghese still used the old-fashioned fountain pen.

He handed the letter to Ayan, and wished them the very best. He also told them to call him and keep him updated about what happened. Ayan told him he would.

Armed with these records, Ayan and Velu reached *Ashrayam Mental Hospital*. This time, Ayan was not scared. He could officially write in the register kept at the entrance, that he was there to see Dr. Jomon.

The security guard looked at him and said, 'Didn't you come yesterday? For shooting the documentary?'

'Yes, we have a few questions for Dr. Jomon,' said Ayan, as he signed the entry register.

When they entered the gates, Velu looked at Ayan and said,

'*Ende Eshwara!*[25] Look at this godforsaken place which Jairaj Sir chose for Gopal Sir. How could he?' He was so emotional, he could barely speak. Ayan touched his arm lightly and told him to compose himself. 'It's even worse inside,' he said quietly.

Sebastian was not in his seat when they entered the office. But Ayan spotted Prakash and called out to him.

'Oh, hello! Good morning,' he trilled and rushed over.

'Hello. We are here for Dr. Jomon,' said Ayan. He was beginning to feel nervous now. What if Dr. Jomon objected? What if there were other formalities? He was beginning to get impatient to get to *muttachan*.

'Dr. Jomon is on his rounds; do you want me to take you inside? Or if you prefer, you can wait in his consultation room,' said Prakash.

Ayan debated for a minute. He wanted to spare Velu the agony of seeing the situation inside. Also, he did not think that he could stomach the visit a second time. The misery and the plight of the people inside depressed him.

'We will wait,' said Ayan.

The twenty minutes that Ayan spent there, ticked so slowly. They were probably the slowest twenty minutes of his life.

Dr. Jomon walked with a brisk stride, and he greeted them as he entered the room. He was tall and lanky. His salt-and-pepper beard was closely trimmed and he wore thick glasses.

'Yes, what can I do for you?' he asked.

Ayan introduced himself and Velu. Then he took out Dr. Varghese's letter, *muttachan's* records and handed them over.

Dr. Jomon read the letter and then went through the medical file quickly. He then looked up at Ayan.

'You know, I did suspect this. This is not unusual. He is Dr. Balakrishnan's patient. I usually do not interfere in such cases.

---

25. A Malayalam expression for 'Oh God'.

But here, it is clear that your grandfather can be discharged immediately. In fact, Dr.Balakrishnan and I had discussed this case. He has been treated for electrolyte imbalance. Dr. Balakrishnan said there was nobody to look after him, which was why he was here.'

'We are here now. We will look after him. And it is nice to hear that he can be discharged immediately,' said a visibly relieved Ayan.

'All you have to do is keep a watch on his electrolyte imbalance. Go for regular check-ups to Dr. Varghese and he should be fine. I will tell the admin to prepare the discharge papers, and you can settle all dues.'

'Thank you ... Thank you so much, Dr. Jomon ... Ever so grateful,' said Ayan.

'Oh, no, no. It is good for us if the families take them home. Many of them are abandoned you know.'

'I know, and it is sad,' said Ayan.

'Yes, we are trying to create social awareness through media. In fact, just the other day, there were people from the media here. The more exposure this issue gets, the better. There is a lot more that needs to be done for these people,' said Dr. Jomon.

Ayan guiltily looked away when he heard that. He considered whether he should tell Dr. Jomon that he was the fake media person. But he quickly decided against it. Roshan would be making the documentary anyway. Also, he just wanted *muttachan* out of here, as soon as possible.

Ayan thanked Dr. Jomon once again and then went to the administrative desk to pay the dues.

The clerk looked at the records and said, 'There is nothing due. It has been paid for one year. But as per our rules and regulations, it is non-refundable, if you take the patient home, earlier.'

'Oh, that's okay; we don't need the amount,' said Ayan, as

he signed the discharge forms which the receptionist gave him.

His anger against his father came back at that moment. Now there was not a shred of doubt that all of this was premeditated. His father had deliberately planned it all. *Muttachan* was right—he just wanted him out of the way.

Prakash said that he would escort Gopal Shanker from his room. Velu handed him the packet of clothes he had brought along.

'Here are freshly laundered clothes for him to change into,' said Velu.

It was a tearful moment when Gopal Shanker emerged, wearing a crisp white *jubba*[26] and a white *mundu*. He was walking very slowly, and he was holding on to Prakash's arm.

Velu couldn't control himself. He ran to Gopal Shanker and said, 'Gopal Sir! Are you okay?'

Gopal Shanker looked at him and said, 'Yes, I am fine. What was the need for you to come?'

Ayan smiled. And so did Velu.

Ayan was ready with two hundred rupee notes and he quietly slipped them into Prakash's hands, and whispered, 'Thank you.'

'No need for this,' said Prakash. But he nonetheless pocketed the money.

Escorted by Velu and Ayan, Gopal Shanker got into the waiting taxi. As the car sped away, Ayan looked back at *Ashrayam Mental Hospital* for the last time, and sank back into the seat, next to his grandfather.

---

26. Upper garment, usually long sleeved, worn commonly in Kerala

23

Gopal Shanker was very quiet through the journey from Erunjipally to Poongavanam. He stared out of the window, not uttering a word.

'*Muttaccha…*' said Ayan. Gopal Shanker did not hear him. Or if he did, he chose to ignore him.

'*Muttaccha*, are you okay?' Ayan tried again.

'Eh? Yes, yes … I am fine. There's nothing wrong with me,' said Gopal Shanker.

'He comes to see me after so many years, and then shoves me into a mental hospital. I still cannot believe the gall. How foolish of me to trust him,' Gopal Shanker's voice shook, as he spoke.

'It's okay, Gopal Sir. We are fine now, aren't we?' said Velu from the front seat.

'Fine? We are fine? What would have happened if Ayan wasn't staying with me? Can you imagine? And I know why he has done this.'

'Why, *muttacha*?' asked Ayan.

'He has been after me to sell *Thekke Madom* for so many years now. He thinks I should move into a flat. Bloody matchboxes if you ask me. But he doesn't care what I think. I am sure he has lined up buyers too. Let them come. I know what to do,' said Gopal Shanker. He was getting angrier and angrier by the minute.

'Gopal Sir, we got a good crop of coconuts, while you were gone. About 600 coconuts, can you believe?' said Velu. Ayan knew at once that it was quick thinking on his part to distract Gopal Shanker.

'Break them over Jairaj's head. One by one. And then when he dies, burn his funeral pyre with them,' said Gopal Shanker.

Ayan and Velu looked at each other. Ayan signalled with his eyes to Velu to keep quiet. They completed the rest of the journey in silence.

Ayan took out his phone and texted Shivani. He told her that they had rescued *muttachan* and that her press card had come in handy. He thanked her for all the help. He told her that he had started reading *muttachan's* diaries at his request and that they were enthralling. He asked her what she was up to. She said that she was flying back home to see her parents. She had taken leave for a few days.

Once they reached *Thekke Madom*, Gopal Shanker climbed up the steps slowly. Ayan was happy to see him walking without any support.

'Get me tea, Velu. The hospital tea tasted like mud-water,' said Gopal Shanker.

'That means Gopal Sir has tasted mud-water,' said Velu cheekily.

Ayan looked startled for a moment at Velu's audacity in cracking a joke. Gopal Shanker was stunned for a moment too. And then he burst into a guffaw.

'Hahaha, Velu. That was a good one I must admit. Go now and make a strong cup of tea,' said Gopal Shanker.

Once they were seated inside the drawing room, Velu appeared with tea and banana chips.

'*Muttacha*—I ... I found the diaries and started reading them,' said Ayan.

'Oh ... Is that so? Then you would know the sequence of events and what Rohini meant to me.'

'It is fascinating, *muttacha*—just fascinating. I couldn't put it down. When did you start keeping a diary? And why did you start one?,' said Ayan

'Keeping diaries—let me see. I think I started the habit way back in school. Have you heard of a writer called John Steinbeck?'

'No *muttacha*, I haven't.'

'Well, look through the books in the old storage room. His books might be there. He used to keep a diary and I was inspired by him. One of my teachers had told me that all great men keep diaries. It gives a sense of direction, it documents where your days went, and it serves as a tool for self-improvement. Hemingway, President Truman, Robert Scott, Franz Kafka—all of them kept diaries. Hence I too started one. It has certainly helped me—to self-reflect, to gather my thoughts. You should also think of keeping a diary, Ayan. It makes you grow.'

Ayan had not considered this. He hadn't written a diary after that episode during his school days, when it had been discovered by his father. As an adult, he couldn't imagine himself writing diary entries like his *muttachan*.

'Hmmm, I will definitely give it a thought, *muttacha*,' said Ayan.

'I must tell you this, Ayan. I haven't spoken to Rohini or kept any contact with her since October 1989. I have been true to my word. A promise is a promise,' said Gopal Shanker.

'Why *muttacha*? What happened? Why did you stop being in touch with her?' asked Ayan.

'You haven't read all the entries then, have you?' Gopal Shanker sighed.

'No *muttacha*. Not yet. I have read upto 1987 November. Then we had to hurry and get you. We had to meet Dr. Varghese. It was he who gave a letter of recommendation for your discharge.'

'Ah, I see. Read the rest. Then things will be clear.'

'I will, *muttacha*. Your life is so interesting. I am curious to know too.'

'You can read and discover for yourself. And as for Dr. Varghese—he is a good man. And Ayan—you have done a good job, to find me and bring me back home. I ... I have to say, thank you. Your mother—she has raised you well. As regards your father—I have no words for him.'

'Oh please, *muttacha*. There is no need to thank me. It was the least I could do ... I just cannot believe *acchan* did this. I was hoping there would be an explanation. But clearly, there isn't.'

'I don't want him to set foot in *Thekke Madom* ever again. Both my children are dead to me now... Shaila—I don't even want to see her face. I thought Jairaj was different. But no—he turned out to be just as terrible as her,' Gopal Shanker's eyes hardened with an icy steel resolve, as he spoke.

'You ... you have every right to say that, *muttacha*... I ... I am on your side. My entire life, I have listened to my father. I have done everything he has ever asked me to. He picked my college for me, I did not protest. He sent me to work at a company he chose, I did not protest. But this, I just cannot condone,' Ayan bristled with indignation on his grandfather's behalf.

'Aaah, that reminds me. What happened to the job interview he sent you for?' asked Gopal Shanker.

'I don't want to work there, *muttacha*. I got the job. It is at a fish factory. I just cannot stand the smell of fish. *Accha* insists that I have to take it up, and he refuses to speak to me now. But I just can't do it.'

Gopal Shanker was thoughtful for a minute. Then he said, 'Have you figured out what you want to do with your life?'

'No, *muttacha* ... I am looking for jobs.'

'Don't worry son … It will all come in good time. There's always a time and place for everything.'

'I sure hope so, *muttacha*.'

'It will all work out. Come, let's have lunch. I want to nap for a while. How good it feels to be back in my own home,' said Gopal Shanker, as he stood up and walked towards the dining area.

As soon as they finished lunch, Gopal Shaker went to his room for his afternoon siesta. Ayan couldn't wait to run upstairs and read the rest of the diary entries.

He opened the book right where he had stopped and began to read.

* * *

25th December 1987
Friday

I am writing this from the hospital. Padmaja was admitted last night. She was hysterical when I got back from work two days ago. I returned home early, as she called me and asked me to come home immediately. She sounded so terrified on the phone that I rushed back. I rang the bell several times. She wouldn't open the door. I fished out the spare key from my office bag, and let myself in.

I found her in the bedroom, crouched on the bed, terrified, sobbing, pale. She refused to get off the bed. She was frightened and screaming. She said she had heard a man outside the door, and that he was waiting with a knife to kill her. She wanted me to check every room in the house. I did. Then she said he was probably under the bed. When I tried to show her that there was nobody, she grabbed my arm, digging her fingers into my flesh. There are scratches all over my arm now. I calmed her down and spoke to the neighbours. They had seen nothing. The ironing chap outside says he has been there the whole time, and nobody had come. Padmaja refused to get off the bed even the next morning.

Then she said that she was certain that I am going to leave

her and marry Rohini. How absurd! I assured her that no such thing will happen. She did not let me go to work, saying she was frightened. I took leave and stayed at home.

In the evening, she said she got a phone call from Bahrain, and that Jairaj had been killed in a car-crash. She said Kamakshi's parents had called her up. I was with her the whole time. I did not hear the phone ring even once. But still, I called Kamakshi's parents. They said they had not called. That was when I decided to take her to the doctor. When I called him up, the first thing he told me was to check her medications.

I discovered that she has not been taking her medications for the last many weeks. She has stuffed it all in the bedside drawer. I was giving her the tablet and a glass of water, every single day before I left for office. She would tell me to keep it on the bedside cabinet and would assure me that she would take it. And this is what she has been doing.

How can she be so irresponsible? I even give her the pills in her hand.

The doctors suspect psychotic depression.

I suppose the only blessing is that we are in the general hospital and the expenses are covered under my medical reimbursement. A mental hospital would have been terrible.

The hospital is full of Christmas Day decorations, and the nurses are cheerful.

But I can't wait to get out of here.

* * *

31st December 1987
Thursday

It is always a good thing to take stock of what has happened the whole year. I don't believe in New Year resolutions, but I think it is important to reflect and learn lessons from mistakes.

Padmaja was discharged on the 29th. The doctors have said that medication is a must and so are constant follow-ups. They said psychotic depression is very different from clinical depression. She was being treated for clinical depression so far, as until now, she had not exhibited any symptoms of delusions nor had she been imagining things. But now she is.

I asked them if there are any triggers—what causes this? They say there is no specific cause. Older adults are at risk. They asked if there is any family history, as it could be genetic. But I don't think there is. I told the doctors that she was always like this—very emotional. They asked if a death or any other incident had occurred in the family. It has been more than thirteen years since her father passed away. So there was no immediate death as such. I told them about Jairaj moving to Bahrain and that she was attached to him. They have advised that she be kept occupied mentally.

I have no idea how to keep her occupied, mentally. I gave her books, but she dislikes reading. I have got her a few magazines, which she leaves untouched. I asked her if she would like to do embroidery or something. She laughed and asked me if in all these years of marriage, had I ever seen her doing anything to do with needle craft. She told me not to worry about her and that she would be fine. She said she was sorry that she had caused all this trouble and that I had to take leave from work. I told her not to worry about it and to call me if she ever gets another episode.

In any case, I did inform her mother about this. Her mother said she was too old to travel and had her husband been alive, they would have come and helped me. She thanked me for taking care of her daughter. I told her there was no need to thank me.

The good things that happened this year:

Rohini getting back in touch.

Jairaj getting married—and he seems to have settled down well.

Looks like I will be getting a promotion at work, to the next level, soon.

I have restarted my exercise regime and I have not missed my morning walks for the past four months.

The bad things:

Padmaja's hospitalization.

But I am glad things are better now.

I think I will start a new diary for next year, even though there are blank pages left in this note book.

New Year, new start.

* * *

The diary ended there. Ayan kept it aside and sat back reflecting. He had no idea that his grandmother had been hospitalised for psychotic depression. His father had never told him, and neither had his mother. But he didn't blame them. He guessed that it came with a stigma. Anything to do with mental health was taboo in most families. He figured that was why they had never talked to him about it.

Ayan then took out the diary that said 1988 and began to read.

24

This morning I had a row with Padmaja. For a few days after her discharge from the hospital, she was taking her medications. But today she once again refused. She said she was fine and did not need them. This is exactly what the doctors warned us about—that the patient will feel better and say they don't need the medication. But they are likely to have a relapse if they discontinue it. All the doctors have stressed on this point. But she just does not listen. She asked me this morning to leave her alone. She said she was perfectly fine, and that I need not mollycoddle her. She went out for a lunch meeting with the Kerala Samajam ladies. They want her to volunteer for activities that they do. They have adopted a few government schools and have plans in place, to improve the facilities. I think it's a good thing. It will keep her occupied. I encouraged her to take it up. But she refused to.

She said she heard the other ladies snickering and gossiping about a lady who wasn't present at the meeting. She says they will do the same to her, if she didn't attend regularly. I asked her what prevented her from attending regularly. She said it was more for socializing and less for social service. I told her it will help her condition if she actively gets involved in something, now that she has so much free time on her hands. That was when she erupted and told me not to be condescending just because I have a job. She reminded me of all the sacrifices she had made to keep this family happy.

I just don't understand her. It was a mere suggestion. What was there to get so upset about it?

Anyway, the end result is that she did not take her medication nor did she join in the volunteering.

Rohini called today, but sadly I couldn't pick up her call, as the RBI officials were right in my cabin. I wanted to call her after work, but Padmaja called me asking when I will get back home. So I hurried home, and then had this row with her.

What an awful day.

* * *

17th February 1988
Wednesday

Shaila called today. She is expecting a baby. The pregnancy results have come out positive.

Padmaja was over the moon to hear the news. She had a whole lot of advice for her. 'Don't eat this ... don't eat that ... Don't lift heavy weights, blah blah blah.' It was amusing to hear them make plans. The baby is still a good eight months away. But they are already discussing the cradle and cloth to be used for nappies.

Jairaj called after a long time. He said he needed money for investing in his friend's company, as he could then become a partner. He asked if I could borrow against my provident fund. I am not comfortable doing this. I told him that if the venture failed, his mother and I would be penniless. It would mean the evaporation of all our savings, and us having to start from scratch. He scoffed and said that I was exaggerating, that I anyway had Thekke Madom coming to me. I did not like his attitude of entitlement. He has no right to speak like this. I made that clear and told him so.

* * *

10th March 1988
Thursday

Shaila called today. She had a miscarriage. She is heartbroken.

Padmaja started wailing as soon as she heard the news. Since I had heard only one side of the telephone conversation, I got a fright thinking that something had happened to Ghanshyam. I grabbed the phone from Padmaja with my heart pounding. When Shaila managed to calm down, she told me she had lost the child.

To be honest, it was a relief that Ghanshyam was okay.

It's a foetus at this stage, not even a baby, I tried telling her. But she sobbed louder when I said that. Padmaja took the phone from me and said, 'You heartless man—you will never know what this loss feels like. Your heart is made of stone.'

Dramatic dialogues. I think she is watching too much TV.

I do feel bad about the miscarriage. But these things happen. She is young. It's not like they cannot try for another child.

* * *

4th April 1988
Monday

Jairaj called again from Bahrain asking if I have changed my mind about giving him money to invest in his friend's firm. I said I haven't changed my mind. I asked him if he has no shame, no backbone. He laughed and said that businesses are not built on morals. He said you can't be so idealistic in business and you have to grab every opportunity.

At what cost?

I asked him that and he said I would never understand.

It's true. I don't understand him. How can he keep asking me for the money? Padmaja wants me to give him the money. I asked her how we will manage after I retire. I pointed out that if we broke up my provident fund, we wouldn't have a fall-back option and that we would be financially dependent on Jairaj. I certainly do not want that. She is upset that I have refused Jairaj the money.

But it is the principle of the whole thing. I have educated him, and he has stood on his own feet now. His engineering college fees cost a small fortune. He had a well-paying job. Now, getting into a start-up was a choice he made. He and his friend can approach banks and take loans for their business.

If refusing to break up my hard-earned provident fund which

I have been saving over the years, makes me a hard-hearted man, so be it. He needs to fund his own venture.

* * *

5th April 1988
Tuesday

In today's phone call with Rohini, I discussed this demand of Jairaj's. She firmly concurs with me that grown adult children have no right to their parents' money—it is wrong to even ask or expect. I felt relieved that she could see my point of view.

Jairaj, Padmaja, and even Shaila—all of them think I am a tyrant for not helping Jairaj.

So be it.

I know I am doing the right thing. It's not like I have unlimited funds at my disposal. If that was the case, I would have helped him. If my PF is gone, almost all the savings are gone.

Rohini says she is going to Germany for a month along with her husband. She leaves on the 20th. Her husband has won the Alexander Von Humboldt Award for his research on something to do with advanced robotics. Rohini was very proud and excited about it. She said he is getting a fellowship at the University of Darmstadt, Germany. She says it's one of the best fellowships around. He gets to teach there, so he has also started learning German. She has never been to Germany. She will go there with him and return after a month.

It was petty of me, but I burnt with jealousy.

'Why don't you also shift to Germany?' I asked.

'No, no ... My work is here in India. Next month, we are starting a second camp in rural Maharashtra,' she said.

'Then why do you even have to go to Germany?' I asked.

I know I was behaving rather boorishly. I don't want her to go away from India—even for a short while. I want those phone calls with her to continue.

She said it was a chance to visit a foreign country and she wanted to watch him receive the award.

I wish she hadn't said that.

It is illogical and utterly nonsensical to feel this way. He is her husband and it is only natural she would want to be there. She says she will call me as soon as she gets back. She did not once ask me what I thought about it, before deciding to accompany him. She does not have to at all. But it has come as a surprise. She has never once mentioned this before.

I should learn to deal with this all-consuming jealousy. I have never experienced this before. I need to learn how to handle this.

* * *

14th May 1988
Saturday

Padmaja has had another episode. I had to take her back to the hospital. This time she said she saw a young girl calling out to her from a river, asking her to join her. There was a strange sense of calm in her when she said this. I have never seen her like this—this controlled, this certain.

When the doctors spoke to her, she said there are ghosts hanging upside down in trees, and they have been photographed too. But only chosen people can see them. She said, contrary to the popular belief, the ghosts are actually our guides and if we learn to listen to them, our lives will change.

She has never talked about paranormal beings before. This is a first.

The doctors have suggested ECT (electro convulsive therapy) twice a week. They say that only one-third of patients respond with tricyclics alone. Right now she is on antidepressants as well as antipsychotic drugs, but she has had a relapse. I pointed out that it could be because she is skipping medication. The ECT procedure was explained to us—all the benefits, side-effects, everything.

Padmaja immediately refused.

The doctors spoke to me in private. They said if I signed the consent form, they can sedate her, and then give the ECT. They said it is either that or I would have to ensure that she takes medication.

Padmaja is dead against the ECT. I don't want to do anything against her wishes.

I spoke to her patiently and explained why it is imperative that she has the medication. She has once again promised to. I told her that now onwards, I will stay back till she swallows the tablets.

I feel so defeated. And so utterly alone.

* * *

10th June 1988
Saturday

I am in a state of utter shock. I am unable to sleep, unable to eat, unable to do anything. Padmaja is no more. My hands tremble as I write this. Nothing makes sense anymore. Nothing registers.

She killed herself on Monday. I came back from work, and she wasn't answering the door. I let myself in. I found her hanging from the ceiling fan in our bedroom. The image refuses to go away from my head. She has used the pink plastic stool from the bathroom to stand on. She has used her maroon nylon saree, the one she wore the other day when she went out with the Kerala Samajam ladies. Her face was slumped forward, her hands hung lifeless, her eyes were closed. I couldn't even understand for a few minutes what was happening.

I ran outside and called the neighbours. They helped me lower her down. We rushed her to the hospital. The duty-doctor couldn't find a pulse. 'Dead on arrival' is what he entered. As per the regulations, they had to send the body for post-mortem. They have registered a case under Section 174, CrPC.

Her psychiatrist came to me and said he was so very sorry that they couldn't save her. He asked me not to worry about the police enquiry. He said it was routine, and the psychiatric case-history would help.

Shaila, Ghanshyam and Jairaj, Kamakshi—all of them arrived before dawn the next day. We got the body back in the evening. We conducted the funeral at Shamshan Ghat at Lower Tank Bund Street. All the Kerala Samajam people helped.

One part of me still cannot believe it. It feels like it is happening to somebody else. The minutes and seconds feel like they are taking forever to pass. I don't remember when I last slept.

The police came today. They said it was a routine enquiry to close the case. They asked questions, and I said she was under psychiatric treatment. They spoke to Jairaj and Shaila too.

When the police asked if I was taking adequate care of her, Jairaj did not hesitate to say that I was there for her 24x7. I was stunned when Shaila said that she believed that if I had not gone to office, her mother would have been alive. That has hurt me deeply. How can she make such a statement to the police? They asked for her medical records then, which I showed them. They will be speaking to the doctors and closing the case.

I feel this infinite guilt. I should have tried a little harder to convince her for ECT. I feel so responsible for her death. Jairaj keeps telling me that it is not my fault.

But Shaila—she looks at me like she wants to murder me. There is hatred in her eyes, which I cannot comprehend.

There are so many thoughts going around in my head right now. But yet it's a vacuum. I feel empty inside.

I am ashamed, sad, angry.

Why didn't Padmaja just call me? I would have dropped everything and come over. What thoughts had haunted her?

I am just filled with so much anguish.

I wish Shaila would understand me.

* * *

Ayan read the entries with a lump in his throat. He had no idea that his grandmother had committed suicide. He had always been told that she died after an illness. He was shocked to find out the truth.

He heard a noise outside his window and peered out. He was pleasantly surprised to see Roshan, Biju and the entire football club walking down the driveway of *Thekke Madom*. He rushed downstairs and greeted them.

'We heard that *muttachan* is back home,' they said.

'Yes, yes. He is. News indeed travels fast here,' smiled Ayan.

'Velu news agency,' said Biju and everybody laughed.

'We have come to see him. Is he around?' asked Shibhu.

'He is fast asleep,' said Ayan.

'Poor guy. That place, it was awful,' Roshan shook his head.

They decided to wait for Gopal Shanker to wake up. All of them sat on the verandah. Velu served them tea and hot capsicum *bhajjis*.

When Gopal Shanker woke up, he was surprised to see all of them sitting there.

'What is with the welcoming committee that has gathered here?' he asked, as he went to his favourite armchair and sank in.

'We just came to tell you that anytime you need us, we are here,' said Roshan.

'Okay ... I think I owe a 'thank you' to all of you. Ayan told me the whole story,' said Gopal Shanker. 'Now you better make that documentary, Roshan. We have to sell it to the youth wing of the BBC,' he added with a straight face.

All of them laughed at that. *Thekke Madom* was filled with the sound of laughter, the smell of hot crispy *bhajjis* and all the boys of the football club chattering away.

Gopal Shanker leaned back in his chair and smiled contentedly.

Ayan talked to them for a while, then began to get restless. His mind was elsewhere. He couldn't wait to get back to the diaries and read about what happened next.

25

As soon as Roshan, Biju and all the members of the football club left, Gopal Shanker said he was going to lie down for a while. Velu hovered around him and expressed his concern. It was unusual for him to take an evening nap, especially since he had just woken up from one.

'Gopal Sir, are you feeling okay?' he asked.

'Yes, yes, I am fine. It's just the events of the last few days that I need to recover from. And sleeping in my own bed, after that nightmarish hospital experience—it is such a comfort. I am going to lie down and read for a while.'

Gopal Shanker walked slowly towards his bedroom. He asked Velu to wake him up an hour later, in case he dozed off.

Ayan went into the kitchen with Velu. He requested Velu to make him another cup of tea. What he had just read in the diaries was weighing heavily on his mind. He wondered if Velu knew of it.

'Velu, do you have any idea how my grandmother died?' he asked.

Velu didn't answer immediately. His back was turned to Ayan. Ayan couldn't see his facial expression. He turned towards Ayan and asked, 'Why do you suddenly ask Ayan Sir, after all this while?'

There was something odd in the manner that he said it. Ayan knew at that moment that Velu knew a lot more than what he was letting on.

'I ... I read the diary, Velu,' Ayan said.

'I do not know what is in the diary, Ayan Sir. But I can tell you one thing, your grandmother was a troubled woman. Gopal Sir did his best to put up with her. But their marriage was a not a happy one. Gopal Sir's parents knew it very well, when they brought the proposal for Gopal. It was more a business deal.'

'What do you mean, a business deal?'

'Gopal Sir's father, Achutan Sir, had a business that dealt with spice exports and also paddy and rice. His warehouse burned down one day. Some people say that it was deliberately done. It left him with huge debts, and he almost became a pauper.'

Velu lowered his voice a little and said, 'Some say it was Padmaja *amma's* father himself who had hired goons to start the fire. He was a prosperous man. He offered to bail out Achutan Sir, provided Gopal Sir got married to his daughter.'

'Oh I see,' said Ayan.

'Isn't all this mentioned in those diaries you are reading?' asked Velu.

'No, I am reading only the later ones I found in his trunk.'

'Aaah, if you had been reading the earlier ones, you would know all this. But I think he destroyed all the old diaries one day. He used to write diaries even when he was very young. A few years back, when I came back from the market one day, I saw Gopal Sir making a bonfire out of a lot of torn books. When I asked him, he said they were his old diaries which he no longer needed.'

'He seems to have saved only the ones I am reading right now.'

'What is in those diaries then?' Velu couldn't contain his curiosity.

'His life in Hyderabad,' said Ayan.

There was a moment of silence.

'Hyderabad. Aaaah. That was where it happened,' Velu said quietly.

Ayan knew that he was referring to his grandmother committing suicide. He nodded.

Velu silently handed him the cup of tea.

By discussing his grandmother's death with Velu, Ayan felt connected in a strange way, by a painful truth which had happened many years in the past. Velu had known all these years and he had never spoken about it till Ayan raised it. It was only the grandchildren who had not been told the truth.

Ayan deliberated on whether he should tell Nithya what he had read in the diaries. But then he decided that his grandfather had given permission only to him. Also, Ayan was becoming fiercely protective about his grandfather. He wasn't ready to share anything about him, to anyone else.

He went back upstairs with his tea. He checked his phone and saw that there were messages from Shivani. She had messaged him saying that her parents had set up meetings for her with 'eligible men'.

'My divorce isn't even finalised and my parents want me to meet other men. How absurd can parents be,' she had typed.

He replied back to her, saying that sometimes parents do things thinking they know what is best for the children, but they do more harm than good.

She called him as soon as he sent that. Ayan answered the phone, and realised quickly that all Shivani wanted to do was vent. She complained about how her parents didn't get her, and how she wanted nothing to do with men for a while.

Ayan listened to her distractedly. His attention was on the diaries that lay open in front of him. The conversation was mostly one-sided.

When she finished, he said he had to go.

Then he opened the diary and began to read.

* * *

26th June 1988
Sunday

Images of Padmaja keep playing in my head. It is like I am awake but I keep dreaming. The images are so clear. It's the oddest thing I have experienced. On one side is the agony and on the other side, the memories. Then the piercing realisation that I will never make another memory with her again. Regret, sorrow, anger, grief—all come in torrents, subsuming me.

I remember how I had taken her on her first flight with my LTC (Leave Travel Concession) allowance, and how excited she had been. We had gone to Goa and stayed in the bank-listed Holiday Home. I keep thinking about our wedding day too. She had been so quiet and I had done nothing to make her feel comfortable.

She had said, 'Whatever may be the relationship between our parents, we are now husband and wife. I think we should forget about our families, and create a fresh start.' I had nodded then. But even at that time, I was in deep pain about Rohini getting married and my not having had the courage to speak to her parents sooner.

Ironic that Rohini is still in my life and Padmaja is gone. I called up her doctor and asked whether if I had insisted on ECT, she could have been saved. The doctor was very pragmatic. 'It is hard to save those with psychotic depression. Suicide is common in these cases. It is a torture for them to live. The risk of suicide is very high in the first year, after the treatment begins. It remains an elevated risk for ten years,' he said.

I told him that this was not the first year. She had been having problems for a long time. He pointed out (rightly) that she had never had hallucinations before, and also earlier, it wasn't psychotic depression. She seemed to have developed those symptoms only recently. He assured me that no matter what I would have done, if it was too torturous for her to live, she would have made that choice. He told me to take care and to do everything possible to cope. He said it is imperative at this point that I pay attention to myself, else, there was a risk that I could slip into depression myself. He highly recommended a change of scene for a few days.

Rohini got back from Germany on Friday. She called. I could barely speak. I told her what had happened, and she was shocked. I hung up after a brief conversation. I did not feel like talking to her.

* * *

2nd July 1988
Saturday

The owner of the house I live in came to see me today. He offered his condolences and said all the polite things. Then he said that he wants me to buy the house and that I have to pay him the market price.

He said, 'Don't mistake me. Your wife—she committed suicide here, and now this property is affected. Nobody will want to rent it, and nobody will stay in it.'

I told him that I simply did not have that kind of money. Also, I do not want to buy a house in Hyderabad. He got upset with me then and was slightly abusive. He did not call me names or anything, but he talked about 'people like me' in a derogatory tone. I did not say anything. He sat there and cursed me saying I have brought ill-luck to him.

The house is on a lease agreement with the bank, and the bank has allotted it to me. It is not like he has to go looking for tenants. The bank has not terminated his lease or any such thing. It is a ten-year lease. It was when I pointed out all the above, reasonably, that he got nasty.

When he saw that I was not retaliating to his abuses or curses, he left.

* * *

10th July 1988
Sunday

Living alone is something I have to slowly get used to. This morning, out of sheer habit, I made two cups of coffee. Only after I made it did I realise that Padmaja is not here anymore.

Weekends are hard. She used to have something or the other going on.

The television would be switched on all the time. Now the house seems silent.

I did not realize until now, how much of my time she was actually taking up. With her around, there was always some kind of a drama or the other. Now it all seems like nothingness.

Days and days of nothingness merging into one another, I don't know where one begins and the other ends.

I told Rohini that I do not want to talk on the phone for some days. She said she understands. She said, 'I KNOW that grief.'

That was when I remembered that she has lost an adult child too, and she too is suffering.

I think she is coping with her grief wonderfully. Her secret seems to be the new projects that she drowns herself in.

Perhaps I should resume my phone calls with her.

* * *

30th July 1988
Saturday

Whoever said it gets easier with time, lied. The weekends seem to drag on and on. I have started walking to the Somajiguda Hanuman temple. I walk a good six kilometres up and down. It is good exercise.

I gave away all Padmaja's sarees and her clothes today. A few ladies from the Kerala Samajam came over and helped me sort out the stuff. All the jewellery she has, I have kept. I will get it evaluated and divide it equally between Kamakshi and Shaila. Shaila wanted her Kanjeevaram sarees, and I have kept them all aside.

The other news is, that Shaila is expecting a baby again. She said, 'I think it is amma coming back to be with us.' Her disdain for me is still evident from the way in which she speaks to me—it's like she is speaking to me because she has to, out of a sense of duty or obligation.

I told her today what the doctors said about psychotic depression. Shaila said, 'Well, she never had it when we were there.'

I asked her what she was implying. Did she think that after she and Jairaj left, I somehow caused Padmaja to have psychosis? What was the point she was making? I told her to speak up directly. She said she had called to share the happy news of her pregnancy and if I have to twist that and make it into a fight, so be it. She told me that I have to deal with it.

I am angry at her tone, and the manner in which she speaks. But I think she is going through a difficult time. Padmaja should have been around for her. She would have been so happy to hear of her pregnancy.

*   *   *

17th August 1988
Wednesday

It is with great pain and distress I write this. Thirty-three years of service and now they want me to move out of this branch because of 'performance issues'. At my review meeting, the MD told me gently that they wanted to ease my stress, and hence they want to move me to a smaller branch. He made it sound like I have a choice. He said he needed good persons in semi-urban branches too, and he was sure I would understand and oblige. He gave me a choice between Pondicherry and Bellary (Karnataka).

What I don't get is, that I have met all my targets. I pointed that out to him. I agree that the number of loan defaulters is slightly high this year, but that is not all that abnormal. It will even out in the next financial year. There has not been any fraud, malpractice or corruption in my branch. The growth rate, when compared to the industry average, is good. He said he knows all this. He knows what I am capable of. He told me that the move had already been decided, and there was nothing else he could do.

Later, I got to know that my post is being given to someone very young. He is apparently related to one of the board members. Extreme nepotism. There seems to be no rationale or logic in terms of transfers or promotions. Usually, all the transfers and promotions are finalised in March/April. In the month of August, it is rare. So it is evident that whoever will be taking over from me, definitely has high connections at the board level.

I strongly think that bank heads with certain years of experience, should not really be posted in rural or semi-urban areas. The management should wake up and do something about it.

The MD suggested that if I was not happy, I could take Voluntary Retirement. I would get a generous package.

Why should I? This is terribly unfair. Throughout my career, I have never been happy about the HR policy, but this really, is the limit.

* * *

19th August 1988
Friday

I spoke to Rohini at length today. It's the first time since Padmaja's death that we are speaking for a long time. I received a letter from her yesterday. In the letter, she had written about how she is there for me, and how she understands. She said it is important to grieve and talked about the five stages of grief which everyone goes through. She said she had read it in a book called 'Death and Dying' by Elizabeth Kubler-Ross.

I called her up today from the STD booth, and we ended up speaking for nearly forty minutes. For once, I did not glance at the metre ticking. I ended up paying a small fortune for that phone call. But the way I look at it, we saved a lot of money by not talking at all for so many months. So this one time, it is okay if I spend a little more.

Rohini is urging me to take the Pondicherry option. She thinks it will be a great idea.

'Just think, it is only about two hours from Chennai. I will be able to come and see you,' she said. She said it was a blessing in disguise. She seemed kind of excited about it. I had never thought of it that way.

On one hand, I do want to leave Hyderabad. I want to leave this house, put all these memories behind me. Everywhere I go in this house, there is something or the other that reminds me of Padmaja. But on the other hand, a semi-urban posting in a small town is not what I had in mind. I was expecting a promotion.

I will still be on the same pay scale. Rohini says that the cost of living will be much less there—so I will end up saving more.

I guess between Bellary and Pondicherry, I would prefer the latter.

* * *

24th September 1988
Monday

I moved to Pondicherry two days ago. I will take charge at the branch from the third of next month. I completed all the handing over formalities at the Somajiguda branch on the 15th. It turned out that Sriram, who is taking over from me, is an only child, and has been raised by his widowed mother. Hyderabad is his hometown. He isn't as young as I thought. He is about forty-eight. His mother is apparently dying of cancer, and he wanted to be posted here. He turned out to be a pleasant person, and extremely apologetic too. He told me his whole life story within ten minutes of meeting me. He hoped I would understand.

Somehow that made this whole transition better.

What a quaint place this town is. The houses all seem to be modelled on French houses. Each house shares a wall with another. There is no cross-ventilation at all. There don't seem to be any stand-alone houses. Just rows and rows of houses, with common shared walls, end to end. The street names are all in French. There are names like Rue Francois Martin, Rue Saint Lois, Rue Labourdonnais and Rue Suffren.

I am told this is White Town, the nicer part of Pondicherry on this side of the canal. I took a little stroll around. The bank offices face the beach. It is not an actual beach, but it is a beautiful promenade.

In the evenings, many men and women wearing white T-shirts and khaki shorts come out. I see them doing various physical activities. I am told they are the Ashram people. There seem to be a lot of Ashram followers here.

I had never read about Mira (The Mother) or Aurobindo (The Father) till I moved here. I plan to go to their final resting places, and I plan to read up about them.

The bank has allotted a house to me. It is an old house with a courtyard. It reminds me of Thekke Madom. The large compound walls are flush with the street pavement. There is a narrow wooden door in this wall, and this is the entrance to my home. What a good thing that I sold off the car before moving here. I had intended to buy a new car here, but everybody here rides cycles. The streets are too narrow for a car. Also, the bank is just walking distance from my house. So I will not buy a car.

The neighbour introduced herself to me. Her name is Shyamala and she has a dual citizenship. She told me she is a Tamil-born French citizen. I am surprised. Her husband served in the French army, and she now gets his pension from the French government. She proudly pointed out the word 'soldat' embossed on her gateway.

She asked too many questions about me, which I didn't like. She clucked her tongue in pity, when I said that I had lost my wife.

'Ready to marry again, eh?' she chuckled.

She seems to be a well-meaning soul, but too inquisitive and too chatty.

Rohini is very excited about my move to Pondicherry. She said she would come and see me next week.

26

The diary entries kept Ayan riveted. In the few days that he was reading them, it felt like he had teleported through time, into his grandfather's world of two decades ago.

He was filled with a longing to know what the younger version of his grandfather looked like. He went to the room which had all the old things and looked through the photo frames resting behind one of the cupboards. They were all black and white photographs, many of them fading with age. One of the photos had a proud-looking Gopal Shanker, posing with Padmaja, Shaila and Jairaj. In the photograph, his father and aunt looked about 17 and 20. It was clicked at a photography studio. The backdrop was a painting of a busy street scene, in front of which they all posed stiffly. Ayan noticed with a smile that both Gopal Shanker and Jairaj wore bell-bottom trousers and polished black shoes. Shailammayi looked distinctly uncomfortable posing in a saree.

Ayan searched for photos from 1987 or 1988, the time of Gopal Shanker writing the diaries. But there were none from that time period.

Ayan decided to return to the diaries as he was eager to know what happened next in his grandfather's life. He was rushing back upstairs, when Velu called out to him asking if he wanted anything.

'Nothing, Velu *chetta*. I just want to go back and read those diaries.'

'So interesting, are they? You are devouring them like you are studying for an exam,' remarked Velu.

'Yes! Can you believe, our Shyamala has made an appearance in the diary pages!'

'*Daivame*[27]! So she was a real person after all?"

'Yes. She was his neighbour in Pondicherry.'

'Pondicherry, eh? Gopal Sir lived in Pondicherry?'

'Yes. Didn't you know about it, Velu?'

'He has never spoken to me about it. I thought, after Padmajamma passed away, he came straight to *Thekke Madom*, and he has been living here ever since. That is what I was given to understand.'

'No Velu, he lived in Pondicherry for a couple of years. From Hyderabad, he moved there.'

'Oh, I see. Very interesting. I never knew that part. Was Gopal Sir happy in Pondicherry? And did Shyamala kill herself there? Is that why he talks about it whenever he is upset?'

'I don't know. I haven't read it fully yet, but I sure intend to find out,' said Ayan, as he made his way upstairs. 'And don't forget to wake up *muttachan* in an hour; He didn't want to sleep too much,' called out Ayan.

'Don't worry, Ayan Sir. Gopal Sir just has to tell me once, and it will be done,' said Velu.

Ayan settled down on the bed once again and opened the diary exactly where he had stopped reading. He once again plunged into Gopal Shanker's world of the yesteryears.

* * *

3rd October 1988
Monday

My first day at work here. The work culture here is very different from that in Hyderabad. The people here seem more committed,

---

27. Malayalam for 'Oh God!'

more disciplined. There is a lot of warmth and a personal touch. They seem to genuinely enjoy interacting with customers.

In Somajiguda, the tellers wouldn't even look up at the clients. Customer satisfaction wasn't their highest priority. Here, it seems to be a part of their persona itself. From my cabin, I see the tellers casually chatting with the customers who come in to deposit cheques or withdraw money.

My colleagues invited me to accompany them to the Ashram canteen today, which is open to the general public too. Wholesome nutritional Satvik food at a very nominal cost. Keeping in line with the Ashram guidelines, we have to wash our own plates after we finish eating. The food itself is prepared by Ashram volunteers, with fresh ingredients that they cultivate themselves—all of it organically. The menu changes every day. It is simple food, and I feel very light after eating it. The canteen is walking distance from my house, and I can take my dinner too there, if I wish. It will save me the trouble of cooking.

When I got back from work today, Shyamala was sitting on the verandah, smoking. I haven't seen too many women smoke really. So I was surprised to see her smoke so openly. She offered me a cigarette and I said I do not smoke. She asked me to sit for a few minutes. I thought it would be impolite to refuse her. She chatted about her late husband and the good old times. The whole time, I was trying not to inhale too deeply, as I dislike second-hand smoke.

She has two sons and both live in Paris. She asked me what I was doing for dinner. She offered to send me rotis. I told her I am going out with colleagues, even though I have no dinner plans

I think she is lonely.

* * *

4th October 1988
Tuesday

Everything in Pondicherry is so much cheaper when compared to Hyderabad. Since it is a Union Territory, a lot of things seem to be subsidized here by the government.

This town seems untouched by time. Many of the buildings

were constructed during the French regime. A lot of people speak French fluently. I am told the medium of instruction in the Ashram school is French.

I went for a walk on the promenade with my colleagues. It was lovely. I started at the north end of the beach, and across the road is a beautiful building, Ecole Francaise d'Extreme-Orient, which is the French Institute of Pondicherry. I also saw the lighthouse, which is about 30 metres tall. I read a plaque which said that it was first lit in 1836. I love lighthouses. There is something mesmerising about them.

Right at the centre of the promenade is a Gandhi statue, flanked by eight exquisitely carved monolithic pillars. I was told by my colleagues that the pillars were brought there from Gingee, after the capture of Gingee Fort in 1751 by the French, who later lost it to the British. (The bloody British take everything). The pillars were erected in 1861. My colleagues, who are residents of Pondicherry, seem to be very proud of their architectural heritage. They are delighted to share these nuggets of information with me.

I found the whole walk very interesting.

What a wonderful coastal town this is. It's a big change from Hyderabad.

It is like life is telling me to slow down and relax here.

I can feel that heaviness of my heart slowly melting away. This place has that effect on people.

Another thing that I discovered—phone calls are so much cheaper from here to Madras!

Rohini says she will come on Saturday morning and spend the day with me.

I look forward to that.

* * *

6th October 1988
Thursday

Shaila called today. Her pregnancy is progressing well. She wanted to know if I had settled down in Pondicherry. I said I had. It was a very short conversation. She is definitely calling me out of a sense of obligation. She couldn't wait to get off the phone.

Today, I went to a temple which is five centuries old. It is the Manakula Vinayagar temple, a beautiful large temple dedicated to Lord Ganesh. Opposite this temple is the final resting place of The Mother, and Shri Aurobindo.

I went there as well. The experience was deep, spiritual and powerful. I sat there with many others who were in deep meditation. I have never meditated until now. I just closed my eyes, and sat in silence, feeling peaceful, content and calm.

The Samadhi is decorated with fabulous flower carpets, the designs done in visually pleasing patterns by the Ashram volunteers.

Twice a year, The Mother's room and Aurobindo's room are open for viewing to the public. I am told people come in busloads and wait in queues to see these rooms. I will definitely join them on those dates.

I bought a book on meditation.

When I returned, Shyamala was waiting. She asked me about the book I had purchased. When she saw it, she went inside and gave me a book called 'Words of long ago' which is a collection of The Mother's writings and talks from 1893 to 1920.

I was curious about the relationship between Aurobindo and The Mother. Shyamala was happy to oblige. She told me that The Mother's actual name was Mira Alfassa. Aurobindo and she met in 1914. She was married to the French politician Paul Richard. In 1920, she left Paul for Aurobindo. Shyamala said it was not a romantic or a sexual relationship. I asked how that is possible if she left her husband for him.

Shyamala laughed and said, it wasn't like that at all, and if you knew her, you would understand. She was his disciple, his 'shakthi'. He saw her as an incarnation of 'The Mother'. Shyamala has met The Mother, a few times, and even served her.

I found it very interesting to know all this.

* * *

8th October 1988
Saturday

Rohini arrived at 8.30 a.m. in the morning. I met her at the bus stop. We took a phat-phati[28] which dropped us off at the tempo stop which is close to my house. Then we walked home.

Shyamala was at her usual spot. I introduced Rohini to her. She scrutinized her carefully and the first thing she asked Rohini was, 'Are you married?'

I was taken aback and so was Rohini.

But she was graceful about it and she replied that she was.

'Children?' asked Shyamala.

I found her behaviour very rude. I was afraid that she had touched a sensitive spot.

But Rohini just smiled and said she had none.

Shyamala clucked her tongue. 'So sad … Children bring such joy,' she said.

I got really angry then, but I did not say anything.

I just took Rohini's elbow and guided her inside. I did not even realise that I had done that, till we were inside the house and Rohini said softly, 'You can let go of my elbow now.'

I apologized and she laughed.

'Come on Gopal, we have known each other long enough to dispense with formalities now, haven't we?' she said.

She then explored the house.

'So beautiful, Gopal, did you do this up yourself? Such lovely antique furniture. Where did you get it from?' she asked.

To be honest, I had not even noticed the furniture. It had come with the house. I told her that it was fully-furnished accommodation that I had been given. She delighted in examining each and every piece. She pointed out the beauty in the carved legs of the tables, the ceramic tile inlay in the headboard of the four-poster bed, the beauty in the architecture of the house.

---

28. A popular mode of transport in the 80's, a closed, three-wheeler vehicle

By the time she finished, I felt I was fortunate to be living here. Funny I had not noticed any of this before.

We went for a meal to the Ashram canteen and she loved it.

She said she wanted to take the 4 p.m. bus back. When we were leaving for the bus stop, I was annoyed to see Shyamala sitting there again, smirking.

'Had a good time?' she winked, as she lit a cigarette.

I was really annoyed, but Rohini laughed and said she had indeed had a good time.

When we were out of earshot I asked Rohini whether she realized what Shyamala had implied. She had suggested that we had slept with each other, and that was why we were meeting. Rohini smiled and said that of course, she had understood.

'Why didn't you deny it?' I asked.

'Why should I explain to her? What do we owe her?' asked Rohini.

She is right. But it still bothers me.

* * *

15th October 1988
Saturday

Rohini again spent the day with me. I asked her what she tells her husband. She said she told him she was travelling on work. I asked her if she feels bad lying to him.

She shrugged and said, 'If I get to spend the day with you, it is worth it.'

She cooked today. I helped her by chopping the vegetables. It felt so strangely intimate. I remembered how Padmaja was very finicky about how I chopped the vendekka[29]. She would give me precise instructions about the exact dimensions that the pieces had to be. Rohini is easy-going in comparison.

Afterwards, we took a walk on the promenade.

Once again, Shyamala annoyed me by making a silly comment about how all husbands are fools and she winked. Rohini just laughed it off, but I am irritated about her not minding her business.

---

29. okra/*bhindi*

Rohini and I had long conversations about life, about the unexpectedness of things that hit us and how we really have no control over anything that happens to us. I disagreed with her and said that all of us definitely have a certain degree of control. She said that we do not. All we can do is put in the work, and hope that things turn out favourably. We argued a little bit about that. She does have a point. But to attribute everything to the Universe or to Destiny, would be foolish.

Later, after she boarded the bus back to Chennai, she looked out of the window and said, 'Don't let Shyamala get to you.'

'What? What?' I asked, as I didn't hear her properly.

'Shyamala means no harm. Let her get her amusement by spying on us,' she said.

* * *

18th November 1988
Friday

Jairaj called from Bahrain. He is calling after very long. He asked if I wanted to invest in his company in my own name. I said I did not. I asked him why is it that he calls only to discuss money. Doesn't he want to know how I am managing, what I am doing? He said he did. He then asked about what I was doing regarding my meals. I don't think he was even paying attention when I told him about the Ashram canteen.

For the first time since Rohini started coming here for the weekends, I am nervous. She is spending the night here tomorrow. She will come tomorrow morning and will leave on Sunday evening. Her husband is going to Germany for three weeks. When she mentioned it on the phone, I asked her, 'Why don't you go with him?'

She said, 'No, I want to spend time with you.'

I felt happy about that. She is choosing me over him. She wants my company.

I feel like a teenager at the moment. When I think about her coming over, my heart sings with joy. It is the one thing I look forward to.

I will give her my bedroom, and I will sleep in the hall, on the sofa, which opens out to become a bed. I shopped today, for bedsheets and pillow covers. I also got extra towels.

* * *

20th November 1988
Sunday

Rohini just left a little while ago. Having her over was wonderful. She said that she would sleep in the hall, but I wouldn't hear of it. Finally, she said thank you and slept in my bedroom. Just the thought of her in my bed fills me with a strange sense of excitement and joy.

In the morning, she woke up before me. She made coffee for both of us.

'This was so nice, Gopal,' she said.

I agreed.

'I bet Shyamala thinks we are having an affair,' she said.

'Aren't we?' I asked, surprised.

'It counts as an affair only if you have sex,' she said and giggled.

'Oh, I didn't know that. I guess most people would presume that that's what we were doing,' I replied.

'This ... this is so hard to explain or understand. But I am happy we have this,' she said.

I couldn't agree more.

I think there are some relationships that just cannot be explained. This deep sense of joy, this camaraderie, this feeling of oneness when I am with her—how many people get to experience this?

It is like I cannot get enough of her. No matter what the topic is, we end up having long discussions, long conversations. This was never the case with Padmaja.

I asked her if she had such conversations with Raman. I had to know. I don't know why I am competing with him. So petty of me.

She said, 'You will not get a word out of him unless it is something highly intellectual and something to do with his research.'

'Aah, so he would consider all these conversations a waste of time?' I asked.

'Yes, pretty much. Imagine how he would react if he met Shyamala,' Rohini smiled.

'Shyamala will straighten him out,' I laughed.

'Shyamala will straighten anybody out,' she too laughed.

When we were returning home after having lunch at the Ashram, Shyamala called out to us and invited us inside for a cup of tea. I did not want to go, but Rohini immediately accepted.

Shyamala's house was crammed with antique furniture. Rohini loved it. I hated the stale smell of cigarette smoke that hung in the air. There were clothes scattered all over the house. There were half-cut vegetables, trays, uncleared ashtrays, used coffee mugs. It seemed like Shyamala never bothered to clean up.

But Rohini—the one quality about her is that she always focuses on the good. She ignored all this and went straight to the tall grandfather clock, which stood in the centre, against the wall. Shyamala said it was a cuckoo clock. and that it was much sought after in those days. She said it worked perfectly, and we could see the cuckoo come out if we hung around till 3 p.m. Next to it was a bed with intricate panels of stained glass. Whoever keeps a bed in a living room? The panels caught the sunlight and reflected a hundred colours all over the living room. It was like a discotheque which I saw on television in a movie. But Rohini was examining each piece and exclaiming in genuine joy. Shyamala was happy to regale her with all kinds of stories about each piece.

Then Rohini saw a hand-held mirror with a wooden frame. She admired the detailed carving. Shyamala made a face and said that it used to belong to her son's mistress. She said it so casually, as though having a mistress was something to be talked about so openly. Rohini wanted to know details. I was gesturing frantically to her, not to ask Shyamala, as I did not want her to go into another long story. But Rohini just ignored me.

Shyamala said that her elder son had a mistress in Paris, a French lady called Alexandrine. Rohini asked what happened to her.

'She died. Her hair caught fire because of the stove. Apparently, she was bending over and cooking something. She ran out on the streets screaming, with flames on her head. She could not be saved. Some say my son's wife had paid her a visit just before this happened, and that they saw her leaving through the back door. She deserved the death, if you ask me,' said Shyamala, as she lit up another cigarette.

Then she gifted the mirror to Rohini.

'I can't take this,' said Rohini.

'Why not?' asked Shyamala.

'Because … Because it probably costs a fortune. It seems like a genuine antique piece.'

'Things are only as expensive as the value you place on them. It doesn't mean a thing to me, and you seem to have an eye for beauty. Really, you can have it. I will be happy for you to have it.'

Just then the cuckoo came out of the clock and chimed thrice.

'See that's a sign. Even the cuckoo wants you to have it,' said Shyamala.

Shyamala wouldn't take no for an answer, and finally, Rohini accepted it.

Later, I teased Rohini about it. 'Alexandria's ghost will come through the mirror and haunt you. Her hair will be burning,' I said.

'Shyamala is already haunting you and she doesn't let you be in peace. I have at least got a mirror in return for the haunting. What have you got?' she asked and laughed.

'I have got a laugh from you, and for me, that is enough,' I said.

It truly is. Rohini is such a delightfully nice person. She only sees the good in people.

27

Ayan took a deep breath and leaned back on the bed. How rich his grandfather's diary entries were! He felt as though he was living in Pondicherry and walking on the promenade alongside Gopal Shanker. And here was the mysterious Shyamala who his grandfather referred to when he was upset. There was indeed an incident which happened that involved hair being set on fire. His grandfather had not been entirely wrong when he had narrated the Shyamala story when Ayan had first come to *Thekke Madom*—except for the fact that Gopal Shanker had jumbled up the two separate incidents. Perhaps the electrolyte imbalance which he had at that time had done that.

'Ayan Sir … Ayan Sir! Dinner is ready,' said Velu.

Ayan went downstairs. The aroma of steamed tapioca and onion chutney made Ayan's mouth water. His grandfather was already seated at the dining table.

'Mmmm—this smells divine, Velu *chetta*. You must start your own restaurant,' said Ayan, as he helped himself to two pieces of tapioca, and the onion chutney.

'Good to see you enjoying traditional food, Ayan. Most children these days don't even know what this kind of cooking is. This is all a generation of people who eat instant noodles from packets,' said Gopal Shanker.

'Mmm … I am different. I like this stuff,' said Ayan, in between bites.

They savoured their meal in affable silence. Then Ayan spoke up.

'*Muttacha*. Your time at Pondicherry, it is fascinating.'

'Oooh yes, I certainly had good times there,' Gopal Shanker said softly.

'That lady Shyamala—she was quite a character, wasn't she?' asked Ayan.

'Aaah … Shyamala. She was a character for sure. Have you read all the diaries then?'

'No *muttacha*. I intend to read them all tonight. You write well, *muttacha*. I felt like I was living in Pondicherry.'

'Oh! That is very kind of you to say, Ayan. I haven't read them in years. It is all history now. Memories are best packed up and put away in boxes.'

There was a tone of bitterness in his grandfather's voice which Ayan instantly recognized.

'Has your father or mother not called you?' Gopal Shanker changed the topic.

'No, *muttacha*. My father hasn't spoken to me ever since I refused to take that job at the prawn factory. He must have forbidden *amma* to talk to me too. I don't know. Anyway, so much has happened in these last few days, that I haven't even thought about them. My focus was on getting you back here.'

'I wonder if Kamakshi knew of this ploy of his, to send me to that mental hospital; I would like to believe she had no role to play in it,' said Gopal Shanker.

Ayan couldn't say for sure. He had no idea if his mother was a part of the plan or not. If she was, then he would lose all respect for her. This was pure evil—leaving his grandfather there. His mother always went along with whatever his father decided. Deep down, he wanted to believe that his mother had nothing to do with it. But then again, he would never have believed that his father was capable of such betrayal, had he not seen it for himself.

After they finished dinner, *muttachan* said he would go to bed early.

Velu was concerned. 'Gopal Sir, are you feeling okay? You have rested a lot today,' he said.

'Yes, yes … Don't worry, I am fine,' said Gopal Shanker as he bade good night to Ayan and retired to his room.

Ayan straightaway went back to reading the rest of the diary entries.

* * *

31st December 1988
Saturday

What a year this has been. Last year, around this time, Padmaja seemed to be getting better. And now she is no more. How fragile life is. How easily it is lost.

I have begun liking life here. Even though I get to see Rohini more often, I miss Padmaja. I suppose when you have been living with somebody for more than half your life, it is only natural to miss them. I did not realise how used I had become to being responsible for her, taking care of her.

Rohini has left for Amboli, near Pune. She is doing a training camp there. She will be back around 10th January. She called once, when she went to Pune from Amboli, for the weekend. There are no STD booths in the village. She loves her work and I am happy it brings her so much joy.

Shaila called two days ago. The baby is due in February. Her in-laws wanted her to have the baby at Calicut. They say that Calicut has good hospitals. But she wants to be in Delhi for the birth. She says Ghanshyam has contacts in the embassy and they can get good staff. Also, she is in the advanced stage of her pregnancy and doctors will not allow her to fly.

'I wish amma was there; I feel so bad,' she said and started crying. I felt helpless. I told her I will fly to Delhi and be there for her delivery. I shall apply for leave now itself, for about fifteen days.

Good things that happened this year:

My move to Pondicherry. It has taught me to slow down. It has shown me that there is an alternative way of life. I love this town.

Shaila's pregnancy going smoothly so far.

Getting to meet Rohini more often.

Bad things:

Padmaja's death.

I hope she is at peace now.

*   *   *

The diary ended there.

Ayan took out the next one, which said 1989. That was the year that both Nithya and he were born. How strange it was, to be able to read about the time when they were both in the womb! What a treasure these diary entries were turning out to be.

Muttachan had started this diary with a collection of quotes.

If you are going through hell, keep going.

—Winston Churchill

Do not pretend. Be. Do not promise. Act.
Do not dream. Realise.

—Mira Alfassa

The word is a great gymnasium where we come
to make ourselves strong.

—Swami Vivekananda.

Ayan reflected on these words. What a wealth of wisdom they contained. He remembered how in school, they had to write a 'Thought for the day' on the blackboard. Each day, a student had to get a new quote. At that time they wouldn't even think about what the words meant. They would look it up in the library hurriedly just before the prayer bell went and write something out.

Seeing these words in his grandfather's writing made Ayan actually think about how deep they were in meaning.

As Ayan turned the page, a single photograph fell out of the diary. He took it out and scrutinized it. It was a photo of a group of people. He looked closely at them. They seemed to be rural artisans, proudly holding up cloth bags that they had stitched. To the far left of the group stood a very beautiful tall lady, wearing a saree, smiling. Ayan stared at the photo. It didn't take him long to realise that this was Rohini. *Muttachan* had been spot-on, in his description of her. She was so beautiful and elegant!

He turned the photo around, and behind it was written: 'Artisan's camp, Amboli, Maharashtra, December 1988.'

He put the photograph back carefully between the last page and the cover. Then he began to read.

* * *

15th January 1989
Sunday

Rohini spent two nights here. She arrived on Friday evening. I met her at the bus stop as usual. This time, when we reached home, Shyamala wasn't there.

'Alexandria's ghost has taken her away,' I quipped.

'Oh? I thought her ghost was supposed to haunt me?' she said.

'She decided Shyamala was a better target. You are too sweet; Ghosts don't like sweet people.'

'Haha, and you have a hotline to the ghost's mind, I suppose?' she laughed.

When she laughs, she looks exactly like she did when we were together in school. It is wonderful having her over, talking, eating meals together. Now there is no awkwardness anymore about her staying. She sleeps in my bedroom, and I make myself comfortable in the living room.

She showed me photos from her camp at Amboli. She said she had to file them and write a report. I told her I was keeping one. She smiled.

'Why do you need a photo when I am with you?' she asked.

But she gave it to me anyway.

I told her that I was feeling very bad about Shaila being all alone for her pregnancy. She offered to come with me to Delhi and help Shaila. How could I tell her that both Shaila and Jairaj would never approve of this?

Most people would never understand this relationship between Rohini and me. This love I feel for her, is pure, genuine. This is exactly how I felt all those years ago. I don't know how it is possible that I still feel the same, but I do. She says it is the same for her.

'Gopal, when we talk, I forget everything. During the time that I am with you, the outside world ceases to exist for me.'

I told her, perhaps, it was because we both suffered deep losses. She had lost a child and I had lost my wife. She pointed out that even before Padmaja died, when we met at Hyderabad, we felt the same. She was right as usual.

I like how she said 'we'.

We left for Gingee Fort the next morning. Shyamala was back at her usual spot on the verandah. She and Rohini chatted away like old friends. I don't know how Rohini can be so friendly with someone who is so interfering.

'She is a harmless chatterbox, Gopal. She is lonely. Can't you see she loves the little drama in her life? Probably, she lives vicariously through us. Who knows?'

'Why should we be the ones to provide her excitement? She has her sons for that.'

'Come on, Gopal. You know how it is when your children live far away. And anyway, it is only a few minutes of our time. How does it matter?' Rohini asked.

When we reached Gingee Fort, we discovered that it was in ruins. But you can clearly visualize how majestic it must have been when it was in its full glory. Rohini enjoyed the visit thoroughly.

We spent Sunday at home.

'How are you able to manage all this time away? Doesn't your husband mind?' I asked her.

'He is very absorbed in his work. He is used to my travelling on camps. He knows it makes me happy. And in any case, there's nothing at home really which needs my attention. We have an efficient housekeeper who also cooks,' she said.

Well, what can I say? Her husband's loss. My gain.

I am fortunate that I get to enjoy Rohini's company.

* * *

16th February 1989
Thursday

Shaila gave birth to a baby girl. She weighs 3.05 kgs. It was a last minute caesarean, as complications developed after the waters broke. Mother and child are doing well.

I am glad I had taken leave from Monday onwards, and had reached Delhi, well ahead of the due date. I was with her when it happened. I rushed her to the hospital. By the time Ghanshyam reached the hospital, the baby was already born.

His parents will not be able to come to Delhi, as his father is ill and doctors have advised him to rest, not travel. Ghanshyam has got a live-in maid. She is there to assist Shaila, twenty-four by seven. She is a sweet lady by the name Paro. She is from the north-east and has two sons of her own, who she has left behind in Darjeeling, with her mother. She seems to be experienced in dealing with babies. She says she can even bathe the baby.

They have decided to name the baby, Nithya. I like the name. It means 'eternal'.

The naming ceremony will be on the 10th day. His parents said that they should name her only on the 28th day, as that was tradition. But Ghanshyam would not hear of it. 'What will I call my daughter till then? The nameless one?' he asked.

He consulted the astrologer, and they have fixed an auspicious day and time.

The baby is delightful. She is no trouble at all and sleeps most of the time. It is wonderful to see Shaila and her. Shaila is handling her with ease. Padmaja should have been here. I miss her more than ever.

I am now a grandfather. I realised that only when Ghanshyam carried baby Nithya, brought her to me and said, 'Here is your muttachan.'

Muttachan. I like the sound of that.

* * *

28 March 1989
Tuesday

I returned from Delhi on 3rd March and joined back work on Monday, the 5th. The day I landed, Rohini met me at the Chennai airport. We travelled back together to Pondicherry.

'How is the baby? Did you also go for the delivery?' Shyamala called out as soon as she saw us.

'The baby is fine,' I said.

'No. I did not go for the delivery. I met him at the Chennai airport,' said Rohini.

Every weekend since then, Rohini has been spending with me. She comes either on Friday evening, or sometimes on Saturday evening. She goes back on Monday. Her Maharashtra project has come to an end. She now wants to start a project in Pondicherry. She was talking about the Auroville administration being legalized. She says the possibilities of doing good work in association with them is immense.

'This way, I can get to see you more. Raman keeps travelling to Germany for two to three weeks at a time. During the time he is in India, I can return to Chennai,' she said.

I remarked that she was having the best of both worlds. She got very upset with that remark. I did not mean anything by it. It was a careless, casual remark which stemmed out of jealousy more than anything else. I did not think she would get so upset. She has always been firm in what she wants. She asked me if I doubted her love for me. I didn't know what to say to that, so I was silent.

She mistook my silence for reticence.

'Look, if you feel that way, we can stop meeting,' she said.

I should have kept quiet then, and told her what she meant

to me. Instead, I said foolishly, 'So, you are ready to stop meeting me now, is it? You are okay with giving this up?'

'What do you want me to do, Gopal? Walk out on my 34-year-old marriage? And then what? We get married to each other?' she asked.

I apologized then.

She said she wants to keep meeting me and that is one thing which she looks forward to. She said her love for me is pure and genuine. I told her I feel the same way too.

Then she made us both coffee.

I suppose that is our version of holding hands, I don't know. All I know is when it comes to me and Rohini, it is just this wonderful and deep bond that we share.

She makes me feel alive, and she says it is the same for her.

I will never raise the topic of her marriage again. That is for her to sort out. I will let her deal with it.

* * *

8th April 1989
Saturday

There has been a new development. Ghanshyam called me today. He has been posted to Ivory Coast on a diplomatic mission for six to eight months. He is a part of the joint trade commission that is investigating the possibilities of setting up an Oil Plant for ONGC in the Ivory Coast. He has to leave by 27th April. He will not be able to take Shaila and the baby with him. It is not advisable, he said.

He said that he and Shaila had a detailed discussion about where she should stay. Shaila is firm that she does not want to stay in Calicut with his parents. She wants to stay with me, here in Pondicherry. He said that Paro was ready to travel with Shaila to Pondicherry and live here, only if I was comfortable. He asked me if I was okay with that. How could I refuse? I told him that she and Paro were most welcome here.

He said his father's health was deteriorating. He requested me to please take Shaila and baby Nithya to Calicut once they moved to Pondicherry and settled down, so that his parents could see the baby. I assured him that I would.

Then he said, 'Uncle, please don't mistake me. Can I please send you money for expenses, as there are three people who will live with you now?'

I told him that my daughter or my granddaughter would never be a burden for me, and while I may not have a job in an embassy, the bank was giving me enough money. I did not require anything from him.

He apologized profusely. He said he didn't mean to insult me. I said it was okay. I wasn't insulted. He said he would be sending money to Shaila every month, and she would pay Paro. I told him that all that was between him and his wife. All I can say is that they are welcome here.

Rohini was with me during the entire conversation. The first thing which struck me was that she would not be able to visit me as long as Shaila was here. But I said nothing.

Rohini was excited.

'Oh, nice! I can finally meet baby Nithya,' she said.

I had to tell her then that neither Jairaj nor Shaila approved of her. In fact, they downright detested her. I told her about the fight in the house after she left, when she had visited me in Hyderabad. She was shocked.

'Why didn't you tell me all this before?' she asked.

'There was no need to. Besides, I had made up my mind that I would meet you, no matter what,' I replied.

'So I am no longer welcome in your house, now is it?'

I could see how hurt she was.

'I am ... I am so sorry Rohini. There will be a lot of stress if you visit. Shaila still looks at me with a kind of revulsion and hatred. This is one chance for us to mend our relationship,' I said.

She was silent for a long time.

Then she asked, 'So do you want to continue meeting me? Or is this 'the end'?'

'Of course, I do. But you won't be able to stay over. For obvious reasons,' I said.

Then she said 'Don't worry. We will continue meeting.'

'How?' I asked.

But she wouldn't tell me.

28

Jairaj called from Bahrain today. For once it wasn't a call about money.

Kamakshi is expecting a baby. The baby is due in the first week of December. I congratulated him. I asked him where she was planning to have the baby—in India or in Bahrain. He said there's a lot of time for that, and they would decide that later.

He sounded pleased and excited. I told him about Shaila shifting to Pondicherry.

'What about their expenses? Has Ghanshyam offered to pay for all that?' he asked.

I said it did not matter whether he did or not. Shaila was my daughter and I would look after her.

I cleaned out the bedroom today. I told my colleagues that my daughter is shifting to Pondicherry with my granddaughter. They were all excited about it. Mrs. Bala from accounts said that she has an old antique cradle and that she would give it to me. She also said she will arrange for a cleaning lady.

'You have to be very careful, Mr. Gopal. Little babies can get infections very soon. And your granddaughter is less than three months old, isn't she?' When I confirmed that she was, she had a whole lot of advice for me. She is like a sweet old granny, I thought. But then I realised I am a grandfather myself now.

And in December, I will be a 'double-grandfather' if there is such a term.

So sad that Padmaja never got to hold her grandchildren. She would have probably made an excellent grandma.

But now, we will never know.

Strange are the vagaries of fate.

* * *

23rd April 1989
Sunday

Shaila, baby Nithya and Paro arrived today. I met them at the Chennai airport. I had hired a car for the same.

Mrs. Bala had helped me set up the bedroom beautifully. On one side, we suspended the antique cradle from the roof. All the old houses come with hooks embedded in the roof, to suspend large wooden swing seats (which are almost like a bed) or for cradles. I hadn't noticed them until now. She insisted we should get new curtains, and she came with me to help me choose. She knew all the shops that sold curtains at good rates, and she wheedled out great deals. She also got cushions and such things.

It has made a huge difference—a woman's touch. I could have asked Rohini to help me, but it didn't even occur to me to 'decorate' till Mrs. Bala insisted.

Shaila looked disappointed with the house.

'Only one bedroom, accha? Where will you sleep?' she asked.

I told her I was comfortable in the hall.

'I can sleep in the hall,' she said.

I asked her not to be silly. She is still breastfeeding the baby. Also, the bathroom is attached to the bedroom.

Shaila kept complaining about the mosquitoes. I told her I would go and get a mosquito net tomorrow. She asked me to get a small umbrella net for the baby. I went out immediately and got that.

It looks like a mini canopy. Baby Nithya is sleeping so peacefully inside it.

Looks like she has settled down here faster than her mother has.

* * *

24th April 1989
Monday

We have identified a good paediatrician here. We took baby Nithya for a check-up. They made a card for her, which had all the due dates for vaccines, etc. printed on it. The next vaccine is due soon.

I had forgotten how much work looking after a baby entails.

'I don't remember taking you or Jairaj, for so many vaccinations,' I remarked to Shaila.

'It was always amma who took us. You were mostly buried in your work,' she said.

The house is spotless. Between the cleaning lady and Paro, they keep it spic and span. It smells of antiseptic all the time. Kind of like a hospital smell. I remarked about this to Paro.

'Germs, sir. We need to protect the baby,' she says.

I dislike that smell. But it cannot be helped.

* * *

30th April 1989
Sunday

I have no idea how such a little baby can occupy so much space. Everywhere I turn, there are the baby's things. Paro does keep it organised—but oh, the number of things needed for babies, these days!

I went to the Sunday Market today and got a 'jhoomer' for the baby. It is a plastic toy which has a key, which you wind. The little plastic orange globe has hanging things spinning round and round, when you release the key.

Shaila said the baby is too young for it. But she will keep it and use it once Nithya is bigger.

I spoke to Rohini on Friday.

She asked me if I could come to Chennai. She said Raman was not at home—he was in Germany for two weeks. I asked her where we would meet. She said we could meet at her house, inside the IIT campus.

I am not comfortable with that at all. I do not want to go to her house when her husband is not around. It seems to be a sneaky thing to do.

She asked me how I could say it was sneaky. She pointed out that it was only as sneaky as her coming to my house every weekend.

'That is different. This is just my house,' I said.

'How is it different? Just because I share my house with Raman, it doesn't make it any less of my house,' she said.

I don't know how to explain to her. But I told her I cannot come to her house when her husband isn't home. I asked her to invite me when he was around, and I would come.

'Then why don't you tell Shaila about our friendship? I can come and see you at your house?' she asked.

I suppose I must.

* * *

4th May 1989
Thursday

There was a massive row between Shaila and me. I told her that I wanted Rohini to come over and see the baby. She threw a fit.

'How can you still be in touch with that woman?' she asked.

'What do you mean—that woman? Please speak with respect. She is my friend,' I said.

'Ha! She doesn't deserve any respect. She is a bitch,' Shaila said.

I was furious. I asked her to mind her language.

'I speak the truth. It is because of her that we lost amma,' she said.

What utter nonsense she was speaking.

I asked her what the logic was in that statement. Didn't she know that her mother had a psychiatric problem?

'That woman ... That bitch—amma's problems started only after she visited. Amma detested her. HOW COULD YOU BRING HER TO OUR HOME? SHAME ON YOU, ACCHA!' Shaila's eyes were icy with hatred as she spat out the words.

I asked her to lower her voice. She started hurling all kinds of accusations at me.

She said I had neglected Padmaja because I was busy serenading Rohini. She said I should be ashamed of myself—that at my age, when I am a grandfather, I am now having an affair.

'SHUT UP ... DONT YOU DARE TALK TO ME THAT WAY,' I yelled. I was so angry, I almost raised my hands to strike her. But I controlled myself.

Shyamala knocked on our door and asked us what the matter was. I said it was nothing and I apologized for the noise. I am certain Shyamala heard everything we spoke. These houses share a wall—and they are so thin.

Shaila kept quiet then, and so did I.

After Shyamala left, she started crying. She said I was selfish and I looked at only my interests. She said if I had paid more attention to her mother she would have been alive.

Her words hurt me immensely. How could she hurl such accusations without even understanding what I am going through?

* * *

10th May 1989
Wednesday

I haven't been speaking to Shaila since the last argument we had. I spoke to Rohini and told her what had transpired.

She was extremely apologetic. I told her it wasn't her fault.

'No, in a way, it was. It was I who goaded you to tell Shaila,' she said.

'But I made that choice. You did not. The decision was mine. It is my house after all,' I said.

'I feel terrible to have caused this divide,' she said.

I said that she had not caused anything.

I told her I would come to Chennai. We could meet at a restaurant or something. She said it wouldn't be as nice as what we were doing—just spending massive amounts of time together. 'We will be able to sit at the restaurant for just an hour or so, and then what will we do?' she asked.

'You come home here, then; Shaila cannot dictate who comes to visit me and who doesn't,' I said.

But she told me not to be foolish, and not to create problems when there were none.

I asked her what we would do then. She said she is working

on it, and that she had started working on it last month itself when she knew Shaila would be staying with me for a while. She said it is a big surprise, and it's almost ready.

She asked me to be patient and I would soon know.

* * *

6th June 1989
Tuesday

Today is Padmaja's first death anniversary. I took leave from work.

We organised a pooja at the Manakular Vinayagar temple. Most people perform poojas in their house, but I do not want the smoke from the pooja to harm baby Nithya in any way. The house is too small for a pooja, and if we have it inside, it will be full of smoke for at least three days.

Shaila and I sat for the pooja, while Paro looked after Nithya. She left halfway through, as Nithya started bawling.

Jairaj called and said that he and Kamakshi had offered prayers in Bahrain.

Ghanshyam had sent a letter and it reached yesterday. His parents called up this morning and said they were remembering Padmaja. His mother asked me to offer rice to the crows, so that her 'atma'[30] would get 'shanti'[31].

Do the atmas of dead people live inside crows?

There must have been a reason why our forefathers had customs like these. But I think we all follow it blindly, without reflecting much on the reasons behind them.

How things change in a year!

* * *

7th July 1989
Friday

Rohini is a magician. She really is.

The 'surprise' turned out to be an apartment in Kuruchikuppam, overlooking the ocean! I cannot believe it.

---

30. soul

31. peace

Everything—the Ashram, the Manakular Vinayagar temple, the handmade paper factory, the promenade—is a stone's throw away. This apartment is in an old building on the third floor. It is a three-storeyed building and it has no lifts. She has bought this apartment.

She bought it just for us. What a grand surprise this turned out to be! Simply incredible.

She said she got her share of money from the sale of her ancestral house in Poongavanam. She had been looking to invest in a property for a long time, in Chennai. But she hadn't been able to find the right one. She spoke to Shyamala about buying property in Pondicherry. Shyamala's sons are never coming back to India. They were looking for a buyer for this apartment of theirs. She has been coordinating with her quietly. They did everything—sale deed, registration, all of it. Shyamala knows people here and she got it done. Rohini visited Pondicherry a couple of times for the formalities. She did not breathe a word of it to me. Nor did Shyamala.

Rohini was so triumphant.

'See how nice it was that I spoke to her? See? You were so sullen. Now we have our own place Gopal!' she said.

'Correction. YOU have your own place. Congratulations,' I said.

'But I bought it just so we could meet here. I hope you realize that,' she said.

She looked so sweet, so earnest then.

I wanted to kiss her on her forehead.

But I did nothing.

'Shall I make coffee?' she asked softly.

I couldn't reply. I just nodded.

The apartment itself is small, but beautiful. It has two bedrooms, and a common bathroom, outside, in between the bedrooms. It has marble floors, and large windows, through which the sea is visible. It has a beautiful terrace too, which again overlooks the ocean. It is bright, windy and airy. It is already furnished with all the essential furniture—all of them antiques, which Rohini loves so much. Shyamala's son had been living here for a while, before he shifted to France. Hence all essentials, including the hot-plate for cooking, are there.

'We have our own hideout now, Gopal. Our sanctuary. I want to do up this place nicely. Shall we do it up together?' she asked.

I said we would.

* * *

9th July 1989
Sunday

Rohini and I have been buying many things for this place for the last two days. I never knew setting up a home can be an enjoyable experience.

The first thing Rohini did, was speak to the neighbours and arrange for a cleaning lady to come on weekends. I like how efficient she is in all these things.

Then we travelled to a nursery and Rohini bought a whole lot of plants, which were delivered home. The plants, which she arranged on the terrace, have made all the difference and has transformed the place. She also bought garden furniture and a huge garden umbrella.

'Now we can sit here and chat over coffee, as we look at the waves,' she said.

We spent Friday and Saturday night here. I told Shaila that I will not be there for the weekend.

She asked if I was travelling on work. I told her I wasn't. I told her that a friend has bought a place and that I am helping my friend set up the place.

Nithya has started smiling at me now. She seems to recognize me. Shaila is a good mother. She reads to her, sings to her, talks to her.

I have started carrying Nithya out for a short evening walk, where I show her the trees and the birds. She gurgles in delight.

Shyamala visits often. Shaila was very clear that if she had just smoked, she could not carry the baby. 'I am sorry aunty, but I feel strongly about it,' she said.

Shyamala just waved her hands and said, 'I have raised two boys. I know.'

Between Shyamala, Shaila, Paro, the cleaning lady and me, this baby is getting so much attention. Shaila asked today if

Nithya would recognize Ghanshyam when he came back. I told her she would, even though I am not sure at all.

* * *

14th July 1989
Friday

Rohini came to Pondicherry today. I met her at the apartment. She insists on calling it 'our apartment'. She has named it 'The Hideaway'.

'What hideaway?' I asked.

'It is our hideaway from the world, our happy place, isn't it?' she replied.

I spent time with her and returned home by around 9 p.m. or so. I am meeting her again tomorrow morning. I told Shaila that my friend is in town, and I might stay over. She didn't ask any questions and I did not volunteer any more information.

* * *

17th July 1989
Monday

I spent Saturday night with Rohini. It was wonderful to sit on the terrace and gaze at a million stars. We could hear the ocean roaring.

'The ocean reminds us of how fragile life is, how small and insignificant our problems are,' said Rohini.

I couldn't agree more. There is a strange sense of comfort to sit in silence, marvel at the stars, and listen to the ocean waves.

'I think buying this apartment was one of the best decisions, I made. Don't you agree?' she asked.

I said I did.

She said Raman will be back the following week and that she would not be able to come to Pondicherry for two or three weeks. She has left a key with me. She asked me to spend time here on weekends, as the cleaning lady would come. I told her I would.

* * *

22nd July 1989
Saturday

Shaila, Nithya and Paro came with me today to the apartment. Shaila fell in love with it.

'Accha, this is such a pretty place! No wonder you like spending time here. Whenever your friend isn't here, why don't you sleep here? It is better than sleeping in the hall there, isn't it? I am sure your friend will not mind at all,' she said

I just smiled and said it was a good idea and that my friend wouldn't mind. I didn't tell her who the friend is, and she didn't ask.

I told her I would do that every now and then.

* * *

Ayan smiled as he read all of this. Absurdly, he did feel a little jealous of Nithya. She had been to 'The Hideaway' as a baby, and he hadn't! He wanted to call up Nithya and tell her all of this. But unless she read all the diary entries, she wouldn't even comprehend how dear 'The Hideaway' was to *Muttachan* and Rohini.

The entries were getting more and more interesting. Since this was the year that he was born, and it was an indescribable feeling to read about it. He knew parts of the story, as he was born in Bahrain, and his grandparents from his mother's side had come to live with them for a while, when he was born. He knew this from the photographs and the things that his mother had told him.

But reading about it in his grandfather's diaries was a mind-blowing experience. Ayan eagerly turned the pages and continued to read.

29

10th August 1989
Thursday

Rohini said that she would be in Pondicherry for the weekend. Raman was off for a conference at IIT Bombay. If I managed to take a Monday off, then she suggested that we could spend four days together. Independence Day falls on Tuesday this year. She said we could travel somewhere close by and we could take a short vacation. The workload here is so little that even if I take two weeks off, everything runs smoothly.

I told her I would take leave.

When I mentioned it to Shaila, she wanted to know where I was going. I told her I hadn't decided yet, and that my friend would be making plans. Shaila said that she was hoping she could go to Calicut. Ghanshyam keeps reminding her that his parents have not yet seen the baby. Nithya is nearly seven-months-old now.

I asked her if she felt confident enough to manage the baby on her own. I suggested that she and Paro travel together. Shaila said that between both of them, they would easily be able to manage the baby on the journey.

I have an agent in the bank who does railway bookings. He booked a train from Madras to Calicut. There is also a reliable taxi service here. I will travel with them to Madras, and see them off.

Shaila spoke to her in-laws. Her mother-in-law will receive her at the station, along with her nephew, who lives with them.

After all the bookings were done, I asked Rohini if she could meet me in Madras on Friday evening, as I would be seeing Shaila off. Rohini said she would, and we would travel back together to Pondicherry on Friday.

I am looking forward to this weekend.

* * *

16th August 1989
Wednesday

What a glorious four days, these were. I don't remember a time when I was this happy, this content, this peaceful.

We ended up spending it in 'The Hideaway' itself. (I too have started referring to it as 'The Hideaway' as Rohini calls it that.) We did not go anywhere. By the time I dropped Shaila, baby Nithya and Paro at the station, it was 5 p.m. By the time I met Rohini outside Madras Central Station and picked her up, it was 6 p.m. already. We travelled back in the same taxi that I had hired to drop them.

The next morning, we decided we would go to Mahabalipuram. We called up three resorts from a PCO at the end of the road. Rohini had all their contact details. But all three said that they were booked to capacity. Since it was a long weekend, they were all running full.

Rohini said, 'Let's spend the four days at 'The Hideaway' itself. Why go anywhere?'

And that is exactly what we did.

We had endless conversations on the terrace, in the living room, in the kitchen while she cooked, on the promenade when we took walks, and on the beach. We talked non-stop, all the time. I am surprised at how we never run out of topics.

I do not enter her bedroom, and she doesn't enter mine. My heart beats so fast when I lie in my bed and think of her sleeping in her room. I long to simply hold her hand. But I do no such thing. Neither does she.

But her eyes speak to me all the time. And I am certain she can see my love for her, in my eyes too.

And yet, there is this barrier I cannot cross. I know that if I take her hand or hug her, she will not stop me. But I simply cannot.

I don't want anything from her, other than just spending time with her, and conversing with her, being around her. It fills me with joy to be able to do that. She says it is the same for her.

We watched an English movie together. There is a person who comes with video cassettes, every other day. The charges are nominal for borrowing a VCD. He rang the doorbell, out of the blue, and when Rohini opened the door, he showed us the collection of the VCDs. He said the people downstairs and on the ground floor were renting from him. He thought he would check if we wanted any movies. Rohini rummaged through his collection and immediately chose 'Children of a Lesser God'. The man said it was an excellent choice, and that it had won many awards. He said he would be back the day after tomorrow to collect it. We could pay him the rental charges either for that single VCD, or we could take a monthly plan. He said this was an original print and not a pirated one.

The movie turned out to be excellent. It is a love story between a deaf woman Sarah, and her speech teacher James. What starts as a simple challenge for James, as Sarah simply refuses to communicate with him even though she can, turns out to be a very poignant love story, as they develop a deep connection with each other. It kept us gripped throughout. During one particularly touching scene, Rohini cried.

I quietly handed her my handkerchief and she took it. She told me to pause the movie, and then made uzhunu vadas[32] for us.

The lady who acted as Sarah, Marlee Martin won the best actress award for her performance. She is deaf-mute in real life too and communicates through sign language. She is beautiful.

Sometimes, love requires no words.

When the four days came to an end, and it was time for me to go back to work, I just did not want to leave. She too felt the same way. But she had to go back before Raman got back.

I asked her when we would meet again. She said she would let me know soon.

* * *

---

32. A deep-fried delicacy made of lentil batter

27th August 1989
Sunday

Shaila returned from Calicut yesterday morning. I picked them up from the Madras Railway Station. Her mother-in-law has sent tonnes of stuff with her—banana chips, accappams, tapioca chips, tender mango pickle, puttu podis and idiyappam podi.[33]

Shaila tells me that Ghanshyam's father's condition is really bad. Ghanshyam's work in the Ivory Coast is coming to an end. He is returning in the second week of September. Shaila is very excited and happy about this. Paro also seems to be happy to go back to Delhi. I remarked that they are acting as though their 'van-vaasam'[34] has ended. Shaila laughed and said it was something like that, to be separated from her husband.

Baby Nithya has grown so much in just a few days. It is astonishing how fast babies grow.

Jairaj called on Friday. They have decided to have the baby in Bahrain itself. Kamakshi's parents will go there and be with them for some time. Jairaj said that Kamakshi's father had decided to invest in the company, along with some of his friends. 'They have more trust in me than you do,' he said.

I explained that it is not that I did not have trust in him, but he should remember that there is a difference between a salaried bank employee and a businessman who has much more income at his disposal.

Whatever money I have earned is clean. It is all white. I pay my taxes and I do not take any bribes. Jairaj asked if I was implying that Kamakshi's parents were dishonest.

I told him that we will not argue about this, and I hung up.

I do not know why every phone call with Jairaj has to end on a sour note, with a discussion of money-matters. That is all he seems to think of.

I wonder if Padmaja and I are responsible in any way, for

---

33. Rice flour for making a Kerala dish

34. Reference from the *Ramayan*, when Lord Ram was banished to the forest

him to be this avaricious about money. We were frugal in raising them, because my salary was just about sufficient to make ends meet. Is that why he is so eager to grow? I do not know. I have never seen naked ambition like this. Some would call it greed.

I suppose it is a good thing to have his drive. He is certain to make the company succeed, and when that happens, I will be delighted. But his talking about money every time he speaks to me, and his implying that I am stingy—that I do not condone.

Padmaja and I have done our best in raising both to the best of our means.

* * *

4th September 1989
Monday

A terrible thing happened on Saturday. I am still a little bit shaken about it.

I was with Rohini at 'The Hideaway'. She was there only for a day and had to get back by evening. She had gifted me a beautiful deep blue linen shirt. I loved it. She said it will look great on me and asked me to try it on. I told her I would try it on, after we had tea. Just as we sat down to our evening tea, Paro rang the bell. We were shocked to see her.

Shaila had sent her, as the rope of the cradle had broken and baby Nithya had fallen out. Paro told me to hurry. I didn't know what to do.

Rohini told me to hurry and run. She said she would come with me if I wanted, but I told her to leave. She had to catch the 4.30 p.m. bus back to Madras, and if she came with me, she would miss the bus. That made sense, as we also didn't want another confrontation with Shaila.

When I reached home, Nithya was bawling. Shaila was in a state of extreme panic. Shyamala was calming her down. I examined Nithya. She was unhurt. The rope had snapped, the cradle had tilted and the baby-mattress had cushioned the fall. But Shaila said it is better to show the child to the doctor. So we rushed to her paediatrician. He checked her and said she was fine. But he asked us to keep a watch on her. If she was sleeping for an unusually long time, then we were to call him up.

Nithya is talking in baby babble as I write this. She seems to be thriving on all the excitement.

Later, Shaila said she was glad she knew where to find me as she had been to my friend's house. She said to give her the phone number the next time I went there.

'The Hideaway' does not have a phone. That is actually one of the many wonderful things about it. I told Shaila that it didn't have a phone and in any case, it is within walking distance, and hence, she could reach me.

* * *

6th September 1989
Wednesday

Shaila and I again had an altercation. Paro had told her that she had seen me with a lady. Shaila wanted to know who she was. I could have easily lied and told her that it was my friend's wife. But I didn't see any reason to lie.

I told her it was Rohini.

Shaila got very agitated then. She asked me how I could do that.

'Do what?' I asked.

'Is that house hers? Is that where you have been spending time and staying over?' she asked, her voice shaking.

I said I was.

'WHAT?! HOW CAN YOU?' she yelled. 'That bitch ... she brings bad luck to our family. The first time she visited, she took my mother. Now she is trying to take my daughter. She ... she is ill-luck personified. You have lost all your senses!' she said.

I told her to mind her language. I chastized her and told her not to be absurd. I told her that all that I had spent on her education was useless if she continued to believe in irrational things.

I also said I know what I am doing and I can decide for myself. I didn't need her interference. If she continued to stay under my roof, this is how it was going to be, whether she liked to or not.

She refuses to talk to me after that.

So be it.

* * *

17th September 1989
Sunday

Ghanshyam got back from the Ivory Coast to Delhi on 15th. Shaila wanted to fly back on 15th itself. But Ghanshyam told her that he had to get the house cleaned and make it ready for the baby. Shaila is still ignoring me completely and talking to me only if she needs something.

She can do what she likes.

She told me today that she is leaving on Thursday 21st, by flight. Ghanshyam has already sent their flight tickets.

I will be taking an off from work, to see her off at the Madras airport.

* * *

20th September 1989
Wednesday

When I got back from work, baby Nithya was with Paro. Shaila was nowhere to be seen. When I asked Paro where she was, she said she had gone to Madras.

I was worried till she got back. She came home only at 6.30 p.m.

'Where were you?' I asked.

She just ignored me. I asked her a second time.

Then she said, 'Didn't Paro tell you? I had gone to Madras.'

'Why?'

'What do you mean, why? I had work there, and so I went. If you do not owe me explanations for your behaviour, I don't think I owe you any explanations about what I do.' Her face was dark with anger.

I said no more to her after that. I told her to keep all her things packed, as we had to leave at 4 a.m. tomorrow, in order to reach the airport on time.

* * *

21st September 1989
Thursday

I saw them all off at the airport today. Shaila didn't speak a word the entire journey. She did not even respond when I told her to let me know once they reached Delhi. Nithya was sleeping, and she continued to sleep through all this.

Paro said, 'Thank you for all the trouble, Gopal Sir. Thank you for having us over.'

My daughter did not even have that courtesy.

The house feels a little empty now. The cleaning lady asked me whether she should continue to clean the house now that they have left. I told her that she could continue. She seemed to be happy to keep her job.

When I got back, Shyamala invited me over for lunch. I thanked her for the invitation and told her that I had work and hence I could not accept. She isn't one to give up easily though. At 12.30 p.m., she rang my bell and again asked me if I wanted to join her for a quick meal. I said I was just leaving. Then I wandered about on the promenade for some time and ended up going to 'The Hideaway,' just to get away from Shyamala.

The place felt empty without Rohini. The plants are blooming.

I wonder when she will be able to come here next.

I spent the whole afternoon there, reading a book. I got back only late at night, by which time Shyamala had disappeared from her usual spot on the verandah.

30

22nd September 1989
Friday

Rohini called today. She said Raman is taking her on a holiday to Goa and they are going for a week. She asked me if I would go to 'The Hideaway', look after the plants and get the place cleaned. I told her that she did not have to remind me of that. I anyway go there once in two days, to water the plants.

I was angry at her going away.

Once again the pettiness, the ugly jealousy, has reared its head. I cannot seem to control myself and instead of telling her to have a good time, I asked her why she hadn't mentioned it to me before. I sounded like a possessive lover, something I definitely did not want to turn into.

The beautiful thing about friendship, is understanding the other person's needs and to find happiness in whatever makes them happy.

But I am unable to.

I burn.

She said he had come up with the plan out of the blue. He felt he had been immersed in his work, and had been neglecting her of late. He wanted to make it up to her and hence had booked this holiday as a surprise.

'What if you had a camp or some other work then? Would you have cancelled that and gone with him?' I asked.

'Come on, Gopal. He is my husband. He knows all the camps that I do. We do talk to each other, every day, you know. He knew that I had no camps at the moment,' she said.

Somehow, that made me even more jealous. If she had told me that he was a self-absorbed workaholic who didn't care about her, I would have felt better.

If she has such a good relationship with him, why does she need me? Why is she hiding from him and meeting me? She says spending time with me gives her joy. Then why can't she tell him that she has a camp, and meet me?

I feel as though she has betrayed me. It is ridiculous to feel this way. I must get a grip on this. This is absurd.

Yet, I still burn.

* * *

24th September 1989
Sunday

I went to 'The Hideaway' and watered the plants. I let the cleaning lady in.

I missed Rohini so much. Then I imagined her and Raman sitting on the beaches of Goa, enjoying themselves. Even though I have never met Raman nor seen pictures of him, I imagined him to be grey-haired and slightly plump. I imagined Rohini touching his arm and laughing at his jokes.

I am acting like a juvenile here. I should stop being an emotional fool.

* * *

29th September 1989
Friday

Not a word from Rohini. She should have been back from her vacation today. Why didn't she call? Perhaps they reached home late, and perhaps he is around.

* * *

1st October 1989
Sunday

I watered the plants at 'The Hideaway', and let the cleaning lady finish her work. As soon as it was done, I rushed back home, just in case Rohini called.

No calls at all. I waited the whole of yesterday and the whole of today. Except for the time I went to 'The Hideaway', I have been home, the entire time.

* * *

13th October 1989
Friday

I am worried now. No calls, no letters, nothing from Rohini. Is she back from Goa? What has happened? Is she okay?

The India-Pakistan-West Indies cricket tournament started today at Sharjah. West Indies beat us by five wickets with 13 balls remaining. We made 169 in 48.1 overs. Viv Richards smashed his way and led them to victory. They deserve it.

* * *

15th October 1989
Sunday

Pakistan beat us. It was very close, though. It was a touch and go. Sidhu was the Man of the Match. Well deserved with his 108.

We were 273 for 4, in 46 overs.

They did it in 44.4 overs with four wickets down.

Wasim Akram is the man to watch out for. His bowling is superb.

Tomorrow we play West Indies.

No news from Rohini, even now.

* * *

16th October 1989
Monday

We beat them hollow. India defeated West Indies by 37 runs. They won the toss and sent us in to bat. We made 211 and got them all out for 174.

Ajay Sharma, Ayub, Kapil Dev—all got two wickets each.

Well done, India.

Still no news from Rohini. I am debating if I should call her and ask what is happening.

* * *

20th October 1989
Friday

Pakistan definitely deserves this victory. They were unstoppable. We won the toss and sent them into bat.

They smashed a 252. Saleem Malik made a century. He was Man of the Match. Shoaib Mohamed's strike rate was good. He made a 51.

Srikkanth got out for 12, and then Sidhu got out for 28.

Azhar made just 12 runs. Awful. I think the pressure of captaincy is too much for him. He performed much better when he was not the captain.

With this match, this series has ended. Pakistan has won the Champions Trophy.

I got a letter from Jairaj today. More like a postcard. It was very brief. His in-laws are arriving there in the first week of November. He said his company has taken off because of the new investors who have come on board, and that he is working hard. He hoped I was doing fine.

I tried Rohini's home number today.

I disconnected after the fifth ring, as I would not know what to say if Raman picked up. She has not spoken to him about me, and I do not want to make it awkward for her.

This wait is killing me. I last heard from her on 22nd September.

I hope she is okay. I am going crazy with worry.

* * *

26th October 1989
Thursday

I have no words to describe what happened today. I think I feel worse than I did when Padmaja died. This agony is exruciating I don't know where to begin. This is the worst situation I have ever been in, in my life. And yet, I have the upper hand here. But I feel miserable now. I want to sink into the earth.

Raman came to the bank today to see me. I had no idea who he was. He just knocked on my cabin door, and walked in, when I gestured for him to enter.

'Hello, I am Raman,' he introduced himself.

Even then it did not strike me as to who he was. I requested him to sit down and asked how I could help him.

He was staring at me. I was unnerved.

Then he said, 'I am Rohini's husband.'

That is when it sank in. I opened my mouth to speak but no words came out.

'I want to talk to you, somewhere in private, if possible. And I am terribly sorry to barge in like this,' he said.

He was soft-spoken, polite, well-mannered. He had a shock of black hair. He was clean-shaven, lean and way taller than I was. He must have been about 6'1". Completely different from what I had imagined he would be. 'Distinguished' is the word that comes to my mind.

I found myself saying, 'Of course, of course. Shall we go out to talk?'

I cleared all my appointments for the day. We went to a restaurant close by.

He was apologizing profusely and I didn't know what to say. He did not confront me, did not get angry, did not raise his voice.

Once we were seated he said, 'I know what has been going on.'

'What do you mean?' I asked.

'Rohini bought a house here in Pondicherry. And I know why she did that.'

I was silent.

'I am sorry. Really sorry,' I found myself saying. 'But it is not what you think. This is not an illicit, torrid affair'.

'Those are strong words. I know her love for you, and your feelings for her run very deep. But I feel grievously wounded here,' he said.

'I am sorry,' I said.

'We also have to think of other people, don't we, Gopal?' he asked.

It felt so strange to be sitting there and having this conversation with him.

I felt like a criminal about to be executed for my crimes.

'I thought long and hard about this. I decided it was best to speak to you directly,' he said.

'How ... how did you know where to find me?' I asked. I felt pathetic as I asked him that.

'Oh ... didn't Rohini tell you?'

'What? No. I have not spoken to her for the last one month.'

'Your daughter, Shaila. She came to see me just before she left. She gave me your residential address, as well as the address of this bank. She told me you and Rohini have been spending a lot of time in the house that she had bought. She told me how Rohini had come to Hyderabad and all this while ... all this while, I thought she was doing a project...' his voice trailed off.

There was so much pain and hurt in his eyes. I couldn't bear to look at him.

'Gopal, I have a request to make. Could I please ask you to stay away from Rohini?'

I wanted to apologize again. I wanted to tell him that I wasn't sleeping with his wife, if that was what he presumed. But all I could do was sit there with a lump in my throat and look away.

'Did you speak to Rohini about this?' I asked.

'Yes, I did. We have been talking about it. I know I have been a little preoccupied with my work. After your daughter came to see me, it was a huge wake-up call. I have been trying to make amends. That was the reason I took her to Goa. It is the first vacation we have had in years,' he said.

'Well, I ... I am glad you had a good time.'

I forced myself to say that.

'No ... not really. I told her that she had to choose between you or me...'

'And?'

'She said she wanted to think about it. She said she needed time to think about all of this calmly. She finally told me her decision yesterday.'

'What did she say?'

'She ... she chose you, Gopal,' his shoulders slumped as he said this. He looked down, staring at the floor.

My heart sang then. Rohini chose me. I felt vindicated. So she did love me.

'That is why I am here... To beg you to stay away ... I ... I cannot bear the thought of not having her in my life. Thirty-five years, we have faced everything together, Gopal, I am sure you know how that feels. How it feels to lose a partner.'

I didn't know what to say.

'Please Gopal ... I have lost a daughter. I do not want to lose my wife too...'

I have never seen a man so helpless. He was pleading with me. He seemed to be on the verge of a breakdown.

I took a while to think. He was silent the entire time. I then took the hardest decision of my life. I gave him my word that I would stay away from Rohini. That I would not contact her again, ever.

He thanked me. He was so grateful. He also had another request to make. He said Rohini shouldn't know of this visit. If she did, she would probably walk out on him.

My hands tremble as I write this. I am not able to write anymore.

I am devastated.

* * *

27th October 1989
Friday

Rohini called me today, when I was at work. She apologized for not being in touch for the last one month. She said that there were a lot of developments and that we had to meet soon. She said she could come to Pondicherry tomorrow.

I said I could not continue this anymore.

She asked me why. She wanted to know if it was because she wasn't in touch for the last one month or whether it was because Shaila had talked to Raman? She had presumed that I knew about that from Shaila.

I said it was neither. I said the decision was mine, and what we were doing wasn't right.

'What is right and wrong, Gopal? Who decides?'

'I don't know,' I said.

'If we were two women wanting to spend time with each

other, would this have been wrong? Is it about sex then? People presume we are having sex, so it is wrong?' she asked.

'I don't know, Rohini,' I said.

'What happened so suddenly that you do not want to talk to me anymore?' she asked.

I couldn't tell her.

All I said was that I am sorry. She tried to call me three more times after that. But I did not answer her calls. I diverted them outside and told them that I should not be disturbed.

I am heartbroken. This grief ... it is too much to bear.

* * *

31st October 1989
Tuesday

I never knew it is possible to miss a person this badly. The pain is physical. I long to talk to Rohini. I want to hear her voice. I want to hear her laugh. I want to just be around her.

This ... this feeling is unbearable. I feel like there is a hole where my heart is.

* * *

10th November 1989
Friday

I joined a yoga class today, near the Ashram. I am in so much pain, I feel like I will go mad with grief. The yoga teacher gives a little talk at the end of the class. He said the mind is like a monkey and we have to control it.

What about the heart? The heart is a wild stallion. It gallops where it wants to go.

* * *

13th November 1989
Monday

I got a letter from Rohini. I am pasting it here.

IIT Madras
10th November '89

Dearest Gopal, my closest friend,

Why? Why do you refuse to speak to me? Is what I did so

terrible? It was only a month that I was silent for. Can you not forgive me, my friend?

Raman confronted me the day we landed in Goa, with all the details from Shaila. She even described 'The Hideaway'. I had no idea that she had even been there. I was stunned when Raman mentioned all this. And I admit, at that moment, I felt ashamed too. He said, 'If you truly wanted all this, all you had to do was ask. Why did you go behind my back?'

I told him it was because I felt he would stop me. I told him that this is not what he presumes it to be. This is a friendship— pure and true. He was so hurt, he couldn't even bear to hear that. He asked me if I loved you. I didn't have the heart to look him in the eye and tell him that I loved another man. It was more to protect him than anything else.

He told me then, to choose between him and you. I told him I wanted to think about it. I was in an emotional vortex, caught in a storm. I wanted time to myself—to reflect and to take a proper decision. I did not want to be in touch with you while I took the decision. I thought, distancing myself will give me clarity. That was the only reason I did not call you or write to you.

I gave him my decision. I told him this was the purest friendship I had. He corrected me and told me this was not a friendship, it was a relationship. I told him he could call it whatever he wanted. If he was making me choose, I choose you.

He told me to think about it carefully, and I told him I did.

The next thing I know, you are refusing to speak to me. Why Gopal why?

Don't you think you owe me an explanation at least, after all that we have shared?

Please Gopal, talk to me. I am waiting for you.

Please call me.

Yours,
Rohini

31

Ayan felt a tightness in his chest when he read the last few entries. Time seemed to slow down and come to a grinding halt. He was filled with sadness. He bit his lower lips and blinked back his tears. He could feel every bit of his grandfather's pain.

What a sacrifice he had made. He could have easily refused Raman. But he chose not to.

Ayan got off the bed and poured himself a glass of water. He looked at the moonlight streaming into the room and gazed at the stars.

Ayan thought about how Rohini and his grandfather had not even held hands, never kissed. It was clear from the entries that they were deeply in love. He thought about how different his grandfather's generation was, when compared to his own. He and Shivani had barely known each other, and they had jumped into bed. He realised now, what a deep and powerful connection you can have with another human being, and how you can be soul-mates, without ever having a physical connection. It was an eye-opener for him, a revelation. He had never thought about it that way.

What he had with Shivani paled in compassion to what *muttachan* had with Rohini.

Ayan took a deep breath and went back to reading the rest of the entries.

* * *

18th November 1989
Saturday

Rohini's letter sits like a time-bomb inside my heart, waiting to explode. I have carried it with me to work every single day, and have read it at least fifteen times over the past few days. Each time I read it, a fresh wave of pain washes over me.

I do not know what to tell her. What do I explain? I feel shattered about this. I am hurting as much as she is. But I definitely cannot, should not, take her away from Raman.

I called Shaila today. I asked her why she had done that.

'Done what?' she asked, pretending not to know what I was talking about.

'You had no business to go and see Raman. How dare you? And how did you find out where he was?'

'You had no business setting up a home with his wife. It's not hard to find an IIT professor. That bitch ... she had proudly flaunted details about him when she had come to our home in Hyderabad. Serves her right. She had no right to cheat,' her tone was icy, cold.

'Who are you to decide what right she can do and what she can't? Do you ... do you even understand the enormity of what you have done?'

'I have done the right thing. If amma was alive, she would have done this too. You know you have wronged her. And you very well know what you are doing is not right at all.'

I hung up then.

I have nothing to say to her anymore.

Is it possible to hate your own children? I don't know. I simply cannot forgive her for this.

* * *

27th November 1989
Monday

Kamakshi gave birth to a baby boy today, at 8.32 a.m., Bahrain time. It is 11.02 a.m. India time. It is a week earlier than the predicted due date of December 4th.

Jairaj is elated. He called me in the evening and said both

Kamakshi and the baby are fine. It was a normal delivery and the baby weighed 3.15 kgs. He said he was a big baby and had a head full of hair.

Kamakshi's mother is handling the baby and helping Kamakshi.

'You should come to Bahrain, accha. Don't you want to meet your grandson?' Jairaj asked. I told him to bring the baby to Kerala.

I asked if they have chosen a name.

'Yes, we will name him Ayan,' he said.

'What a rare and unusual name,' I remarked.

'Yes, Kamakshi chose it. It means 'pathway to the sun'. But every Bahraini national who has heard it says it means 'Allah's gift'. Whatever it is, both are good meanings and that is what he will be called,' said Jairaj.

'It's a good name,' I said.

I am now the grandfather of two.

A pity Padmaja didn't get to meet either grandchild.

I longed to share the news with Rohini. Instead, I write here, in this diary.

* * *

6th December 1989
Wednesday

I got a short letter from Rohini. She said she is shifting to Germany with Raman in two weeks. She said she would like to be in touch and she hoped I had forgiven her by now.

She begged me to write to her. She left me her address in Germany.

I tore up the letter and threw it into the dustbin, because in a moment of weakness, I do not want to write to her, and break my promise to stay out of their lives.

I feel utterly numb with pain now. This is by far the hardest thing I have ever done in my life. My heart feels broken into shards. I don't even have the energy left to gather the pieces anymore.

Bon Voyage, my precious Rohini. May you be safe and happy.

May Raman keep you happy—always. You deserve all the joy that life gifts.

* * *

21st December 1989
Thursday

Shyamala caught me today when I was leaving for my yoga class. She asked me if I have been avoiding her. I have been. I would leave very quickly in the opposite direction, so that I did not have to pass her house, and would take the longer route, around the street corner. But today, she was standing outside my door, and I came face-to-face with her, the moment I emerged.

'Aah. There you are, finally. I have something to tell you,' she said.

'What is it?' I asked, glancing at my watch hoping she would get the message that I was getting late for class. The subtlety of such gestures is lost on her.

'I got a phone call from Rohini a few days back. She was leaving for Germany the next day.'

'I know,' I said.

'That is strange, then. She was asking a lot of questions about you. What you were doing, how you were, etc.'

'What did you tell her?' I asked

'I said you were fine, and you had joined yoga class and all of that. I asked her why she was calling me instead of asking you directly.'

'She must have tried my number and must not have through to me. I think my phone is out of order,' I lied.

'That's what she said too,' said Shyamala.

Even the lies that Rohini and I make up independently, are similar. How much more in sync can two people be?

I am drowning in grief. I find it hard to even speak her name to Shyamala. I do not know when I will learn to live with this.

* * *

31st December 1989
Sunday

Another year comes to an end. I had a regional meeting with the senior management committee a week back, in Chennai. For the last few years, financial markets are witnessing revolutionary changes, in terms of financial instruments as well as in terms of lenders and borrowers. The role of banks in direct financial intervention is steadily declining. Foreign banks have started opening branches in India. There is growth of innovative techniques—interest rates, foreign exchange futures, all of it will see massive changes in the next few years. They will be reducing manpower by offering Voluntary Retirement Schemes (VRS), as all the PSUs are currently burdened with a lot of staff.

I have just two and a half years of service left. If I look at the package that they are offering, it makes a lot of sense for me to opt for a VRS right now.

There is nothing left for me in Pondicherry anymore.

Every nook and cranny here reminds me of Rohini. I walk on the promenade and pain sears through my heart like a million poisoned arrows. I walk to my yoga class and think about how I had walked down the path with her.

I cannot bear the thought of going to 'The Hideaway'. When I enter my kitchen, I remember how she had first come to this house and exclaimed in delight over the furniture. Even looking at Shyamala's face reminds me of how she used to speak to Shyamala, and how I used to get annoyed.

Considering all of the above, I have decided that I will opt for VRS and will shift to Poongavanam soon.

The good things that happened this year:

The creation of 'The Hideaway' and the time spent there.
Birth of my grand-daughter Nithya and grandson Ayan.

The bad things that happened this year:

The creation of 'The Hideaway' and the time spent there.
(Had it never happened, I would never have to face this grief.)
The greatest loss of my life—losing my Rohini.

A second time.

The diary ended there.

There were no more diaries after that.

It was nearly dawn by the time Ayan finished reading it. He lay in bed, thinking about his grandfather's greatest loss. Sleep eluded him. His thoughts were a tornado inside his head. How could Shailammayi betray *muttachan* like that? That too after he took her in, looked after her and after everything he had done for her? No wonder *muttachan* wouldn't even look at her face now. What she did was unforgivable.

It felt very surreal to Ayan, reading about his own birth, and his *muttachan's* joy on his birth. He was tempted to message Nithya and tell her about all of this. But then, it would be painting her mother in a bad light. Also, she would never understand the enormity of this relationship between *muttachan* and Rohini. Anyone who had not read these diaries would presume it was an illicit affair. Only Gopal Shanker knew the truth.

And now Ayan too.

* * *

After tossing and turning for a very long time, Ayan fell into a dreamless sleep.

He was woken up by Velu. He sat up and looked the time. It was 9 a.m.

'What deep sleep, Ayan Sir! You need to have a certain kind of luck to be able to sleep like this. Not everyone is blessed with the gift of sleep,' said Velu.

Ayan sat up bolt upright. Velu handed him the coffee and Ayan gratefully took a sip.

'Sorry to wake you up, Ayan Sir. Gopal Sir has asked for you three times since morning. That is why I came upstairs,' he said.

'Please tell him I will be downstairs, as soon as I freshen up,' said Ayan.

Ayan hurriedly ate his breakfast and then found his grandfather sitting in his favourite spot on the verandah, in his armchair overlooking the fields.

'*Muttacha*, good morning,' he greeted him.

'Ah, good morning, Ayan. Did you sleep well?' he asked.

'I did, *muttacha*. What about you?'

'Like a baby in a cradle,' he said with a twinkle in his eye and laughed.

'I read all your diaries, *muttacha*. Every single entry,' said Ayan.

'Aaah. The song of despair,' smiled *muttachan*. Even though he was smiling, Ayan did not miss the sadness in his eyes.

'Song of despair?' asked Ayan.

'It is a poem, Young man. Look it up on your Internet. It is by Pablo Neruda.'

'I will, *muttacha* ... I wanted to ask you something. Did you never ever get in touch with Rohini again?'

'Never. I am a man of my word. I have had no contact with her since that day.'

'How, *muttacha*? How? How could you stay away? Don't you think of her?'

'I do. Every single day I do. I live with the happy memories we once had.'

Ayan was quiet for a while. Then he said, 'How can you let go just like that, *muttacha*? Why don't we get in touch with her now?'

Gopal Shanker said, 'Get in touch with her? How? I don't even know where she lives. Or whether she is even alive. It has been twenty-six years now.'

'Don't say that, *muttacha* ... I know she is fine. I want your permission for something.'

'What?'

'To find her. I want to find her and meet her once. Please do not say no. You have given your word. But I haven't.'

Gopal Shanker leaned back in his chair and knitted his brow in deep thought.

Then he said, 'How will you find her?'

'I don't know. But I want to try. Wouldn't you like to meet her?'

Gopal Shanker took a few minutes to speak. When he spoke, his voice was so low that Ayan had to listen carefully to hear him.

'I want to. But I do not know if I can bear the disappointment of knowing something happened to her.'

'So you prefer to simply sit here and think about her, and do nothing?'

Gopal Shanker said nothing.

'Please, *muttacha*. This is … this is probably the world's greatest friendship. It is the best thing ever that has happened to you. You cannot just give it up. You said yourself that it is the greatest loss of your life. You can't just give up on your friend. Please allow me to.'

At last Gopal Shanker spoke. 'All right. You have my permission. Go find her. But if you discover that she is no more, spare me the agony. I do not want to know.'

'Yes! Thank you, *muttacha*. Let me go and get my laptop,' said Ayan.

He rushed downstairs with the laptop and sat next to his grandfather. He opened the browser and typed 'Rohini Raman'.

Mission 'Finding Rohini' had officially begun.

BOOK FOUR

A Hundred Little Flames

The capacity for friendship is God's way of apologizing for our families.

—Jay McInerney,
'The Last of the Savages'

32

The search engine threw up a whole lot of results for Rohini Raman. But none of the profiles was the right one. Gopal Shanker peered over Ayan's shoulder and said, 'My God—so many people by the same name?'

'Yes, *muttacha*,' Ayan smiled.

'What do all these people do? Who are they? Where do they work? ' he asked.

Ayan clicked on a few profiles and explained each one to his grandfather. 'This one is a nutritionist. This one is working in a multinational. And this one here, seems like she is a housewife.'

For the next forty minutes, Ayan painstakingly checked out each and every profile named Rohini Raman, on Facebook. As he was browsing, he glanced at his Facebook messenger. There were a few messages from Dhiraj. They were casual messages asking if everything was fine and why he had not been in touch. The last message from Dhiraj read, 'Dude! Do you ever check your phone?'

Ayan thought about the last time they had all come to Kerala. It seemed like ages ago. There was so much that had happened since then. He realised that he had not checked his phone at all, ever since his last conversation with Shivani. He had been so lost in *muttachan's* world.

He opened the Instant Messenger app on his phone. He found about ten messages from Shivani and a couple from

Dhiraj. The first few messages from Shivani were updates about her situation at home. The next few were asking him why he had not replied. He was a bit irked at the deluge of messages. He had spoken to her on the phone just a couple of days ago, when she had ranted to him. He didn't like the tone of her messages. She sounded annoyed that he had not replied. He did not like it when girls did that and acted as though he owed them a reply. His last relationship when he was in college, had been a disaster as he had to report every detail of his life to his then girlfriend. If he didn't, she would throw a fit. She was clingy and possessive. He felt that what he had with Shivani was not a relationship. They were just good friends. And so her messages irked him and raised a red-flag. He thought she was acting like his girlfriend, which she definitely was not.

Had he been sending wrong signals to her?

'Sorry—been busy,' he typed.

Then he went back to his laptop. He began looking at LinkedIn. Even if Rohini did not have a profile on Facebook, perhaps she would have a profile there? Gopal Shanker asked him what LinkedIn was and Ayan explained it to him.

'Oh, so basically it is a collection of CVs but listed publicly. And you can send messages, is that right?' he asked.

'Yes, *muttacha*. You got it right,' said Ayan.

Here too, there were many Rohini Ramans but there was no listing for the right Rohini Raman.

'These days you can find anyone on the Internet, *muttacha*. I am surprised there is absolutely no reference to her at all,' said Ayan.

'Aaaah my boy ... For you youngsters, having all these things is so important. But we come from a different generation where we did not even have computers. Take me as an example. I do not even have a mobile phone. I suspect it is the same for her,' Gopal Shanker said.

'*Muttacha*—if she shifted to Germany, surely she would know how to use the computer? '

'It was so many years back that she was in Germany. God knows where she is now. Also, just because you know to use a computer, it doesn't mean she will have a social media profile right?'

'Right, right ... *muttacha*,' said Ayan.

He then remembered the organization that Rohini worked for. He went upstairs and checked the name of the organisation in the letter that Rohini had sent all those years ago. Unnati International Rural Cultural Centre. That was it. He searched for it and found the website. The site took ages to load. Ayan found himself getting more and more impatient. At last, it opened. But there was no mention of Rohini Raman anywhere on the site. There was only general information about when it was established, what its objectives were and things like that. Ayan went through the archives and discovered photos of the workshops that they had done. The photographs on the site were all from 2001 onwards. There were no photos clicked before that. Ayan saw that they had a phone number listed, and he decided to call them up.

He explained what he wanted, to the person who picked up the phone. He said he was trying to trace a Rohini Raman who had worked there many years ago.

'Sorry. I don't have access to the employee archives. Also if it was in 1987-89, they will not be computerized. The records are all stored in another facility, and I am not even sure if they exist,' the lady at the other end said.

Ayan asked if there was any way by which he could get the contact details.

She said she couldn't help.

It was only after he hung up that Ayan realised what a foolish attempt that was. Even if they had her records on file, she had shifted to Germany, and her phone number would have definitely changed, unless she was staying in the same house inside the IIT campus.

'*Muttacha*—do you think she might be staying inside the IIT campus even now?' he asked.

'I am not sure, Ayan. Wouldn't her husband have retired by now?'

That was when it occurred to Ayan that there must be a mention of her husband on the Internet. He asked *muttachan* what her husband's full name was.

'Raman Mahadevan,' said Gopal Shanker.

Ayan typed 'Raman Mahadevan, IIT Chennai' into the search engine, and there he was. There were several mentions of Prof. Raman on the Internet along with photos. He had even written a foreword to a scientific book. There were several papers which he had published, all of which Ayan skimmed through. There was even a chair endowed in his name at IIT Chennai, for a research-related activity. And then on the third page of the results, Ayan came across a news item which made his heart skip a beat.

"*Former IIT-M director Prof. Raman Mahadevan dies in Germany*"

Ayan's eyes widened as he read the news item quickly. It was from twelve years ago. It said that Raman had passed away peacefully in his sleep, and that his body would be flown to Chennai. There were quotes from professors who worked with him. One of them said, 'Under Prof. Raman's tenure, several academic reforms were pioneered.' Another said, 'He was known for being a change-maker. He brought in a lot of flexibility for students to choose their electives. He was always very friendly and approachable. More than anything, he knew each and every student by name and he truly cared about their welfare and well-being.'

There were a few more quotes about the brilliant work that he had done, and how he had made India proud. Ayan was surprised to read that he had even got the Padma Bhushan award from the Government of India.

Of all the sentences in the news item, there was one that caught Ayan's eye. 'He is survived by his wife Rohini Raman, who was present with him at the time of his death.'

Ayan said, '*Muttacha* ... there is a mention of her,'

'Oh, is it?' asked Gopal Shanker. He sounded like an eager child. Ayan could feel the excitement in his voice, even though Gopal Shanker was trying to sound casual about it. 'Where is she?' he asked.

'It doesn't say where she is, *muttacha* ... But Raman ... He passed away twelve years ago. She was with him in Germany when he passed. That's what this news item says.'

Gopal Shanker then made Ayan read out the entire news item. He listened to it carefully.

Then he said, 'What a pity. She has faced so many deaths now. Everyone close to her, she has lost.'

'*Muttacha*, she knows the address of this place, does she not? Why didn't she get in touch with you?' Ayan asked.

'Probably because she is...' Gopal Shanker trailed off.

'No!' said Ayan. He didn't want to hear it or believe it.

'Do you have any old contact number for her?' asked Ayan.

'Only her residence number from many years ago.'

'There must be a way to find out, *muttacha*... What about Shyamala?' he asked.

'I do not have a number for her. Also, it was so long ago,' said *muttachan*.

Ayan's phone rang then. It was Shivani. Ayan sighed. Then he answered it.

'Hey! How are you? And what are you so busy about, you busy man?' she asked.

'I was talking to my grandpa.'

'Is he fine? Is he doing well?'

'Yes, he is fine.'

'Are you angry with me or something? I just felt that from your messages.'

Ayan hesitated for a moment. Then he said, 'No, I am not angry, Shivani. Just busy.'

'Oh,' she said. 'Fine, I will call you another time then,' she said and hung up.

Ayan felt a little bad when she did that. He didn't mean to sound curt, and yet that was what he must have come across as.

These last few days of reading *muttachan's* dairy had transformed him in a strange kind of way which he wasn't able to put his finger on. The one relationship that he had in college, and now this new friendship with Shivani, was nothing in comparison to what his grandfather had with Rohini. That was true love. This—he had no idea what this was, but it wasn't on the scale or magnitude of Gopal and Rohini's feelings for each other.

'Who is it? That girl you went to meet at that resort?' asked Gopal Shanker.

'Yes, *muttacha*,' he said.

'Why didn't you speak to her, if I may ask?'

'I don't know, *muttacha*. I felt like she wasn't giving me space. She was trying to get into things which I am not ready to share.'

'I think it is important to not chase somebody. If they want to be in touch with you, they will find a way. Just because you keep calling someone, it does not mean they will respond to you,' said Gopal Shanker.

There was a strange sort of intimacy now between Gopal Shanker and Ayan. It was as though by laying open his diary, and sharing his treasured memories with Ayan, an unspoken understanding had developed between them, where they could discuss relationships as equals. Ayan did not mind talking to Gopal Shanker about his relationships now. He felt he could tell his grandfather anything, and he would understand. He saw his grandfather in a different light now.

'You are so right, *muttacha*. And you know what? I don't want to tell her about Rohini. She will not understand the depth of this. She will just not get why I want to find Rohini,' said Ayan.

'Yes, nobody will understand. My own children do not get it, then how will the world?' asked Gopal Shanker.

Ayan thought for a long time about what other steps he could take to find Rohini.

Then he asked his grandfather, '*Muttacha*, what happened to 'The Hideaway'?'

'What do you mean by that?'

'I mean, does it still exist?'

'I don't know, Ayan. Like I said, I haven't spoken even once to Rohini after that day.'

'Do you have the key?'

'The key?'

'Yes, the key to 'The Hideaway'?'

'Oh yes, Ayan, I do. It sits in the wooden box on my desk. I have kept it as a relic from those times.'

'Will you give it to me, *muttacha*?'

'Why? Why do you want it?'

'I intend going to Pondicherry. I want to find her.'

'But ... but ... how do you know 'The Hideaway' still exists? She could have sold it, anything could have happened.'

'Yes, *muttacha*. I am aware of that. But unless I go and see, we won't find out, will we?'

'I don't know Ayan, if it will be of any use.'

'Let me try *muttacha*—please let me try.'

'All right then. If you insist, you can go. I shall give you the key.'

'Perhaps it will be the key to a new life,' said Ayan.

'New life? My life is almost over. One foot is in the grave.'

'No, *muttacha*. That's not what you say. What you say is: How many new lives can you have? As many as you like,' said Ayan.

Gopal Shanker thought about that for a few seconds, and then he said, 'That is a lovely thought. When did you become so wise?'

'Ha ha! It's a line from a movie, *muttacha*. It's from the sequel to this film called *Best Exotic Marigold Hotel*. It's about a group of senior citizens who travel to India and find a new life.'

'Oh, I see. It must be an interesting movie,' remarked Gopal Shanker.

Ayan browsed through all the travel options from Pondicherry to Poongavanam. There was a direct bus from Kottayam to Pondicherry. The travel time was about eleven hours. One boarded the bus at night, and the next morning you were there. Ayan saw that the site had photographs and discovered that they were sleeper buses with berths, where you could lie down, and go to sleep. There were four berths available.

He did not hesitate and booked a ticket for the same night.

'*Muttacha*, I am leaving for Pondicherry tonight,' he announced.

'What? So soon?'

'Yes, *muttacha*. There is no point waiting. Do write down the address and please give me the key to 'The Hideaway',' said Ayan.

'Oh! I do not remember the address of 'The Hideaway', Ayan. But I can give you the address where I used to live. And

I can draw you a map to go from there to Kuruchikuppam. It is a straight road and about six minutes' walk. You will find it easily. If it still exists that is...' Gopal Shanker trailed off.

'We will find out soon,' said Ayan, as he packed his bags to leave for Pondicherry.

33

Ayan had never travelled on a sleeper bus. He discovered that the berth was large and comfortable. It came with bedsheets, a pillow, and a blanket. When he drew the curtain, it was like a little private room. He could even sit up erect, without bumping his head against the top berth. He loved looking out of the window, into the darkness of the road, punctuated by a few lights, whenever the bus passed through villages. He loved watching the dark silhouettes of the trees speeding by. At times when the bus driver suddenly rammed the brakes, there was a jerk and he got a start. But by and large, the ride was smooth. He did not know when he fell asleep as he stared out of the window. They halted at a point, and the helper in the bus announced that people could use toilets if they wanted. Ayan peeped out and saw that they had stopped at a highway restaurant. Several people were getting out of the bus to stretch themselves. Some were having warm beverages at the restaurant. Some others moved on to use the restrooms. Ayan glanced at his phone. It was already 4 a.m. He went to the front of the bus and asked the assistant what time they could be expected to hit Pondicherry. The man said that they would arrive by 7 or 7.30 a.m. He debated whether to get off the bus and grab a cup of coffee or not and then decided against it. He went back to his berth. When the bus started moving, he was lulled into sleep.

When he next opened his eyes, they had arrived. Passengers were getting off the bus with their luggage. Ayan had just carried his backpack. He had packed light. When he alighted from the bus, he was surrounded by a mass of auto-rickshaw drivers jostling with each other, trying to get him to ride with them. They were all pushing each other and saying, 'Sir—auto?' He gestured to one of them, who immediately tried to take his backpack from him, indicating that he would carry it to the auto.

'No! I will take it,' said Ayan as he clutched his backpack tightly. The last thing he wanted was for someone to steal his backpack. Once he was seated in the auto, he told the driver to take him to a good hotel in white town.

'Sir, budget or luxury?' he asked.

'Budget hotel—but a good one. Near White Town or in White Town,' said Ayan

The man nodded.

As the auto sped along, Ayan got his first glimpses of Pondicherry. It was like any other small Indian town. He was a little disappointed as he had expected it to be exotic.

But as the auto approached White Town and crossed the canal, the buildings and streets dramatically changed. Ayan noted the distinct French architecture, the neat streets lined with shady trees. He felt as though he was transported to a little French town, where people walked or rode bicycles through the tree-lined boulevards. He noticed a group of people playing a game with metal balls. His auto driver told him it was a game of *Boules*.

Ayan quickly read up about it on his phone and was surprised to discover that it had an ancient history dating back to the middle ages. It involved throwing metal balls towards a target called the 'pig'.

The auto-driver brought him to the hotel which was more

like a large mansion with a courtyard. When he walked in, the auto-driver walked in with him and helped him check in. He saw the auto-driver pocketing a few currency notes which the receptionist handed over. The auto-driver saw Ayan watching him. He grinned and said, 'Commission sir,' as he shrugged his shoulders and left.

The hotel was a boutique one, housed in an old colonial building built around a courtyard. It was a pretty place and yet, not too expensive. Ayan checked into a single room, which was tiny. It had a four-poster bed, a side table and an attached bathroom which was clean and spotless. He quickly brushed his teeth, had a shower and rushed downstairs. The hotel had a restaurant in the courtyard and he ordered a plate of *idlis* and a cup of filter coffee, which was served piping hot. Ayan enjoyed his meal. Once he was done, he typed the address which his grandfather had given, into Google maps on his phone.

He discovered that it was just an eight-minute walk.

Ayan walked through the streets of White Town, admiring the beautiful architecture just like his grandfather had done years ago. It seemed like Time had stood still. What a lovely place this was. No wonder *muttachan* had loved this quaint idyllic town.

The map on his phone announced that he had arrived and that the destination was on his left.

Ayan looked to his left, puzzled. There was no house at that location. The building he saw appeared to be an art gallery. It had a verandah. Next to it stood a door, flush with the wall, which sported a board indicating that it was a children's activity centre.

As he stood there, uncertain of what to do, an old woman emerged from the gallery. Her steely grey hair was bobbed and she wore thick glasses, through which she squinted to look at Ayan. She wore khaki shorts and a white T-shirt. She had a walking stick and was taking slow, measured steps.

'Yes? May I help you?' she asked.

'I … I am looking for an address, but I am not sure if this is the right place,' he said.

'What is the address?' she asked.

Ayan told her the address that his grandfather had given.

'Yes, this is the building. The address is correct. Who are you looking for?' she asked.

'I … I am looking for Shyamala… Err… Mrs. Shyamala,' said Ayan. 'My grandfather used to live here a long time ago,' he said.

The old woman looked at him carefully and then said, 'Gopal Shanker! Are you his…?'

'I am Ayan Shanker, Gopal Shanker's grandson,' he said.

Her face broke into a grin and it instantly transformed her.

'My … my … my… what a pleasant surprise. Come in, come in,' she said. Then she asked, 'Are you his daughter's son or his son's son?'

'His son is my father,' said Ayan.

'Ooooh, lovely! And congratulations—you have found her!' she said.

'Eh? What?' asked Ayan.

'I am Shyamala … I believe you were looking for me?' she said.

'Ooooh … Hello … Hello, ma'am… Forgive me, I did not recognize you.'

'Haha … how would you? We have never met, have we? Come on inside,' she said, as she led the way.

Ayan followed her inside. He saw that the rooms were all empty. Beautiful artwork hung on the wall. She led him through the gallery to the back of the house. They stepped out through a cemented arch into another annexe, which consisted of a two-room apartment. She led him in. The place was exactly like how his grandfather had described. Ayan felt like he was walking into the pages of his grandfather's diary. He could even smell the cigarette smoke which his grandfather had written about.

'This is where I live. And when your grandfather was my neighbour, the main building, the art gallery which we just walked through, was my home. I have rented it out to the Ashram folks, and as you can see, they use it as an art gallery now. Mind if I smoke?' she asked.

She lit a cigarette even before Ayan could answer, and took a puff.

'How is he? Is he alive?' she asked and chuckled.

Ayan was shocked at her direct question.

'Yes, yes, he is alive and doing fine. Thank you,' he said.

'Tea?' she asked.

'No, thank you. I just had my breakfast,' he said.

'Drink up, boy. You can never have too much tea,' she said, and proceeded to make a cup anyway.

Ayan looked around the flat. He nearly jumped up in excitement when he spotted the grandfather clock in the room.

'Is that ... is that a cuckoo clock?' he asked.

'Yes. An original antique piece and it still works. Made in France,' she said proudly.

She placed the steaming mug of milky tea in front of Ayan.

'Thank you,' he said as he took a sip.

'Are you married?' she asked.

'Eh ... No, no! I am not married.'

'Working?'

'Umm. In between jobs.'

'Girlfriend? You are a handsome young man. Women must be swarming around you, eh?'

'Er ... No girlfriends.'

'Gay?'

'What?! No! I am not gay!'

'Nothing to be ashamed of. It is high time the government legalized it,' she said, as she took another puff.

'Yes. But I am straight,' said Ayan.

She chuckled. 'I was only teasing you,' she said and Ayan gave her a half-smile.

Shyamala was nosy. Just like his grandfather described.

'You look like your grandfather. Exactly like him,' she said, as she scrutinised his face.

'Do I?' Ayan was pleased to hear that.

'Yes. Very much. Now tell me, what brings you to my doorstep? Why were you looking for me?'

'I ... I was actually looking for Ms. Rohini,' Ayan admitted.

'Aaaah ... That explains it. Your grandfather sent you, eh?'

'No, no. My grandfather didn't send me. I ... I just want to find her. Any idea how I can find her? Do you know where she is?'

Shyamala closed her eyes and frowned, as she tried to remember.

'She wrote to me from Germany many years ago. She wanted to know about your grandfather. She wanted to know how he was and she wanted me to find out why he wasn't talking to her.'

'And what did you reply?'

'What could I reply? Your grandfather had shifted out of Pondicherry by then. He said he was taking VR and he moved back to Kerala. I replied to her saying I did not have his contact details, and that he had vacated. I moved to France for a few years after that. After that, I have not heard from her.'

Ayan's face fell when he heard that. He was hoping Shyamala would lead him to Rohini. But now he had reached a dead end.

'Do you have any idea if that apartment which she bought

from your son still exists?'

'What do you mean 'still exists'?' Of course, it does. The tsunami didn't take it away.'

'No ... I mean does she still own it?'

'Aaah. You should be specific about what you say. That I wouldn't know. I know that the building is still very much there. In fact, one of my oldest friends lives in that building on the ground floor. If Rohini has sold her apartment, I will have no idea who she sold it to. You could perhaps go there and find out? The present occupants might be able to help you,' said Shyamala.

'Thank you so much for all your help, ma'am,' said Ayan as he stood up.

'Wait ... before you go, give me your phone number, and also your grandfather's number. And yes—how is Shaila?' she asked.

'She is doing well. They are in Pretoria now.'

'What is her daughter doing? What was her name? She was a little baby when she was here.'

'Nithya. She is in the US now. They are all doing fine.'

Shyamala whipped out a mobile phone and told Ayan to add his number as well as his grandfather's number.

'My *muttachan* ... I mean my grandfather—he does not have a mobile. I will give you my number,' said Ayan as he opened her contacts and keyed it in.

'What? Does not own a mobile? He is getting old. Tell him he will turn into a dinosaur,' she said and laughed.

Ayan laughed with her.

'I will give you his residence number,' said Ayan as he keyed that in as well.

'All right, thank you. I shall give him a call one of these days,' said Shyamala.

'I am sure he will like that,' said Ayan.

He also saved her number on his phone. She asked him to be in touch and to keep her posted when he got in touch with Rohini.

Ayan was happy that she said 'when you get in touch' and not 'IF you get in touch.' He saw that as a sign.

He thanked her. She accompanied him to the street. On his way out, he looked at all the paintings on display in the gallery.

'They are all made by local artists. All students of fine arts. Some of them are brilliant works. In a few years, when they become big names, these paintings will cost a fortune,' said Shyamala.

Ayan was drawn to a painting of the promenade. There was the Gandhi statue which his grandfather had described in the diary. The brush strokes were bold and fluid and the transparency of the water colours was shining through.

'How much does this one cost?' he asked.

'Do you like it?' asked Shyamala.

'Yes, very much. I think I will gift it to *muttachan*,' he said.

She took it off the wall and packed it up for him.

'It is a gift from me,' she said.

'What? Let me pay for this. I want to buy it,' he said.

'No. It is a gift from the heart,' she said. She wouldn't hear of any payment for it.

Ayan thanked her and carefully placed the painting in his backpack.

Then he took out the map which his grandfather had drawn and set out towards 'The Hideaway'.

34

The map which his grandfather had drawn for him was accurate. Ayan looked at each of the landmarks which his grandfather marked, as he passed them.

He decided that he would pay a quick visit to the temple that his grandfather had described—the Manakular Vinayagar temple. He walked to the temple and saw a large elephant tethered at the entrance. People were offering jaggery and bananas to it. The elephant would take the offering in its trunk, eat it and then the person making the offering would bow to the elephant. The elephant would then lift its trunk and 'bless' him by giving a thump on the bowed head. Ayan stared in wonder and surprise. A little boy came up to him and asked him if he wanted to buy a packet for the elephant. The cane basket that the boy was holding out to him, contained two bananas, a ball of jaggery and a lotus flower.

'It brings good luck, sir. Elephant blessing—all wishes come true,' he said.

Ayan smiled. He couldn't resist buying a packet.

'Come sir … come,' said the little boy as he pushed the cane basket into Ayan's hands and led him towards the elephant.

Ayan was a little startled as the elephant reached out, grabbed the bananas, and the jaggery. They vanished in a jiffy.

He bowed down and 'thump'! He received the blessing.

The boy took the cane basket back.

'Your wish will come true sir!' said the boy.

Ayan sure hoped so. He needed all the luck he could get to trace Rohini. He then joined the long line of devotees inside the temple. He offered a prayer to Lord Ganesh, the remover of obstacles.

Ayan also made a quick detour to the Ashram and saw the samadhis which his grandfather had described. What a serene place this was. Peaceful. He felt different here. It was as though life had slowed down. He sat for a few moments in silence just like grandfather had, so many years ago.

He then walked down Francois Martin Street, reached the intersection of the main road, and looked to his left. Just as his grandfather had described, to his left, down the road about 800 metres away, was the handmade paper factory. He walked straight on, crossed the road and entered a narrow lane. In the distance, he could see a few tall multi-storeyed buildings. He guessed correctly that the first one of these must be the Troth Apartment building, which housed 'The Hideaway'. His pace quickened as he walked towards it. This road was not very clean compared to the roads in White Town. It was just as narrow, but uncleared garbage lay overflowing in large round cement dustbins. There were slums on one side of the road. Pigs were feasting on the garbage. The road was lined with small shops selling everything from provisions to electric light bulbs.

As he neared the building, he saw the marble logo on the wall which said 'Troth Apartments—Phase 1'. Next to it, stood Troth—2 and Troth—3. His grandfather hadn't mentioned anything about the other two buildings. He presumed they must have come up in the later years.

As he walked into the apartment complex, a security guard sitting on a chair who was half asleep, stopped him.

'Yes? Who do you want to meet?' he asked.

'I am the owner's grandson. Third floor,' said Ayan.

'Mr. Mukherjee is your grandfather?' asked the guard.

'No. Mrs. Rohini Raman,' said Ayan and bit his lip.

'Ooooh. I have never seen you, sir. You don't live here?'

'No I don't live here. I live in ... London. I am working there,' said Ayan. 'I work with the youth wing of the BBC,' he added unnecessarily. He clenched his fists. He had blurted out the first thing that came to mind. He cursed Roshan inwardly for planting the absurd idea of 'youth wing of the BBC' inside his head.

The security guard couldn't be bothered though and where he was working did not interest him.

'Madam isn't coming? How is madam?' he asked.

'Fine. She is fine ... no, she will come later,' Ayan said, his heartbeats quickening.

So Rohini did come to the flat! Bingo—he had hit jackpot here. Excitedly he took two steps at a time, and ran to the third floor. His mouth was dry. He was breathless. He took out the key which his grandfather had given him. The door itself was antique with brass inlays, with a carved wooden wheel prominently placed at eye-level. The lock was embedded on the door itself. He put the key inside. It turned easily. Then he pushed the handle down. Opening the door, he entered the apartment.

There it was! The apartment he had been reading about all this while. He couldn't believe it. There was not a speck of dust anywhere. It was neat and spotless. Clearly, this apartment was being cleaned often.

The furniture was all made of rosewood. A tall chest of drawers stood at one end, with brass handles that glistened, catching the light of the day. The living room had period furniture, with carved legs and woven cane backing, framed with rich deep dark brown wood. The curtains were white, thin linen ones that let the sunlight in. Ayan walked towards the terrace door and opened it. There were potted plants that were well cared for. A row of sunflowers welcomed him, swaying gently in the ocean breeze. What a fabulous view of the ocean! The sun was shining so brightly that Ayan shielded his eyes with his hands as he gazed out at the ocean. The bright blue of the ocean was dazzling. In the horizon, he saw a few sailboats. This was where *muttachan* and Rohini must have spent many happy hours.

After a few minutes, he returned inside and peeped into the bedrooms. The beds were neatly made, with fresh sheets in block printed fabric. The curtains matched the bedspreads and the colour co-ordinated rugs on the floor added an extra touch of warmth. Both the rooms had very pleasing interiors. The atmosphere of the house was serene, warm, welcoming.

The kitchen was equipped with a gas stove. He opened the kitchen drawers and found steel utensils neatly stacked. The cupboards were well-stocked, with all the kitchen supplies— grains, legumes, rice, spices. This was clearly a house where someone lived, most likely Rohini herself. Once the initial excitement of discovering 'The Hideaway' died down, Ayan began feeling a little apprehensive. What if she walked in? How would he explain who he was to her? He had to somehow reach her, before she got here.

He began frantically looking around for a clue as to where to reach her. He rummaged through the chest of drawers. They just held a few table mats made of fabric, rolled up neatly and cutlery for the dining table. He felt like a thief as he went through the drawers in the side stand beside the bed. They contained a toiletry kit and a few knick-knacks. There was nothing else. There was not a single scrap of paper which gave any indication of what Rohini's phone number might be.

Ayan was growing desperate by the minute. He was so near, and yet so far. He considered his options. He could wait here in the flat till she showed up. If she visited this flat, then she was bound to turn up sometime. He wondered how often she came here. But how could he possibly live in someone else's house without their knowledge? He was trespassing, and he wasn't comfortable at all about this.

Ayan felt thirsty and helped himself to a glass of water from the water filter in the kitchen. Just as he was sipping it, he heard the doorbell ring. Ayan's heartbeats quickened again. He went to the door and squinted out through the peephole. He saw a short, stout balding old man with thin white hair and a bulbous nose, dressed in white kurta pyjamas standing at the door. He rang the bell a second time. Ayan nearly jumped out of his skin.

He cautiously opened the door and peered out.

'Hello, I am Mr. Mukherjee. I live in the flat opposite. And you are?' he asked

'I am Ayan. Ayan Shanker.'

'The watchman told me that you are Rohini's grandson?'

'Er... actually I am Gopal Shanker's grandson.'

'Eh? Gopal Shanker—who is he? May I come inside?'

Ayan had no choice but to let him inside.

'You see, Rohini has left a key with us. Our maid waters the plants here and keeps this house clean. Whenever Rohini is coming over, she calls us up in advance and informs us.'

'Err ... yes ... This visit is a bit of a surprise actually.'

Mr. Mukherjee looked at Ayan suspiciously.

'Does she know you are here? How are you related to her? How did you get the key?'

'Uncle, my grandfather gave me the key. He is a close friend of Rohini's,' said Ayan.

'Aaah—so you should say that right in the beginning, isn't it?' said Mr. Mukherjee as he visibly relaxed and leaned back in the chair.

Ayan wanted to tell him that he hadn't given him a chance to explain. But he bit back his words. Mr. Mukherjee was sure to have Rohini's number. But how could he ask him for it, as he had just mentioned that Rohini was a close friend of his grandfather's. Ayan's brain was furiously working, trying to figure out a way to get it, while Mr. Mukherjee was saying something. He had zoned out and he realised Mr. Mukherjee was looking at him, expecting him to answer.

'Sorry uncle ... what did you say?' asked Ayan.

'How long are you going to be staying here? And what do you do?'

Ayan was about to say that he worked for the youth wing of the BBC but he stopped himself, just before the words could slip out. He might have fooled the security guard with this, but Mr. Mukherjee looked like a sharp man.

'I work in Pune, for a multinational,' he found himself saying. Somehow he did not want to tell Mr. Mukherjee that he had no job.

'And what brings you to Pondicherry?' he asked.

'I ... I have a job interview tomorrow. And my grandfather said I could stay here.'

'Ooh, I see. And you leave tomorrow evening?'

'Yes, uncle I will.'

And then it occurred to Ayan, the perfect way to get Rohini's number.

'Uncle, I have been trying to reach Ms. Rohini but I think my grandfather might have missed a digit when he gave me her number. Can you please tell me the correct number?' asked Ayan.

'Oh, certainly,' said Mr. Mukherjee. He took out his phone from the pocket of his kurta.

He called out Rohini's number and as he did that, Ayan keyed it in his phone.

'Aaah—that's it! The last digit was wrong. Thank you so much, uncle,' said Ayan as he stood up.

That forced Mr. Mukherjee to stand up too.

'I have to prepare for tomorrow's interview uncle. I am so sorry, I need to go.'

'Not at all. There is no need to apologize. You must go prepared. Please carry on,' he said.

Just as he was leaving, he said, 'No need to prepare dinner. We will send you food from our house.'

'Oh, no, no. Uncle. You don't have to do that, please. I will manage.'

'I insist. Any guest of Rohini's is a guest of ours. Please concentrate on your interview. Good luck!' he said, as he left.

Ayan bolted the door and slumped back on the sofa. His forehead was covered with a thin film of sweat. How easily he had lied! He had surprised himself. He had no idea where all these quick lies were coming from, but he was thankful that he had thought on his feet.

Ayan wanted to shout with glee and dance. He wanted to stand on the terrace and scream out in joy. He had done it! His trip was not in vain. He had tracked her down and got her phone number. Perhaps the elephant's blessing had brought him luck after all.

Ayan inhaled deeply. Then with his heart pounding like drums inside him, he took out his phone and dialled Rohini's number.

35

Ayan held his breath as the phone rang. After what seemed like an eternity, a voice at the other end said, 'Hello.'

Ayan was tongue-tied. The drumming inside his chest increased in intensity.

'Hello? Yes…?'

'Hello … Ms. Rohini?'

'Yes, who is speaking please?' She sounded gentle, soft, kind, dignified and at the same time, full of energy. It was a voice that invoked respect. She didn't sound like she was in her seventies.

'This is Ayan … ma'am. I am … I am Gopal Shanker's grandson.'

There was a pause at the other end. Ayan could hear the clock ticking.

Then she said, 'Good Lord! Are you Nithya's brother?'

'No ma'am. Nithya is my cousin.'

'Aaah, Jairaj's son then?'

'Yes, m'am'.

'How is Gopal Shanker? Is he…?'

Ayan cut her short before she could complete the sentence.

'He is fine, ma'am … he is fine. I … I am calling you from your home in Pondicherry.' The words came out in a torrent.

'What? My home? 'The Hideaway'?'

'Yes, ma'am.'

'Oh ... Oh ... I see... But ... but how? And... why?'

'Ma'am I am terribly sorry for letting myself in ... *muttachan* ... my grandfather—he gave me the key. But only because I asked him to. It's ... It's a long story, ma'am.'

'Ayan, you needn't call me ma'am. It makes me feel like a school teacher, you know. You can just call me Rohini.'

'Oh, okay ... ma'am. I mean ... Okay.'

It was only then that Ayan exhaled.

'For how long are you there in Pondicherry?' asked Rohini

'I have come only to find you. It is a long story. Where are you right now?'

'I am in Chennai. I just got back here from a camp. Whenever I have work at Auroville, I come to Pondicherry, and I stay there. At other times, it's locked up.'

'I want to meet you. Is it ... is it possible? Would you be able to give me your address in Chennai? I can come and see you there.'

There was a pause from Rohini. Ayan licked his lips nervously.

'You know Ayan, I want to meet you too. I had anyway planned a visit to Pondicherry as I have a follow-up on one of my projects there. It is fortuitous that you happen to be there.'

Ayan heaved a sigh of relief. 'Is it? Would you be able to come here then?'

'Yes, I will. Can you stay back there tonight? I can start out right this evening and be there by 8 p.m. Is that fine?'

'Yes ... yes. That's great. It is fine. It would be an absolute honour to meet you.'

She laughed then and said, 'How did you find my number?'

'It's again a long story. May I tell you in person when you get here?'

'Of course. I will see you tonight,' she said and hung up.

As soon as she hung up, Ayan went to the terrace and

jumped up and down shouting, 'Yay! Yeah!' He punched the air, just like he had seen football players do, after hitting a goal. His joy knew no bounds. He felt as though he had climbed a huge mountain and was now at its peak, looking down at the view. A sense of exhilaration and joy washed over him.

He rummaged in the kitchen and found a kettle. He whistled as he made himself a cup of tea. Once he had calmed down a bit, he dialled the landline at *Thekke Madom*. Nobody answered the phone. So he dialled Velu's mobile number.

Velu answered immediately.

'Velu *chetta*! Where is *muttachan*?' he asked.

'He is sleeping. He has started sleeping at odd times these days, Ayan Sir. Did you reach safely? How is Pondicherry?' he asked.

'Yes, Velu *chetta*. I reached safely. And not only did I reach safely, I have found Rohini.'

'What? Incredible, Ayan Sir! That is wonderful news. Is she there?'

'No, not yet. But I want to be the one to tell *muttachan*. Please have him call me as soon as he wakes up, okay?'

'I will Ayan Sir ... and one more thing ... I am not sure if I should tell you now or when you get back. It can wait actually, It is nothing urgent.'

'Please tell me now, Velu ... I have all the time in the world.'

'Your father ... He called, Ayan Sir. He spoke to me.'

Ayan's blood froze when he heard that.

'And what did he have to say?'

'He wanted to know how things were at *Thekke Madom* and how you were doing.'

'What did you tell him?'

'I said everything was fine, and you were fine.'

'And didn't he ask about *muttachan*?'

'He did, Ayan Sir. I didn't want to tell him that *muttachan* was here and that we had got him back. But he already knew about it.'

'How?'

'My guess is that he spoke to the doctors at *Ashrayam*. Your father asked how *muttachan* was doing. I said he was doing fine. So obviously he knew that Gopal Sir was home.'

'Oh, I see ... What else did he say? And why doesn't he call me?'

'He is furious with you, Ayan Sir. He said you were meddling in things that didn't concern you. He asked me to advise you to go and take up the job which he had got for you. He ranted about what you can possibly do in life without a job. He asked me if you intended to stay the whole while at *Thekke Madom*, eating hot *puttu* and drinking the *chaya* that I make. He was very upset.'

'Let him be. Did you tell him that I am in Pondicherry?'

'No, no, Ayan Sir. Why will I do that? It will be like pouring ghee into a burning fire. I told him nothing.'

'Okay, good you didn't say anything. Have *muttachan* call me as soon as he wakes up, okay Velu?'

'I will, Ayan Sir.'

After he hung up, there was nothing for Ayan to do but wait. Ayan was upset with his father. He didn't want to speak to him. He was now using Velu to send messages to him. Ayan didn't know what the future held for him or when he would get a job. But he was certain that he did not want to join the prawn factory and he wasn't going to budge from that stance. Anger coursed through his veins when he thought about how his father had pushed Gopal Shanker into a mental hospital under a false pretext. Ayan wanted to have nothing to do with his father. He was disgusted, repelled. His father was heartless.

Now that Ayan had read Gopal Shanker's diaries, he thought that perhaps his father was angry with *muttachan* for not lending him money for his business venture in Bahrain. Maybe that was why he was mean to him. But whatever it was, in Ayan's book, this was unforgivable.

There was no television in the house. Ayan wished he had brought something with him to read. He looked around the living room. He noticed that the centre piece was actually an old wooden trunk. He opened it and saw a few old novels by Wilbur Smith, an author he had never heard of. He read the back blurbs and they seemed interesting. He chose one which said 'River God'. It was about a kingdom in ancient Egypt. He settled back and began to read.

He had read a few chapters when the doorbell rang. He jumped up to answer it. How could Rohini have got here so fast? But it wasn't Rohini.

It was Mr. Mukherjee, who handed him a three-tiered lunch box made of steel. '*Dal, roti* and salad. We didn't know if you are veg or non-veg. So we didn't include the fish,' he said. He pronounced veg as *bej*.

Ayan said, 'Oh. Thank you, uncle! But honestly, you shouldn't have. I am fine.'

'No ... no ... Eat well. Prepared for your interview?'

'Eh?'

That was when Ayan remembered he had mentioned an interview to him. In the excitement of speaking to Rohini, he had forgotten that.

'Yes, yes ... Prepared well. By the way, Ms. Rohini is coming tonight,' said Ayan.

'Oh ... strange. She never mentioned anything to us. Usually, she always calls us.'

'I spoke to her a little while ago. She must be on her way.'

'All right. We will see her tomorrow then. Goodnight, son,' said Mr. Mukherjee, as he left.

Ayan decided that he would wait for Rohini, just in case she hadn't eaten. He wondered if she used WhatsApp. He opened his phone and checked—and there she was. He was impressed that she knew how to use the messaging apps. She was only a couple of years younger than his grandfather. His grandfather didn't even have a mobile phone. She was so different from him.

He messaged her and asked her if she would join him for dinner.

She responded back within a few minutes asking, 'Are you cooking?' She had thrown in an emoji as well.

Ayan was delighted at her ease in the use of technology. Even his father didn't use the instant messaging apps—and here she was, not only using it, but also using smileys. She had also told him to call her by her first name. He didn't know anyone in their seventies who had said that to him before. He thought about whether a person was automatically entitled to respect and special treatment just because they were old. He felt respect had to be earned. One couldn't demand it, just because of age.

He replied back that food was waiting. She said in that case, she would join him.

The exhaustion of the previous night's the bus-travel and the day's events—meeting Shyamala, visiting the Ashram, walking in the hot sun from Shyamala's house to 'The Hideaway', getting inside by lying to the watchman, and then finally finding Rohini through Mr. Mukherjee—caught up with him. Ayan felt his eyes closing. He fell asleep on the sofa itself.

He was woken up by the sound of the doorbell. Ayan sat up with a jerk. He was a little disoriented. And then it came back to him. Rohini was at the door. He rushed into the bathroom and splashed water on his face hurriedly. He wiped it using the face towel that hung in the bathroom, and hurried to the door. He opened it.

There stood Rohini. Her suitcase rested at her feet. She looked beautiful! Her hair was salt-and-pepper, cut in a stylish manner. It fell below her shoulders. She wore trendy glasses with black frames. She was wearing a white sleeveless blouse and a lemon yellow saree. She looked so much younger than he expected.

As soon as she saw Ayan, her face lit up in joy. A dazzling smile spread across her face, her eyes crinkling in delight. She held out both her hands and said, 'Ayan!'

Ayan was taken aback by the warmth and unbridled joy with which she greeted him. She enveloped him in a big hug and didn't let go of him for a few seconds. It was as though she had known him all her life. Ayan could smell a pleasant flowery fragrance and he instantly loved her perfume.

At last, she broke the embrace and said, 'How wonderful to see you!' Ayan carried her suitcase into the living room. He was tongue-tied. She was so sweet and warm, and he didn't expect such a genuine and a loving welcome. She was so classy.

'Welcome to my home Ayan. This is … incredible. Gopal's grandson coming to see me,' she said, as she sat down.

'I am … I am overjoyed too, ma'am … I mean … I am happy too, Ro–Rohini,' Ayan stammered.

She laughed again. 'Don't be so nervous. Your grandfather and I—we were such good friends. I would like to believe we still are. Else you wouldn't be here, would you?'

'No … I mean … yes.' Ayan wasn't finding the words and he was embarrassed about coming across as an idiot. He kicked himself mentally.

'I hope you made yourself comfortable at home.'

'I did … I did. You have a beautiful home.' Ayan was relieved that he had at last managed to utter one coherent sentence in her presence.

'Oh, thank you. You know, Gopal and I chose some of these pieces together,' she said softly. Rohini had a way of speaking which made Ayan relax. Her voice was gentle, comforting. Ayan found himself feeling a bit more at ease with her.

'Yes ... I know. I read his diaries. He wanted me to read them,' he confessed.

'Oh,' said Rohini. She was silent for a few seconds.

Then she said, 'I knew that he maintained diaries. But I never knew he would preserve them. And that he would mention me.'

'Mention you? You are the star of his diaries! He has kept only the ones from 1987 to 1989. I think he burnt the rest. These, I suppose were too special and so he kept them. I ... I really think you have a precious, powerful connection. I can't tell you how moved I was reading his diaries.'

'What did he write about me?'

'Everything ... He deeply loves you...'

Rohini didn't say anything. Her eyes misted. She stood up and said, 'Have you had dinner?' Ayan could see that she was trying to control her emotions.

'Thanks to Mr. Mukherjee, dinner is waiting for us,' said Ayan as he led her to the dining table.

'Oh, bless that man. He always does this when I come to stay over too.'

Rohini fetched two plates from the kitchen. They ate their meal together. He asked about her work, and she explained in detail the projects that she was spearheading at the moment. One of them involved providing portable toilets to construction workers at labour sites in Bangalore, and on the outskirts of Tamilnadu. The other involved organising life-skills workshops for school children from impoverished sections of society. This was in Auroville. She was passionate about it, and she spoke with deep feeling.

'You know, *muttachan* was spot-on when he described you in his diaries,' he said.

'Is it?' she laughed.

'Yes, the only thing is, you seem not to have aged at all.

You are exactly as he described. You ... you seem so young!'

'Haha ... I work with young people. They keep me energized. The secret of staying young forever is to drown yourself in work that recharges you,' she said.

Ayan thought that there might be some truth in that statement. His grandfather looked so old, in comparison to Rohini.

After dinner, they sat in the drawing room. Rohini wanted to know all details. Ayan said it was a very long story. She said she wanted to hear every single thing. So he started with how he had lost his job, how he had shifted to Kerala as his grandfather had a fall. He told her about how he had slowly fallen in love with *Thekke Madom* and Kerala. He talked about how his father had arrived and put *muttachan* in the mental hospital under a false pretext.

Her eyes filled with tears when she heard that. She made no attempt to conceal them, and they flowed.

'Excuse me,' she said as she dabbed at her eyes with her handkerchief.

Then he told her about how he, Roshan and the boys had formed a gang and how he had found him in the mental hospital. 'That was when *muttachan* told me about the diaries. He wanted me to read them ... I think he wanted to prove to me that you exist, as my father had told them he was talking about an imaginary person named Rohini.'

Rohini nodded. She couldn't speak. The look of pain on her face made Ayan want to comfort her.

'He is fine now. After reading all the diaries, and knowing the truth, I just had to find you.'

He told her about how he had found her, and how he had met Shyamala.

'Oh is she back here? I was told she had moved to France.'

'Yes, she was in France and now she's back. Her house is

now an art gallery.'

'You know, I have never ever gone to that part of town. Whenever I come to Pondicherry I stay here, finish my work and then get back to Chennai. Too many painful memories.'

'I know.'

'So now that you have read his diaries, Ayan, tell me did he ever mention why he decided to cut off from me, all those years ago?' Rohini asked.

Ayan couldn't meet her gaze.

'Tell me, Ayan. This was all so long ago. Why did he stay away? What happened?' She was looking directly into his eyes, searching his face for answers.

Ayan felt he owed it to her.

'It ... it was your husband... He met *muttachan* and asked him to stay away from you,' he said.

Rohini sat there stunned, speechless. They sat in silence, Ayan looking down and Rohini leaning back against the sofa, her head thrown up.

When she spoke, there was a ring of deep sorrow in her voice. 'He was always a man of his word. Your grandfather.'

Then she said softly. 'I wish he was not. We could have been together many years back... But now... Now, I love him all the more for it.'

36

Ayan and Rohini talked late into the night. Rohini told him about all the childhood memories she had with Gopal Shanker. Ayan had already heard some of the stories from his grandfather. But he listened enthralled, as Rohini narrated them. He laughed with her. Her eyes twinkled as she spoke. She was a remarkable woman. She was a great conversationalist and easy to talk to.

When Rohini glanced at the clock, she saw that it was past midnight.

'I think we should call it a night, Ayan. I am beginning to feel sleepy now,' she said, as she stood up.

'Yes, me too,' said Ayan.

'Did you speak to Gopal Shanker? Does he know that you tracked me down?' asked Rohini.

'Not yet. I called him but he was asleep. I left word that he should call me the moment he wakes up. I am surprised why Velu *chettan* hasn't called,' said Ayan, as he checked the phone. He saw that the phone had shut down as it was drained of battery. It needed to be recharged.

No wonder Velu hadn't called him till now. In the excitement of meeting Rohini, he had forgotten to charge his phone.

'It's been wonderful talking to you, Ayan. I am beginning to feel tired now.'

'Yes, me too. The pleasure is all mine,' said Ayan.

Rohini asked him which bedroom he would like to use.

'Both are the same to me,' said Ayan.

'Choose one then, and I will take the other,' Rohini said.

Ayan chose the one to the left of the bathroom.

'That was the very same which Gopal chose all those years ago,' remarked Rohini.

Ayan noticed that her voice dropped whenever she mentioned *muttachan*. She said his name so tenderly. It was almost like a whisper, when she spoke about him. How fortunate they were to have experienced this remarkable connection.

He plugged his phone into the charger, and when it came on, he messaged Velu that his phone was drained of battery and that he would call *muttachan* tomorrow.

Ayan lay in his room and thought about how *muttachan* lay in this very room, on this very bed all those years ago, thinking about Rohini in the next room, and how they had never even kissed. He was certain if he could never be able to do that with someone he truly loved. He thought about his first girlfriend. At that time he did believe that he loved her with all his heart. Then after they broke up, there was nobody else, till Shivani. And now he had been slightly curt with her. He checked his phone—there were no messages from her. He texted her saying he was sorry if he sounded rude. It was just that he was in the middle of something very important when she had called.

Ayan fell asleep with a smile on his face, thinking about all that he and Rohini had talked about. What a lovely woman she had turned out to be. Not a single person who met her for the first time would be able to tell that she had faced such big tragedies in life—losing her parents, her grown-up daughter, her husband ... and then *muttachan* had cut off from her too. Despite all of this, she was so full of life and positivity. Ayan was very happy that he had made this journey and found her.

Early next morning, at 6.30 a.m., Ayan was woken up by

the phone ringing in his ears. He grabbed it with his eyes still shut and mumbled, 'Hello...'

'Ayan Sir? Sorry. Did I wake you?' said Velu.

'Mmm... No Velu *chetta*. What is it?'

'Ayan Sir—I have been trying your number since yesterday. It kept telling me it was switched off. I saw your message only this morning.'

'Yes. Sorry about that. The battery drained out,' Ayan yawned, stretched and sat up leaning against the headboard of the bed.

'No problem, Ayan Sir. You wanted me to call you as soon as Gopal Sir woke up. Shall I give the phone to him?'

Ayan thought about Rohini in the other room. He wasn't sure if she was awake or still sleeping.

'Does *muttachan* know you are calling me? Is he around you?'

'No, no, Ayan Sir. I am calling from the kitchen. I am making his morning coffee just now. He is waiting for his coffee on the verandah.'

'Oh, good. No. Don't give the phone to him just yet. I will call him soon,' said Ayan, and hung up.

When he went outside to use the bathroom, he found that Rohini was already awake.

'Yooohooo. Is that you, Ayan? Good morning,' she called out in a sing song voice.

Ayan smiled. 'Good morning,' he imitated her tone.

'Coffee or tea?'

'Coffee, please. I have read about the legendary coffee you make.'

'Really? He even wrote about that?'

'Yes, he loved it.'

'Coming right up. You go freshen up and come to the terrace.'

'Yes, ma'am.'

'Yes, Rohini… Not ma'am.'

'Errr … yes. Okay!'

When Ayan joined her on the terrace, there was a steaming cup of filter coffee waiting for him. He sniffed and inhaled the freshly brewed smell of coffee. The mug that she served it in, was made of stone.

'Nice mug,' he said.

'Stone earth pottery. You get it only in this region in India. I love them too,' she replied.

Then she pointed towards the ocean.

Ayan looked and took a deep breath. Stretching before him was the sun rising from the ocean, like a giant orange ball of fire. He could see only a quarter of the circle. He gaped open-mouthed, staring in wonder at the magnificent sight unfolding in front of him. The ocean was a golden orange, and the water shimmered like gold.

'It's my favourite part of the day,' said Rohini in hushed tones.

Ayan was so much in awe of the spectacular sunrise that he couldn't utter a word. The crimson, orange, yellow and the gold in the sky mingled like paints from an artist's canvas. They both watched in silence, spellbound, as the ball grew bigger and bigger. Finally, a blazing yellow golden ball arose, moving upwards in the sky. As it rose, the oranges and yellows slowly started fading, the brightness of the sun eclipsing the colours.

It was only after the sky was a light yellow and tinges of blue started appearing, that Ayan spoke.

'Wow—that must be the most fabulous thing I have ever witnessed,' he said.

'In Kerala, you will be seeing better sunsets, as it's on the west coast of India. There, it is the Arabian Sea. Here, you are watching it over the Bay of Bengal,' said Rohini.

'Breathtaking. I should have at least taken a photo,' said Ayan.

'There's always a sunrise tomorrow!' said Rohini.

'True... Once, when I was in Bahrain, my father had taken us all to Riffa Fort where he woke us up to make us watch the sunrise. I was too young to appreciate it then.'

'Finer things in life take time,' said Rohini.

'I agree ... I guess I have a long time to wait,' sighed Ayan.

'But once you get them, they are yours forever to treasure. Just like true friendship and true love.'

Ayan nodded in agreement.

'You know, if I hadn't read *muttachan's* diaries, I would have never believed that something this wonderful exists,' he said.

'We are fortunate, yes, to have experienced this, even once in our lifetime. People go through their entire lives searching for this, and never finding it,' she said.

'Speaking of which, I have to call the man himself,' said Ayan.

The sun had started shining brightly now.

'Come, let's go inside,' said Rohini.

Once they were seated in the living room, Ayan took out his phone and dialled Velu.

'Velu—give the phone to *muttachan*,' he said, as soon as Velu picked up.

Ayan was smiling broadly when Gopal Shanker came on the line.

'*Muttacha*! How are you?' he asked.

'I should be asking you that question, young man. Not a single phone call to even let us know you reached safely? I have to get to know through Velu, is it? Couldn't you call me up directly?'

'I did, *muttacha*—but nobody picked up the landline. And then you were sleeping when I spoke to Velu.'

'Excuses, excuses ...' said Gopal Shanker. 'Anyway—what did you discover there? Where are you staying?'

'*Muttacha*—you will never believe it if I tell you.'

'What?'

'Here ... speak to her yourself.'

'What? To who?'

'Rohini, *muttacha* ... I found her. She is here.'

There was a stunned silence at the other end. Ayan grinned even wider. Then he handed over the phone to Rohini.

'Hello, Gopal. How are you?' she said. Her smile lit up her entire face.

Ayan went into his bedroom as he wanted to give them some privacy. But he needn't have bothered. Gopal Shanker and Rohini were once again in a world of their own. They had the events of so many years to catch up on. He started by telling her how very sorry he was that he had stopped talking, and she silenced him saying he did not have to apologize. She said that Ayan was a fine young man, and he had told her the reason why Gopal had stayed away.

'You are a man of your word, Gopal. You are amazing. I don't think I would have ever done anything like that,' she said.

'Oh, you would have done the same if it was Padmaja who came to you,' said Gopal.

'I don't know. I am selfish. I wouldn't give you up for anything in the world.'

'And yet, you never got in touch with me after you moved to Germany.'

'No Gopal. I did. I wrote to you three letters a year, like I always have done. But I never posted them.'

'Why?'

'I didn't know what it would set in motion. Had the letters reached you, I wouldn't have been strong enough to stay away. I would have broken away from Raman, and that would have crushed his heart. He would never have been able to endure losing me.'

'And after he died?'

'I still wrote to you, Gopal. But I didn't want to send them because I did not want you to think that I had come running to you just because I had lost my husband. I wanted to wait and see if you would ever reach out to me.'

'And what if I hadn't?'

'Well—you still haven't! It was Ayan who insisted on looking for me.'

'I had given my word. How could I break it?'

'You haven't broken it still. I haven't called you. You haven't called me. It was Ayan who called you, and then gave the phone to me, remember?' she laughed.

Gopal Shanker laughed along with her.

It was almost forty-five minutes later that Rohini gently knocked on Ayan's door.

'Finished your call?' asked Ayan as he came out.

'Yes,' said Rohini, dabbing away at her eyes. 'Forgive me, at my age, I get emotional very quickly.'

Ayan couldn't stop smiling. He was overjoyed that his *muttachan* and Rohini had spoken.

'God bless you, Ayan,' she said.

'God bless this fabulous friendship,' Ayan replied.

Rohini said that she knew a lovely place on the beach where they served a delicious South Indian breakfast. She and Ayan walked to the hotel. Ayan thoroughly enjoyed the meal.

'You know, I told Gopal that I want to meet him,' said Rohini, as they were walking back to 'The Hideaway'.

'That would be wonderful! And what did he say?' asked Ayan.

'He said he wanted to meet too. But he said he was bald and old and wrinkly. And that he has lost all his teeth, and I would be disappointed if I saw him.'

'That's not true! He is not bald!'

'Haha … I knew he was just teasing me. I told him I didn't care how he looked.'

'And? Are you coming to Kerala? Why don't you come with me? I will take you to *Thekke Madom*.'

'You forget I know where *Thekke Madom* is; it's just a three-minute walk from where my ancestral home used to be.'

'Aaah—right … right. I had forgotten you are from Poongavanam too.'

'I haven't gone back to that place in years. Not since I lost my parents. The house too was sold long back. I don't have too many happy associations with that place. That was where I got married.'

'Oh. I can only imagine how it must have been.'

'It was terrible. I had no choice. Your grandfather was in Bombay those days. I had written so many letters to him, begging him to approach my father to ask for my hand.'

'I know. It remains the greatest regret of his life.'

'Is there anything you don't know?' she smiled.

'I know pretty much everything now about *muttachan*,' said Ayan, and smiled back at Rohini.

When they reached 'The Hideaway', they met the same security guard who had questioned Ayan the previous day. He was just taking over duty from the guard who was being relieved.

'Rohini Madam!' he called out, 'When did you come?'

'Yesterday night.'

'That's why I didn't see you. I was not on duty,' he said.

'I must tell you, madam, you are lucky to have him as your grandson. God has blessed him. Good looks. A job in London. It's all your good karma,' he continued his monologue.

Rohini looked at Ayan quizzically. He mouthed, 'I will tell you later,' and she nodded.

'And he looks exactly like you, madam. Carbon copy of you,' the security guard proclaimed.

Ayan and Rohini burst out laughing when he said that.

He looked at them puzzled as they walked up the stairs, still laughing.

37

Ayan climbed the stairs easily, but Rohini was a little out of breath.

'Why don't they put a lift in here?' asked Ayan.

'It's good exercise. And at the time of construction of this building, lifts were a luxury. That's why there are only three floors,' said Rohini.

'That security guard. What a guy,' said Ayan.

'He is a sweet chap. Well-meaning. What was all that about London?' she asked.

Ayan then told her the whole story and she laughed when she heard about Roshan's BBC youth wing.

Now that Ayan had found her and connected her to his grandfather, there was nothing for him to do in Pondicherry. He told Rohini that he would take the bus back that night.

'Why don't you stay for a while more? Take a break from everything?' she suggested.

'I want to get back to *muttachan*. The last time I left him alone for a day, we all know what happened,' he said.

'Hmm ... I don't think your father will suddenly appear, and ship him off somewhere. But yes, go back; I know you must be wanting to get back home,' said Rohini.

He looked at the bus schedule. There was one which left around 6 p.m. Ayan decided he would take that one.

Rohini asked him what he would like to do for the rest of

the day. He said that he would love to explore White Town some more. He asked her whether she knew where the Ashram canteen was and where his grandfather's bank was. She knew the places, and they spent the rest of the day walking around White Town. The Ashram canteen still served meals, and for Ayan, it was a fulfilling experience to sit and eat at that very place which his grandfather used to frequent.

'Isn't it amazing that all of this still exists?' he asked Rohini.

'Some things never change. They still remain, Ayan. This is an old, established order. It is likely to remain this way even for the next hundred years,' she said.

When it was time for Ayan to leave, Rohini hugged him tightly. She gave him a package neatly wrapped in exquisite handmade paper.

'This is for Gopal. Do give it to him,' she said.

'What is it?' asked Ayan.

'Letters from me. I wrote three letters to him, each year. I never broke that tradition.'

'Wow,' said Ayan. 'It will be my honour and privilege to get them across to him.'

'Thank you, Ayan. God bless you,' she said, her eyes misting again.

'So if you will not come to Kerala, how will you meet *muttachan*?' he asked.

'Oh—I guess I forgot to tell you. He said he would come here. To "The Hideaway".'

'Really?!'

'Yes. This is where our happiest memories are. And he feels the same way,' she said. 'Will you come with him?'

'Of course, I will … But I … I don't want to come in between you two.'

She laughed when she heard that. 'We are not young teenagers madly in love. Come with him. It will be good,' she said.

Ayan said he would.

'See you soon,' he said and left for the bus stop.

* * *

Ayan reached Kottayam at the crack of dawn. His back hurt as this sleeper bus wasn't as comfortable as the earlier one. He took a taxi and reached Poongavanam. His grandfather and Velu were sleeping. Ayan called on Velu's mobile and told him he had arrived. Velu opened the doors and let him in.

'Good morning, Velu *chetta*,' said Ayan

'Good morning, Ayan Sir. How does it feel to be a Pondicherry-returned?'

'Eh? What is that?'

In Kerala, we usually have 'Gulf-returned' when people come back home from the Middle East. But this Pondicherry-returned is a first,' said Velu.

'It sure feels good. The place is just fabulous,' said Ayan.

Velu wanted to hear all the details about Ayan's trip. Ayan spent the next half an hour filling in Velu. By the time he finished his narrative, he had finished two cups of coffee as well. He told him how he had met the legendary Shyamala and then what a delightful person Rohini was. He couldn't stop praising Rohini.

'You know, ever since that phone call yesterday, it seems like Gopal Sir has become twenty years younger. You should see him and hear him now. He sounds like a totally different man. I have never seen him this excited or happy. He has transformed overnight,' said Velu.

'Such is the power of true love. Some call it friendship,' said Ayan.

'He was talking about going to Pondicherry. Are you going with him?'

'Yes, of course. I will go with him, said Ayan.

'Good ... good. That will be good then. I was worried about how he would manage. His leg has just healed.'

'Don't worry Velu *chetta*, I will take care of him,' said Ayan.

When Gopal Shanker woke up, he greeted Ayan with enthusiasm.

'Hello Hero,' he said.

Ayan smiled. 'That's a first,' he said.

'What?'

'Calling me a hero.'

'There's a first time for everything, young man.'

Velu was right. It was as though Gopal Shanker had suddenly become ten years younger. Ayan could have sworn that his grandfather was standing up straighter too, and walking faster than before. Earlier his movements had been slow, deliberate and careful. Now there was a spring in his step.

'*Muttacha*—Rohini is a remarkable person. I feel so privileged to have met her and interacted with her. And 'The Hideaway'—*muttacha*, you should see it. She has maintained it so well. It's this warm happy place. So many sunflowers on the terrace too. And the sunrise—oh, it is to die for. Breathtakingly beautiful.'

'I know. I know, young man. You forget I have lived there,' Gopal Shanker was smiling at Ayan's enthusiasm and his animated, vivid descriptions.

'So when are we going there?' asked Ayan.

'Going where?'

'Pondicherry, *muttacha*.'

'Why should I go to Pondicherry? What is there anyway?' asked Gopal Shanker with a straight face.

'What?! After all this, you don't want to go there? Rohini said you were meeting there?' Ayan couldn't keep the disappointment and outrage out of his voice.

'Hahah ... Fooled you, didn't I?' chuckled Gopal Shanker. 'Sorry Ayan, I was just teasing you. Of course, I want to go. A big thank you for going all the way there and finding her. I don't think we would have ever spoken otherwise,' said Gopal.

'Oh. You did fool me for a moment, *muttacha*,' smiled Ayan.

'For a while, Rohini and I fooled everybody,' said Gopal Shanker as his eyes twinkled.

As they sat having their breakfast, Ayan and Gopal Shanker spoke about love, marriage and finding the right partner.

'You know, I have always loved Rohini. I think it is important to act when you are convinced that you have found the right person.'

'But how do you know for sure? You keep thinking that there might be somebody else, someone more suited.'

'That is probably a problem of the present generation. I think you young folks are never happy with anything. You are not willing to give time to a relationship. You should allow it to breathe. To grow. You should nurture it. Above all, you should be patient.'

'So true, *muttacha*. Our generation definitely does not know to be patient.'

'Then again, probably my generation was slow to act. I know that all those years ago, if I had taken one bold step in the right direction, my life would have been completely different. Rohini was my best friend back then. She is my best friend right now too. We should all marry our best friends,'

'What if your best friend is of the same sex?'

'Then you will either have sex or you won't, depending on your orientation. You can still marry them though,' chuckled Gopal Shanker.

The landline rang and Ayan asked Velu to answer it.

'If it is my father, please tell him I don't want to talk to him,' instructed Ayan.

But it wasn't his father. It was Shyamala who was asking for Gopal Shanker.

'Oh, the return of the pesky Shyamala!' said Gopal Shanker as he walked towards the phone.

'Hello-hello, Shyamala. Been so long,' he boomed. For the

next ten minutes or so, Gopal Shanker had a conversation with Shyamala.

Ayan just sat there staring at this version of his grandfather. Who was this happy, extroverted person full of energy and life? Where was the grumpy old man he had met when he had first come to *Thekke Madom*? His connection with Rohini was indeed magical.

When he hung up, Gopal Shanker said, 'She hasn't changed at all. She is still curious and wanted to know every detail about my life,' Gopal Shanker shook his head in mock disapproval.

Ayan wanted to go back to Pondicherry immediately. He asked his grandfather if he could book the bus tickets.

But Gopal Shanker said, 'Patience, Ayan, patience.'

'Why *muttacha*? Why should we wait?'

'Good things come to those who wait.'

'You waited for so long. You stayed away all these years. Why don't we travel immediately?' Ayan persisted.

'I need a little time to mentally prepare myself, Ayan. I guess you will understand only when you reach my age,' said Gopal Shanker.

'Oh, I nearly forgot, *muttacha*. Rohini sent you something,' said Ayan.

He reached into his backpack and took out the bundle of letters that Rohini had given him.

'She said she wrote to you every year, but she didn't post them.'

'Did she say why?'

'She said you had mentioned that you didn't want to be in touch. She had moved to Germany, and she felt by sending the letters, she would be tormenting you. After her husband passed away, she didn't want you to think that she was coming back to you because it was convenient for her. She was waiting for you to reach out, *muttacha*.'

Gopal Shanker couldn't form the words even though there

were so many things that came to his mind. 'Oh, Rohini ...
If only...' he muttered. But overcome with emotions, he was
unable to speak.

He told Ayan that he wanted to read them. He walked back
to his room with the bundle in his hand. It was a treasure for
him. He read them slowly, one after the other. Rohini had
numbered them and arranged them in chronological order.

He opened each one, and read it, blinking back tears several
times. He lived through all those missed years with Rohini. In
those few hours, he re-lived the past two-and-a-half decades
with her. Her initial letters were all questions, asking him how
he could do this to her. In the later ones, her tone changed.
She had grown and evolved as a person and learnt to accept
the things that one could not change. She had also written in
detail about Germany, her life there and what she had been
up to. It was like watching somebody's life on television in
fast forward mode. She had signed off each letter with: 'Your
friend, Rohini'.

Gopal savoured them all. Each and every detail he took
in. He laughed when he read some of the letters. Rohini was
witty. He dabbed away his tears when he read about how she
had to fly back from Germany with Raman's body in the hold.

'It was so routine for them, Gopal. It was a long box with
him inside and labelled 'Handle with care'. That was it. Also,
what I found terrible was that I still had to give his passport.
The embassy helped with the embalming procedure, death
certificate, no objection certificate from the local police and
all that. But oh, the agony.'

The letters changed over the years, as Rohini came to terms
with the death, and began getting over her grief. There was
a mention of the paperwork involved in getting all his bank
accounts closed, getting the property he owned in Chennai
transferred to her name. After she started taking up new

projects, the letters had detailed descriptions of her work, and the joy she derived from them.

She had never stopped thinking of Gopal. What astonished him was the way she had addressed him in the letters—as though they had never stopped talking. It was like she was sitting in front of him, and narrating all that had happened, every few months.

It took Gopal Shanker a few hours to finish reading them all. Then he carefully put them back in the package she had sent and kept them next to the wooden box on his desk.

Rohini had never given up on him. He thought about all the years lost when they were not in touch. He thought about how she had faced all of it alone. He wished she had reached out sooner, and told him. But he was also filled with a sense of deep contentment to know that Rohini had not forgotten him at all.

He was still her best friend, and she was his.

38

It was a week later that Gopal Shanker asked Ayan to book the bus tickets to Pondicherry. He and Rohini had been talking every single day on the phone. They would talk for nearly an hour.

'Do you know what a luxury this is? The rates were so high back then, when we had to watch every single paisa we spent. And now—we don't have to watch the metre anymore and we can speak for as long as we like,' remarked Gopal Shanker.

'*Muttacha*—if you get a smartphone and an Internet plan, you can talk for free.'

'Really? For free? How is that even possible?'

'You pay only for the data, *muttacha*.'

'Data?'

'The Internet that you use. You use that and you can call the other person's phone.'

'But they too should have this Internet on their phone, am I right?'

'Right, Rohini does, *muttacha*.'

'Oh, does she?'

'Yes! And she knows how to use even the Instant Messenger. I have been chatting with her.'

'Oh, I see. She is smart then. You have to be smart to use a smartphone. I am dumb.'

'No, you are not!'

'Haha … Now use that smartphone of yours, and book us both tickets to Pondicherry,' Gopal Shanker said.

* * *

Velu fluttered around like a bee, packing Gopal Shanker's clothes.

'Look here—I have kept your toothbrush here. And this pouch has your shaving kit. Do not forget, okay?' he fussed.

'Velu, I am perfectly capable of locating these things inside the box. It's a tiny suitcase, not the Sahara desert,' said Gopal Shanker.

Gopal Shanker had shaved. He wore a smart trouser and a deep blue linen shirt.

'Looking smart, Gopal Sir! I have never seen you wear this shirt before,' he remarked.

'Yes, I haven't worn it for a long time now,' he said.

Ayan smiled. He knew from the diaries that this was the shirt which Rohini had gifted him all those years ago.

'Mmmm … Mmmmm. Gopal Sir has dressed like a bridegroom,' Velu said cheekily.

'Are you jealous that you don't have a blue shirt like *muttachan's*?' retorted Ayan.

Gopal Shanker laughed and said, 'Yes. That is it. He has always been that jealous kind.'

Velu just gaped in surprise, and then he laughed too.

Velu had booked a taxi.

'The last time I got into a taxi to leave *Thekke Madom*, was with your father,' remarked Gopal Shanker.

'Haven't you spoken to him since then?' asked Ayan.

Velu loaded the suitcases into the boot of the vehicle and slammed it shut.

He waved as the cab drove off, and Ayan waved back.

'No, I do not want to speak to either of my children. Nor do I wish to see them,' said Gopal Shanker, as he sank into the back seat of the car.

Ayan could imagine why.

'Do you feel bad about it? About cutting off from both your children?'

Gopal Shanker thought about that.

Then he said, 'They left me with no choice. With Jairaj, it was because I did not want to invest in his company in the initial days. I felt a distance growing then. With Shaila—what she did was unforgivable. Meddling in things that do not concern her. I suppose other people would see this as harsh. After all, we live in a culture where parents sacrifice their all for their children. But what about the parents' needs? Do children ever pause to think about it?'

Ayan just squeezed his grandfather's hand in response.

'Are you excited about this trip to Pondicherry?' asked Ayan, changing the topic.

'Excited? No ... Not excited. But I am happy we are going. It will be nice to see 'The Hideaway' again, after all these years. I never imagined I would go back. Life is full of surprises. We do things which we never thought we would.'

Ayan had booked a double berth for him and Gopal Shanker. It was twice as wide as the one he had travelled on last time. He checked in his bag as well as Gopal Shanker's suitcase, and they were loaded in the hold.

'Are they safe there?' he asked the loaders.

'Yes, nobody will touch them, sir. The hold is locked and it is opened only at the end point,' said the helper in the bus.

Gopal Shanker had never travelled on a sleeper bus. It had been many years since his last travel. After he had shifted to *Thekke Madom*, he had not travelled at all.

'My ... my... look at all these. All of this luxury—it was never there in my times,' he said.

'Yes, *muttacha*. These are nice and comfortable,' Ayan agreed, as they settled in.

Ayan took the berth near the aisle. Gopal Shanker lay down and went to sleep even before the bus started off. Ayan smiled and settled down beside his grandfather.

When the bus stopped for the usual break, Gopal Shanker was awake. Ayan and he got down from the bus and walked to the highway restaurant where several buses had stopped. It was a busy place bustling with activity despite the early hour of the day. Ayan ordered a cup of tea for his grandfather, as well as himself.

They went back to the bus after they finished the tea.

'How much more time? I am feeling a little claustrophobic now,' said Gopal Shanker.

'Just a couple of more hours and we are there,' said Ayan.

As soon as they settled back, Gopal Shanker started snoozing again.

Ayan took out his phone and texted Rohini.

'We are on our way,' he typed.

'Can't wait! See you soon,' she replied.

'Up so early?' he asked.

'Unable to sleep,' she typed back.

When the bus reached Pondicherry, Ayan saw all the suitcases being unloaded.

'Got your suitcase?' asked the helper.

'Yes. Thank you,' said Ayan, as he identified his bag and *muttachan's* suitcase.

Ayan did not want to take *muttachan* by an auto, even though the auto-drivers were milling around, trying to coax them into riding with them.

Ayan pushed his way out of the swarm of people and told Gopal Shanker to wait with the luggage. He walked to the taxi stand opposite the bus stop. In a minute, he had arranged a taxi which would take them to Troth Apartments.

'Oh, this place has totally changed since I was last here,' remarked Gopal Shanker.

He looked at the shiny, glass exteriors of the multi-storeyed malls that had come up. He talked about the building which used to be there in its place earlier. Each time he saw some familiar landmarks, he made comments about how they needed to be maintained properly, and how they were so old. When he found something that was no longer there, he exclaimed that it was gone. He was excited and garrulous. Just like a child who had discovered something new, he wouldn't stop talking.

'You used to live here earlier, sir?' asked the taxi driver, speaking Tamil. He turned back to look at Gopal Shanker.

'Yes, keep your eyes on the road. And go through the White Town,' commanded Gopal Shanker.

When the car reached the White Town area, Gopal Shanker saw that nothing much had changed.

'*Muttacha*, it is exactly like how you described in your diaries,' said Ayan.

'Yes. I feel like I have been transported back to 1989,' said Gopal Shanker.

When they reached Troth Apartments, Ayan looked up to the third floor. He saw Rohini waving to them from the terrace. He smiled and waved back.

Gopal Shanker squinted as he looked up. He saw her waving.

He smiled and looked away. Ayan could have sworn that his grandfather was actually blushing. He couldn't believe it.

'Let me take the bags,' said Ayan, as he took his bag and Gopal Shanker's suitcase and started climbing up.

Gopal Shanker followed him.

'*Muttacha*, can you manage the stairs? Your leg?' asked Ayan

'Yes, yes. I will climb slowly but I can manage all right. You go ahead,' said Gopal Shanker.

* * *

It was after climbing two flights of stairs that Ayan heard a noise, a little groan. He turned back, and saw his grandfather holding on to the railing, leaning forward. He was almost at the landing, halfway through the stairs to the second floor.

Ayan watched in shock and disbelief as Gopal Shanker climbed that last step to the landing, leaned forward and stumbled, losing his balance momentarily. He saw him clutching the railing. His face was distorted and he seemed to be in great pain.

'*Muttacha*! Are you okay?' he yelled as he deposited the bags on the stairs and rushed down.

Gopal Shanker had hit his head on the balustrade when he had leaned forward. There was a cut, with blood gushing out. Before Ayan could reach him, he had collapsed on the landing. He lay flat, sprawled out on his back, his legs dangling over the steps he had just climbed.

'*Muttacha ... muttacha*,' Ayan called out, as he tried to help him up.

Gopal Shanker's eyes did not open. Ayan looked around desperately for help.

He rushed up the stairs and rang the bell on every flat on the second floor, and in a jiffy, he was at 'The Hideaway'. He rang the bell and rushed down to his grandfather, leaping over the bags placed there. The whole exercise took him less than seven seconds.

Gopal Shanker lay still, without the slightest trace of movement.

By then, the doors to the apartments had opened and people were peeping out.

Rohini too had opened the door when the doorbell rang and when she found no one there, she came out to look, as she heard the commotion.

'Call the ambulance,' someone yelled.

She hurried downstairs and gasped in shock when she saw Gopal Shanker sprawled out.

'What happened, Ayan?' she asked.

'I don't know. He was fine, and suddenly he collapsed.'

'Move back ... give him air to breathe,' said a lady who was dressed in a purple salwar. 'I have called the ambulance, and they will be here soon,' she added.

The blood gushing from Gopal Shanker's head was a steady trickle. Someone had got ice-cubes, a bandage strip and cotton.

Ayan dabbed his grandfather's forehead and tried stemming the flow of blood with the cotton.

Mr. Mukherjee had come out as well. He had got a newspaper and he gave it to Rohini.

'Fan him. That will help.'

Rohini fanned him but Gopal Shanker's eyes remained shut.

'Sprinkle water on him,' said somebody and handed a bottle of water to the lady in the purple salwar. She sprinkled a few drops but there was not a flicker of movement on Gopal Shanker's face.

The ambulance arrived. The paramedics brought out the stretcher and rushed up the stairs. They lifted Gopal Shanker and placed him gently on the stretcher, carrying him to the ambulance.

'Who is the family?' one of them asked.

'I am ... I am his grandson,' said Ayan.

'You can come with us in the ambulance,' they said and Ayan followed them.

'Come, let's follow them in my car,' said Mr. Mukherjee to Rohini.

* * *

When Rohini and Mr. Mukherjee reached the hospital, Ayan was waiting outside the emergency section.

'What happened? Is he okay?' asked Rohini.

'I don't know. They told me to wait here. I filled up all the forms required. The doctor will come out soon,' said Ayan.

They waited for a few minutes, worry writ large on their faces.

'I hope he is okay. He has just recovered from a fall,' said Ayan.

'He will be fine. Don't worry,' Mr. Mukherjee reassured them.

Rohini was too upset to speak. She found a chair and sat there, covering her mouth with a handkerchief.

After a few minutes, the doctor emerged and walked towards them.

'Who is the family of Gopal Shanker?' he asked, as he consulted the sheaf of papers clipped on to a pad in his hand.

'We are,' answered Rohini and Ayan simultaneously.

Rohini clutched Ayan's hand. Her hands were cold and clammy.

'Sorry. He is no more. He ... he was dead on arrival,' said the doctor.

Rohini clutched Ayan's hand even tighter, and they stood there, dumbfounded, shell-shocked, unable to speak, the doctor's words resonating in their ears.

39

'Did ... did he ... was it because of the fall?' Ayan managed to ask. His voice was hoarse.

'No. It was a cardiac arrest. The cut on his forehead was just superficial. Not very deep,' said the doctor. 'You can collect the medical reports from the reception. You will need it when you apply for the death certificate. There are not too many formalities and we can release the body, once the paperwork is done.'

The doctor was very calm and spoke in a matter-of-fact manner, just the way he was trained to do. 'I am so sorry for your loss,' he said.

Ayan sat down then, with his head in his hands, not knowing what to do. He was in a state of shock.

Mr. Mukherjee consoled him. 'It's all God's will. We have no control over these things, Ayan.'

The words barely registered.

'I am a member in the Ashram's managing committee. I have called and already informed my fellow members. Don't worry, Ayan. We have volunteers for all this. We will all help you,' said Mr. Mukherjee.

* * *

The ambulance brought Gopal Shanker's body back to 'The Hideaway'.

Mr. Mukherjee was true to his word.

Everybody in the building, as well as the neighbouring buildings, had come. It looked like there were at least a fifty people in the room. The furniture in the drawing room had all been cleared away and moved to the sides.

Somebody got a white sheet and wrapped Gopal Shanker's body in it.

Someone else got incense sticks, lit a bunch of them and placed them on either side of his head. They got flowers and garlanded him.

Rohini was inconsolable. She hugged Ayan and she wept, making no attempt to wipe away her tears.

'Perhaps it was the strain of the journey ... I should have come to Kerala. To meet him instead of asking him to see me here,' she kept repeating over and over.

Ayan was too distraught to console her. He put his arm around her and gently patted her back. He did not trust himself to speak.

Mr. Mukherjee took charge of the situation.

'No, no, Rohiniji. If it had to happen, it would have happened, even if he was in Kerala,' he said.

Ayan said, 'He was happy to travel. He was ... he was excited like a child and he was fine on the bus.' His voice was shaking as he said it.

Rohini kept sobbing silently.

Ayan sat staring at his grandfather's body. The cut had been cleaned up, and it looked as though Gopal Shanker was sleeping. There seemed to be a half-smile on his face. It looked like he would get up any minute and say that all this was a joke.

Ayan touched his grandfather's forehead. It was cold. He had never touched a dead person before.

He pursed his lips and looked away.

'Your father's number, Ayan? We will have to call him,' Mr. Mukherjee said.

'He doesn't live in India. He is in Bahrain,' said Ayan, as he gave him the numbers.

'I have to call Velu,' said Ayan as he stood up and went to the terrace. There were a whole lot of people on the terrace too.

Velu answered on the first ring itself.

'Ayan Sir! Did you reach safely? I have been waiting for your phone call,' he said.

Ayan broke down then.

'Hello? Ayan Sir? Ayan Sir?' asked Velu. He knew immediately that something was amiss.

After Ayan managed to control his emotions, he said, 'Velu *chetta* ... Pack your bags and come to Pondicherry immediately. Take a taxi. I am messaging you the address.'

'Okay, Ayan Sir,' said Velu. He did not ask any further questions.

Ayan walked back into the living room. There were more visitors streaming in. Mr. Mukherjee was greeting them. They were going around Gopal Shanker's body. Some were touching his feet.

Ayan's phone rang then. It was his father.

He stared at it for a few seconds and then he answered it.

'YOU BLOODY FOOL ... YOU BRAINLESS COLT ... What the hell do you think you were doing? You took him to Pondicherry?' his voice boomed.

Something in Ayan snapped at that moment. All the days of pent-up anger against his father for what he had done, the deep sorrow that was inside him on losing Gopal Shanker, the unfairness of life where *muttachan* had almost reached 'The Hideaway'—it all rose like an enormous wave and exploded within him.

'SHUT THE FUCK UP ... YOU ... YOU FUCKING MONSTER ... SHUT UP ... HE WANTED NOTHING TO DO WITH YOU ... OR YOUR SISTER. DO YOU UNDERSTAND?

NOTHING. I DESPISE YOU ... ALL ... ALL OF YOU
SELFISH MANIPULATIVE LOT ... FUCK OFF!' Ayan was
screaming.

There was stunned silence as Ayan's voice rang loud and
clear through the house. Every single person in the room had
heard him. The whispers, the talking, all of it died down in
an instant.

At the other end of the world, Jairaj was too shocked to
speak as well.

But Ayan wasn't done yet.

'All my life I have trusted you. Listened to you. You
BETRAYED that TRUST. Do you even KNOW what that
word means? YOU HAVE LOST me FOREVER. Do you
understand? What kind of a heartless monster makes a false
case and shoves his own father into a mental asylum, eh? And
you made it out as though Rohini did not exist? Let me tell you
something—it is under her roof that I am standing right now.
DO YOU HEAR ME? She is with me as I speak. I am taking
charge of my life from now on. DO YOU UNDERSTAND?
And don't even bother coming for the funeral, please. We will
be having it here in Pondicherry. And it will be today. So it
will all be over even if you decide to come. You ... you will
NEVER KNOW what true love is. You are incapable of that.
YOUR LOSS. I DON'T GIVE A FUCK ANYMORE.'

With that, Ayan cut the call. His eyes were blazing with rage
and grief. He was breathing hard. Then he composed himself.

He walked to Mr. Mukherjee and said, 'Let's make all
arrangements for the funeral. We will go ahead and have it
here itself. Whoever wants to come from Kerala, can come
here if they want to see him for the last time.'

Velu reached just in time for the last rites. He broke down
when he saw Ayan.

'Hush, Velu *chetta* ... Hush. He wouldn't want to see you
sending him off with tears,' said Ayan.

People kept pouring in to pay their last respects. Ayan did not know from where they came or who called them. He was in a daze. At one point, he saw Shyamala hugging Rohini. Then she came up to him and hugged him as well.

When it was time to take the body to the funeral pyre, Ayan was completely calm and in control. He lifted his grandfather for the last time, along with three other people, and carried the body to the waiting ambulance.

Then he climbed in and left for the crematorium.

40

Three months later

19th October 2015
Monday

I have decided to start writing a diary today. Just like muttachan did. The idea occurred to me only today while I was reading his diaries again. I don't think I will ever get tired of reading them over and over again. Each time I read them, I discover something new. It is a great day to start, as it is Rohini's birthday too.

Then I thought to myself that it was only because he wrote these diaries, that I was able to meet Rohini. My life is richer because of them.

I will make the entries in my diary just like he did. I won't make it a daily log, as that would be boring. I will write only when I feel a need to. I have got a leather-bound notebook just like muttachan's and I love it. There is a strange sense of peace in making scratches on this paper with muttachan's fountain pen, and watching the words form. This diary-writing business—it is like meditation. We look inwards and we express our innermost thoughts. And not only is it comforting, it also helps in giving me clarity of vision.I like it. No wonder muttachan wrote for so many years.

After the last rites were over, Rohini said she couldn't bear to be at 'The Hideaway' alone. I stayed with her for two days. Then she accompanied me back to Kerala. Velu returned immediately as the house couldn't be locked up.

My father, mother, Akshu, Shailammayi, Ghanshyam

ammavan[35]—all of them came down to Thekke Madom. What a pity that Akshu didn't get to meet Muttachan ever.

I didn't want my father to enter the premises. But Rohini said that wouldn't be right.

Shailammayi wouldn't look at Rohini. It was an awkward situation.

They organized a prayer meeting for muttachan. They kept a huge framed photograph of his and put a garland around it. I hate it when they do that. Rohini agreed with me that this was the kind of thing that muttachan would have hated too.

Apparently, there are some poojas to be performed for his soul to obtain peace. Tonnes of relatives whom I have never met, turned up. They all spoke about how good muttachan was. Bullshit. They didn't even know him. And if they cared so much for him, how is it that not one of them visited when he was alive? I detest them ... the whole lot of them. I couldn't wait for them to leave.

It turned out muttachan had made a will. Dr. Varghese had signed as one of the witnesses. When I came back and informed him of his demise, he notified the lawyer. I didn't even know he had a lawyer. His lawyer is Roshan's father. Muttachan has cut my father and Shailammayi completely from his will. He has left them nothing. A big zero is what they get. I am the sole inheritor of Thekke Madom. He left Rs. 3 lakhs to Nithya.

My father was hopping mad when he heard the will being read. The lawyer was very calm, while my father raved and ranted. My father said that the will is not valid and that since Thekke Madom is ancestral property, muttachan cannot will it. But it turns out that Achutan Shanker, muttachan's father had lost this property, because of debts. It was bought back by muttashi's father. He registered it in muttashi's name, with muttachan as joint owner. It was his wedding gift to them. That was apparently one of the conditions of their marriage.

I don't care what my father feels. I have stopped caring for him. All my life, he has told me what to do and I have obeyed him. I didn't speak a word to him. I do not know whether this

---

35. 'Uncle' in Malayalam

loathing I feel will reduce in intensity, as the years go by. But right now, I cannot bear to even look at him.

They left soon after. Returned to their lives.

That they never really cared about muttachan is clear from their behaviour.

Rohini said she had a project at Auroville and that as soon as she finished it, she would come back to Thekke Madom.

I haven't spoken to my father even once since the day they left. My mother called me twice after they returned. Akshu has taught her how to call on Skype. I video chatted with both of them. I told them I don't want to speak to my father. She said I wasn't understanding him. She said all he wanted to do was shift muttachan to a flat, as that was the only way Thekke Madom could be sold. She said he had simply admitted him to the hospital for a check-up and that he was to bring him back soon. I don't believe her. I think she is simply covering up for my father.

It's been three months now, since muttachan left us. But the pain is still raw.

It hurts like crazy. I miss him every single day.

I sit in his chair on the verandah and stare at the fields.

* * *

25th October 2015
Sunday

Shivani called me today. The messages and phone calls between us are now erratic. It is mostly my fault. I have been bad at keeping in touch. She was shocked to hear of muttachan's demise. She kept saying that she is there for me if I wanted to talk.

I don't want to talk. Talking will not bring muttachan back. I know she is just trying to be a good friend, but it feels like I have retreated into a cocoon, and I want time to myself.

I had to force myself to talk to her today. She noticed the change in tone. She asked me if I was still upset and how I am coping.

I said I was fine, and that the void would always be there.

She told me to call her, when I felt like talking. I said I would, but I don't foresee that happening anytime soon.

I do not know why I keep comparing every relationship with what muttachan and Rohini had.

Correction: Still have.

Even death cannot steal the treasured memories.

* * *

18th November 2015
Wednesday

Rohini has been living here for the past two weeks now. She and Velu get along so well. Velu worships her.

Rohini had a great idea today. She said when she had gone back to Pondicherry, she had visited Shyamala, and she had seen the beautiful art gallery. She asked how I felt about opening a similar one at Thekke Madom.

'It will be a huge encouragement to the local artists,' she said.

That was when I remembered the painting which Shyamala had given me to give to muttachan. I gifted it to her today. She loved it.

I love her idea of opening an art gallery here. There are so many rooms that are vacant.

I am also thinking I can rent out many of these rooms on Air BnB. There will be enough takers. It will be a source of income for me as well.

I picked up my paints and canvas today. I made a painting of the paddy fields. I want to paint more often.

* * *

10th December 2015
Thursday

Thekke Madom is listed as an Air BnB destination now. Shyamala told her sons and we have got our first booking for three rooms already! It is a party from France. Velu is excited about it.

'It will be nice to have visitors here, Ayan Sir,' he said.

Rohini is delighted too. She has written to the Kerala government, asking for support to open an art gallery. She has made a detailed proposal.

* * *

31st December 2015
Thursday

Last day of the year. Time to take stock of good things and bad things that happened this year, just like muttachan used to do.

<u>Good things that happened this year:</u>

Rohini moving to Thekke Madom. She is my family now.
Muttachan getting to see Rohini one last time, before he died. Agreed it was not the ideal circumstance as they didn't even get to talk. But sometimes, life doesn't let you choose.
Me finally having the courage to stand up to my father and tell him to fuck off. All my life I was afraid of him. Now the only person I answer to, is myself.
(Okay—Rohini is the other person I will listen to.)
We have been told unofficially that Rohini's proposal has been accepted!! We will inaugurate the gallery next year, in March!

<u>Bad things:</u>

Losing Muttachan.

But like Rohini says, when those we love die, they live on inside us.

Like a hundred little flames.

Author's Note

Poongavanam exists only in the pages of this book, and you are not likely to find it on Google maps, even though Ayan put it there. However it closely resembles my mother's village in Kerala. Erunjipally, a fictional place, could be any small town in Kerala. Again, you will not be able to spot in on a map.

My association with Kerala is a special one. I am not a Malayalee, though I can speak the language, and even read it. I learnt it outside my school curriculum, simply out of interest. Growing up, every summer vacation, was spent at my grandparents ancestral home, which closely resembles *Thekke Madom.*

My love-affair with Kerala continues to this day, and this book is a tribute to a thousand cherished memories that I hold like a treasure within my heart.

Acknowledgements

To my mother Priya Kamath, with whom I discussed the details of this novel, at length.

To my father K. V. J. Kamath—for everything.

To my early readers (you know who you are), especially my daughter Purvi Shenoy, my son Atul Shenoy and Satish Shenoy, without whose encouragement this book wouldn't just be the same.

To S. K. V. Prabhu for all the facts about Mumbai and Kerala.

To Dr. Oliver for the medical inputs.

To my wonderful editors Sandhya Sridhar (for the brilliant editing and the inputs) and Karthik Venkatesh (for the special touches).

To Pooja and Pankaj, for the cover.

To Lostris for being my arm support

To Manjula Venkatswamy, my one-woman cheer-leader and support factory.

To the wonderful HarperCollins India team.

About the Author

Preeti Shenoy, among the highest selling authors in India, is on the Forbes longlist of the most influential celebrities in India. Her books include *When Love Came Calling, Wake Up Life Is Calling, Life Is What You Make It, The Rule Breakers, A Hundred Little Flames, It's All in the Planets, Why We Love the Way We Do, The Secret Wish List, The One You Cannot Have* and many others. Her work has been translated into many Indian languages. Preeti is also a motivational speaker, and has given talks at many premier educational institutions and corporate organizations like KPMG, ISRO, Infosys and Accenture, among others. An avid fitness enthusiast, she is also an artist specializing in portraiture and illustrated journalling.

30 Years *of*

HarperCollins *Publishers* India

At HarperCollins, we believe in telling the best stories and finding the widest possible readership for our books in every format possible. We started publishing 30 years ago; a great deal has changed since then, but what has remained constant is the passion with which our authors write their books, the love with which readers receive them, and the sheer joy and excitement that we as publishers feel in being a part of the publishing process.

Over the years, we've had the pleasure of publishing some of the finest writing from the subcontinent and around the world, and some of the biggest bestsellers in India's publishing history. Our books and authors have won a phenomenal range of awards, and we ourselves have been named Publisher of the Year the greatest number of times. But nothing has meant more to us than the fact that millions of people have read the books we published, and somewhere, a book of ours might have made a difference.

As we step into our fourth decade, we go back to that one word – a word which has been a driving force for us all these years.

Read.

Harper
Collins

HARPER
PERENNIAL

HARPER
BUSINESS

HARPER
BLACK

हार्पर
हिन्दी

HarperCollins
Children'sBooks

HARPER
DESIGN

HARPER
VANTAGE

Harper
Sport